Also by Ava Miles

The Dare Valley Series:
NORA ROBERTS LAND
FRENCH ROAST
THE GRAND OPENING
THE HOLIDAY SERENADE
THE TOWN SQUARE
THE PARK OF SUNSET DREAMS

DARING DECLARATIONS:
An Anthology including THE HOLIDAY SERENADE AND THE
TOWN SQUARE

The Dare River Series:
COUNTRY HEAVEN
COUNTRY HEAVEN SONG BOOK
COUNTRY HEAVEN COOKBOOK
THE CHOCOLATE GARDEN

COUNTRY Heaven

AVA MILES

www.avamiles.com
Ava Miles

ISBN-13:

To my sister, Tabitha, for her inexhaustible sense of humor, her kind heart, and for telling me how to ride the bull. For her husband, Mark, the best brother-in-law imaginable—who feels like one of my brothers; for teaching me Texas Hold 'em and showing me how the big boys play poker. And to blessed, darling Alexis, my niece, for making me laugh and for being a woman who already knows her own mind. I can't wait to see how your life unfolds and will always be here to cheer you on. I love you guys.

And to my divine entourage, who paves the way for my highest good always.

ACKNOWLEDGEMENTS

I want to thank the following people for supporting me on this amazing journey:

My editor, the magnificent Angela Polidoro; my incredible assistant, Maggie Mae Gallagher; the awesome Gregory Stewart for always supporting me; the Killion Group for the eye-catching cover art; my wonderful copy editor, Helen Hester-Ossa; Jennifer Fusco and Melanie Meadors for support spreading the word; Bemis Promotions for my website; and my aunt for answering all my law enforcement questions.

It might sound strange, but art inspires art, and I want to thank Carrie Underwood for turning me onto country music, and Tim McGraw for singing "Real Good Man." Rye might not exist otherwise, and I certainly wouldn't have written country music songs to go with this novel.

T.F. My hope rests in you.

To all my readers who have been asking for Rye's book! You are a blessing. Happy reading.

Obligations make my stomach hurt.

They're no fun.
Make me want to run.
Feel too up-pity.

Don't make me go.
Forget about the show.
I'm not for display.

Obligations just aren't for me.
No more obligations please.

Rye Crenshaw's first Top Twenty Hit, "No More Obligations"

PROLOGUE

Nashville's Disadvantaged Children's Association's Annual May Day Charity event at one of the city's finest country clubs didn't have a whiff of disadvantage, in Rye Crenshaw's opinion.

Ice sculptures of unicorns and cherub-faced children were dripping in the hot sun on the plush buffet table. The silver flatware fairly blinded him, and the plates gleamed so brightly they looked like they'd been shined with furniture polish. At least the food appealed to him, the succulent beef tenderloin and slow-roasted pork being sliced delicately by black-tie waiters while others carried around silver trays with champagne, mint juleps—this was Nashville, after all—and delicate canapés of crab and caviar. An assortment of European cheeses from bleu to goat caught his eye, and his stomach grumbled. Food was one of Rye's greatest pleasures in life, and he loved indulging in it.

Thank God the only thing the chairperson of the DCA wanted from him today was his presence, his pocket book, and for him to take some pictures with the disadvantaged kids they'd brought to the event. No live performance singing songs from his new album, *Cracks in the Glass House*, which continued to rise to the top of the charts.

His had been a wild ride to stardom after a childhood spent without any autonomy. Now, he did exactly what he wanted, went where he wanted.

Except on days like today, when his manager, Georgia Chandler, arranged for him to attend a hobnob charity event. He liked giving back to the community and hated seeing kids treated poorly, but he didn't like being put on display like some zoo animal.

And he downright hated hoity toity events like these, having had his fill of them growing up in blue-blood Meade, Mississippi, before breaking the family tradition of being a lawyer in the family practice to pursue country music.

Of course, his family hadn't liked that one bit. And events like these made him think about them...and how they'd disowned him when he stepped out of line.

Georgia made her way toward him, wearing a leopard-print mini skirt, a black blouse, a black cowboy hat, and five-inch black cowboy boots that left punctures resembling bullet holes in the finely manicured lawn as she meandered through the crowd.

"Are you ready to work your magic?" she asked when she reached him.

"Yes," he said, and joined her to stroll through the crowd of Nashville's finest, being stopped for an occasional autograph or a more personal proposition from some of the elegant ladies in attendance.

He had just finished shaking hands with the mayor when his cell phone vibrated in his jeans, and since Georgia was busy chatting with the politicos, he stepped away. He dug his smart phone out of his pocket, and his heart just about stopped...

It was the number from his family's house, which he hadn't stepped foot in for five years.

A spear of fear drove straight into his heart.

"Hello?" he said, hurrying away from the crowd, the sun beating down on his black cowboy hat.

"Rye, I hope this is a convenient time to call," she said.

Mama? The reason she was calling must be dire. She must have gotten his number from his sister, the only person in his family with whom he still communicated. And just as he remembered, Mama's tone was so cold it could have kept the ice sculptures from melting.

"Of course," he woodenly replied. Manners must always be observed.

"Good. Well, then. I've learned that you plan to attend Amelia Ann's graduation from Ole Miss, and I'm calling to tell you not to come."

Anger sparked inside him, hot and fierce. "She's my baby sister, Mama, and I'll come see her graduate if I want." It wasn't like he'd planned on sitting with them anyway.

A brittle laugh echoed on the line. "I thought you might say that. Rye, when you left this family and turned your back on everything we stood for, your Daddy and I made it crystal clear you were to have no contact with any of us again. And wasn't it a surprise to hear that you've been secretly in contact with Amelia Ann for some years now. Well, I forbid it."

One of his songs suddenly erupted from the speakers, and he had to put his finger in his ear to hear her. "Too bad. She's an adult now, and I'll see her if I want."

Amelia Ann had reached out to him five years ago when he'd been disowned, sending him an email, and they'd kept up a secret correspondence ever since. When she started at Ole Miss, they began talking on the phone now and again, and Rye had even visited her periodically. But they'd been careful, both of them well aware that Mama wouldn't approve.

"Rye, I won't have my baby sullied by your lifestyle or your unconventional belief system. Amelia Ann will take her rightful place back home in Meade after graduating, and she'll marry a fine Southern gentleman and have babies, just like Tammy has done."

Yeah, his older sister, Tammy, had toed the line. She was so much like Mama they might as well be twins.

"Mama, I'm going to that graduation," he said, an edge in his voice.

"If you do, Rye, or if you have any more contact with her at all, I will disown her too."

The punch of that threat rolled across his solar plexus.

"I won't tolerate another rotten apple in my barrel."

"You wouldn't," he said, even though he knew she would. Mama was the kind who would eat her own young at any provocation.

"Try me, Rye. You didn't use to underestimate me."

No, he hadn't. Her weapons were sharp and unforgiving. And he had the scars to prove it. "Fine," he said. "I won't go to her graduation." It cost him to consent, but he couldn't bear to see Amelia Ann hurt. She had a gentle, loving heart, which is why she loved her black sheep brother against the family's wishes. They would find a way to be in touch.

"And no more phone calls," Mama added, as if reading his mind. "I'll be monitoring her phone bill in the future."

Christ.

"Don't mess with me on this, Rye. I've spoken to Amelia Ann, and she has accepted my dictate. You'd best do the same."

His sister had caved? The hurt of never again seeing her bright smile or hearing her laugh on the phone almost brought him to his knees. "You're a goddamn mean-spirited bitch," he spat.

"I love you too, son. Bye now."

The phone went dead, and he fought the urge to hurl it across the yard. Goddammit! He punched the air instead, wanting to strike out at something, anything.

He didn't often feel helpless in his life anymore, but he did now. And it was pure hemlock, hearing the utter hatred in Mama's voice again, like he was a whelp she'd brought into the world and hoped would simply disappear from existence.

Getting out of this charity event was the first order of business. He didn't care if it was early. Georgia could write them a fat check to smooth over any complaints.

He texted her to say he was leaving and that he'd explain later. As he reached the side entrance to the country club's lobby, a heavily built man grabbed his arm.

"Leaving so soon?" the man drawled, his mouth an ugly sneer. "A hot shot like you can't even stay to help disadvantaged kids?"

Since he'd been harassed by strangers before, he knew better than to reply. He tried to step around the guy without comment, but the man was bold and blocked him. Rye could guess at the reason for that boldness when the stench of alcohol wafted over him.

"Best get out of my face today, boy. I'm not feeling too nice today."

"You're just some country whelp." Little did this man know how thick the blue blood ran in Rye's veins, even if he went out of his way to conceal that fact. "You don't belong among good family folk," he continued.

"Your opinion."

The man only scratched his fat belly with his other hand. "You're a good-for-nothing son of a bitch, and you don't deserve to be here."

The words echoed in Rye's head, but this time it was his mama's voice he heard. The towering inferno of rage erupted inside him, spewing like a dormant volcano that had just come awake after sleeping for years. He shoved the man out of his way, and the man fell to the side and started howling.

Rye immediately reached to help him up, but the guy jerked away and yelled, "He hit me! Rye Crenshaw hit me."

Of course, a crowd gathered at the noise, the man yelling about how violent Rye had been. How he wasn't fit to be around children. And wouldn't you know it, a few of the disadvantaged children the association had brought for the event teared up and cried like in some frickin' Dickens novel.

Camera phones flashed everywhere.

He was screwed.

Striding out of the country club, hounded by the man's shouts, he waited for his truck to come around to the valet stand and called his lawyer on the way home to tell him what had happened so he could call the police and give Rye's account. He'd bet the farm the man was going to press charges. Good God, the whole rigmarole made his head swim.

By the time he made it home to Dare River, Twitter had

exploded with pictures of the fat man writhing on the floor, Rye standing over him looking dark and foreboding. And then there were the accusations.

Rye Crenshaw Punches Innocent Man at a Charity Event
Rye Crenshaw Mean to Children.
Rye Crenshaw Violent Around Kids.

He threw his phone against the wall of the den, the crack of it breaking doing nothing to comfort him. Georgia would be wild to talk to him, as would the rest of his staff, but he couldn't handle that now. Grabbing a bottle of Wild Turkey, he headed out to the river and stood by the bank. But the usual delight he took at seeing the water turn to diamonds in the light was gone.

His reputation had just taken a devastating blow. He might cultivate a bad-boy image, but what was being said in the media would shock his fans. And it wouldn't matter if the police didn't press charges. Like the old phrase went: a picture is worth a thousand words.

Even he knew that.

And just as he was starting his tour at the end of the month.

His career could be in trouble, but all he could think about was that his baby sister, his precious heart, was lost to him.

He hung his head and sank to his knees by the river.

Daily specials make a real man's day.
Gimme that fresh food.
Gimme that cooking crea-tiv-ity.

Let me drink that sweet, sweet tea.
Let me savor what you have in store for me.

Serve me up butter-dotted cornbread,
With some juicy, tangy ribs,
And a side of collard greens,
Finish me off with a coconut cream cake as tall as weeds.
Sate me well.

Make 'em all just like my Granny,
You steamin' hot, apron-clad woman,
And I'll surely make you mine.

Rye Crenshaw's Top Twenty Hit, "Daily Specials"

CHAPTER 1

Over a month later...

The run-down appearance of Diner Heaven just outside
Lawrence, Kansas, didn't concern Rye. Everyone knew diners
were hidden food gems.

Through a grime-encrusted window, he could see a lone
redheaded waitress bustling around under harsh fluorescent lights,
wiping down white countertops. That the diner looked to be empty
was a bonus. He wouldn't have to contend with any of his country
music fans and their worried glances, pinched mouths, or flat-out
nosy questions about whether he'd *plumb lost his mind* at the
charity event on May Day. The man whom Rye had shoved, a
wealthy businessman, had pressed charges for assault and blabbed
to anyone who would listen about how Rye didn't have family values
and was too wild to be around "decent people."

He'd had to go to the downtown police precinct for questioning,
and there were pictures all over the media of him alongside the men
in blue. Few cared that the police hadn't charged him, finding little
evidence and observing the man had been drunk.

Tonight, he'd fled the stage after his concert and was
immediately attacked by a rabid female fan and swarmed by
journalists with cameras who asked him rude questions while
shoving cameras in his face. Over a month after *The Incident*, they
were still asking him if he had anger management issues, if he
needed counseling, and whether he hated kids and families.

So here he was, craving a little comfort food and peace since
he'd recently fired his tour cook—another disaster he didn't want to
think about. And he was crammed into a beat-up muscle car, two
decades old if it was a day, that he'd borrowed from a member of
their local crew, wearing a ball cap instead of his black Stetson.
Trying to be all *incognito-like*.

No one ever saw him without his cowboy hat, so he should be

able to fly beneath the radar. Plus he met the restaurant's high standards. He had on shoes *and* a shirt. Bully for him.

The sooner he got inside, the sooner he could get back to the tour bus and start the drive to the next concert stop. He slammed the car door, rubbing the bite mark on his neck from the overzealous fan. Darn kids read too many vampire books these days. A cat the color of his beloved Oreo cookies shot past him.

And then he saw the striped tail.

He lunged for the car, but it was too late. A menacing hiss punctuated the silent parking lot, and a filmy spray misted his clothes. He gagged at the rotten smell and pinched his nose.

Rye knew Kansas had a reputation for being rural, but seriously. His stomach growled. God, he was rank, but he was *starving*! Grateful the wind wasn't behind him, he prayed the waitress would have seasonal allergies and a plugged nose.

He pulled the cap lower, hoping he could pass for an innocent college student with his jeans and black T-shirt. He snorted. Innocent he wasn't.

The door chimed when he eased it open, and he nudged the doorstop down with his foot. Maybe fresh air would help. The air conditioner blasted more of a tepid tropical breeze than a meatlocker chill anyway. He sighed, even over *eau de skunk*, he could pick up the heavenly odors of garlic, onions, and grilled meat.

The middle-aged waitress gave him a once-over like a bad private investigator keeping tabs on her target. She was wearing a gold uniform with a monogram of clouds and a halo under her name tag. Myra. He nodded a greeting and shuffled forward. "I'm just gonna head to the men's room to see if I can wash off this skunk's stink. It got me in the parking lot."

Her nose twitched, and then her face scrunched up. "Oh, good heavens!" She bustled over, pressing a white lace handkerchief to her tired face like he had cholera or something. "That darn thing. We've had two customers sprayed this week. Bill can't catch it, and I hate to see it shot. I watched Pepé Le Pew growing up."

A cartoon was stopping her from getting rid of it? Well, didn't that beat all?

"Don't bother to try washing it off. It won't help," she said.

"I'm sorry," he said. God, he must be the unluckiest son of a bitch on the planet.

"It *sure* is rank." She shifted on her feet, the handkerchief morphing like a sock puppet as she breathed through it. "Umm... We were about ready to close. Our cook's cleaning the grill." Her eyes darted to the kitchen.

AVA MILES

Her voice had the flat, articulate cadence of a TV anchorperson. People in the Midwest teased him about his slow drawl, but he was simply too lazy to finish pronouncing the end of most words. He hoped he could tone down the Southern in his voice tonight, though. The last thing he needed was for this situation to end up in the tabloids.

"I'm sorry to put you out, but I wouldn't ask if I wasn't starving. I couldn't get here any earlier." He kept his head down, looking at her white shoes. Her right shoelace was untied.

"All right, but only because our skunk got you."

Whew. "Wonderful. What do you recommend, Myra?" Rye eased into a cracked fake red leather booth.

"Why don't I see what our cook can whip up for you? Tory's awfully inventive." She bit her lip as her nose wrinkled. "She'd be more inclined if you smelled better. We used Febreze on the last person. It works as good as tomato juice and isn't as messy. Do you mind?"

Might as well give it a try. "Sure. Go ahead."

She disappeared around the counter, and then popped back up with a blue bottle. He'd been sprayed with a few things in his life, but this was new. The things a guy did for a good meal. He stood up and forced a smile as she edged toward him slowly, like the smell might be contagious. She pinched her nose and went to work, the handle cranking. Mist filled the air, making him cough. She was thorough, he'd give her that. Now Rye was covered in Febreze *and* skunk. Things couldn't be peachier. He'd have to burn the clothes.

Myra's eyes were watering, so at least he wasn't the only one suffering. Setting the bottle down, she flexed her hand. "That's better. Amazing what this stuff can do. I keep it around the house. Wait, I got some on your face." She took her handkerchief and wiped his cheek like he was a kid. He jerked his head back, his eyes meeting hers for the first time.

Her own narrowed and then popped open as wide as the silver dollars his granddaddy used to give him for Christmas. "My God! I'd know those long-lashed eyes anywhere." Her pale, heart-shaped face transformed. "You're Rye Crenshaw! You had a concert tonight. I wanted to go, but I couldn't find anyone to cover my shift. There were some tickets available last minute because of what happened last month." She pressed her hand to her mouth. "Oh, I'm so sorry. I shouldn't have said that."

Rye fought back a growl. Like he didn't know some of his more conservative fans thought he'd crossed the line and were dumping their tickets.

20

"I'm sorry. I know I screwed up," he muttered.

Hadn't he practiced saying the words every morning since *The Incident*? Georgia, his manager, had written them in bold red letters on yellow legal paper and taped it to his bathroom mirror in the tour bus. They'd made an official announcement about the drunken man harassing him, but the media kept running those pictures of the disadvantaged kids crying over and over again. So, he kept apologizing—even though it burned his ass each and every time.

Myra lifted the blue bottle in her hand. "This would...ah, make a funny commercial. Maybe you could become a Febreze spokesperson." She shrugged. "It would be a family item. Might help restore your reputation."

Like hell. He and Georgia hadn't figured out how to turn the tide of negative press, but he doubted an air freshener endorsement would do it. If Corona, a brand that suited his bad boy image to a T, had decided he was too much of a liability, why would some hygiene-concerned wife and mother buy this Febreze stuff because of him?

"I'll mention it to my manager." He lied to be polite.

His stomach gave a hungry gurgle.

She looked at his belly like there was a monster about ready to break out. "I'll get Tory." She scurried off toward the swinging kitchen door, her sensible shoes squeaking with each step.

He took a seat again.

A woman with jet black hair peered through the glass hole in the door just before Myra sailed into the kitchen. He caught whispers of heated conversation and then the door slammed open, smacking the wall, and a petite woman charged toward him with a hand towel over her nose. She had on faded jeans with a hole in the knee and a smudged white apron over a red T-shirt. Her big eyes peeked out at him from under a messy pageboy haircut.

"We close at midnight, and it's..." She lifted her wrist to look at her watch. "Exactly seven minutes to—not enough time to make you something. I don't care if you're that infamous singer everyone's talking about or what. I don't even listen to country." She studied him for a moment. "You don't look anything like your picture."

Rye's mouth lifted at the corners. "That was the idea. Look, I'm sorry you're about ready to close. Tonight hasn't been a party for me either." He lifted the damp, Febrezed T-shirt clinging to his chest, hating the flowery, skunky smell of it. "I didn't do anything to your skunk." He dug out his wallet and thumbed through it. "I'll pay you five hundred dollars to stay open and feed me."

Her eyes narrowed a fraction, and she put her hands on her

slim hips. "You think throwing your money around here will get you a meal?" Her gaze zeroed in on the red mark on his neck.

He didn't cover it with his palm like some embarrassed teenager, but defending himself seemed a good idea. "Some fan decided to make a spontaneous audition for Bram Stoker's *Dracula* after tonight's concert. Sunk her teeth into my neck before I knew what hit me."

Stories made people comfortable, so he pretended he was giving an interview. He'd charm the pants off Barbara Walters to get a meal tonight.

"Security went crazy, dragging the woman away kicking and screaming. Luckily she didn't break the skin, or I'd have to worry about rabies and communicable diseases. Can you imagine? After that, I burned rubber and came here. According to Yelp, you're the best diner in town. Over a hundred reviews with a 4.5 rating. Impressive."

She didn't look amused—or like she believed him for a second. He did have a reputation with the ladies, after all.

"Nevertheless, it's late, and I'm tired. I'll need more incentive than that."

Myra, who had trailed out after the spunky chef, gasped. "Tory! What has gotten into you?"

He couldn't contain the grin. He wasn't often treated poorly by people—present scandal aside—so she was a welcome change. Fame had a way of making people kiss his ass faster than he could say dandy. He settled back into the booth, which was about as uncomfortable as stadium bleachers.

"I like your spunk, and the reviews on Yelp did say a meal here is worth every penny. What would you say to a thousand?"

Her eyes fluttered before narrowing again. They were as green as his favorite beer bottle and almond-shaped. So, she hadn't thought he'd agree to up the ante. Wasn't that interesting?

"That works," she replied.

The amount was over-the-top, but it would be good PR. Stories like this tended to get out. His people could spin it into something good. He was helping out some ladies who'd served him a great meal.

Myra clutched her hands, muttering something he couldn't make out.

Rye counted out ten crisp one-hundred dollar bills. "So, what can you make me?" He caught the shake in Tory's fingers before she shoved the money into her pocket.

She crossed her arms in a cocky stance. "What do you like?"

Oh, did he have some inventive responses to that one. "I'm a meat and potatoes kind of guy, but after Myra's praise for your intuitiveness, I'll take whatever you want to make me."

She started tapping her tennis shoe on the linoleum. "You like chicken fried steak?"

He gave her a smile. "Yes, Tory, I do. Thanks." How had his life gotten to the point where he was casually spending a grand on a meal at a greasy spoon?

She turned and walked past Myra, who was shaking her head like a disapproving schoolmarm. "Not a word," the pixie said.

Still muttering to herself, Myra poured him a glass of tea, which he immediately sweetened. Then she picked up her dishrag and started scrubbing the stainless steel counters by the cash register, keeping at it until Rye could see her reflection in them. As he waited for his food, he flapped his damp shirt against his chest, hoping it would air dry. The stickiness against his skin was cold and uncomfortable.

Fifteen minutes later, he heard a shout from the kitchen. Myra raced back and came through the doors moments later with a heaping plate. She smiled when she set it in front of him.

"I hope you like it."

The chicken was fried to perfection, all golden and crisp. Rye closed his eyes as the smell and steam wafted up to him, taking a moment to be grateful. Food always pleased him, and tonight he needed the comfort of it more than usual. He cut into the chicken fried steak, eyeing the buttery mashed potatoes and creamed beans. The first bite was just as advertised. Heaven. He fought the urge to gobble the whole plate up like a hog. Some things were worth savoring. The food was incredible, but then again, he'd always thought diner food had something on those snooty five-star restaurants where his mama used to drag them.

He ate slowly as his belly warmed and filled. The noise in his head—like New York City at rush hour—faded away. If he didn't know better, he'd say there was something special in this food. He hadn't been this calm and focused since *The Incident*.

Myra hurried over with a pitcher of tea and refilled his glass. He dumped in half a cup of sugar and stirred.

"Someone's got a sweet tooth." She grabbed his empty plate. "Do you want lemon meringue pie or carrot cake for dessert?"

Rye leaned back against the booth, sated. "If it's as good as the meal, how about a slice of both? I nearly licked my plate."

"Sure thing. Tory might be sassy, but she's a damn good cook. She's just more stressed than usual. Her grandfather died four months ago, and she's trying to make things work with the hospital bills, mortgage, and school. That's why she pushed you for more money for the meal, I think." She grimaced. "I wanted to tell you as a way of apology. She's a good girl."

"It's no problem."

Myra slid his newest CD out of her apron and shyly extended it toward him with a pen. "I was listening to your music earlier tonight since I didn't get to go to your concert. Would you autograph it for me?"

He studied the cover. *Cracks in the Glass House* showed him swinging his guitar like a nine iron at a glass house covered in spider fractures. They'd taken a hundred pictures of him before declaring they had the winner. Personally, he couldn't tell why this one was any better than the ninety-nine others.

"I'd be happy to. What would you like me to write?"

"For continued courage."

He tapped the ballpoint on the table. "You having a tough time too, Myra?"

Her face turned red. "I have two kids in college and another graduating next year. Always seems to be another bill in the mail. That's why I understand Tory. She's a survivor. Sometimes I wish I had her courage."

"I'll bet you have more courage than you think," he said as he signed the CD.

Myra touched the case reverently after Rye pushed it toward her. "About what happened in Nashville..." she whispered. "Those of us who love your music know the media is blowing this whole thing out of proportion. I hope you find a way to deal with the bad press. Your music inspires us." Her face beamed like soft lamplight. "I'll get your dessert now."

He watched her go, his fingers gripping the table. How could he undo that moment of idiotic recklessness? If he hadn't pushed the man aside, the guy would never have fallen. Yes, there had been reason enough for his moodiness, but it wasn't any of *People* magazine's business. He never talked about where he was from and his life before country music, and it was that life that had risen up to kick him in the nuts once again. And break his heart. Oh, Amelia Ann.

His career was all he had left, and right now he needed some positive publicity, and he needed it pronto.

Strategies rolled around in his mind as Myra brought him dessert. The lemon meringue had to be about four inches tall. This meringue melted like cotton candy in his mouth, and the tangy lemon filling made him think *za za zing*, lifting his spirits again. Then came the carrot cake. The cream cheese frosting coated his tongue, and the cake—loaded with raisins, shredded carrots, and nuts—hit his taste buds like a flavor bomb. His eyes fluttered shut, and he groaned, chewing slowly. God, sometimes food was as great as sex.

The cake crumbs called to him, and he swiped them up with the last trail of frosting before pushing his plate away. He couldn't remember eating anything that good since he'd been at his Granny Crenshaw's house.

And all from the hands of a cranky, down-on-her luck cook.

"Down-on-her luck," he muttered.

An idea started to piece itself together like the first verse of a song. Why leave everything to Georgia or fate? He could kill two birds with one stone. Eat well *and* improve his image.

"Myra, could you have Tory come on out?"

"Sure, Mr. Crenshaw. I'll be right back."

She left before he could tell her to call him Rye. Or how he planned to thank Tory for the incredible meal, which was worth every penny of the thousand dollars she'd negotiated, just like Yelp had said.

***

Tory scrubbed the grill in furious strokes, ignoring her aching muscles. God, she hated cleaning it, and twice in one night royally sucked.

And all for that stinking redneck—literally. She didn't care what Myra said. Febreze might be magical stuff, but it did *not* completely obliterate skunk smell.

The grayish dishwater coated her hands and soap and grease bubbles danced and popped across her skin. She closed her eyes, hoping to relax. Her head was too full, her thoughts like a sprinter racing relays from one mark to the next.

She couldn't ignore the facts anymore. She was on a one-way path to bankruptcy. The thousand dollars would help, but she'd give Myra half. Her family was having troubles too.

What was happening to her? Part of her couldn't believe she'd hit the guy up for more money, but seeing him throwing the bills around like they were Monopoly money had set her teeth on edge. Why were the most undeserving the most successful? Seriously, every major media outlet had covered Rye Crenshaw's attack on that man, at an event for children, no less. Myra swore up and down the man had been inebriated, just like Rye had said in his official statement. Like she knew.

Deep down, Tory knew it wasn't just Rye's presence that had set her off. Another hospital bill had arrived in the mail yesterday, and the tight-knotted terror of that number at the bottom of the page had overwhelmed her. Her grandpa hadn't had supplemental insurance, so Medicare hadn't covered everything.

Scrubbing faster, she told herself she'd get through. Maybe she could pick up a second job. She curled over the sink, making her lower back twinge. When? Now that the semester had ended, her time at the diner began at breakfast and, after a short break in the afternoon, she was back until midnight. With her student loans and the mortgage to the family house she couldn't sell, the bank wasn't about to give her any more money. She'd have to take out another credit card, and pray she could handle the payments and horrible interest rates.

"Tory?" Myra called when she came through the door. "Mr. Crenshaw wants to see you."

"Isn't he finished yet? I'm beat."

"I know, dear. I need to get home too. He's just had his dessert. I think he just wants to pay his compliments."

She was gone before Tory could reply. Finishing off the grill, she wiped her hands on a faded blue dish towel. There were new black streaks across her apron, but what did she care?

Her knees hurt like she had a sprain when she trudged out of the kitchen. Even though he sure seemed to like food, he was fit, built. Broad shoulders. Firm chest. The ball cap looked strange on him after the pictures she'd seen of him in a cowboy hat, but she liked it. Without the cowboy getup, he was attractive—someone she would have looked at twice in a bar. His ash blond goatee framed some seriously chiseled lips. God she must be exhausted to be thinking like this. He was the last person she'd ever go for... And Lord wasn't it funny that she'd even think of that—it was hardly like he'd go for her either.

"You liked the meal?" she said when she reached his booth.

His mouth kicked up. "More than any I've had in a long time. I wanted to thank you."

Maybe it was because she'd spent the break in her shift packing up her grandpa's liquor cabinet, but Rye Crenshaw's voice made her think of the small batch bourbon her Grandpa drank before he got sick. All dark and smoky and...

What was it about good looking men and deep, throaty voices?

Okay, now she really needed to get to bed.

"If my granny were here, she'd ask you for the secret to your carrot cake," he said.

A man who punched people at charity events was asking her about secret ingredients? Wasn't that a first? "I usually peel the carrots, but I can't remember if I did today. Maybe it added texture." Yes, she'd been that tired.

"Oh..."

He blinked rapidly, making her notice his heavily lashed eyes. To say they were hazel wasn't enough. The browns, golds, and greens reminded her of a forest at dusk.

"Myra said you wanted something," she said.

"Like I said, the meal was incredible. Best I've had in some time. Thank you."

Well, she could be civil too, when the situation called for it. "You're welcome."

"She tells me you've had some tough times recently. You're in school?"

Tory turned her head to glare at Myra, who ducked into the kitchen. The diner was quiet save for the whooshing of the swinging door and the hum of the fluorescent lights.

"She shouldn't have said anything."

"She was trying to explain your..."

"Bitchiness?" she supplied, a bit of laughter creeping into her voice.

Rye cleared his throat and broke eye contact for a moment. "I'd never use that word to describe a lady."

Wasn't he full of it? "Right."

"What I wanted to say is that I'm sorry for keeping you open. You have to go to school tomorrow?"

She shifted her feet to ease her back ache. "No, I'm off for the summer. I work here full-time now."

"You're at the University of Kansas, right?"

"Yep."

Rye reached for his dessert fork and tapped it on the table. "When does school start back up?"

"After Labor Day. Why?"

He turned a bit to get a better look at her. "Look, I need a new cook. Mine just quit. My last concert is July 30. My manager has started making inquiries for a replacement, but why make it hard when it could be simple? Would you consider being my cook on the tour? I'd give you a good salary and cover all your expenses."

Her legs wobbled like Jell-O. "Do you mind if I sit down?"

"Of course not."

She slid into the booth across from him and scrubbed her face with both hands, trying to wake up. "You're offering me a job?"

"Well, you're out of school. We could help each other."

Wow. Okay, this was a surprise. Tory rested her head on one hand. "God knows I need the money. I can't sell my family's house. It's a serious fixer upper. I inherited the mortgage and my grandfather's hospital bills when he died. And then the grant didn't come through for my research, and the tuition and loan payments keep coming due." She compressed her lips. "I must be tired. I don't usually babble."

Rye shifted in his seat like he was super uncomfortable. Who could blame him?

She rubbed her temples—his drumming was beating in time with the beginnings of a headache. "Tell me more about this job." Was she actually considering his offer? Was he really violent? He didn't seem to be.

"Our cross-country tour started ten days ago in Nashville and lasts until the end of the summer."

"What would I have to do?"

Rye shrugged and put down the fork. Finally!

"If you joined the tour, you'd be on my bus. You'd cook me three meals a day and have a day off every week." The salary he named made her jaw drop.

The thousand dollars he'd paid for dinner was peanuts in comparison. "You're kidding."

"I never joke about money. You'll earn every penny as my cook. I love to eat." He chuckled. "My last cook's pie couldn't compete with yours."

"You said your cook quit. Seems a little strange since you just started the tour—"

"Ten days ago," he finished, rubbing a hand over his goatee, grimacing. "Smart, aren't you? Well, I don't like to talk out of school, but she slept with someone in my band. It was a big mistake—for both of them. She heaved a chocolate cream pie at him on the way out. I'd need to know you wouldn't follow in her footsteps, so to speak."

"So all I have to do is cook for you three times a day and not sleep with anyone in your band?"

A dark laugh escaped. "Well, when you put it that way, it *does* sound like an unusual stipulation."

She turned sideways and drew her knees to her chest, crossing her ankles on the seat of the booth. "Well, that won't be too hard."

Rye hummed in his throat and reached for the fork. He started tapping again. The man couldn't sit still. Would it be rude to grab the fork and hide it?

"You haven't seen them yet—only me."

"Do they look like you?" Oops, did she just say that?

His head drew back sharply. The tapping stopped, thank God.

"I mean, do they look like cowboys?" she qualified.

He cleared his throat and glanced over her shoulder. Tory followed his gaze. Myra was watching them through the window in the kitchen door.

"Well, I guess so."

Tory waved a hand dismissively. "No problem then. Marlboro men don't appeal to me." They were attractive in an Alpha way, but she liked her men smart and sensitive, not afraid of their feelings.

He twirled the fork around. From the way his mouth was pinched, she could tell he hadn't liked her response. When he rapped the fork against the table again, she finally darted out a hand.

"Could you..."

He settled back against the booth and crossed his arms, but a few seconds later his foot started tapping. Did he have attention deficit disorder in addition to anger issues?

"So, are you game? It'll be tons of traveling. You'll see more of the great U.S. of A. than you've ever wanted. We have twenty-four more concerts in twenty-three states. It's a merry-go-round, but it can be fun. But you'll need to decide now. I'd like you to start tonight. We're heading out shortly to the next stop."

Now? That was like...

The kitchen door burst open and Myra bustled out, her panty hose making that awful rubbing sound, reminding Tory why she never wore them.

"Tory, you have to do it, honey. It's the answer to your prayers."

Tory wasn't so sure the big man upstairs bothered answering her prayers anymore. "You shouldn't be eavesdropping," she said, but there was no censure in her voice. She rubbed the tense muscles in her neck. "Anyway, I'm not so sure I should be considering this after recent events."

Myra's face turned red. "Well, I'm sure he had a good reason for pushing that man. Didn't you, Mr. Crenshaw?"

His nod was as stiff as her back.

Tory raised an eyebrow at him. "Nice to have such loyal fans, isn't it?" God, what kind of wild behavior would she witness? Her grandma had always warned her about things that sounded too good to be true...but the money. She'd be crazy to pass it up. It would go a long way toward solving her financial woes.

His stare didn't waver. "Myra, could you give us a second here?"

"Of course," she said, heading back into the kitchen without another word.

"You have something you want to ask me?" he growled once they were alone together.

Her fingers curled around the fork she'd taken from him. "Well...if I'm going to take the job, I need to be comfortable, I guess. I'd like to know that you had a good reason, like Myra thinks, that you aren't violent."

He didn't say anything for a long while, and the long seconds were marked by the tapping of his knee. Tory tried not to fidget under his angry stare.

"I'm not violent, and I had a good reason," he muttered.

When he didn't continue, she leaned forward. "And..."

He yanked on his ball cap again. "Christ, I miss my Stetson. Look, I don't have to tell you shit."

"You do if you want me to take the job."

He leaned his elbows on the table. "It was a family matter, all right?" he hissed. "It made me crazy upset, and I shoved that man out of my way when he got in my face. He fell and started yelling and...oh hell."

Tory pressed her lips together to keep from asking more questions. Myra talked about him all the time, giving her the latest updates from the tabloids. There had been no mention of his family in the news, and she knew he wasn't married. He was considered one of those famous sexy bachelors, and yet tonight he looked like a normal guy, much less arrogant and cocky than all those pictures in the tabloids. She studied him closer. She wasn't sure when it had happened in their conversation, but underneath the anger, there was hurt. His face had fallen. His color had gone from tan to pale. He looked away from her.

"I'm sorry," she said, lowering her voice.

He snorted. "Forget it. I'm a bad boy, honey, but I'm no criminal. Does that reassure you?"

"Okay, I'll do it." God help her, and then she remembered she wasn't convinced that God cared about people like her, the ones who'd lost everything. Her stomach jumped like a pond of frogs, excitement and terror warring inside her.

Rye stroked his goatee. "Good. The buses leave in about an hour," he said, telling her where to meet him. "I can stretch it to two, but we have another concert tomorrow night in Minneapolis. Now, go tell your friend, so you can get going."

Right. Tory darted into the kitchen. Myra was dancing an Irish jig when she walked through the door. "Oh my God! You'll be famous, Tory. Maybe this will help you get your cookbook published. Wouldn't your grandma love that?"

Could her grandma love that from heaven? She wasn't so sure, but she liked the idea. "I don't want fame, Myra. I only want the money."

Myra placed her hands on Tory's shoulders. "Everything's going to be fine now. You'll see. I'll take care of the house while you're gone. And when you figure out how your mail should be directed, let me know, and I'll forward it to you." She pulled Tory in for a hug. "You call and tell me how everything is going. Your grandma would get a kick out of this if she were still with us. Gosh, I still can't believe she's been gone three years."

Tears filled Tory's eyes, making the kitchen look like she was viewing it through a half-empty fish bowl. But she didn't let them run over. She'd almost mastered burying her emotions, but there were still hits and misses.

"Thanks, Myra. I wouldn't have gotten through any of this..." While taking care of her grandparents these past four years, she'd made few friends. All of her friends growing up had moved away for college. Myra's presence in her life had lessened the blow of not being able to socialize with people her own age.

Myra leaned back and framed Tory's face. "Your grandma helped me get my job at this diner when I was your age. I owe her. And it's not hard to look out for you, Tory."

"I need to go pack and make some arrangements," she said in a hoarse voice.

Myra kissed her cheek and then stepped back. "I'll talk to Mel tomorrow and let him know you won't be with us this summer. He'll be so happy for you, Tory. I heard him say how he wished he could pay you more. He loved your grandma like we all did."

"I feel like I'm leaving him in the lurch."

"Don't worry. I can't cook as good as you, but I can help out until he hires someone. Now, let's get you back to Rye Crenshaw. If I were twenty years younger, I'd fight you for this opportunity, dear."

Rye was standing by the door when they emerged.

Tory drew in a breath. "It's all so fast." And she'd have to call Connie Perkins, her realtor, in the morning to tell her what was happening.

"Life works that way sometimes," he said with an enigmatic smile. "Myra, it was a real pleasure." And he tipped his finger to his ball cap.

Myra pulled him into a hug.

Still in a daze—this was just about the last thing Tory had expected to happen when she woke up this morning—she followed Rye out to the parking lot. He stopped by an ugly car and dug out his keys.

"That's your ride?" Of all the things she'd imagined a famous singer might drive, a dented muscle car wasn't one of them.

"I borrowed it. I'm traveling on a tour bus, remember? Do you have a pen and piece of paper?"

She dug into her purse and handed over a grocery slip and ballpoint. He scribbled on the crumpled paper in bold strokes before handing them back.

"That's my cell if you have any trouble finding me. I'll tell Clayton, my deputy, to keep an eye out for you. He handles all the hiring, so he'll go over all the details with you. Be there in two hours," he instructed, ducking into the car. His head hit the ceiling. Cursing, he slammed the door. The car turned over once before the engine started.

Tory had to bite her lip when it backfired as he reversed and left the parking lot. When she turned back toward the diner, Myra was standing in the doorway. She felt a shimmer of warmth crest over her. Myra's mothering had started when Tory was a kid, after her mom and dad died in a car crash. The diner, where her grandma had been the cook, had been her second home.

"I'll miss you." She dug into her pocket and counted out five bills. "Take half. I don't want to hear a word of protest."

Myra took the money and brushed a hand over her face to wipe away a tear. "Thank you. Do you want me to help you pack and give you a ride to the fairgrounds?"

"No, go on home. I have cab money, remember?"

Myra laughed and pulled her in for a hug. Tory relaxed into her embrace before breaking away and heading for her car.

The H in the diner's sign sputtered to life as she started the engine, making her halt. The word *Heaven* lit up for the first time in months before going dark again. Even with all her doubts, the sight sent a shock through her system. It seemed like an omen of something...she just wasn't sure what. Rubbing her arms, she climbed in her car and waved goodbye.

Grandma Simmons had one traditional cornbread recipe she would make either sweet or savory, depending on Grandpa's mood. When he had a bad day, she'd make maple cornbread to sweeten his disposition. When he was feisty—or she wanted him to be—she'd make Mexican, adding grated cheddar cheese and jalapeños from our garden. The secret is the buttermilk, the frothy elixir that makes it super moist and rise like crazy. You can make more variations than maple or Mexican cornbread. Be bold. Experiment. Find out what makes your man sweeter or spicier. Believe me, deep down, you know.

Basic Cornbread Recipe

1 cup cornmeal
½ tsp. salt
½ tsp. baking soda
2 tsp. baking powder
1/3 cup flour
2 Tbs. melted butter
2 eggs
1 cup buttermilk (fresh or from powder)

Combine the dry ingredients. Add the butter, beaten eggs, and buttermilk. {For maple: add 1/3 cup maple syrup. For spicy: add 2 Tbs. chopped jalapeños and 1 cup cheddar cheese.} Stir. Pour into a greased pan and bake for 20 minutes at 450 degrees. A cast iron skillet works best.

Tory Simmons' Simmering Family Cookbook

CHAPTER 2

Four tour buses hummed in the parking lot behind Liberty Hall. They almost looked like alien ships that had landed on an ocean of asphalt. She paid the cabbie and thanked him after he hefted her three suitcases out of the trunk. God, she hoped she hadn't forgotten anything important. Two hours wasn't a lot of time when it came to planning the next few months of her life.

The taxi chugged off. She grabbed the closest suitcase and quickly pulled it behind her, hoping she wouldn't have any problem finding this Clayton. Even in the nearly abandoned lot, she wasn't about to leave her other suitcases alone for too long. A security perimeter had kept the cab from getting as close as she wanted. Her legs had been achy and rubbery at the restaurant. Now they were numb like the rest of her body. She just wanted to lie on a flat surface. Even the asphalt looked tempting.

A string of die-hard fans milled about, shouting for Rye.

Her suitcase caught on something and turned over. "Shit," she muttered as she pulled it upright.

"Hello there," someone drawled. "You must be Tory,"

She straightened. Her purse slid down her shoulder. A tall man in boots, jeans, and a white dress shirt strode toward her and tipped back his matching white cowboy hat, giving her a big smile.

"Rye told me to keep an eye out for a dark-haired pixie with suitcases. I'm Clayton Chandler, his deputy manager."

She pulled up her purse and shoved her hair behind her ear. "Hi. I'm Tory." Great. Hadn't he already said her name?

"Let me help you with your bags and then we'll get you hired all formal-like." He reached for her suitcase. "I'll bet you're fried."

Like a donut. "Yes, it's pretty late. I have two more suitcases." She pointed across the way.

"I'll have someone get them. Why don't you follow me?"

His boots clicked on the pavement as he rolled her suitcase to the perimeter, where a bulky man waved them through. When

Clayton stopped at one of the buses, he set her suitcase against the side to keep it from toppling. She'd jammed it so full she'd had to sit on it to make the zippers meet.

"This is the bus I'm on, and it's where we keep the employment papers." He gestured for her to ascend the steps. "Your bag will be fine. Don't worry."

She trudged up the four steps. At this hour, it took as much effort as ten minutes on a Stair Climber. Pathetic.

"Down the hall," he instructed.

After the driver's seat, she passed a closed door. Someone was playing the guitar inside. There was a bathroom next to it, the door open. It looked as tiny as the one in her old college dorm.

"My room's the next one."

The door was open, so she wandered in. The snug space made Clayton seem gigantic when he joined her. The light from a silver floor lamp gave her a better view of him than she'd had outside. Apparently, Rye's band members weren't the only attractive ones on the tour, she noticed. Clayton had chiseled features and the grayest eyes she'd ever seen. He unfolded a desk from the wall and pulled out some papers.

"I know there's not a lot of space, but you'll get used to it. We'll stop at some hotels along the way when we're at a location for more than a night. It's always a nice change of pace." He handed her the stack. "These are our standard employment contracts. Rye told me the salary he offered you. I've already added in that information. Just fill in the personal information and sign it."

Her skill at speed reading helped. One of the papers gave her pause. "Is this really necessary?" she asked, gesturing to the confidentiality agreement.

"All our employees sign one," he explained, pushing back his cowboy hat. "Rye's real concerned about his privacy. We don't want anyone giving an exposé to the tabloids, especially after recent events."

So, that's what they were calling it?

"You'll be approached by reporters—even fans," Clayton explained. "Especially since you're going to be on Rye's bus. You seem like a nice girl. Just keep your nose clean, your mouth shut, and you'll be fine."

She tried to give him a reassuring smile. "You don't have to worry about me." Still, she read the entire agreement, wondering why lawyers had to use such complicated language. It seemed even more foreign at this hour. It took her fifteen minutes to complete the paperwork. Clayton worked quietly in a chair in the corner while he waited. When she handed them to him, he winked.

"Welcome aboard, Tory Simmons. Now, I'll introduce you to Georgia, my mama. She's Rye's manager."

So it was a family affair, she thought, as she tugged her purse up and followed him to the last door in the narrow hallway. His knuckles rapped on it before he opened it. "Mama, this is the lovely lady that Rye's hired as his cook." He made the introductions.

Georgia sat smoking on a mini leather couch in front of a window. She had fiery, dyed red hair and three-inch long blood-red nails. She didn't look like anybody's mama.

"Well, Rye says you cook like a dream, and he's a good judge," she said in a voice so husky she must have been smoking for decades. "I hear you're having a tough time. I'm glad this is going to work to everyone's benefit."

Tory fought the urge to choke from the smoke. This room was larger than Clayton's, but it reeked like a backed-up chimney.

Georgia stubbed out the cigarette. "I imagine you want to get settled. I'll see you in the morning." She stood and rose onto her tiptoes to kiss Clayton's cheek. "Night, son."

"Night, Mama."

"Goodnight, Mrs. Chandler," Tory added, trying not to run for clean air. She took deep breaths as she left the room.

"She's perfect," she heard Georgia whisper to Clayton before he left the room.

Perfect? What an odd comment. "Why did your mom say I'm perfect?" she asked, turning to Clayton.

He tugged his cowboy hat lower. "She thinks you're perfect for the job, I guess. I'll show you to your room in Rye's bus now."

Whistling softly to himself, Clayton led her to the second bus. Once again, he stepped aside and gestured for her to precede him. So far, his manners had been exquisite. Must be that southern gentility everyone talked about. She nodded to the driver tapping the steering wheel.

"Hi. You must be Tory," he said. "I'm Bill."

Did everyone know her name? It was a surreal feeling, particularly since she'd only met Rye Crenshaw a few hours ago. She shook the man's hand. "Good to meet you."

"We can take off in a few minutes," Clayton told him as they walked away. "First open door on your right, Tory."

She walked down the hallway, and Clayton flicked on the light when they reached the opening. "Here's your new office."

Tory stepped into the kitchen. The space wasn't too bad. She could work with this. A touch larger than a galley kitchen, it opened onto a small eating area. The honey brown tile floors blended into honey-colored cabinets fitted with a stainless steel sink in the middle. The appliances were stainless steel too, and so clean they sparkled. The side-by-side door refrigerator was nestled in the corner. She was grateful to see the dishwasher. Washing dishes by hand sucked. The stove drew her attention next.

"It's gas," she whispered. And there were five burners. Oh yeah.

"Yes, it's a gas grill setup with a tank," Clayton said. "I think it's a fire hazard, but Rye's convinced it cooks food better."

"I agree with him." She studied the tan leather booth in the corner, the table decorated with blue placemats. There was a plasma television mounted on the wall. Probably, like most men, he watched the tube while he ate.

She smiled at the white Kitchen Aid mixer on the counter. Good. The kitchen might be small, but it had everything she needed.

Clayton walked by her. "Just tell me what you want grocery-wise, and I'll have someone swing by the store for you."

She trailed her fingers over the microwave above the stove. "I prefer to do my own shopping," she said.

"Fine. I'll get you some petty cash. You can do it in Minneapolis tomorrow morning. There should be enough fixings for breakfast."

Tory let out a bone-cracking yawn.

He chuckled. "Let me show you your other room."

The light was already on in the bedroom. It was as small as Clayton's, but there was a coziness to it that appealed to her. Her suitcases were already lined up against the wall, she noticed. He walked past her.

"So, tour buses are all about efficiency. We can store your suitcases below once you unpack. Your clothes can go in this closet," he gestured. "And the bed folds out like this." He opened the compartment, demonstrating.

It reminded her of the bed Eva Marie Saint had crammed Cary Grant into on the train in *North by Northwest*. She was rather like his character, Roger Thornhill—one moment she had been leading an ordinary life, the next she was on this incredible cross-country adventure.

"The desk folds out the same way in front of the windows." He pulled open yet another cabinet. "TV."

Someone had given the room feminine touches. Yellow sunflowers graced the white bed linens, and the curtains lining the windows were a pale blue. "It's great," she said, even though the size would be an adjustment. Because heck, this whole situation would be an adjustment.

"It looks bigger when the curtains are open. And people can't see in."

She dropped her purse and rubbed her shoulder. "Thanks. Good to know."

"Come on. Rye wants to see you before you hit the hay."

Her feet dragged as she followed him to the closed door. When Clayton knocked, Tory heard a giggle.

"Come on in," Rye called.

Clayton let out a sigh as loud as a wind gust and opened the door. Even though the giggle had sounded an alarm in her head, Tory's mouth still dropped open. Rye was sitting in the ugliest hot tub ever created, a blond woman snuggled up to his side. As if the bright teal color of the tub wasn't bad enough, the thing was actually studded with rhinestones. Fortunately, they weren't arranged to spell Rye's name. The hot tub was smaller than average, arranged smack dab in the middle of the far side of the bathroom.

Her eyes flicked back to Rye. He had on a black cowboy hat and, as far as she could tell, nothing else. His bare-chest was covered with water droplets and was as utterly gorgeous in the flesh as it was on his albums.

Holy loving Mary.

"Hi there, Tory," he drawled, tipping his beer at her.

The blond gave a half wave and ran her hands through the bubbles frothing all around her. She didn't appear to be wearing anything either.

Heat flushed her face in the humid room. For heaven's sake, her new boss was greeting her while he basked in a hideous hot tub with some groupie? Was he going to be doing something like this every night?

"I see you got rid of the ball cap," she commented dryly, striving for the same calm she used as a graduate assistant teacher before a classroom of freshmen.

The blond giggled. "I would have loved to see that."

Keeping her gaze fixed on anything but them, she took in the rest of the bathroom, which was much more luxurious than the one on the other bus. A shower and toilet were to the right, and a two-sink vanity lined the wall on the left. Sharing this bathroom with him was going to be a heck of a lot weirder than sharing one with the six girls in her old dorm. And Myra wasn't going to believe her about the hot tub.

"Cozy set up you have here." Embarrassment burned away her fatigue, and regrets started to swirl like the currents in the hot tub. "I'm having second thoughts about this," she said.

"Who could blame you?" Clayton muttered by her side.

Rye nudged his black Stetson up, water dripping from his fingers. "About what, darlin'?"

Was he dense or was this just a regular conversation to him? It was certainly the first conversation *she'd* ever had with two naked strangers. Heck, make that *one* naked stranger. "Being your cook. This situation is a bit..."

Rye shrugged out of the woman's grip and started to stand.

"No! Don't get up." She threw a hand over her eyes.

His chuckle was dark and dirty. "Don't worry. I usually wait until the third date to get naked."

"Right," Clayton snorted.

Tory opened her fingers a crack and peeked through them. Her breath rushed out in a sigh of relief when she saw his black swim trunks, but then her insides heated as she took in his dripping wet, muscular body.

Rye tugged a towel from a nearby stand and strode forward like a gleaming wet god. "Did she sign the papers?"

Clayton tugged on his hat. "Yep."

Threading his arm through Tory's, Rye led her into the hall. "Well, then it's all official-like. What's the problem, sweetheart?"

"First, don't call me that." She pulled away and rubbed the watery fingerprints he'd left on her shirt. "Second, I'm having second thoughts about our arrangement. I'm not going to be comfortable with this kind of...incident happening all the time."

"Only happens a couple times a week," he drawled.

Her glare didn't diminish his naughty smile.

"You're a bit of a prude, aren't you?" he asked, his gaze wandering over her face.

Her mouth parted in shock. "By your standards, absolutely. My mother was a Catholic school teacher, and my father was the principal."

"We're leaving in five, Rye," Clayton said from behind them.

Tory didn't miss the stern note in his voice.

Rye rolled his eyes. "Best send the blond back home then. I'm talking to Tory."

Shaking his head, Clayton wandered back into the bathroom. Seconds later, a high-pitched shriek sounded, followed by a string of curses.

"This could get ugly." Rye started chuckling. "Let's head back to my room."

This was the type of thing that amused him? What kind of man played footsie with a woman in a hot tub before making another man give her the kiss off?

"No, here's fine," she said.

Another piercing shriek punctuated the silence, then a loud slap. The blond streaked out wearing nothing, and would have collided with Tory if Rye hadn't pulled her against him. Coming into contact with his bare chest propelled her even further out of her comfort zone.

"You bastard," the blond shouted and then streaked off. Literally.

Clayton emerged, rubbing his cheek. "Harder to catch than a greased pig," he commented.

"Then you'll be ready for the state fair this fall," Rye said with a smirk.

His deputy glared at him as he left the bus. "I'll make sure no one sees her running around the parking lot buck naked."

"Thanks, man," Rye said and then turned to Tory. "So, you're a prude and don't much like my shenanigans."

The urge to lower her head was strong, but she met his gaze instead. "You want me to be comfortable, right? I'm going to be living here too, and I cook better when I'm comfortable." It wasn't exactly a lie, and it was the only leverage she had.

"Fine. We can set some ground rules. First, no frolicking in my hot tub with strange men."

She blinked. "You're talking about me?"

"What's good for the goose..."

He could not be serious. "Trust me. It won't be a problem."

"Then I'll try to limit my...interactions on the bus and be more discreet. You think you can live with that?"

Well, it wasn't like she was working for a monk. This was probably the best offer she was going to get. "Okay. We can revisit things if necessary."

His eyes gleamed. "Oh, I revisit things all the time. Now go to bed," he commanded and headed down the hall. "Wouldn't mind blueberry pancakes for breakfast. Say ten o'clock? Night, now." Turning, he tipped his hat and shut the door behind him.

Blueberry pancakes? She'd do something to his blueberries all right.

Without any warning, the bus started moving. She wove at the sudden movement. With increasing dread, she found her room and shut the door, flipping the lock for good measure. She tapped her forehead against the wood of the door.

Why did she feel like tonight's hot tub craziness was only the beginning?

She'd made a pact with a devil—a *crazy* devil—and now she'd have to cook for him in country hell.

What had she gotten herself into?

***

Rye was tugging on a shirt when Clayton opened his bedroom door. He closed it, leaning against the wood with crossed arms in that insolent stance he'd perfected their first year together at Vanderbilt University when they were both barely eighteen.

"We're moving. How'd you get back on?" he asked.

"I called Bill to let me on at a stop sign. I've got five minutes to get back on my bus before we get on the interstate."

Since he felt a lecture coming on, Rye picked up his beer. "Pretty blond, huh?"

Clayton rubbed the red mark on his cheek. "What were you *thinking*?"

The beer was lukewarm. Rye didn't want to drink it, but he wanted something to do with his hands. "I was thinking she was hot."

"Bullshit. You were playacting for your new cook," Clayton growled. "A girl next door with her kind of background? She's the perfect way for you to restore your image, and you just gave her cold feet."

Yeah, because her dark-smudged green eyes had made him feel a hint of responsibility for her, so not his speed. Rye took a sip of the beer for show. "No worries. I'll sue her if she breaks her contract." It was a joke. Mostly.

Clayton shoved away from the door and took a step closer to Rye. "You'll what?" He stopped in front of his friend and crossed his arms again. "Look, I know you're still upset about Amelia Ann, but you have to think about your career. Stunts like this are dangerous after what happened in Nashville. If that blond decides to tell all to some tabloid or someone got a picture of her running naked off your bus, we could be in big trouble. That's certainly not a family values picture."

He was so goddamned sick of being reminded of what a screw up he was. "You forgetting who's boss here?" he asked, setting the beer aside.

Clayton pulled off his hat and slapped it against his jeans, the sound like a crack of thunder. "You planning on throwing away a twelve-year friendship right now? Seems to me you need all the friends you got."

Rye casually reached for a mint from the crystal bowl on his dresser, his hand shaking a little from the realization that he'd gone too far. "Shit. Come on, man. I didn't mean that. I'm just tired…"

"So are the rest of us! Do you think you're the only one under pressure here? Look, I'm saying this for your own good. You'd better start acting right or everything you've worked for—*we've* worked for—will go up in smoke." He ran his hand through his hair. "Do you want your family to have the last laugh?"

Not in a million years. Rye popped the mint in his mouth and bit into it hard enough to make his teeth hurt. "That's below the belt."

Clayton shook his head. "Listen. You need to shape up and execute that brilliant plan you thought up tonight. Tory is perfect for improving your image. Wholesome."

Hadn't he had the same realization in Diner Heaven? But now he wasn't nearly as certain he'd made the right decision. Tory seemed like a nice woman, and it would be wrong to use her.

"She admitted to being a prude," he remarked.

"Good. We need more family values around here."

"Fine, we'll show my good side to the world by helping her, but I don't like Georgia's idea."

"Too damned bad. It's genius. If we make it look like you're involved with her, people will think you're settling down a bit, maybe thinking about having a family. It'll look like you actually like kids."

"Jesus, it sounds like you want me to marry her." Rye reached for a fireball from the crystal bowl. The flavor was as strong as five-alarm salsa. His eyes watered. "Doesn't seem right, using her that way. Besides, she's not even my type."

Clayton slapped his hat on his head. "She's pretty and petite. I've always liked that in a woman."

"Then why don't you go after her?"

"I'm not the one with the image problem." He slung his hands from his belt loops. "So, we'll leak a story about what you did at the diner with the thousand dollars and how you're helping this down-on-her-luck cook."

He'd had to do a lot of crap in the business, but he'd never pretended to date anyone like other celebrities did. Wasn't it just his luck that he'd be using a nice woman who was going to find the whole thing repellant. "I hate this."

"You have to turn the tide now. Rye, we lost another sponsor."

"Who?" he asked, dread heavy in his belly.

"Levis."

"Shit." No one had to tell him how huge that was. "Okay, we'll try, but if the press doesn't help, I'm putting a stop to it."

"Well, well, someone sounds a little guilty. I haven't seen any signs of a conscience from you in years."

Rye flipped him the bird.

Clayton moved to the door. "And *try* to be charming. If we're going to suggest you're falling for your anti-type, it would help if she actually *looks* like she's into you."

"No need to worry about that. Women fall for me all the time."

Clayton had the audacity to tip his hat as he left. "Somehow I think she'll be a tougher nut to crack. The girl's got spine, and you haven't come across that in some while."

Rye picked up a boot from the floor and pelted it against the closing door. Jackass. Interfering son of a bitch. What the hell did he know? He could make anyone fall for him. Soon she'd be eating out of his hands—even if she was the one doing the cooking.

Being the cook at Diner Heaven for nearly thirty years, my Grandma Simmons dealt with some pretty mean truck drivers. They'd come in off the highway with bloodshot eyes and bark at the waitresses. One particular man was so mean, she fixed him a special stack of pancakes, certain they'd improve his disposition. Grandma believed the way to a man's heart was through his stomach, but she didn't think food's power stopped there. She talked about the emotional reactions all people had to food. The mean truck driver wasn't growling anymore after eating her special pancakes, so she added them to the menu with great success.

Truck Driver Pancakes

1½ cups flour
1 tsp. baking soda
¼ cup sugar
½ tsp. salt
¼ cup cocoa
2 eggs, beaten
1 cup milk
½ cup butter, melted and cooled
½ cup chocolate chips

Combine the dry ingredients. Add the eggs, milk, and butter. Stir. Add the chocolate chips. Shape into pancakes on the griddle and cook. Serve with maple syrup or bittersweet chocolate ganache.
Tory Simmons' Simmering Family Cookbook

Chapter 3

Maple bacon strips crackled and popped on the stove. Tory arranged the bowls holding the wet and dry ingredients for the pancakes and strained to hear if her boss was coming down the hall. His guitar had broadcast an angry melody not long ago, so she knew he was awake. Plus, he'd said he wanted to eat at ten o'clock. Her fork whisked the eggs for the tenth time.

Today's breakfast was critical. She planned to have him eating out of her hands.

Her finger trailed down her grandma's recipe in the makeshift binder she'd created. She could tame the beast with food—just like her grandma had taught her. And she'd start with her Truck Driver pancakes.

Boots clunked down the hall, and then Rye appeared in the doorway, his face cleanly shaven save for the goatee. He tipped his hat—a white one today—and smiled.

"Mornin'. Smells good in here." And then his gaze dipped lower.

She tucked her hands into the pockets of the only apron she'd found in the kitchen—a frilly confection of white lace and pink fabric that made her want to blush. Who made aprons like this, anyway? Frederick's of Hollywood? She wasn't surprised the former cook had slept with someone in the band. This was an apron with an agenda, and the only reason she was wearing it was because bacon grease stained like ballpoint pen ink. But you could bet your britches that a new apron was at the top of her shopping list.

"I'll...have breakfast up in a second."

She swiveled around and mixed the two bowls together. She added the chocolate chips to the batter and checked the griddle. It was smoking hot. Perfect.

Tory looked over her shoulder. He was already sitting at the booth, reaching for the remote, and morning news filled the silence.

"You look kinda cute in that apron."

Oh, great. Of course he had a comment.

"It's not what I would call a normal apron," she muttered. "It's the only one I could find."

"Looks fine to me."

Of course it did. It was a costume straight out of one of his country music videos. Sighing, she picked up the bowl and dobbed batter on the griddle. After making four circles, she shut the heat off under the bacon and dropped the glistening, steaming strips on a paper-toweled plate. The apron came off, and she gleefully stuffed it back into its drawer, hopefully forever.

"You want coffee?"

"That'd be great. And orange juice."

She served up his requests, watching the pancakes bubble as they cooked.

He reached for the coffee and sipped. "I'm sorry about last night. You're right. This will be your home for the next few months, and I don't want you to be uncomfortable. Won't happen again."

Well, that was much more agreeable than she'd expected. "Thank you." Her sensitive nose detected that the pancakes were ready to be flipped, so she turned them over. She started the microwave to heat the maple syrup.

Minutes later, she set everything in front of him. He grabbed a bacon strip and popped it in his mouth. "Nothing better than bacon in the morning." He looked at the pancakes. "Those aren't blueberries."

"No. Chocolate chips. It's my Grandma's recipe."

Rye bowed his head and then forked the whole stack onto his plate, pouring enough maple syrup on them to drown a city. Tory started to clean up, listening for his reaction. The first groan soothed the ball of tangled Christmas lights in her stomach.

"Like them?" she asked, smiling easier.

He gave a humming sound. "They're like chocolate chip cookies, but spongier. Incredible."

Thank you, Grandma. She loaded the dishwasher and scrubbed the pans.

"You're not eating?"

When she turned to look at him, he was wiping his mouth with the blue cloth napkin.

"No, I..."

He pointed to the feast in front of him. "You eat everything you make, okay? Unless you don't like it."

She noticed his orange juice was gone, so she poured him more. "I don't make anything I don't like."

He leaned back in the booth. "That your cookbook?" he asked, gesturing to the thick blue binder on the counter.

"Well...it's a family cookbook I've been working on it since my grandma died. It's a collection of recipes with stories about her and her philosophy."

Rye drained half the orange juice before setting his glass down with a thunk. "You should publish it. If the other recipes are anything like these pancakes or the meal you made for me last night, you'd make a mint. Got any of your own recipes in there?"

Standing while he was sitting felt awkward. "Yes, I'm an intuitive cook—just like she was."

His brow furrowed. "What does that mean?"

"Well, I seem to have a knack for inventing food. Knowing what people like." She wouldn't discuss her grandmother's belief that good food could sway people's moods and emotions. That was like talking about acupuncture to a doctor. "My grandma said it was a gift, like knowing how to play the piano."

Rye nodded and stroked his goatee. "I like that. That's how I feel about playing Old Faithful."

The geyser at Yellowstone Park? "Excuse me?"

He picked up another strip of bacon. "My guitar. The only thing a man can count on in life besides a dog."

Tory disagreed, but then again, she and dogs didn't get along.

His fork drew circles in the remaining syrup on his plate. "Why don't you quit college and go to cooking school? You'd make an incredible chef."

That's what everybody said, and she'd always given the same answer. "My grandma wanted me to have an education. She was the cook at Diner Heaven for three decades, and she wanted better for me."

Rye broke the bacon in two. "Well, let me give you some advice. You should listen to your own gut and not your family when it comes to your future."

There was bitterness in his voice, and she remembered what he had said about his family. Clearly it was a sore subject, which only made her more curious. "And you know this how?"

He looked away. "Personal experience. So, what are you in school for?"

"Anthropology."

"What's that?" he drawled.

Something about the way he asked made her suspect he was playing dumb. While she hadn't known him long, she already had the impression that there were a dozen different Ryes that he took out for the right occasion, rather like a man selecting his daily tie to accompany his suit.

"It's the study of the origins of physical and cultural development. I specialize in cultural anthropology, which looks at social norms and customs."

"What the hell are you going to do with it?"

"Teach college, I guess.

He popped in another piece of bacon and chewed. "What year are you?"

"My coursework is finished, so I just need to wrap up my dissertation. I'm studying the effects of tourism on the Maasai people's traditional way of life in Kenya." She turned away to start the dishwasher.

That was a mouthful. And it sounded as dull as dishwater, even to her. "You're in graduate school? How old are you?"

She pivoted at the surprise in his voice. "Twenty-eight. Why?"

He rubbed his fingers on his napkin. "Well, shoot, you're damn near my age."

"How old are you?" she asked.

"I'm turning thirty this year."

"Oh." For some reason she'd thought he was younger. Maybe because of the way he acted.

He walked over with his mug to pour himself some more coffee. "Aren't you a little old to still be in school?"

"I had to take some time off when my grandparents got sick."

"How long is it going to take you to write your dissertation?"

"Well, that's kinda up in the air. My grant hasn't come through yet, but I can do my field research and finish my dissertation as soon as it does." Even thinking about the grant made her heart race. She'd never traveled outside the U.S. before, but soon she'd be heading to rural Africa.

"So, you're a smarty pants." He shook his head slowly. "I don't know how I feel about that."

"Why?" she asked, scrunching her forehead. "You have something against education?"

"No," he said, taking a swig of coffee. "It's just that some folks with too much schooling get it into their heads that they're better than those who don't have much. I don't like that."

"I agree. You know, I've always hated studying." And wasn't it odd that she'd told him that? She'd never said it out loud before.

"So why do it?"

"Because it was Grandma's wish for me." More like her deathbed wish. Of course, Tory had been happy enough to grant it. Her parents had been educators, after all, and she knew from her grandma's struggles that working in a restaurant was harder than teaching. This way she could be home in the evenings with the family she dreamed about having. Not serving up dinner specials like her grandma had done all her life, missing bath and bedtime.

"So what's your full name going to be when you get your degree?"

She lifted a shoulder, a tad embarrassed. "Dr. Victoria Simmons."

He gave her a slow up and down look that made her jumpy. "Suits you."

Since that wasn't worth debating, she walked over to the refrigerator and pointed to the paper pinned with a magnet. "This is the Food Wish List, so you can let me know what you'd like to eat, including snacks and such. I'll consider it when I make the menu and buy the groceries, but you have to give me a little freedom with the menu planning."

"After what I've had of your cooking, I trust you." He took out a pen from his pocket and wrote on the paper while standing up.

"Veal piccata and taco salad?" she read aloud. "Dr. Pepper and Perrier?"

"I have an eclectic palate. I'm going to make some calls." He looked at his watch. "We should be getting to Minneapolis pretty soon. I'll introduce you to the band tonight before the concert."

She straightened the magnet and the paper in a perfect line. "I told you I'm not a fan of country music."

"I'd like you to meet everybody anyway. You'll be running into them, and I like a cohesive tour. Plus, you know you want to see me in concert." He leaned against the refrigerator and undid the order she'd just achieved.

It was hard to restrain the eye roll, but she managed. "Who's cooking for everyone else by the way?"

"A caterer. They're good, but nothing like you. Just go once. You'll be *backstage*," he drawled.

Like that would tempt her. "Fine, I'll go."

"Good. I've gotta run. We'll get to know each other better later." He sauntered out.

Get to know each other? What in the world did he mean by that?

As she watched him leave, she realized he had a great butt.

Definitely not a thought she needed to be having in these close quarters.

***

Tory was dipping chocolate cupcakes into espresso frosting when Clayton came to take her backstage before the concert. He didn't have a hat on this time, and he was wearing a gray dress shirt and black slacks.

49

"Those look so good they should be illegal," he said, waving his hand at the cooling rack stacked with cupcakes.

Taking her knife, she smoothed frosting along the edges of one of them and set it aside. "The receipt from the cab I took to get the groceries is over there," she said, nodding to the counter. Plucking up a cupcake, she held it out to him with a smile.

"Oh, Rye's going to be jealous I had the first taste."

"We won't tell him. So, I've never been to a concert before," she confessed.

"You're kidding?" he said, removing the liner from the treat. "Why not?"

"Just not a priority, I guess. Plus tickets can be expensive." And money had always been an issue.

"Well, you'll have the best seat in the house tonight." And then he took a bite. His eyelids fluttered shut for a moment. "Oh, yeah. I can now see why Rye hired you."

They stepped off the bus, Clayton still eating the cupcake, and made their way through a scattering of people, some dragging heavy equipment.

"It's always crazy," Clayton commented when someone almost ran into them. "We have our own set-up crew, but there's always a local one as well. Coordination can be a challenge."

He led her through the back door of the stadium. Groups of people were milling about, shouting back and forth about the lighting. There were wires running everywhere, taped to the scuffed wooden floor by duct tape. Wearing a yellow dress with cowboy boots, Georgia stood in the middle of the madness talking with a man in a suit with some leather-like tie at his neck secured with a silver and turquoise clasp. Tory tried not to ogle their fashion choices as she tugged at her plain red T-shirt.

Music thrummed in the distance beneath the roar of the gathered crowd. Her eyes widened when she saw the black curtain in front of them. It was as tall as a small mountain.

"We pipe the music in to get the crowd in the mood," Clayton said, raising his voice to be heard over the noise. He gestured to a door that said *Private*. "Rye and the band are chilling in the lounge."

He didn't knock before entering. Tory stepped inside and came to an immediate halt. Rye and his band were all decked out and looked ready to face down the bad guys at high noon in a gun fight. She'd read Louis L'Amour books as a kid, but she'd never seen so many cowboys in real life. They looked...well, foreign. And imposing.

Rye grinned when he saw her and sauntered forward. "Boys, this here's Tory, my new cook. She's never been to one of our concerts, so we'll have to play extra good tonight."

He stopped in front of her, his smile reminding her of a wicked sorcerer. There it was again, that unwanted but undeniable thrill of attraction. She edged back until she hit the door. She hadn't seen Clayton close it. How embarrassing.

He only smiled wider. "She's not easily impressed," he murmured, "but that's part of her charm."

Her charm? What was wrong with him? He was looking at her like she was...a Twinkie he wanted to eat, sucking the cream out of the middle. Her wave was a light flutter of her hand.

"Hi," she said lamely.

Rye introduced her to six men. She didn't catch all the names, but she caught most of the instruments—violin, drums, piano, and three types of guitars.

"So which one of you had the pie heaved at him?"

The one guy whose name she did remember—he'd been the first in line—started laughing. Tucker pointed at Rye. "You blaming us for your misdeeds now?"

Her mouth gaped open as she turned to look at Rye.

His eyes narrowed, and that unnerving smile vanished. "Shut up," he ordered.

Tucker held up his hands before reaching for his beer. The other band members looked away and picked up their own longnecks.

"*You* slept with your cook?" She checked her foot from kicking him, but oh, how she wanted to. "You lied to me!"

"No, I said she slept with someone in the band." He pointed at his chest. "*I'm* in the band."

She turned to Clayton. He lifted his shoulders as if to say *don't blame me.*

"Well, that explains the apron. There's no way anyone with an ounce of talent would cook in that."

His shoulders started to shake. "Oh, she cooked in it all right."

The other men started laughing.

She put her hands on her hips. "You deliberately lied to me. I'll bet you lied about the little family matter that made you get into it with that man at the charity event."

Laughter ceased. The whole room grew quiet save for the outside music and the noise of the crowd.

The gold ring around his hazel eyes looked like fire. "I didn't lie about that. Wish I had," he murmured, only loud enough for her to hear.

She scanned the room. No one would meet her eyes.

Someone pounded on the door and yelled, "Five minutes."

"Excuse me," Rye said, striding out of the room without a backward glance. The band followed.

Clayton stared down his nose at her. "Well, that went well. I hope we don't have *another* incident tonight."

Well didn't that beat all! "Don't guilt-trip me here. He's the one who didn't tell the truth. How am I supposed to know what he does and doesn't lie about?"

"Let me give you some advice about Rye. Don't judge a book by its cover." He gestured to the door. "We should get out there."

He led her through a tunnel to the stage area. "The best place to see a concert, in my opinion, is from the wings. If you don't mind standing."

"No," she muttered as the bass reverberated through her body and the lights nearly blinded her.

Her heart skipped a beat when the hall went totally black, and the crowd began to clap and scream. When a spotlight pierced the darkness and illuminated Rye, he was standing on a slender silver platform a hundred feet above the stage.

The crowd went wild. He sang three words, "Take the fall."

She only had a moment to marvel at how beautiful his singing voice was before a haunting silver light arced up behind the stage. He lifted his arms and fell backwards. Tory screamed, joining the rest of the astonished crowd. For a moment she thought she'd witnessed a public suicide, but then his body bounced off a net that had been obscured by the darkness. The band started to play as Rye crawled to the end, flipped off the net, and jogged to the front of the stage.

"How're ya'll doing tonight?" he drawled.

The noise became deafening. Tory raised her hands to cover her ears.

"That good? Well, I want to dedicate this concert to all of you who are struggling right now. I know times are tough, and you paid your hard-earned money to be here tonight. We appreciate you coming and plan to give you the show of your lives."

The crowd applauded, and whistles and screams filled the stadium from men and women wearing cowboy hats. Tory looked up at the gigantic TV in the corner of the stadium. Rye's handsome face filled the screen.

"You know, I went to a diner last night after a show. Y'all ever need some comfort food?"

He paused and let the crowd answer.

"Well, I had the best food of my life last night and found out the cook was having a hard time. She was out of school for the summer like many of you and working a tough job to pay the bills." He tugged on his guitar strap. "I decided then and there to hire her. Help her out some."

Tory lowered her hands from her ears. Could he be...was he talking about *her*?

"Tory Simmons, where the heck are you?"

All the sudden the spotlight flooded her, and she had to lift her hands to shield her eyes.

"Cute, ain't she? And her mama was a Catholic school teacher and her daddy the principal. So if I don't mind my Ps and Qs from now on, I'll be getting detention."

As her eyes adjusted, she realized her image was on the big screen, and her whole body flushed red with embarrassment. A hundred thousand people were staring at her! And he'd just told them her business.

"So here's my challenge to you," he continued as the spotlight shifted back to him. "We can all help each other get through these tough times. If you can do something for someone, don't hesitate." He played a few strands on his guitar. "Now, are you ready for some music?"

He didn't wait for a response. The band started playing a fast, hard-edged intro.

Georgia appeared beside Tory and Clayton. "Brilliant! This is going to be incredible PR."

So, she was a PR campaign? He was using her? She was a proud and private person who never shared her troubles with strangers. How dare he! And worse, by talking about her parents like that, he was implying she was more than just his cook. Many of his fans were church-going people, and after the charity event incident, something like this might help reassure them.

She no longer had any desire to see the concert. The music pounded through her like blows as she got up and started to walk away.

Clayton stood and grabbed her arm. "Tory, there's no reason to be upset."

"Do you really believe that? He humiliated me in front of all these people, and he's using me to restore his image."

Clayton put his hands on her shoulders. "He didn't humiliate you. He's helping you."

She shoved his hands away. "No, he made me out to be a

charity case."

"Look, Rye's trying to save his career. You're good press. I'm sorry if that upsets you."

She wrapped her arms around herself. Suddenly all she wanted was to be back home in her comfortable life, where people said what they meant and meant what they said. "I want out of my contract, Clayton."

"We won't break the contract, especially not after what Rye said tonight. Look, having his career tank is the last thing he needs. He's having problems with his family right now."

"And what about me? You don't think I have troubles?"

"I know you do, and I'm sorry. Come on," he murmured, his voice soft. "I'll take you back to the bus."

Once she was tucked away in her tiny room, she called Myra and poured her heart out. Hearing her friend's voice made her long for home. When she ended the call, she stared out the bus window.

Suddenly the summer seemed too long, and she felt more alone than she had since her grandpa's death.

Take the fall,
Hit that wall,
Sometimes it's all you've got.

The pain inside,
Rages like fire,
And there's no extinguisher nearby.

You won't break,
You won't burn,
Don't be afraid.

Take the fall.

Rye Crenshaw's Number One Hit, "Take the Fall"

CHAPTER 4

Avoiding Tory the next morning seemed to be the best approach, particularly after what Clayton had told him. He couldn't blame her for feeling used, but he hated that she'd felt humiliated too.

It was hard not to think about her and feel guilty with the bacon smell wafting through his closed door.

Rye set his guitar on his lap, looked out the window, and studied the passing cornfields. He spied what looked like an invisible man racing through the tall green stalks, trying to outrun the bus. Rye knew the image wasn't real, that it could be explained away by some physics thing, but he liked watching it.

When his cell phone rang, he reached for it and his heart burst when he saw his sister's number on the display. Thank God she'd finally called. He'd hoped she would find a way to defy Mama.

"Amelia Ann. I'm so glad you called. I missed—"

Crying and hiccupping was the only answer.

"Rye, Daddy collapsed on the golf course this morning. He had a heart attack and needs a quadruple bypass. We're all at the hospital."

His daddy? No way. He was as fit as a fiddle. "What happened?"

"I don't know! The doctor said he's been working too hard. Mama said it was all the stress you put the family through with your business with the police, which is the meanest comment ever. I'm scared, Rye." She started crying again. "I wish you could come home."

Home? His home was Dare River now or this tour bus. Not the place where he'd been born and raised. "Amelia Ann, you know I can't. Mama's made that very clear."

"I know. She was awful to me after Taylor Benint let it slip that I'd been in touch with you. I shouldn't have told her. Mama threatened to disown me if I contacted you again, but I had to tell you about Daddy." A ragged chain of sobs sounded on the line.

His knuckles whitened on his guitar.

"I don't know if I can take it, Rye. Mama's still planning to push me into some semi-arranged marriage, just like she did with Tammy. And now Daddy's sick."

The pounding in his head crested to epic proportions, and his helplessness left a gaping hole in his chest. "Honey, you know I want to be there for you." Only the threat of his Mama's actions kept him from having Bill turn the bus toward his hometown in Mississippi. "Besides, I'm not sure Daddy would want me there anyway." God knows, his presence might even harm his father's recovery, given the fallout between them.

"Rye, you know it wasn't Daddy's idea to disown you. That was all Mama."

What did it matter? The result had been permanent banishment. No one messed with a crème de la crème family like his and survived. And he'd done that when he chose country music over following in the footsteps of his male ancestors, all of whom had joined the family firm after graduating from Vanderbilt Law.

"Well, he didn't do anything to stop it," he said.

Her crying tinkled like a soft bell. "Oh, Rye."

"Please stop crying," he whispered, his eyes tracking to the picture of them on his bureau right before he returned to Nashville after his last spring break in law school. It had been at a karaoke bar in Nashville where he'd met his fate. Clayton's mom had met them there for drinks a few weeks before graduation, and being one of the major country singer managers in the business, she'd instantly picked up on his raw talent. The rest, as they say, was history. He and Georgia always laughed about the fact that he'd been under her nose for years. "You're breaking my heart."

"I miss you."

God, he missed her too, but saying so would only add to her pain. "You be strong for me."

An ambulance siren sounded on the line. He drew the phone away from his ear.

"Tammy! No!" Amelia Ann suddenly cried. Then the line went dead.

So Tammy was still Mama's enforcer. His Stepford-wife sister had turned her back on him with a posture so perfect a book wouldn't have fallen off her head. Having been best friends with Rye's fiancée, Emeline, Tammy had felt doubly betrayed by his defection from family tradition and his cancelled engagement.

Pain seared Rye's heart, and he stood tall, trying to close it out. To occupy his mind, he studied the invisible runner in the fields for a moment, but then he shoved the sheet music off his desk in a rage.

You stupid bastard, he thought. *You can't outrun anything.*

Even though they were estranged, he wanted his Daddy to be okay. It was hard to imagine the lean, tanned golfing lawyer being sick. The man never succumbed to so much as a simple cold.

Could it be true? Had *The Incident* stressed his old man enough to make him collapse?

A whiff of bacon touched his nose, promising comfort, but he only wanted to be alone. He caressed Old Faithful's burnished wood and hugged it to his hollow chest. The first strums on the guitar were violent and angry. A string broke, and he swore.

***

The rolling green of Michigan passed by as Tory shoved the ribs into the oven to keep them warm and tapped her foot on the tile floor. They had a few more hours before they'd arrive in Detroit, the next concert stop. Rye hadn't responded to her summons to breakfast and lunch. He hadn't even come out. Was *he* really ignoring *her*?

She yanked off her new apron, a normal white one courtesy of yesterday's shopping trip, and stalked down the hallway. She wouldn't let him hide any longer. His door was shut. She pounded hard enough to make her palm hurt.

"If you're not going to eat, at least be respectful enough to tell me as much."

When he didn't respond, the first ripple of worry ran through her. Pressing her ear to the door, she heard nothing. Was something wrong? "Rye? Is everything okay?"

No response.

She cracked the door open, seriously concerned now. His big body lay huddled on a brown leather sofa under a caramel and white striped blanket.

"What's the matter?" she asked, walking forward. His face was white and haggard. She darted a hand out to touch his forehead for fever.

"I don't feel good," he whispered, pushing her hand away.

"Are you sick?"

He tugged the blanket up to his neck. "Just leave me alone."

She picked up his phone off the floor. "I'm calling Clayton. Give me your passcode."

He muttered it, and she located Clayton's number in his contacts and dialed. Told him what was going on and hung up.

"You just need to eat," she said to Rye. "I bet that's part of the problem. I'll make you some mashed potatoes and applesauce.

That's what my grandma always made me when I was feeling sick."

A half-empty glass of amber liquid sat on the floor. She picked it up and sniffed. "Are you drunk?"

"No, started to get that way, but couldn't choke it down." He groaned. "Christ, I wish I were drunk. I don't want to think."

The bus stopped, and she realized they'd pulled onto the shoulder of the interstate.

Clayton and Georgia burst into Rye's room moments later.

"He's not feeling well."

"We'll take care of it," Clayton said.

She left, her anger fading. What he'd done last night wasn't right, but there was clearly something wrong with him. He looked more sad than sick to her. And his comment about not wanting to think? Well...

Tory had potatoes and cored apples boiling in separate pots when Clayton and Georgia emerged and walked past the kitchen.

"Do you think we should cancel Detroit?" Clayton asked.

"No, it would be devastating to the tour, especially since we couldn't release the reason. If you have to get him drunk to get him onstage, do it." Georgia walked past the kitchen. Her snakeskin boots seemed an appropriate choice after that comment.

They were going to liquor him up to perform? It seemed cruel. Well, she'd try to get some food into him first.

She checked the apples with a fork to see if they were soft. Yep. All ready. She drained them, reserving a few tablespoons of the liquid. After dumping the mix into the blender, she added nutmeg and honey, pressed down on the lid, and hit the On button.

She looked back when she felt a tap on her shoulder. Clayton was standing behind her. She turned the blender off. "Yes?"

He cleared his throat. "I understand you aren't feeling too friendly toward any of us, so I'm grateful you called me."

"I'm not inhuman. He's not feeling well." She popped the lid and poured the mixture into a bowl. "Would you let me try and get some food in him before...?"

"I get him drunk? I know our measures seem harsh to you, but it's all for his benefit." He slapped his hat against his knee. "Yes, please give him some food. It won't stop the reason he's upset, but maybe it will help a little."

So, it was as she'd thought. He was sad.

"Thanks, Tory." He strode out of the kitchen, boots clicking like a metronome, and the bus started moving again some moments later.

She blended the steaming potatoes next, adding butter, heavy cream, sour cream, and salt. When she tasted them, she smiled. Was there anything better than mashed potatoes? She dished up both concoctions and headed to Rye's room.

He was lying on his back with the blanket tucked around his waist. He rolled his head, saw her, and grunted. "Go away."

She placed a napkin and the bowl of mashed potatoes on his chest. "Why don't you try this? You'll feel better if you get something substantial in your stomach."

He sniffed and then reached for the spoon. "Smells good." When he took a bite, his eyelids fluttered closed.

It was impossible to be angry with him when he was like this. The energy that usually poured from him had all been leached out. He ate with slow determination at first, but by the time he finished the potatoes and she handed him the applesauce, his pace picked up. She sat in silence, cross legged on the floor by the sofa. Somehow she knew he didn't want to be alone.

"Tastes good," he murmured.

When he handed her the empty dishes, their eyes met. She didn't look away. She couldn't say why.

"My Daddy had a heart attack," he whispered.

She gripped the bowls. Oh goodness, no wonder he was so upset.

"I'm so sorry. When are you going home to see him?" She pushed off the floor, balancing the bowls, and nearly tripped. She looked down. *Leaves of Grass* lay at an angle. Rye Crenshaw read Walt Whitman?

"I can't go home. Gonna rest now. Have to sing...later." His eyes closed, and he slipped into sleep.

He couldn't go home? The thought was abhorrent to her. Her family had been everything to her.

She tucked the blanket up to his neck and left the room.

***

The sound of someone stomping down the hall woke Tory up. She gazed at the green glow of the clock. 12:47. Rye must be coming back from the concert. She was glad he'd been able to sing.

She tunneled her head into the pillow, but when a loud curse punctuated the silence of the tour bus, she decided to check on Rye. She pulled on her lavender silk robe, wishing she had something less revealing, and hurried out. When she entered the kitchen, he was bent over at the waist, breathing hard. He turned the sink on and stuck his mouth under it.

"Are you sick again?" she asked.

60

He whirled around and breathed out of his mouth like a panting dog. He pointed to the table. "No. The ribs!"

Uh-oh. "I might have added a bit too much spice," she said, knowing that in her anger, she'd been liberal with the cayenne pepper. Opening the refrigerator, she pulled out a slice of bread. "Here. It'll help counteract the heat better than water."

He shoved half a slice in his mouth and chewed. "Those are the hottest ribs I've ever tasted," he said finally.

That was the idea, my friend. She tapped the Food Wish List. "Do you see ribs here? I do."

He made a growling sound.

She tugged on her sash. "Well, I guess we'll need to communicate better. If you specify hot, medium, or mild, I'm happy to make the food to your liking. You must be feeling better if you wanted ribs."

He downed another glass of water. "I was until I ate them. Christ, woman. They almost killed me."

"Eat some more bread. And don't brush your teeth. It's the worst thing you can do. I'm going back to bed." Considering the mood he was in, it would be too friendly to say she was glad he was feeling better, so she didn't. She just turned and left.

"Tory," he called when she was two steps from her door. "Thank you for earlier. I know I've...been a prize jerk. You didn't have to be nice to me."

"Your daddy was hurt. I...know how that feels. Have you gotten any more news?"

His fingers squashed the bread in his hand. "No."

Since she didn't know what to say, she only responded, "Well, good night."

"Wait a sec. Do you always wear stuff like that to bed?" he asked.

Turning around, it was hard to miss his lazy perusal. But she knew he was just trying to hide the sadness he felt for his father under other emotions. Still, his gaze skated across her skin, sending tingles down her spine. "Sorry, I would have changed, but I heard you curse and thought I'd better check on you."

His fingers ripped off a piece of the squashed bread. "Never figured you for the lingerie type."

Why did his eyes make her feel this way?

"I never figured you for a spice wimp," she responded, trying to stay on level ground. "Maybe I'll only make you soft food from now on."

"Don't count on it," she heard him say before she disappeared into her room.

She tossed the robe aside, promising herself she'd change into something more proper next time—even if things sounded dire.

***

Clayton woke him the next morning, calling way too early. Rye swiped his hand across his unshaven face, sitting up. "This had better be good."

"It is. A tabloid reported online that you left the charity event early and got into a scrap with that man because of a family matter, and now they're asking questions about your family."

His hands fell to his sides. "You're kidding me," he said, wide awake now.

There was silence on the line for a few beats, and then Clayton said, "Mama and I talked, and the only person who knew that—"

"Was Tory," Rye finished, pushing aside the covers. Hell, it was so hush-hush he hadn't even told anyone in the band. "Dammit! I knew she was angry, but..."

"We don't know it was her, Rye, but she needs money, and she was totally pissed about being used as PR in Minneapolis."

Hadn't she coolly negotiated with him for his meal in the diner? Of course this would happen...and just when he'd started to trust her, a rarity for him. So much for her being a wholesome Catholic school teacher's daughter. "Did she say anything about Daddy's heart attack?" he asked, his stomach sinking at the thought.

"No. There was only a vague allusion to a family matter. Nothing more."

Well, at least she hadn't gone that far. He would have tossed her off the bus if she'd mentioned that. "I'll find out the details," he growled, "and put a stop to it."

"I think you should let me handle this."

"No. I brought her on. I'll take care of it. Bury the rest of the story, Clayton. I don't want anyone to start talking about Hollinswood and Meade." His past fit his image about as well as if he'd decided to wear his old blue and white striped seersucker pants.

"Don't outright accuse her. There's legal—"

"Did we or did we not attend the same law school?"

"You dropped out," his friend reminded him. "I didn't."

"It was three weeks before graduation. We'd covered everything by then." And the memories of tort law and all of the other kinds of law he'd studied made him shudder. He was so glad those days were over.

"Rye, I'm sorry about this, but let's look on the bright side. Maybe this will help your image. It might be good for everyone to know why you responded to that man's harassment like you did."

After ending the call, Rye yanked on a pair of jeans and a shirt. Maybe Clayton was right, but he frankly didn't care. He didn't want any talk surfacing about his past. His record label had done everything in the beginning to bury his roots, using their influence to shape his image into a low-country bad boy.

All this talk did was churn up more hurt inside him.

His past needed to stay buried where he'd left it.

***

Tory was humming and removing cornbread from the oven when Rye walked into the kitchen. She had on a plain white apron over jeans and a green T-shirt.

He studied her, still shocked by the thought that she'd probably sold him out. But what did he really know about her? While he was getting dressed, he'd come to the conclusion that she'd intentionally made those ribs Texas-scorching hot. Wasn't that additional evidence that he'd pissed her off with his little speech in Minneapolis? Talking to the tabloids might have been another form of revenge, and Clayton was right. She did need the money.

But it still didn't fit with what he knew of her, with the way she'd treated him when he was feeling poorly. She'd been nice. She *was* nice. But still, he didn't trust anyone except a handful of people who'd proven themselves to him time and again, and other than Georgia and Amelia Ann, there wasn't a single woman in the mix. All the other women he'd known had tried to use him at some point.

"Looks like you've made yourself at home, darlin'."

She turned to face him. "Don't call me 'darlin'," she said, scrunching up her nose like she smelled something bad.

"Honey, I'm from the South. I call every woman I meet darlin'. It's not personal." He waited a beat. "But it seems you might have something personal against me."

"Like what?" she asked, planting her hands on her hips.

"I'm gonna ask you straight out, and I want the truth. Did you tell the tabloids that I was upset over a family matter on the day of the charity event?"

Her mouth parted. "Of course not! I would *never* do that."

"Then do you want to tell me how they got wind of it? How an article saying that very thing was printed right after I pissed you off by using you for good PR?"

"No, because I don't know anything about it," she said, eyes narrowed. "And I can't believe you're accusing me. I've been nicer to you than you deserve after everything you've done to me."

Studying her, he couldn't detect a trace of deceit, but that didn't mean it wasn't there. "But you need the money, and when I told you that in the diner, it was the only time..." And then he trailed off. That waitress had been there too. Myra.

"Don't you even think it," Tory said, making a chopping gesture with her hand. "Myra would never do that. She loves you."

He sighed deeply. "Well, Myra didn't know to keep it secret, did she?" Rye mused. "You didn't until I had you sign that confidentiality agreement."

Her hand trembled when she pushed her bangs to the side. "Listen, if Myra said anything—"

"She wouldn't have done it on purpose," he said, coming to the same conclusion. "Call her, will you? See if she remembers anything." His mind started playing out scenarios. "Once we told the press about you, the tenacious ones might have cosied up to her at the diner to see if they could find out more. She might not have known she was talking to a reporter. The good ones blend in."

When she crossed to the counter and picked up her phone, Rye shook his head. What a mess. He listened as Tory spoke with Myra on speaker phone—and hadn't she given him an indignant look when she punched the button? Sure enough, Myra said a nice young college student, a huge fan of Rye's, had come into the diner. They'd gotten to talking about *The Incident*, and she'd stood up for Rye, telling the kid he'd been upset over a family matter. When Tory explained who the kid really was, the woman started crying and apologizing. Rye wanted to flee the kitchen, but he stayed while Tory calmed her down. He said nothing because what could he say?

Tory looked like she wanted to bean him with a rolling pin when she finished the call. "Satisfied?" she hissed.

"I didn't like your friend getting upset, but I'm glad we discovered it was an innocent mistake."

"Upset? She adores you and thinks she's betrayed you. Is all this really worth it?" Her hand swept across the bus.

If she'd known what he'd sacrificed to get where he was, she wouldn't ask. "My private life is mine, and it's not for public consumption. Ever. Anyone who wants to be around me for any period of time understands that."

"Fine," she said. "It's understood. Why don't you eat some breakfast?"

Was Ms. Simmons simmering? Yes, it seemed she was, and who could blame her? He edged closer to the cornbread, his appetite restored.

She swatted his hand from touching the steaming pan. "Don't touch that. It's still hot."

He sniffed. "I have a weakness for cornbread."

"We'll let it cool. Now that you're done accusing me of putting you in the tabloids, we need to talk about *you* putting *me* in them." She put her hands on her hips. "It won't come as a surprise, but I don't like you using me for PR. I read Minneapolis' *Star Tribune* online yesterday. Guess what it said."

"I can't imagine," he said, although he knew darn well what the reporter had written.

"It gave more details about what you said at the concert in Minneapolis. Clayton even gave the journalist a comment about me being a positive influence on you." She threw up her hands. "Like that's possible."

But she *had* been a positive influence. If she hadn't made him eat that food yesterday, he wasn't sure he would have been able to sing Detroit. But he couldn't tell her that, especially not after all of the morning's miscommunications. "Look, I'm sorry. It's only business. There's nothing personal." What a crock of shit.

"Nothing personal?"

Yeah, that wouldn't wash with him either. Her voice fairly grated on his ears. "Look at it this way. You're inspiring thousands of people to help each other."

"Like that was your motivation."

He was surprised by how much her words smarted. "Okay, so you think I'm a total fraud. Why don't we agree to disagree on this one?"

Her gaze fell to the floor. "I wasn't calling you a fraud. I was only trying to tell you how I feel about being used for PR. Seems to me you should understand, being a private person and all."

His heart chugged like an old steam engine at that. "I'm sorry," he repeated.

She slipped on a potholder and cut off a big piece of cornbread, serving it to him dotted with butter. Her face was crestfallen. "Here's your cornbread."

"Thank you," he said, unsure of what else to say. He bit into the cornbread and munched a mouthful. Best to find a balance, and with her, that meant food. "You're going to spoil me. What's the secret to your cornbread?"

She shoved her hands into her apron and frowned. "It's maple. I grind up bark from the tree. Be careful not to choke."

He almost laughed as he popped the last piece in his mouth.

Her sass gratified him, even though it had an edge to it this morning. The rest of the cornbread drew his gaze, and he suddenly wanted more.

When he reached for it, she said, "Here, let me. The pan's still hot."

"No, I can do it."

They reached for the cast-iron skillet at the same time, and her finger touched the side.

"Ouch." She ran to the sink and turned the faucet on, letting the cool water run over her hand.

"Oh Christ, I'm sorry." Rye yanked the freezer open for some ice and came up behind her. As he leaned over to grab her hand, he noticed that the top of her head only reached his shoulders. "Let me see."

"It's fine," she said, but he ignored her and pressed the ice to her burn. She shuddered.

He turned his head, noticing how her eyelashes fluttered against her cheek from this angle. "Does it hurt?"

She pulled her hand from his and stepped away, reaching for a paper towel and wrapping the ice in it. "It's okay. It's only a small burn."

He stood with his hands dripping, still feeling the impression of her small body pressed against his.

"You'd better get back to rehearsing," she commented without looking at him. "*Detroit Free Press* said you sounded rusty last night."

He had, but he'd never admit it. He tapped his Stetson with a wet hand in a salute. "I'm never rusty, darlin'. You must be confusing me with a nail."

"Too bad I'm without my hammer today."

Yeah she was still mad at him all right, but the anger was fading. Even he could tell. "Take care of that burn. And don't worry about cooking lunch. I'll have someone get me take-out."

She held her dripping hand over the sink. "I'll be fine."

He shook his finger. "No arguing. I'm the boss." His eyes fell to the paper-towel wrapped hand against her chest. The apron fit her snugly, accentuating the small slope of her breasts. He hadn't noticed them before. Funny how the plain white apron accentuated Tory's petite figure in such a sexy way. Something about it was so much more appealing than the obvious flash of his former chef's pink frilly apron.

Was he crazy or had his mouth gone dry? He'd gone from accusing her of blabbing to the tabloids to finding her attractive. He needed to get out of here.

He was confused enough about his life as it was.

Some men have fancy offices.
Well, I have my truck.
I don't want no corporate digs.

My truck's souped up,
Jacked up,
With wheels the size of an old tree trunk.

It spews mud.
Makes bunnies run.
And my smokin' women clutch,
The dashboard of my dreams.

So, hold on, sweet thing.
Let me show you how it's done.

I'll take you for a ride, all right.
In my truck.

Rye Crenshaw's Top Ten Hit, "My Truck"

CHAPTER 5

A week later, Rye still felt guilty about what had happened with Tory. A two-day break between concerts was coming up, so he decided to take her off-roading with him as something of an apology.

They were somewhere in New York on the way to Boston after playing the Big Apple last night. His fingers itched to get behind the wheel of a vehicle, and part of him wanted to race out all the worry and anguish he felt over not knowing how his daddy was doing. Was he out of danger? Out of the hospital? There was no way of knowing.

Thoughts of home plagued him, and all he wanted to do was forget. Eating Tory's food and bantering with her seemed to be the only thing besides music that helped him do that.

After finishing up some business calls after breakfast, he knocked on her door and entered when she bade him. He'd been seeking her out frequently for conversation, and she never disappointed. Today, she was sitting on her bunk, reading in silver-rimmed glasses he'd never seen before, which were appealing in an odd way. When had he ever thought studious was sexy before? He'd run from smart girls in college. He felt off balance, so he hooked his fingers in his belt loops.

Her mouth slowly dropped open, and her book tumbled to the floor. He had a feeling his state of dress bothered her. He'd left his shirt off to rile her—and clearly it had.

"Put a shirt on," she said sounding all prim and bookish.

"I conduct business better while shirtless." Her reaction only made him want to poke at her more. He leaned down to pick the book up. "Well, doesn't this look like a page turner. *Cultural Messages of The Maasai People*." Bor-ing.

She reached over and wrenched the book from his hand. "You should try it some time."

He sat down on the bunk's end, enjoying her warning glare, feeling the sudden urge to really throw her off balance by tickling her stockinged feet. "What?"

She scooted back and pulled her knees up. "Reading. It might improve your Neanderthal disposition."

Their banter was like diving into a cool lake on a hot, muggy day. He'd come to rely on it. "Ah darlin', but the women I know like that whole caveman routine." He pounded his chest playfully.

"Are you auditioning for a Hanes commercial? If not, I'd appreciate it if you'd put on a shirt."

"You are *such* a liar." He fought a grin as her eyes shot fire at him.

"The whole 'Me, Tarzan, You, Jane' routine is tedious." Not to him. That persona had shot him straight to the top of the charts.

And while she sounded bored, her voice was breathy.

Tory set the book aside and studied him intently. "Wait a minute. I seem to remember seeing *Leaves of Grass* in your room."

There was no way he was confirming that. It didn't suit his image. "I seduced it off a librarian outside Mobile, Alabama, and kept it as a reminder of a lovely night. She was just as prim as you are."

"Hmmm..." she responded, like she thought he was full of it, but wasn't completely sure. After all, if he did read Walt Whitman, she'd have to see him differently, and he knew she wasn't ready for that. Neither was he.

"So why are you here in my room without a shirt on?"

"Georgia's scheduled a break at this campground for everyone to blow off some steam. A few people are going hiking and canoeing, and another group is going to play horseshoes and drink beer. I want to take you off-roading. I think you'd like it."

There was this desire inside him to hear her laugh and watch her clutch the dashboard as the truck Georgia had rented for him hit the deep crevices. Together they could race away from everything that was bothering him, at least for a day.

"You're crazy." Exasperation was becoming her normal tone of voice when he was around. She blinked up at him through the sexy frames. "You want me to go off-roading?"

"You know, for someone who's smart, you repeat what I say an awful lot. There's a great off-roading site not far from the campground. Come on." He forcibly pulled her off the bed. She resisted, but he was stronger.

"That's because most of what comes out of your mouth *defies* rationality." She tore off her glasses and looked down her nose at him—even though he was a foot taller. "No thank you. Unlike you, I do not possess a death wish."

She had a point. He didn't seem to care much about what happened to himself these days. Even less so after what had happened to his father.

"Okay, how about I give you an advance on your salary?" he asked, hoping she could be bribed with money even though he felt bad for bringing it up. "That'll help you pay some bills faster, right?"

Her mouth worked as she was thinking, her eyes downcast. "All right, but I want fifty percent of my salary upfront."

It was a paltry sum to him, but he loved to negotiate. So he countered. "Twenty."

"Thirty."

"You really are going to have to meet my friend, Rhett Butler Blaylock. He's a poker player, and I'm beginning to think you might be good at the game."

"I don't believe in gambling."

"Why am I not surprised?" he responded, loving that prim tone.

"So are you going to give me my thirty percent or go off into the woods in your Freudian truck by yourself?"

Ah, she'd resorted to Freud. Suddenly he had the urge to kiss her and show her how wrong the psychiatrist was about him feeling inadequate.

"You win," he said, and as if on cue, his stomach growled. "I *could* use a sandwich. It's getting close to lunchtime."

"I'll make something. But you have to promise me no crazy antics," she said, her mouth pinched.

"Haven't you heard? I've turned over a new leaf."

"Right."

He winked. "Be ready in twenty."

"I can't wait," she said drolly.

***

The shiny red truck had gigantic tires and a gun rack. She wrung her hands together. If Myra hadn't just called about another whopping hospital bill, telling her again how sorry she was for talking to that reporter, she wouldn't have given into his bribe. Wasn't she the girl who never went over the speed limit?

Plus, spending time with Rye socially was unprofessional. And deep down, she had to wonder if he'd suggested the outing for some more PR buzz. The fact that a cluster of photographers was milling around and talking to Georgia was a pretty strong tip off. The whole thing stank, but she needed the money.

Well, no one who knew her would believe she'd be in a relationship with Rye Crenshaw, so it was no skin off her back. And she could set anyone who did straight once she returned to Kansas.

Her hands clutched the bag holding their lunch as Rye exited the bus. He was wearing lethal-looking black sunglasses and looked about as delicious as her dark chocolate cupcakes.

"Damn Georgia and Clayton," he muttered, waving to the press. "I should have known they'd use this outing for a photo op." Rye took her arm and led her to the truck, which was parked behind their bus. "Smile, now. You can frown when we get inside."

Smile? "Like you didn't know."

"This time I didn't. I promise."

The passenger door was too high for a normal person to reach it. At this rate, she'd need a stepping stool. "I can't even get in. How big are those tires anyway?"

"I'd guess the standard forty nine inches. And quit your whining. Aren't anthropologists supposed to be open to new experiences?"

"I'm not whining."

Her mouth dropped open as he gave her a boost, one of his hands curving around her waist while the other slid under her bottom.

"Grab the handle."

Suspended in midair, she could do little else, the bag with their lunches in it still clutched in her other hand. "I like activities that don't cause brain damage." Or accidents. Like the one that had ended her parents' lives. Being in an out-of-control car scared her more than anything.

He pushed her into her seat, and she immediately reached for the seatbelt, tightening the strap until it cut into her chest. Her breathing was already shallow and it only worsened with each inhale.

"This is going to be fun," he said, sliding in next to her.

She lurched as he shot the truck forward. "I hope so," she prayed. And squeezed her eyes shut. Maybe it would be better if she couldn't see.

"Look, try and relax, and open your eyes for crying out loud. You're going to be sore if you stay that stiff. It's like riding a horse. You need to go with the flow. How about I let you listen to NPR? I heard you listening to it this morning."

She nodded mutely and reached for the dial. They drove a few miles until he finally turned onto a dirt road that looked like it had been created for the Lollipop Guild's go-carts. And ahead there was a series of mammoth-looking hills. She clutched her seat belt and grabbed the dashboard, preparing for the worst.

"Well, at least there aren't any trees," she said, trying for a silver lining.

"I thought that might be too much for your first time. There's a great site outside Little Rock, Arkansas that's heavily wooded and has some death-defying hills. We play there in a few weeks. We can go if you take a shine to this."

Her lungs seemed to collapse as he hit the gas. "You'd have to pay me a lot more for that."

"Good. I love negotiating with you."

She cried out as he jerked the truck to the right, heading for a rut in the road. The car shuddered when it struck.

"Do you have to drive this aggressively?" she asked, and her voice was soft, like she didn't have enough energy for more volume.

Yeah, fear had a way of stealing that.

His loud and wicked laugh was his only response. The car lurched forward when he pressed the pedal to the floor. "Oh, yeah! Let me show you how this is done, honey. God, I needed this."

With NPR droning in the background about the environmental concerns of ozone depletion, Rye certainly showed her. They dipped, jarred, and flew, spewing dust and dirt with each turn of the wheel. His arms showed off impressive muscles as he clutched the steering wheel, navigating the deep depressions in the earth like a demented NASCAR driver.

Her heart beat like Morse code. Adrenaline spiked as she gazed out the passenger window, which was smeared with her fingerprints. She squealed when he veered sharply, weaving off the narrow, Lilliputian road.

She could hear the deep rumble of his laugh over the ringing in her ears. Her eyes clenched shut again, and the contents of her stomach felt like a snow globe shaken by an overzealous five-year-old.

She wasn't sure how long he raced them around—it could have been five minutes or an hour. He suddenly slammed on the brake, causing the seatbelt to cut into her chest. She grabbed the dash with two hands and looked over at him with wide eyes, panting.

"Are you okay?"

She shook her head in the negative.

"You do look a bit peaked. Here I'll come help you down. I'm hungry." He grabbed their lunch and hopped out of the truck.

Of course he was. He was like those people who could eat a chili dog after riding a roller coaster, whereas she just wanted to throw up. Not that she ever went on roller coasters. After all, you never knew when something could go wrong.

He opened her door and had to climb up and unlock her seat belt for her. Her hands were frozen against her chest.

"Hey, now. It's gonna be all right." His brows knit together as he cradled her to him and jumped down. "You okay?" he asked.

The hot air hit her flushed face, her knees trembled, and she suddenly sank to the ground. "Not really."

He knelt beside her. "This isn't your usual nerves, is it? What's wrong?"

"My parents...they died in a car accident." Her throat felt thick. She wasn't sure why she was telling him so much. If anyone asked about them, which was rare, she usually just said they were dead. Never how. She hated to remember that day.

His face fell. "And I was driving like a lunatic. Christ, Tory, I'm so sorry. Why didn't you say anything?"

The pressure in her chest was pulverizing. "I didn't think it would be this bad, and I needed the money."

The arm he wrapped around her was gentle. "Next time just ask for an advance. I would have given it to you anyway. Shit, I feel awful."

"We're a pair. I can't handle crazy because of what happened to my parents and you do it for that very reason."

His mouth twisted. "Can you stand?" His hands helped her up, and she leaned against him for a moment as her legs trembled.

Pulling away, she stood on her own two feet. "I feel like an idiot," she whispered.

His finger tipped up her chin. "Don't. I'm deathly afraid of flying. I'm telling you that to make you feel better, but you'd better not tell a soul."

"Really?" she muttered, watching his ears turn red.

"Yes. I don't even do concerts across the pond. We do live events and broadcast them. More marketing. Now why don't we sit a spell? Then I'll call Clayton and have him come pick you up."

His regard helped smooth out her breathing. "Thanks, Rye."

"No problem. Now let me give you a boost into the truck bed. You'll be more comfortable sitting there."

He lowered the tail gate and helped her up. Then jumped up beside her. It was weird, having her feet dangle so far up, so she scooted until her back was pressed against the side.

Rye pulled out a Dr. Pepper, which he promptly chugged. Then he handed her the water bottle. The food was quickly arranged between them. She held her sandwich in her lap, needing to let her stomach settle more before eating.

"I like the quiet," Rye said finally. "Everything feels far away. It makes me miss my home in Dare River. This sandwich is incredible, by the way."

The first makings of a smile touched her mouth. "It was my grandfather's favorite. Ham, spicy mustard, and sharp cheddar"

Rye turned and raised a knee, letting the other dangle. "When did he pass away?"

She leaned back, grateful the burn of tears wasn't as strong as it used to be. "On Valentine's Day, of all things. He wanted to die at home, so we had a hospice nurse. He slipped away in the evening. I remember watching my neighbors go off for a romantic evening in fancy clothes, chocolates and balloons in their hands."

"I'm sorry." He paused for a moment. "Did he enjoy NPR like you?"

"No, but he tolerated it. My grandma was a devoted listener. After she died three years ago, he kept it on all the time. He was lost without her. We both were. When he got sick last year, he tried to hold on." She had to sniff when her nose started to run. "He didn't want me to be alone, but he wanted to be with her too."

He cleared his throat. "Sounds like a good man."

Being reminded of her fear today, and of how her parents had been taken, had made her raw inside. She fiddled with a potato chip bag to keep her hands busy. "He was, especially at the end. Didn't want to be a burden. He was so upset the house hadn't sold before he died. But like he always said to me, life is a long series of sucking it up when things don't go your way."

"He sounds like my Granddaddy Crenshaw," Rye said after finishing off his sandwich.

There was a smile on his face that hinted at affection. "Is he still around?"

"No, he passed away three years ago."

So he knew his share of loss too. Funny how little he resembled his bad-boy country singer persona now. He was like her, another human being who'd experienced the loss of a loved one. "What was he like?"

He rubbed his neck, almost as if chagrined. "Larger-than-life, funny—brave."

"Why brave?"

His gaze tracked off to the horizon. "Well, he was from a pretty traditional family, but he stood against them to be his own man."

"And you respected him for it."

He tucked his knee closer to his chest. "Yes, it helped me do the same when I had to. He supported my decision to strike out on my own."

A light bulb went on, and with it a spurt of compassion flooded her heart. "Your family didn't like you going into country music, did they?" It explained his refusal to talk about them.

"Ah..." His jaw clenched, and she knew he felt exposed.

"It explains why you can't go home and see your Daddy."

His face closed up like an old beach house after summer. "I don't like to talk about it."

Her image of him was evolving even as they spoke. This was no charming but superficial man—there were depths to him that people rarely saw. "I hope this family problem turns out okay so you can go see your father. Still no word?"

"No," he said, his voice measured, almost like he didn't want to say the word. "You'll remember I'm...not very trusting about private matters, so back to your grandpa. What was he like?"

Since changing the subject meant so much to him, she didn't press the issue. "He loved to read. Laugh. Take chances." She paused. "I bet you two would have gotten along." A strange realization, but true.

Rye stuffed his garbage into the bag. "Well, we both like ham sandwiches."

"You were separated at birth, I'm sure." Tory rolled her eyes, the joke lightening her load somehow.

"You'd better eat something. I'll go call Clayton."

No, she decided, she could suck it up. "It's okay. I should be able to drive back with you. I'm tougher than I look."

His smile started out slow but continued to grow until it filled his whole face, making his eyes twinkle under the brim of his black cowboy hat.

"Don't I know it, but I promise to drive real slow on the way back."

She picked at her sandwich while they sat in silence. After eating at least eight bites, she tucked the leftovers into the bag.

"I'm ready," she said.

He jumped down and plucked her off the truck. After setting her on the ground, his hands lingered for a moment longer than necessary, and there was comfort in the connection. His body cast a long shadow, shading her from the sun. And a familiar tingle of awareness spread through her. Needing to break the spell, she flicked up his cowboy hat playfully. Rye's brows rose as she pulled away.

"Better get me back. I have your supper to prepare," she said as if to remind them both.

"Right," he drawled and helped her back into the truck.

She clicked on her seat belt as he turned the key. But instead of gunning the engine like he had before, he eased forward like he was pushing a sleeping baby in a stroller.

Her eyes tracked to the speedometer. "Twenty miles per hour, huh?"

"I promised you a safe ride back."

A couple of cars passed them along the main road, some honking in frustration, and while his mouth twisted now and again, he didn't speed once—a gesture that felt like the first makings of friendship.

It had been a long while since she'd felt that kind of consideration.

Our house's got cracks licking up the side,
Squeezing the life outta the people inside.

Don't wanna live in a glass house no more.
Nosy neighbors peering in from the outside.

Put on a show.
Like a mannequin in Ms. Jenkins' country store.
I can't take it no more.

Ignore the pain,
There's nowhere to hide.
There's cracks in the glass house,
Licking up the side.

Rye Crenshaw's Number One Hit, "Cracks in the Glass House"

CHAPTER 6

The first two weeks of June rolled by in a blur as they covered the upper Eastern seaboard and then cut across the south. Rye sang in a new city every night or every other night, depending on the travel distance, sleeping in a hotel room once in a blue moon. Before too long, he fell into this tour's rhythm. Each tour had one, he'd discovered, and he was happy to learn that the defining feature of this one was food. He'd called his good friend, Rhett Butler Blaylock, to thank him for suggesting he hire his own tour cook. It was something he was going to do from now on, though he couldn't imagine finding a better one than Tory.

Her food was magical, and it seemed to affect his mood. If he were tired after a late concert, breakfast had him feeling bright eyed and bushy tailed. If he were cross because he was worrying about his daddy, dinner made him feel peaceful before he went onstage. And her sassy and delightful company only added to his enjoyment of her food.

Sure, he'd had to work out more, but then again, he'd always loved feeling that particular burn.

When he strolled into the kitchen en route to Dallas and eyed the fried chicken sizzling in the cast iron skillet, he rubbed his hands together in anticipation. Creamy scalloped potatoes covered with cheddar cheese and steaming corn dotted with butter already stood waiting on the counter. It was going to be another incredible meal—something that never failed to raise his spirits.

"Hey," he said.

Tory jumped. "You scared me."

"Sorry. Dinner about ready?"

"Yes." She forked the chicken off the skillet and set the pieces on a plate lined with paper towels.

Rye carried the corn and potatoes over to the booth and sat down. "We don't play until tomorrow, so the band and the crew are going out tonight. Dallas has one of the best cowboy bars around.

Georgia rented it and has invited some locals. Come celebrate with us."

Her eyes narrowed as she brought the chicken over to the booth. "I don't know. I'm not really into the bar scene."

While he wasn't surprised, he wasn't giving up. "Ah, come on. You need some fun." He didn't think it was good for her to spend so much time alone.

Rye reached for the chicken immediately. Swore at the heat. Blew on the piece hovering near his mouth and took a bite. The juices hit his taste buds, and the crunch of the breading was so succulent that he chewed slowly just to savor it. "God, this is incredible."

Tory wiped her hands on her apron. "Glad you like it."

"You got any cornbread?"

"No, I have buttermilk biscuits in the oven."

His gaze traveled over her slim behind as she opened the stove and bent over to take them out. Well, he didn't want to bribe her, but he wasn't throwing in the towel just yet. "I looked up that thing you study." He almost laughed—he knew perfectly well what she was studying, but he was so used to playing the fool that it came more naturally sometimes. "Cultural anthropology. This bar is gonna fascinate you. It's all about social customs and culture."

"I'll bet," she said, and he could almost hear her rolling her eyes.

The potatoes made him groan when he tried them, and that familiar sense of peace spread through him. He couldn't say why, but eating her food made him feel at home—a place he'd never felt off stage other than in Dare River.

"Hey, watch it over there. You're sounding a little hot and bothered."

He made a humming noise. "Honey, I am hot. For your food. What'd you put on the corn?"

"Cajun seasoning. You strike me as someone who likes spice, despite the whole rib incident. Now, what were you saying?"

Right, what *was* he saying? "The bar, Cowboys Red River, has a mechanical bull. We all take turns riding it. Men and women. The one that lasts the longest gets a special reward."

Tory's mouth parted, but she edged closer, setting a plate of steaming biscuits on the table. "A mechanical bull? So what's the prize?"

"Well, for the men it's a bottle of Johnnie Walker Black. The prize for the ladies hasn't changed since my first tour."

"And that would be?"

His all-time favorite. "A kiss from me."

Her sexy lips curled into a frown. "That seems like a raw deal compared to the Johnnie."

He wiped his mouth with a napkin. "You've never kissed me before. Trust me. The men are getting the raw deal."

And wouldn't he love to prove that now? But he wouldn't. He liked her and respected her. Plus, she was his cook, and he didn't want to mess that up. Even if she was proving more tempting than expected.

She shoved her hands into her apron pockets, her eyes fairly dancing. "You could always kiss them, too."

Rye chuckled. Wasn't she cute, smirking in her white apron? "You *have* to see the bull. It's pretty funny watching people trying to hang on."

Tory just smiled as she fixed herself a plate. Even though he'd told her she could eat with him, she'd declined. So far he hadn't pushed.

"All right then. Sounds educational. Leave the plates out when you're done. I'll clean up later."

As she left with her food, Rye bit into a biscuit and moaned. If he were a marrying man, he might be tempted to get hitched to Tory just to keep her feeding him for the rest of his life.

But he wasn't ever getting married. Was never planning on letting another woman have the chance to control and manipulate him day in and day out like his mama did to his daddy, and to him growing up. And Tory was definitely the settle-down type.

They'd just have to be friends, and wasn't that a first for him with a woman?

***

Hours later, after admitting defeat when Rye wouldn't end his campaign for her to join the festivities, she was leaning against a wooden beam in the dark, smoky Cowboys Red River bar. Well, Rye had been right about one thing. She was fascinated. And downright appalled.

A hoard of scantily clad women had cornered Rye near the entrance to the fenced off bull ring. Cleavage was at a premium. And Rye was eating it up like a sultan prince.

Watching these women ride the enormous robotic bull—with a fake head and horns and everything—was like watching that old John Travolta movie, *Urban Cowboy*. Most wore jean mini-skirts, making Tory wonder about chafing. She winced each time one of them took a tumble onto the squishy black gym mats, their breasts bouncing. Of course, the men just hooted and laughed.

Including Rye, and unease began to spread over her. She'd become used to seeing a different side of him in the privacy of the bus, one she liked. This Rye? Well, she didn't care for him at all.

She tried to take the high road, using her anthropological tool kit to analyze this strange mating dance in front of her. But she couldn't keep it going. As the women wove out of the ring, she only had one academic conclusion: whiplash and alcohol did not mix. One poor beauty queen lost her dinner on a handsome cowboy.

The serpentine line to the mechanical bull dwindled as the night went on. Rye stood at the entrance to the ring with Clayton, who was in charge of the stopwatch and writing down the final time per rider.

"Can you believe this?" said an older man to Tory's right. "I come from a pretty small town and a very different generation, and I have to say I'm a little shocked by all this."

Tory angled her head. The man was in his fifties, a bit portly, and had on a John Deere baseball hat. "I was just thinking the same thing."

"I'm Luke," he said, holding out his hand. "I'm one of the crew. Lighting."

"Oh. Hi, I'm Tory."

"Yeah, everyone knows about you. You're cooking for Rye and reforming him, right?" he asked.

How was she supposed to respond to that? "I just work for Rye."

He smiled easily. "You know, you remind me of my eldest daughter. She doesn't like to talk out of school either. I can't wait for the tour to be over so I can visit her."

"That's nice," she responded.

"Clayton mentioned you're from Lawrence," Luke said. "Great town. Love the Jayhawks. My daughter lives in Kansas City. Hey, I'm heading back to the buses now. Do you want to catch a ride with me? Seems we're both a little out of our element here."

It was true, and she wasn't having much fun. "Sure." It was nice to talk to someone. She'd been on her own for most of the night, without anyone approaching her for conversation. At first she'd assumed it was because she didn't look like one of them, but given what Luke had told her about Rye, she wondered if they were staying clear of her because they thought she was some boring Mary Sue bent on changing their bad-boy hero. The people here wouldn't want that, and it explained some of the hostile looks she'd received from the women in the bar.

As she was weaving her way through the crowd, a hand grabbed her arm. When she looked over her shoulder, Rye tipped back his black Stetson. "Your turn, honey."

Luke continued to make his way to the front of the bar, and there were too many people in between them for her to stop him. Stuck, her eyes swept to the ring as another woman took a dive off the bull.

"Not in a million years," she told Rye.

His hazel eyes twinkled, even in the dim light of the bar. "Come on. I promised you some fun. Riding a bull is something everyone needs to check off their bucket list."

The music changed to something twangy, and she had to raise her voice to be heard. "I don't have one."

"Well, you should."

A lush blond appeared at Rye's side. "What are you doing with *her*, Rye?"

The distasteful once-over she gave Tory made Tory straighten her spine. Okay, so she didn't want to be like Rye's bimbo fans, but being found wanting because of it ticked her off.

"Come back and party with us," the woman pleaded, sliding her hand up Rye's chest. "Clayton's almost ready to announce the winner. I think I might be the lucky girl tonight."

"I'll find you in a minute, Lola," he countered, not paying any attention to her hand tickling the skin above his collar. "I'm trying to talk Tory here into giving the bull a ride."

Lola gave her another haughty glance, making Tory feel like she was back in high school, being insulted by the popular girls. "This pathetic little thing, Rye? Why, I bet she couldn't grip the bull for two seconds with those chicken legs."

"Shut up, Lola." His hand stopped her exploration of his skin. "She's a friend of mine."

And somehow, hearing him say that was all the incentive she needed. The woman's insult to her legs was not going to be ignored. "Okay, let's give this a go then."

She strode forward, weaving around the women who surrounded the bull, wrinkling her nose as it was assaulted by a cloud of different perfumes.

"Clayton?" she called.

He looked up from the clipboard.

"Time me."

"You've got it, honey," he said and gave her a wink.

Her feet sank into the gym mats. The bull suddenly seemed larger than life, from the tip of its fake snout to the well-worn saddle on its fake hairy back. God, she hoped it was fake. She put her foot in the stirrup, grabbed the pommel, and swung her leg over, finding the other stirrup. Then she eased her hand around the pommel and wedged it under the saddle. Curving forward, she gripped the bull's body with her thighs, keeping her head low. Seconds later, the contraption tipped forward and started to rock.

The bucking increased. She squeezed her thighs as tight as she could, digging her heels under the beast's belly. She heard shouts and cat calls, but could barely make them out over the ringing in her ears. The bull jackknifed and then turned in a circle. Tory's thighs screamed, but she kept chanting *a few more seconds, a few more seconds*. Finally her grip slackened, and she went flying. The breath whooshed out of her lungs when she hit the mat. She lay there for a second, stunned.

She'd done it, and while it felt like she'd only stayed on for a blink of an eye, she knew it had been several seconds. The noise in the bar was deafening as she used her hand to lever herself up. Determined not to weave like everyone else had, she took it slow and walked to the gate.

Rye was gaping at her.

Clayton held out the stopwatch. "Seven seconds! Jesus, Tory. You won!"

She'd won? She couldn't remember ever winning anything! She was looking around for Lola to give the woman a smirk when she realized what winning meant.

Oh no.

A kiss from Rye Crenshaw. Her boss.

Rye grabbed the stopwatch from Clayton's hand. "You're kidding me?"

Yeah, he was probably thinking the same thing. Kissing her? It was totally off limits. He'd said so himself that night in Diner Heaven.

Clayton slapped his white hat against his thigh. "Says right there. It's a record. Maybe it's because she's such a little thing. We've got a winner," he called out more loudly, pointing at her.

Protests started to pour in from the Cleavage Covey.

Tory gave them all a cheeky grin and a mock bow and then decided to hustle out of there. If she left, he wouldn't have to kiss her. Be better all 'round.

"Hey, sweetheart, you come back here." Clayton swung her around before she made it two steps. "You're the winner. That means you get the prize."

Her gaze flew to Rye. He stood against the bull pen, kicking at the black mats surrounding the beast. Yeah, he didn't want to do this anymore than she did.

Tory pulled away, her heart beating faster. "That's okay, really. I don't want the prize."

"Don't work that way, honey," Clayton said, dragging her forward while women continued to call her inventive names from the sidelines.

She pulled back. "You only want this for your PR campaign, admit it."

He just laughed and continued pulling her along. "I've never seen a woman so hesitant to kiss you, Rye. Maybe it'll teach you some humility." His hands propelled her into Rye.

There was no smile or wicked gleam in his eyes when he pulled her to him. In fact, his face was totally blank.

"You'd better be careful, partner. She'd as soon bite you as kiss you."

"Look, it's just a kiss," he murmured.

Right. She was making too much of this, wasn't she?

But she hadn't kissed a lot of men, so it didn't seem insignificant to her.

"Fine," she said. "Just do it."

His mouth twitched at that. People whistled and screamed and heckled all around them. Her face grew hot. He lowered his head and pressed his lips to hers. The touch was electric, and she jumped, bumping their noses together.

"Settle down," he growled, caging her waist with his hands.

She started laughing, a strange impulse that seemed to come out of nowhere. "That had to be the worst kiss on the planet." What had she been so worried about?

Patting his chest, she took a step away.

His hands gripped her hips again and yanked her close. Her breath rushed out when she found herself pressed full length against his rock-hard body. Those hazel eyes gleamed down at her as they scanned her face. "Can't have you impugning my reputation."

It was a pretty impressive word, she thought, and then he pressed her back a few steps until she hit the fence, throwing all thoughts aside. He yanked off his hat and threw it.

Uh-oh. Laughing had been a bad idea.

"I didn't mean—"

"Shut up," he commanded and cupped her face, fitting his mouth to hers.

Oh no. The intimacy of it stole her breath. His lips were soft, his body hard as he leaned against her, ducking at the knees to fit his pelvis against her own. A delicious spurt of desire flashed through her belly, and the surprise of it made her open her mouth. His tongue swept lazily inside, engaging hers in a wicked dance.

Her heart rapped against her ribs, and she became lost in sensation. His mouth. The hands tickling her waist, slipping under her T-shirt to stroke her skin.

Her hands slid up his chest on instinct, as much to hold on as to touch him. A moan erupted from deep within her, and primal heat flooded her body.

The man kissed like he ate. With slow, determined, sensual enjoyment. No one had ever kissed her this way. No one. When he tugged on her bottom lip, ending the kiss, she leaned in instead of stepping away, caught up in the sensual storm he'd created. Rye indulged her, taking the kiss even deeper, giving her the connection she craved.

His hands slid down her bottom, and the hard line of his desire brought her back to her senses. The crowd was shouting and laughing over the buzzing in her head, and a few people were pointing at them. Luke gave her a wink from the periphery of the room. So he hadn't left after all. Camera flashes made her blink.

Yeah, they probably couldn't believe she was kissing the infamous Rye Crenshaw. And Clayton was getting the PR of his dreams, no doubt.

Realizing she was still clutching at Rye's shirt like she had the bull, she pushed away. He staggered back, his mouth parted in surprise.

Darting through the laughing hordes, she made her way to the front of the room, deciding not to detour and go back with Luke. She didn't know him well, after all, and she really didn't want to be around anyone right now.

Not when she'd just been kissed senseless by Rye Crenshaw. When someone kissed women all the time, he was bound to be good at it.

But it didn't mean anything to him. Even if it had rocked her world.

She simply had to remember that it couldn't mean anything to her either.

***

Rye watched Tory's red shirt until he lost it in the crowd. He stepped forward to pursue her, but to what end?

He ran his hand over the back of his neck because it still tingled from her touch. That kiss had been much more than he'd bargained for.

Maybe he'd had too much to drink. He grabbed his hat from a grinning Clayton and slapped it on his head.

"Well, now. That didn't look difficult at all, and the press loved it. Who would have guessed she'd win on her own without me rigging the thing? The girl's got thighs of steel."

Rye gripped his friend's shirt. "You were going to set me up?"

"Come on, now, we talked about this weeks ago."

It was true, but it hadn't come up at all in the last two weeks. He'd hoped it was enough for them to just be seen together occasionally. Somehow it took the spontaneity of the kiss away and left a bad taste in his mouth "I wouldn't have agreed to that, Clayton."

"Tory's helping your image, but we needed something more. We haven't had any pictures of you two acting like a couple since you went off-roading. And we couldn't have pictures of you kissing another woman, now could we?"

"She's off limits, Clayton. Starting right now."

"Dammit, I hate it when you go noble on me. You can tell Mama. She's gonna be pissed."

"I'll take care of it," he said and headed to the main bar for a beer.

Blonds, brunettes, and redheads all made excuses to touch him as he walked to the bar, their invitations as obvious as their outfits. Anger and lust waged inside him. She had made him hard as hell. And now Rye was arguing with his old friend and business manager over using a little kiss to boost his image.

Well, it hadn't felt like a little kiss.

A blond in desperate need of a root job gave him a slow smile and slid across the bar to stand next to him.

"Hi there," she said, running her hands up his shirt like she was playing *The Itsy Bitsy Spider*.

Her touch didn't diminish his desire for Tory, so he nudged her away. Usually, he had no qualms about grabbing anything women offered him.

He took his hat off and picked up a water pitcher from a nearby table, upending it on his head, hoping it would clear his mind of all the swirling thoughts about his family and the kiss with Tory. Shaking himself like a dog, he slapped his hat on again and forced his best knowing grin. He didn't want anyone to know he was upset, and everyone was laughing uproariously now beside him. Well, he was a performer, wasn't he?

"Time for us bubbas to show you ladies how it's done," he called out as he started toward the bull.

He got a firm grip and dug his heels in, so he was ready when the bull started bucking. Or so he thought. His body slammed into the mat after what must have been his worst time ever. He used the opportunity to get his breath back.

He reached for his damp hat and smacked it on his wet head. Christ, he needed another drink. Anything to forget that soft mouth and the tiny body that fit perfectly against his.

*****

Tory was humming to herself when Rye showed up for a late breakfast. They'd both stayed at the hotel last night, but he liked her food so much that she always cooked for him on the bus unless it was her day off.

After tossing and turning all night, she was ready to execute her plan. There was bound to be some awkwardness after their kiss. He'd responded. So had she. Better to put it out on the table and say it meant nothing.

Even though it wasn't true, at least not for her.

The urgent need for this discussion had been underscored when Tory saw pictures of her kissing Rye with that horrible bull in the background on the Internet earlier in the morning. The media was speculating that Rye was getting cozy with the struggling cook he'd hired. The reports mentioned how she'd accompanied him on an off-roading outing. Comments about her not being his type were prolific, but several accounts attributed his interest in her to him wanting to settle down with a good woman. Even Myra had called this morning to ask about the romance, promising she'd never tell a soul. Tory had adamantly denied it, of course.

The PR machine was speeding along like a Eurorail train, trampling her privacy, and she knew there was little she could do about it. Or complain to Rye about. Especially when she suspected Georgia and Clayton were pushing it more than he was.

And it wasn't like she was completely innocent. She'd fed the media beast by kissing him in the first place.

"Good morning," she said in a measured tone. "Breakfast is about ready. I made biscuits and gravy since we had leftover ones from last night."

Rye sat at the table and grabbed the remote control, flicking on the morning news. "Great," he responded, not saying anything else.

After she served him, he cut into the piping hot biscuit swimming in sausage gravy and took a bite. His eyelids fluttered shut like they always did, and a low groan filled the kitchen. It was hard not to notice those lips after their kiss, so she turned to wash the pans.

"So that whole kissing thing last night was pretty embarrassing." She scrubbed the gravy off the pan under a stream of hot water. "I don't want there to be any weirdness between us. I mean, I work for you. Besides, it wasn't a big deal. We got carried away since the crowd was watching."

She picked up a hand towel and dried off the pan. "I mean, if that's what it's like for you on stage, it must be incredible. All those people looking on, screaming and shouting. Pretty heady stuff. It's called the public effect. It's a known phenomenon."

"Could you turn around a minute?" he asked in that rumbling, deep baritone that raised goose bumps on her skin.

Tory complied and forced a smile. His gray T-shirt clung to his body and the slight tear in the right sleeve only made him look hotter. When had clothes ready for the garbage ever turned her on before?

"Are you saying my kiss was a *phenomenon*?"

"No, I mean the phenomenon was kissing you *in public*. I'm sure it wouldn't have been half as interesting in private." Yeah, right.

Rye stood up and walked toward her with a gleam in his hazel eyes. "Are you saying the kiss would have been less...eventful if we'd been alone?"

Oh, the mere thought of it made her want to rip the rest of his T-shirt into threads and run her hands up his bare chest. Instead, she held the dishrag in front of her like a shield.

"No offense, but we're not each other's type. I mean, you like big-breasted women in tight clothes with big hair. And I don't go for cowboys."

Even though she knew that his cowboy side was just one of many hats he wore.

He leaned against the counter and pulled his Stetson down. "Honey, I've been told by tons of women I'm the best kisser they've ever experienced."

"So you've said."

Rye frowned. "And here I was planning to tell you not to get all clingy this morning. You really know how to knock a man's ego."

Clingy? Her? No way. Talk about insulting. "I didn't intend to hurt your ego," she said, brandishing the dishrag in one hand. "I only wanted to assure you the kiss was no big deal."

Rye grabbed the dishrag from her, and when his fingers

brushed hers, she felt sparks where their skin touched. He leaned around her and threw the rag on the counter, the movement brushing their bodies together. Oh, that primal desire was back, dag nab it, and it just wasn't fair.

He smiled when he leaned back. "Of course it wasn't a big deal. As you said, kissing women is practically part of my job description. But you do make a man want to prove you wrong about this public phenomenon theory."

Oh, her lips tingled at the thought of his mouth on hers again. She watched as he strolled back to the booth to finish his breakfast, her eyes glued to his incredible butt.

"But you're right," he drawled, forking another piece of biscuit. "We'd best let it go."

Thank goodness he stopped speaking when he slid the food into his mouth, giving another moan instead.

It pinged throughout her body.

He scooped another forkful into his mouth.

She clasped her hands together like a school marm, trying to ignore the electricity coursing through her body. "Good, I'm glad we've got that settled. Well, I've got to go. There's a special program about the challenges of organic farming on NPR this morning." Lame. So lame.

Rye waved her away. "Well, I wouldn't want you to miss *that*."

As she left, she found herself wondering if there would be another mechanical bull bar along the concert circuit.

Like eating a piece of bittersweet chocolate, she found herself craving more of him.

My Grandma Simmons made incredible pies. There are two mediums you have to master to do the same. A flaky crust is essential. Here's a tip if you're making it from scratch: use Butter Crisco™. It really does make an incomparably flaky, golden crust. But you can't stop there. You have to make a filling that doesn't crack or weep. Lemon meringue is my favorite of all the pies she used to make. The secret to her meringue was the extra egg whites she used to create those four inches of magic that swirled on top as puffy as clouds. Add fresh lemon zest, and you have a real winner—a comforting yet tangy treat for a hot, humid day. I've never met a person whose mood didn't improve after having a slice of this pie. Its magic is potent.

Lemon Meringue Pie

Pie Crust

1 crust for the bottom (you can buy a prepared crust or make one from scratch). Here's our family recipe.

1 c. flour
½ tsp. salt
1/3 c. regular or Butter Crisco™
¼ c. cold ice water (we put ¼ in a 1 c. measuring cup and add ice to it)

Mix until incorporated (not too much, but just until it comes together). Then roll the dough into a circle on a floured surface. Lay into the pie plate and flute the edges by pinching the dough on the top and sides between your two index fingers.

Lemon filling:

1½ cups sugar
3 Tbs. cornstarch
3 Tbs. flour
Dash of salt
1½ cups boiling water
3 egg yolks beaten
2 Tbs. butter
½ tsp. grated lemon peel (fresh is best)
1/3 cup lemon juice
1 tbsp. lime juice

Mix sugar, cornstarch, flour, and salt. Add boiling water.

Cook over stove until the mixture boils and thickens, about 2 minutes. Temper the egg yolks with the hot mixture and add to the saucepan. Cook for 2 additional minutes and remove from the stove. Add butter, lemon peel, and lemon juice. Pour into crust.

Meringue

5 egg whites
½ tsp. vanilla
¼ tsp. cream of tartar
½ cup sugar

Beat egg whites with an automatic beater until they form peaks. Slowly add sugar until dissolved.

Add meringue to the pie and seal it to the corners.

Cook at 350 degrees for 12-15 minutes until meringue is lightly brown.

Tory Simmons' Simmering Family Cookbook

CHAPTER 7

Tammy Hollins Morrison clutched her buttercream Coach handbag, surveying the line of tour buses wedged behind the auditorium in Richmond, Virginia. Her hands shook violently as she dialed Rye's cell phone again. Amelia Ann had given her the number. When it immediately went to voice mail, she pressed it to her stomach. She would have to find him on her own.

Fans, mostly women, clustered together behind the cordon in the hot July sun, all of them hoping for a glimpse of their hero. The Fourth of July had come and gone a week ago, yet his fans were still decked out in T-shirts with American flags on them, tied at the waist to show their bellies. A shocking spectacle. She wrinkled her nose at a woman in a short, stretchy jean dress and cowboy boots—sans panty hose, of course, and likely sans panties as well. In her conservative celery green linen dress, Tammy was receiving more than a few stares of her own. The scene was exactly what she would have expected of her black sheep brother.

Fiery resentment rose up in her belly, but she took a deep, calming breath. Daddy wanted to reconcile with his son after his brush with death, and he firmly believed you couldn't deliver that sort of message over the phone. It had taken Daddy three weeks to wear Mama down, and since she hadn't wanted to hurt her husband's recovery by forbidding it, she'd finally agreed. But she'd put her foot down on one thing. *She* would not be the messenger. Daddy had thought it would be a more significant gesture if Tammy came calling rather than Amelia Ann, so here she was.

The whole idea was insane after everything Rye had done to their family. And then there was his recent brush with the law...

Tammy had seen Rye only once since he broke his engagement with Emeline Williams, her dear friend and the perfect Southern debutante from a respected Natchez, Mississippi, family, and left Vanderbilt law school just weeks before graduating. All to launch a record label as a bad-boy, low country hick, shaming the family.

He'd come to Granddaddy Crenshaw's funeral three years ago, but he hadn't stood with the family. And he'd mocked them by wearing a black cowboy hat with his suit.

She caressed the bruise on her arm, concealed by her long sleeves. Soon it would be too hot to wear concealing clothing, so she'd have to be more careful not to provoke Sterling. Her husband hadn't liked the idea of her making this trip alone and leaving their two children behind, but he never went against her family's wishes. The value he placed on their connections was too high.

As she strolled through the crowd, looking for someone official to help her, she thought of what she knew of Rye now. In his interviews, he always said he was happy to be living his own life, not letting anyone else define him. Secretly she envied that. Her husband and Mama had her wrapped around their fingers. More like clutched in their claws. Conforming was her only recourse.

She smoothed back her hair and made sure her dress seams were in perfect alignment. With a posture courtesy of Mrs. Augusta Keller's Comportment School for Girls, she went to find her brother and execute her duty like a good Hollins girl.

***

Tory was pulling a mile-high lemon meringue pie out of the oven when Georgia walked in with a well coiffed blond woman in a light green linen dress.

Georgia's worry lines showed through her heavy make-up. "Tory, this is Rye's sister, Tammy. Rye's still in rehearsal, so I'd appreciate it if you'd give her a glass of sweet tea while I get him."

He had *another* sister? And from the looks of her, this wasn't going to be a happy family reunion. Apparently, the family matter had plopped right into the middle of the tour.

"I'd be happy to," Tory forced a smile at Tammy. "Please sit down."

Georgia escaped before she had the refrigerator open. Tory walked over with the tea, and when she handed it to Tammy, she noticed the woman's flawless French manicure and the large diamond winking in a shiny white gold setting on her wedding ring finger.

This was Rye's sister? She looked nothing like him and had all the warmth of a block of ice. Her sleek blond hair was swept carefully over her shoulders, and pearls glowed at her neck and ears. Her understated make-up showcased a classically beautiful heart-shaped face.

"I'm Tory Simmons. Rye's cook."

The woman eyed her outstretched hand like it was a rat before loosely grasping it. "I'm Tammy Morrison." Her tone was dismissive.

Had she seen the pictures of them or was just being rude?

"It's nice to meet you." Tory shifted on her feet. "I know it's a little early in the day, but would you like some pie? It's fresh out of the oven."

Tammy's mouth tightened a fraction. "No, I wouldn't want to impose."

Rye's sister looked like she could use a piece of pie. Perhaps it would chip away at that rigid posture of hers. It made Tory's muscles hurt to look at her.

"It's no trouble. Really, I insist. There's nothing better than lemon meringue on a hot day."

"My mama says the same thing," Tammy murmured. Her voice was like fresh cream shot with a touch of Southern Comfort.

After serving her a thick slice, Tory went to work on Rye's dinner, rubbing the chicken with fresh lemon and rosemary before shoving it in the oven. From the corner of her eye, she watched Tammy eat the pie in small bites. Unlike Rye, she didn't show any enjoyment in eating. And she wiped the corners of her mouth as regularly as clock-work.

"This is wonderful pie," she said after a moment. "Rye is lucky...to have you."

The words were at odds with the tone. Yeah, she must have seen those pictures at Cowboys Red River. Great. Now she was being judged by this all-too-proper woman.

"Thank you." Tory took a step toward her. "So, did you have a good trip? Where did you come from?"

"I took a plane from Jackson—Mississippi."

"Oh, I've never been there. Is that where Rye's from?" Okay, so sue her, she had to ask.

The woman's spine went ramrod straight. "Rye doesn't like to acknowledge where he's from."

Even though she'd been prepped by Rye about his family problems, her eyes widened at the woman's harsh tone. Clearly Tammy didn't like to talk about "the family matter" anymore than Rye did. "Do you have children?" she said, changing the subject.

Tammy clutched her hands. "Yes, I have two."

"Do you have pictures?" she asked.

"Yes, of course." And Rye's sister gave her first genuine smile.

In the picture she pulled from her billfold, two children were smiling in their Sunday best. Both had blond hair like their mother and looked picture-perfect. They could have modeled for a box of Southern grits.

"What are their names and ages?"

"Rory is six. Annabelle is four."

"Do you mind if I sit down?" She slid into the booth before Tammy could reply. "They're beautiful kids. Is this your husband?" Tory ran a finger over another picture. "He's very handsome."

Tammy didn't smile this time. "Thank you."

Boots pounded down the hall, and then Rye appeared in the doorway of the bus. Georgia was right behind him, but she retreated quickly after giving his bicep a squeeze.

The look on his face was as dark as the clouds in the sky before a thunderstorm.

"What the hell are you doing here, Tammy Lynn? Is Daddy all right?"

"He's better," she responded, the muscles in her face not moving a millimeter.

His frown loosened a fraction, his relief palpable. "Thank God."

"Please remove your hat, Rye. You're inside."

"You sound like Mama when you say that." He swept the hat off and bowed, his mouth curling. "Is that better?"

"Rye, where are your manners?" Tammy said, hoisting herself out of the booth.

He strode forward. "You're on my turf, Tammy, so don't start spouting off about *manners*. I'll throw you out on your finely pressed linen ass."

Tammy's hand flew to her throat.

The tension between them crackled, and Tory's stomach rippled with unease. "Rye—" she said.

"Stay out of it, Tory," he spat. "So, if Daddy is fine, why are you here?"

"If you'd act civilized, I'd tell you," she responded.

Tory jumped up from the booth and put a hand on Rye's forearm. "Come on, Rye, why don't you sit down? I'll get you some sweet tea and a piece of pie, and your sister can tell you why she came all this way to visit you."

His hazel eyes regarded her for a long moment. "All right. No reason we can't be *civilized*." He gave the word a hateful emphasis, but he sat down all the same, and so did Tammy.

Tory hurried to serve him. He grunted in acknowledgment and downed the tea in three gulps, wiping his mouth with his hand, barely restrained rage in his every gesture. He didn't touch the pie. Backing out of the kitchen seemed like a great plan, since she was sure he wouldn't want her to know his business.

"Good to meet you, Tammy. I'll let you two catch up."

"No, please stay," Tammy said, her eyes locking with Tory's, her fear visible. "Please."

Rye's eyes narrowed, and in that moment, he looked trapped. Like he didn't want her to stay, but couldn't see another way to assuage his sister's discomfort.

"Well, seems my sister wants you to stay, so sit on down, honey," he drawled. "We know you're trustworthy. Seems you're going to join our little program of family dysfunction."

When she reached the booth, his hand clamped around her forearm and pulled her down beside him. Yeah, there was a warning there.

"Rye, our family is not dysfunctional," Tammy countered. "We're just not terribly close."

His laughter was hard edged. "Oh, that's rich. Is that what you tell your country club friends?"

Tammy's mouth trembled. "Rye, Daddy wants you to come home and make peace with him."

His body turned into a wooden statue, and he glanced at Tory for a long moment before responding. "Mama made it clear she doesn't want that."

"I know. But Daddy's had a change of heart since his hospitalization, and Mama will do anything to help his recovery."

Tory wanted to crawl under the table to escape their discussion. Only family should be around for such a personal conversation. Witnessing it was awkward, and her eyes tracked to Rye to see how he was taking the news. His whole face had tightened in pain.

"Why you?" he hissed. "Why not send Amelia Ann?"

She looked at her watch. "Because Daddy's asked me to reconsider my feelings about you."

"That won't take long, right?" he growled, mean as a rabid dog now.

"I knew you wouldn't come," Tammy said, standing up. "You walked away from this family long ago. Daddy will be crushed, of course, and I can only pray it won't hurt his recovery."

Tory moved to stand so Rye could slide out of the booth, but his hand gripped her thigh, holding her in place. "Don't pull this kind of bullshit on me."

"I need to get back to the airport." Tammy picked up her purse. "You know, Rye, perhaps Mama was right about you all along. You're a lost cause, unwilling to do anything for anybody but yourself."

With that parting shot, she pirouetted and walked out of the kitchen. Tory tried again to slide out, and this time Rye's hand fell away.

"Do you want me to find Georgia or Clayton?" she asked.

The arm he slung across the back of the booth was meant to convey disinterest, but his eyes told a different story. "Why?"

She cleared her throat. "So you can make arrangements to leave and see your father. I know it will be hard with the tour, but you'll work it out."

Silence descended, thick and suffocating.

"Honey, I don't know what you're talking about. I'm not leaving the tour."

For some reason, she'd hoped for a different answer. If her father had survived his car crash and wanted to see her, she would have dropped everything to go to him. "What? How could you not after what Tammy said?"

"Didn't you hear?" he scoffed. "My daddy's going to live. There's no reason for me to go home. And I don't want to remind you not to say a word of what you just heard...to anyone." He dug his fork into the pie, tearing the meringue into shreds.

Tory put her hands on her hips, not even bothering to respond to the implied insult. "But he wants to make peace, Rye."

"Too bad." He shoved in another bite and choked.

She pounded his back until he cleared his windpipe and then yanked the plate away. There was no way he could eat pie right now. Not after this news.

"Rye, it's your *family*."

"Darlin', you don't know nothing about my family."

Oh that odious endearment. "You're right, I don't know much, but I do know that your dad, who just had a heart attack, is asking to see you. If I had the chance to see my father again, I wouldn't hesitate."

There, she'd said it, and there was no unsaying it.

He stood up and towered over her, his boot tips touching her toes. "Don't confuse my family with yours, honey."

His snarl pushed her over the edge. She shoved his chest to make him step back. "You only use words like *honey* and *darlin'* when you're pushing the image of the impenetrable Rye Crenshaw. Well, screw you. You're right! I don't have a family anymore, so there's nothing to confuse."

He swore, reaching out for her, but she darted away.

"Tory—"

"No, you're acting like a jerk. It's clear you have problems with

98

your family. Fine. Lots of people do. Nothing is a lost cause while everyone's still living, do you hear? Your daddy has changed his mind, and Tammy came to see you, even if it was only for him. Isn't that proof that there's still hope?"

"Leave it alone, Tory."

A shadow passed over her heart. "You sing about being a big tough man and doing what's right. What a bunch of bull."

He froze for a moment before storming out of the kitchen.

***

When Rye didn't return for dinner, Tory wrapped up the food. She'd gone too far earlier, but her hurting heart hadn't let her stop. How could he not want to reconcile when his father was finally extending an olive branch?

She listened to NPR, trying not to think about Rye's family. It didn't help.

Shutting the radio off, she punched her pillow and tried to sleep. She was still awake an hour later when she heard Rye crash into the wall outside her door, followed by the click of bottles hitting the floor.

Wonderful. Alcohol had been his go-to this time. Well, at least she knew where he was. Tory pulled the pillow over her head and squeezed her eyes shut, finally managing to fall asleep.

A hand shaking her shoulder nudged her out of her dreams. She pushed it aside only for it to shake her harder. She rolled onto her back and cracked open one eye. Rye sat on her bed, backlit by the morning light curling around the window blinds.

Clutching her covers to her chest, she asked, "What are you doing?"

He was shirtless, hatless, and badly needed a shave. His eyes were bloodshot and puffy from drinking. She'd seen him shirtless before, but the sight still moved her. Then her gaze fell to his black boxers, and she edged back against the wall.

"Look, I've barely slept," he said. "I drank too much, and my head is splitting. I thought about what you said, okay? I'll go home during the next concert break—but *only* on one condition." His voice was shades deeper than normal, like he'd used gravel for mouthwash.

She smoothed back the hair falling in her eyes. "What is it?"

"You have to come with me."

Any vestiges of sleep evaporated with that statement. "What? Are you crazy? You don't trust anyone with information about your family. Plus, I'm your cook."

"Don't yell, honey. I can hear you just fine." He pressed his fingers to his temples. "Look, I trust you plenty. You've seen how it is with my family—heck, you know more about the situation than almost anyone. Plus, I need food there, so if you don't go, neither do I."

Her hands gripped the sheets as a dark thought skated into her head. "Is this another of Clayton and Georgia's PR schemes? Your sweet cook, going home to meet the family?"

His head jerked back. "No! God. Why would you think that?"

She searched his face and found only blank astonishment there. "Then why in the world would you want me to go?"

He lifted a shoulder. "Because it was your idea, darlin'."

Okay, so she'd urged him to go, but it wasn't like his decision was resting on her shoulders. "My idea! And stop using that darlin' crap. You know I don't buy that put-on charm of yours. You want a buffer, right? Because your sister asked me to stay."

When he didn't meet her eyes, she knew it was true. "That's not my job description. *Honey.*"

His face creased into a frown. "Fine. I need a buffer. And I do need to eat. Plus, you're good with people."

What was she going to do with him? He acted impervious and cocky one moment and then showed moments of vulnerability that made it impossible for her to step away.

"Why not take one of your friends? Clayton's good with people too."

He looked away and was silent for a long time. "This isn't something you take a guy friend to deal with. And I thought...Well..."

"What?" she asked in exasperation.

"That you and I had...become friends."

His words made warmth bloom in her heart. She felt the same way, even after that crazy kiss in Dallas. At some point, bantering with him had become the highlight of her days.

"Forget it!" He stood, the sight of his almost naked body stealing her breath again. "It was a stupid idea anyway. You're right."

As he turned to leave, she said, "Okay, I'll go."

That gorgeous body swung around. "You will?"

"Yes."

The corners of his mouth turned up. "I suppose I'll have to double your salary for hazard pay," he said softly.

Suddenly it was like she'd eaten a spoonful of peanut butter. "I wouldn't protest."

Silence descended.

"Well, I... Thank you, Tory." He headed for the door again.

"I'll start breakfast," she called after him.

He gave her a pained smile over his shoulder. "Don't bother. I couldn't force it down this morning. I'm going to shower and start rehearsing. I'll see you later."

"Rye?" she called.

Again he paused and craned his neck to look at her.

"I'm glad you think we're friends."

His mouth turned up briefly. "Me, too."

Then he finally left. She tumbled back onto her bed and stared at the ceiling, breathing deeply to calm her racing heart.

They seemed like the two least likely people to become friends. And yet they had.

Was there hope for Rye and his family? What if she were wrong, and there was just more pain in store for him, for all of them?

Rye wasn't the only one who skipped breakfast.

I cut my teeth on tradition,
With my Grandmama's rattle in my mouth.
Tiptoed around my own house.

Grew up like a puppet.
Got pushed into something I didn't want to be.
Followed in the family footsteps.
No one listened to me.

But the music wouldn't stop.
My collar wanted to pop.
I couldn't breathe.
So I fought.

My own kin hated the thought.
They set me aside.
It broke my heart.

I broke tradition.
But it didn't break me.

Rye Crenshaw's First Release from his Debut Album,
Breaking Tradition

CHAPTER 8

Five days later, Rye stood next to his truck in Fort Lauderdale, Florida, at dawn, waiting for Tory. There was about to be a six-day break, the longest that had been scheduled, since everyone needed some time to recharge before the final month. The tour would end in Memphis just before Labor Day weekend.

He'd called Amelia Ann to let his family know he was coming, and she'd squealed on the phone like a little girl, easing the crushing pressure in his chest a fraction. At least one person would be delighted to see him. His mind spewed out various ways his meeting with his daddy could go, not all of them pleasant.

The drive to Meade would take a day each way, so he planned to spend four full days with his family. He wished he weren't so afraid of flying. The twelve-hour car trip would be interminable, particularly after all the traveling they'd been doing. But how could he deny his daddy? Maybe his old man really did want to reconcile. Time would tell. And if not, they could always leave early.

Clayton exited his bus and strolled to where Rye was standing. "All set?"

Rye adjusted his dark sunglasses. "Sure. Thanks for having someone drive my truck up here from Dare River."

"Know how much you like driving it." His friend stroked his chin.

Rye felt a frown spread across his face. When Clayton stroked his chin like that, it meant he was thinking about something he wanted to keep to himself.

"Are you sure you want to take Tory with you?" his friend asked. "You've always been really private about your family, and after what happened in the beginning—"

"That was easily explained." Rye's lip curled. "And she's been nothing but wonderful since."

"Fine," he replied. "Let's change the subject. I won't tell you to give your family my regards since they still blame me for luring you into that karaoke bar."

"Which is bullshit."

They both laughed, and it felt good.

"Yeah, it was more like Mama. She had plans for you the minute she heard you sing."

"Thank God." He couldn't imagine what his life would look like now if Georgia hadn't entered his life like a fairy godmother, finding him an agent, becoming his manager, and shaping his image, making him into the star he was today.

Would he still be married to Emeline, maybe with a couple of kids? Would his Saturdays be spent on the golf course in a polo shirt, pressed cotton pants, and loafers? God. His eye twitched just thinking about it.

Rye heaved a sigh of relief when he saw Tory emerge from their bus. Good. It was time to get on the road. He didn't want to think about this crap anymore. Bill carried her suitcase down the four steps, and he must have offered to help her carry it the rest of the way because she waved his hands away and smiled before wheeling the bag toward them. Rye's impulse was to go over there and grab it, but he didn't—he knew she valued her independence.

"I haven't said it in a long time, but thanks, Clayton. For everything."

Clayton looked over as Tory arrived. "Ah, cut it out, or you'll make me cry. "

"As if," Rye responded. "All ready?" He stopped himself from saying *darlin'* since she'd called him on it the other day.

"Yes," she responded, ceding her suitcase to him when he reached for it.

Their hands brushed, and a ping ran up his arm. It had become a familiar reaction to her.

"Y'all have a safe drive now," Clayton said.

Rye stored Tory's bag in the cab. "I'll check in when I can."

"Don't worry. We'll take care of everything. Just..."

His mouth twitched. "I know." And he did. *Don't do anything stupid.* The phrase had been running in his head since he woke up that morning, as nervous as he'd been before performing on stage the first time.

Rye opened Tory's door, and once she was settled, he jumped into the driver's side.

As he turned the key, he took a deep breath.

"You're doing the right thing, Rye," she said quietly. "When you have doubts, remember that."

Going home wasn't going to be the easiest thing he'd ever done, but he was glad he wasn't doing it alone.

His gaze slid to his pint-sized *friend*, for whom he felt more than simple friendship.

Yeah, he was real glad he wasn't heading down this path by himself.

***

Rye's refusal to let her help drive ticked her off. Apparently only he drove his truck. Lovely. She found her escape, reading a new book on primitive tribes in Africa and their experiences with tourism, something that was in the sweet spot of her research. Her earbud headphones cocooned her in her own world of sound. Rye alternated between blaring country music and driving in silence.

Flying would have been faster, but given his fear, they'd *had* to take a car. Fortunately, he didn't speed, and she recognized with gratitude that it was because she was with him.

When they reached Meade, Mississippi, about twelve hours later, she finally pulled out her earbuds. The green population sign said it was a town of 3,241 people. As they drove through a historic brick Main Street, which had three stoplights and an array of small businesses decorated with blooming plant containers out front, she could see the polish. Feel the class. This was a wealthy town still celebrating– or clinging to—its heyday.

She noticed Rye's hands clenching the steering wheel as they headed out of town through a maze of country roads. Tory caught sight of a muddy river and clusters of majestic Spanish moss hanging from the trees. She didn't ask him about any of it. His expression, which had become progressively surlier as the hours passed, demanded silence.

Rye slowed the truck at the entrance to a private driveway. Flanked in brick, a name plate was inscribed with the word *Hollinswood* in fancy cursive. Great oaks lined the gravel road, so it felt like the truck was easing through a shady tunnel.

Tory's eyes widened when the white antebellum house came into view. It was arresting in the waning evening light. From everything he'd told her, she'd been prepared for old money, but the reality was something different. Because Rye was watching her out of the corner of his eyes, she forced her expression to relax.

"It looks like something out of *Gone with the Wind*," she said in awe.

"Yeah, and we know how that movie ended," he said.

"I liked it."

He only snorted.

The house was an old plantation mansion, gleaming white, two-story, and flanked by four large pillars lining the massive entrance. Enormous wrought-iron lanterns hung along a veranda piped with trailing ferns and puckered-leaf hostas in greens and blues. Beds packed with multi-colored flowers angled under dogwood and crepe myrtle trees, brightening up a lush, manicured lawn as green as the Emerald Isle. The blooms in the rose garden were the size of her hand.

Hollinswood bespoke of wealth, tradition, and another world.

Rye drove around the circular driveway and parked in the shade of an old magnolia resplendent with white flowers. He was breathing audibly, almost hyperventilating, as he yanked the keys from the ignition.

"Well? Any other movie strike your fancy? Maybe *North and South*?"

Tory slid her reading glasses off. Not wanting to add to the charged silence, she evaded the question. "Let's go inside, shall we?"

The smell of fresh-cut grass and magnolia flowers greeted her when she exited the truck. Her khaki Capri pants and red top seemed much too informal now, as did the gold sandals showcasing the red toes she'd painted in a fit of boredom yesterday.

Rye headed toward the door, his boots dragging on the gravel. If this was where he was from, no wonder he never talked about it. Plantation-style money was a far cry from the rabble-rousing cowboy he presented himself to be. When he'd said they'd disowned him, she'd thought it a strange term. Seeing his family's home, she understood. People with this kind of money had something *to* disown.

She followed him and was watching the door when it suddenly burst open.

"Rye!"

A young blond woman in a pale cream suit and matching heels catapulted herself at him after dashing down the front steps of the veranda.

He caught her with a grunt. "Amelia Ann."

His sister squeezed her eyes shut and wrapped her arms tight around his neck. "I'm so glad you're here!"

Tory stood quietly to the side. She caught sight of Tammy, who was standing in front of the floor-length windows. There was a strange expression on her face as she watched her siblings—a combination of envy and hurt.

Two young children marched out the door a few moments later, and Tory recognized them instantly from the photos Tammy had shown her. The young boy had on a pale blue shirt and matching shorts with a red bow tie that didn't look like a clip-on. The young girl, a few years younger, had yellow butterfly barrettes in her hair and was wearing a pale pink dress. Both stared at their aunt and uncle before turning to look at Tory.

"Hi, I'm Tory. I'm your Uncle Rye's friend."

The boy held out his hand. "I'm Rory Morrison and this is my sister, Annabelle."

Tory sank to her haunches and gently took his hand. "Nice to meet you." She looked up as Tammy stepped through the front door after her kids. "Hello, Tammy."

Annabelle stood behind her brother. "Mama, her name sounds like Rory's. You know, like in my Dr. Seuss books."

"Yes, honey. It's called a rhyme."

Annabelle shuffled forward. "Our Granddaddy is sick."

Tory nodded. "Yes, your mother told us. That's why we're here."

"Thank you for coming, Rye," Tammy said softly, her eyes widening a bit, like she couldn't believe he was actually there.

Rye tucked Amelia Ann against his side. "Where is he?"

"He's upstairs. With Mama."

His jaw clenched. "Amelia Ann, this is Tory Simmons. She's getting her doctorate in cultural anthropology, but she's cooking for me while she's on summer vacation and is the best cook I've ever met. She's also a good friend."

Amelia Ann reached out a hand, surprise flitting across her face before polite regard won out. "Nice to meet you."

So he hadn't mentioned he was bringing her.

"And these must be my nephew and niece," Rye said. "Hey, kids. I'm your Uncle Rye. Last time I saw you was at Granddaddy Crenshaw's funeral a few years back. You've grown quite a bit since then."

Rory did not hold out his hand to Rye like he had with her. He went over and took Tammy's. "Our daddy calls you bad names."

"Rory!" Tammy rebuked.

Rye's smile was tight. "It's okay. I'm sure your daddy does, son. I probably deserve them." He knelt on one knee in front of the boy. "I used to say things I wasn't supposed to at your age too. Still do. But I'm your uncle, and I don't have any problem with you. Okay?"

The boy's brows scrunched together. "Yes. *Sir.*"

"Good." He turned to Annabelle. "And aren't you the prettiest little darlin' I've ever seen? You look just like your mama did at your age. Come give your Uncle Rye a kiss."

Annabelle waited for Tammy's nod and then sashayed forward,

leaning in to kiss Rye's cheek. "Your goatee tickles."

"Well, let's go inside then, shall we?" Amelia Ann declared.

"Yes, by all means," he said, standing. His drawl was exaggerated. "Ladies."

His gallantry was as false as his image, and Tory knew he was acting like that just to rile Tammy. But his sister refrained from sniping back at him. She led the way, only stopping to throw a warning glance at him over her shoulder. Tory crossed the threshold, wanting desperately to give them some privacy.

Amelia Ann took her elbow and gave her a friendly smile. "We'll get you some rosemary lemonade while Rye visits Daddy, and you can tell us about life on tour."

Thank heavens. Being in the room when Rye saw his father for the first time in god knows how long didn't seem appropriate. She gave him a half-hearted wave as his sister pulled her through the door and steered her toward the kitchen, Tammy and Annabelle trailing in their wake. Rye didn't even seem to notice.

***

His nephew hung back, letting the ladies file through the door first. Rye lightly squeezed the boy's shoulder. "After you, son."

The way he tiptoed inside made Rye tug at his collar for air. His mama had always hated noise, and she'd ordered them to be as silent as possible. Seemed some things hadn't changed.

"Welcome," he read aloud as he stepped onto the yellow-stenciled mat. "Yeah, right."

Inhaling deeply, he stepped into his childhood home. In a reflexive gesture, he took off his cowboy hat and slapped it on a table in the foyer before heading up the curving staircase. There was a new gray carpet runner on the black walnut hardwood stairs, but the railing was still white. His Mama must have redecorated. When he was a kid, she'd averaged about five years between projects. Family antiques remained where they always did, but details like furniture, curtains, art work, knickknacks, lamps, and paint color changed. The house was his Mama's canvas. He'd always found her endless quest for perfection stifling.

His palms turned damp suddenly, and he wiped them on his jeans.

His parents' bedroom lay at the end of the hall.

Memories washed over him as he walked down the hall, none of them pleasant. Well, he was here, wasn't he? No turning back now. His stomach pitched as he entered their bedroom. His mama's signature rose fragrance drifted to his nose. The mahogany four-poster bed where his daddy lay had been in the family for four generations.

Hampton Hollins looked commanding even in a navy polo and tan slacks, propped up against the headboard by fluffy white pillows, a John Grisham paperback at his side. His color was a shade lighter than the healthy tan Rye remembered, but while his blue eyes looked tired, he seemed as alert as if he were facing one of his jury trials.

Mama was perched on the bed next to him in a sage green suit, her grandmama's pink pearls on her slender neck. Her hair was coiffed in a French twist, showcasing the lustrous blond highlights she had faithfully applied twice a month since turning thirty. Seeing her, he felt that old hurt of never having measured up.

"Sir. Mama." The words were stilted, but he could think of nothing more to say.

His daddy's face grew taut, and he reached for his wife's hand. "It's good to see you, Rye. Thank you for coming." He tried to smile. "It means a lot."

Rye shifted on his feet. There was no mistaking the uncharacteristic emotion in his daddy's voice, so at least someone here wanted him besides Amelia Ann. Silence descended, save the ticking of his mama's antique clock on her armoire.

Yeah, his mama wasn't going to greet him, and his daddy seemed to understand that.

"How are you feeling, sir?" he asked.

"Better. Margaret, why don't you go downstairs? I'd like to speak to Rye alone."

Mama smoothed the coverlet after she stood, erasing the wrinkle in the embroidered blue and white bedspread. "Of course, darlin'." She leaned over and kissed his cheek. "Just ring the bell if you need anything. I'll be up to check on you when you've finished chatting."

Again, no reference to Rye. He might as well have been invisible. Well, he hadn't expected anything else.

Her posture was the same—ramrod straight, shoulders pulled back. A lady never slouched. As she passed him on the way out, she gave him a sharp glance, which triggered his old response to her.

He hooked his hands in his belt, slouching. "I promise not to have him carousin' or drinkin', Mama. At least not yet."

She straightened, appearing an inch taller. "Well, at least you had the sense not to wear your cowboy hat in the house."

"Oh, don't worry, Mama. It's downstairs. I'll be sure to put it on later when we have tea in the parlor."

"All right, that's enough," his daddy said. "Margaret, please go downstairs. Rye, why don't you come over here?"

Mama walked stiffly out of the bedroom.

"And shut the door, Rye. It wouldn't surprise me if your mama tried to eavesdrop on our conversation. Did you think I didn't know?" he said, clearly noticing Rye's shocked expression. "I know your Mama's tactics, just as she knows mine. Usually I let her listen, but not this time. Come sit down."

Rye walked over and froze when his daddy patted the place his mama had left. The seat he took was half on the bed, half off.

His daddy's hands joined prayer-style on his stomach. "I've had some time to think about what I wanted to say to you... Well, I figured the best way to get through to you was to produce some evidence. My key chain is on my dresser. Would you mind retrieving it?"

Rye did as instructed, his heart pounding in his ears. The keys jingled when he gave the chain back to his daddy.

"Thank you. Now, take the lock box out of the bottom drawer of my nightstand and set it down beside me."

After he did as he was asked, Hampton inserted the key and opened the lid.

His breathing hitched when he saw what was inside—a collection of his CDs. Oh, dear Lord.

Daddy's hands trembled as he removed them. "I've bought every CD you've put out, and I listen to them in my car on the way to work. I even downloaded your music onto my phone."

A barrage of conflicting emotions swept through Rye. Confusion. Hurt. Anger. He'd never expected to learn that his daddy had given his career a single thought.

The older man suddenly looked his age. "I bought your CDs in the beginning because I wanted to see what meant so much to you that you would break off your engagement, leave Vandy right before graduating from law school, and turn your back on my business."

His voice grew hoarse, and he coughed to clear it. Rye clutched the bedspread.

"The first time I heard your voice," Daddy continued, "I had to pull the car over to the shoulder. I couldn't believe that it was my son singing."

The acceptance he'd craved for years grabbed him by the throat. Rye didn't realize he'd stopped blinking until his eyes started smarting.

"I've tried to understand who you really are by listening to your music... Still, I'm sure it's not the full picture."

No, but it was as honest as he ever let himself be.

"I don't want things to be the way they've been, Rye," Daddy continued. "For a long while, I didn't know what to do about you, and then there's your mama... She has definite opinions, and I don't like to go against her. But after that quadruple bypass, life doesn't look the same."

Rye had to look away from the entreaty in his father's eyes. Lord, he was feeling a world of hurt.

Daddy leaned back against the pillows, his face turning from milk white to gray. "I'm sorry, Rye. For disowning you." Their gazes finally met, and his father's eyes were wet, something Rye had never seen before, not even at Granddaddy Crenshaw's funeral. "For everything."

The antique clock ticked loudly in the silence. Rye rubbed his raw throat. "It's okay, sir," he whispered. Even to his own ears, the words sounded too simple.

"It was hard, Rye. When you broke your engagement so close to the wedding and announced you were leaving law school to become a country singer, it seemed like you were spitting in the face of everything we'd ever wanted for you. I'd hoped we'd...work together...with the law."

"I know that, sir. But none of those things..." Ah, dammit, he might as well tell the truth. "I didn't want them."

"Well, it's pretty clear that you've found something that makes you happy. And you're incredibly successful at it. I don't rightly know where we go from here, but I want you to know that I'm proud of you."

Rye's head jerked up. That he hadn't expected. At one time, he'd hungered for those words.

Daddy fiddled with his collar, drawing Rye's attention to the bandage underneath.

"It must have taken a hell of a lot of courage to go against our expectations, the life we'd laid out for you. I never understood until I heard you sing. You love music like I love the law. So, good for you. Granddaddy Crenshaw was right. I should have listened to him, but I was too upset to see straight."

Chaos had been their music back then, but now Rye was removed enough from it to understand his own complicity. "I didn't handle things particularly well either."

Daddy held out his hand. "I hope you'll forgive me, Rye. I don't expect it, but I'm asking you to think about it. I'll understand if you can't shake my hand just now, but I hope you will one day."

Rye took his hand.

Hampton squeezed it firmly and held it for a few moments. "Thank you."

No... Thank you, *Daddy*, he wanted to say, but couldn't squeeze the words out.

"When the doctor gives me leave to travel," he continued, "I'm going to come see you in concert. I don't care what your mama says. Things are going to be different from now on, and she's just going to have to get used to it."

Rye's mouth parted. A concert? This was more than a private reconciliation. Daddy was willing to acknowledge him in public. It was more than he'd ever imagined.

"I'd be honored, sir."

He glanced down again at the pile of CDs. *Breaking Tradition*, his first album, was on top. It had been an instant hit. He'd poured himself into it like a drowning man, not knowing it would resonate with millions of fans and turn him into a star. If he hadn't been estranged from his family, he wouldn't have had anything to write.

"I have to admit I'm at a loss for words. I...never expected this."

"I wasn't a good father to you or the girls, and I want to change that now, even though I don't exactly know how." Hampton sighed. "But I'm trying. Maybe you can sing me something a little later on. If it wouldn't be an imposition."

His throat squeezed shut another inch. "I'd be happy to, sir."

Daddy laid his hand over Rye's again. "Good. I'll see you later then, son." And the last word was uttered with hesitation. And hope.

The term seemed foreign after so long. He'd stopped thinking of himself as anyone's son, but now he'd been offered that role again, by a man he barely recognized. Rye rose on shaky legs and headed to the bedroom door.

"Oh, and you can wear your hat in here when we're alone," Daddy called. "Just don't do it in front of your Mama. You know what a stickler she is about that kind of thing."

As a gesture, it was telling. His father had always stood on ceremony, too. "Yes, sir. Rest now." He let himself out of the room, closing the door behind him. All his energy exhausted, he sagged against the wall and closed his eyes.

God. His head was spinning like he'd been doing wheelies with his truck.

"Rye, is there something wrong?"

Rye jerked upright. His mama stood by the staircase with her hand on the carved newel post, her wedding and Crenshaw family rings glittering in the light from the second floor front window. He took a moment before responding. He'd bet twenty bucks she'd been hovering upstairs, waiting for him to come out.

"No, Mama, everything is fine," he said as he passed her, heading down the stairs. She'd trained him well. Never show true emotion and say everything was *fine* even if the house was on fire and you'd just caught your fiancé in bed with another man.

When he reached the foyer, he called, "Tory," since no one was sitting in the front parlor.

"In the kitchen," came her reply.

She was sitting at the table with Amelia Ann and the children, having a glass of the standard Hollins rosemary lemonade, if he had to guess, and boy didn't that take him back. When was the last time he'd had lemonade?

"What are y'all talking about?" Rye asked, striding forward.

"We were just asking Tory about her favorite recipes," Amelia Ann said.

Which meant his sister hadn't really known how to engage their guest and had selected a safe topic. Well, it had probably surprised her to see Tory. He hadn't mentioned he was bringing her because he hadn't wanted any push-back. Or questions about why he was bringing his cook.

"How nice."

"Speaking of which. Are you hungry, Rye?" Tory asked. "It's well past dinnertime."

And it was clear no one had planned a supper for them. Mama's doing, no doubt.

"Ah...we thought you'd get in later," Amelia Ann murmured, trying to cover up the rudeness.

Tory rose fluidly from the chair. "No worries. Amelia Ann, do you have any sandwich fixings?"

"I'm not hungry," he said, suddenly needing to escape. He wanted to spend time with Amelia Ann, but he was too raw after talking to Daddy.

"Well, you're growling like a bear," Tory said, "and it's best to feed you when you're like that."

"Tory, I said I'm not hungry." He scanned the kitchen. The gleaming perfection made his stomach curdle, like he'd been struck with the flu. The counters sparkled without clutter. There were green pears ripening in a silver decorator bowl. Stainless steel appliances shone without smudges. Mama still didn't allow pictures or school drawings to mar her canvas, he noticed.

Nothing had changed.

He turned to walk out, but halted when he saw Mama standing stricken behind him.

"Rye, your Daddy would like you to stay in the guest house."

His heart hurt again. It was an honor, that, especially since it was Granddaddy Crenshaw's old place. He hadn't expected hospitality, so had secured them reservations at the motel in town.

"Thank you. That would be nice," he responded, not wanting to refuse Daddy.

When Tory came through the doorway, Rye said, "Mama, this is Tory Simmons. She's a friend of mine who's studying for her Ph.D. at the University of Kansas. She's a Yankee, so I hope you'll show her the lovely Southern hospitality she's read about."

"Of course," Mama singsonged, the perfect hostess. "It's lovely to meet you, Ms. Simmons. We've seen your...picture in the paper. Such a lovely story, Rye helping you and all. And you two...becoming close because of it, especially since you're the daughter of a schoolteacher and such. We couldn't have been more delighted to hear that Rye's been spending time with you. You are most welcome here."

His mama could make bullshit sound like apple pie.

"Thank you," Tory said, glancing his way, a question in her eyes. "As I told Amelia Ann, the media tends toward embellishment."

"We'd better get settled in the guest house," Rye said. "We'll just say goodnight to everyone else."

"No need to disturb your daddy," Mama responded. "I'm sure he's just plain tuckered out." She sailed up the stairs.

Rye grabbed Tory's arm and drew her toward the kitchen door.

"We're heading to the guest house. See y'all later," he called.

"Good night, everybody," Tory said. "Rory and Annabelle, remember what I said."

His cowboy hat was on the hat rack now—courtesy of Mama, no doubt. Anger and other emotions pounded him like hail. He slapped it on his head and let go of Tory, the door looking like a sanctuary now.

Stalking to the truck, he realized his face was hot. Even his ears were burning. The minute they'd buckled their seatbelts, he shoved the car into gear and floored the gas.

"Hey," she called as she braced a hand against the dash.

While he knew he should slow down, he just couldn't manage it. He drove like a maniac, taking the turns fast and hard. When he pulled up in front of a smaller white house with slate blue shutters and a wrap-around porch, Tory was breathing shallowly, her face white.

A spurt of guilt shot through his gut, but it was like a raindrop in an ocean of emotion. He flew out of the truck and ran for the house, sucking in deep breaths of hot, muggy air. The meadow beckoned, making his eyes sting. So many memories.

God, he hadn't been prepared. He knew now that *nothing* could have prepared him.

Everything was raw again, and he felt like he was back in the same place he'd been when he left five years ago.

There was just no escaping the past.

***

Tory leaned her head against the truck's window as Rye strode off, and it seemed wise to just take a moment to settle herself. The terror from his reckless driving had her heart pounding a two-step in her chest. As she took slow, steady breaths, it finally returned to a normal cadence. When she finally left the truck, her gaze tracked to Rye, and she headed in his direction. No one needed a friend right now more than he did.

He stood by a white fence with his head pressed against a black stallion's neck, stroking the animal's mane. His cowboy hat was perched on a fence post.

The meadow rose onto a hill lined with wildflowers, flanked on both sides by trees. Three horses roamed in the distance, their tails flapping in the gentle breeze, warding off flies. The black stallion near Rye playfully nudged him in the shoulder and then ran off to join a buttermilk-colored mare.

Rye was leaning his arms over the fence when Tory reached him. Putting her shoe on the bottom rung, she turned to face the horses.

"Do you want to talk about it?" she asked.

His hand ripped away a vine wrapped around one of the fence posts. "Not right now."

They were quiet for a long while until Tory whirled around to look at him. She placed her hand on his arm. His muscles bunched, but he didn't meet her gaze. "Come on, let's go see what I can scrounge up for you to eat."

He laid his hand over hers before returning to his pose at the fence, the only sign he'd given that her presence was comforting. "You go on ahead. I'll be there in a while."

As she walked toward the house, she realized devastation had been the main note in his beautiful voice.

She didn't think it would go platinum.

I've never cared for vegetables. I suppose I should say plain vegetables. Whoever said they were good for you really ruined my life. There's a whole host of other foods I'd rather be eating. Being from the Midwest, we didn't do much to our veggies. So I decided to try something new one day. One of my favorite veggies is asparagus. Alone, I'm not sure I'd care for it, but I've learned one of life's essential truths—heavy whipping cream makes everything better. If calories bother you, stop reading now. But if you're like me and willing to indulge every once in a while, give this a try. You'll never look at asparagus again in the same way. Oh, and here's a helpful hint: the sauce also works wonders on green beans.

Tory's Creamy Vegetable Sauce

1 tsp. olive oil
2 cloves garlic, mashed
1 cup heavy whipping cream
½ tsp. fresh ground pepper
¼ cup feta cheese
¼ tsp. Greek seasoning
2 tbsp. Brandy
1 tsp. lemon juice (fresh)

Heat the olive oil and sauté the garlic until brown. Add the next four ingredients until the cream bubbles around the sauce pan and reduces. Add the brandy, and if you're lucky enough to have a gas stove, dip it toward the flame. The mixture should ignite and further reduce the cream. Add the lemon juice. Cook 1 more minute. Remove and serve over your vegetable of choice.

Tory Simmons' Simmering Family Cookbook

CHAPTER 9

With nothing to do, Tory explored the house, pausing to marvel at the luxurious rich fabrics and heated towel racks in the bathrooms. There were two guest bedrooms, and she chose the gold and cream one for herself, leaving the room decorated in navy blue and white to Rye. It was like staying in the Ritz Carlton, not something she'd ever done, but she'd seen pictures. The kitchen had stainless steel appliances, a gas stove, and beautiful caramel granite countertops. But there wasn't a single thing in the refrigerator save sweet and sour pickles, mayonnaise, and mustard. Either his family hadn't expected him to stay, or their welcome had its limits. Rye hadn't come back yet, and she didn't have the heart to bother him. Since it was nearing nine o'clock, she didn't even know if there were a local grocery store open in a town this small.

The anthropology book she was trying to read just wouldn't hold her attention. When she heard a knock at the door, it puzzled her. Why would Rye knock? Sighing, she headed to the front of the house and answered it.

It was Amelia Ann. "Hope I'm not interrupting, but we realized after you left that there wasn't any food stocked in the guest house." Even under the porch light, Tory could see the flush of embarrassment on her cheeks.

"Good thing Rye didn't want to eat." But she did, and her stomach grumbled on cue.

"Speaking of which, where is he? I thought he could bring in the groceries."

"He's watching the horses. I can help you."

Amelia Ann stopped her with a hand. "One thing you'll learn about these parts is that men do the heavy lifting. He won't like us taking them in. And I brought a lot of stuff down from the main house."

Rye wouldn't like it, huh? Well, that was news. "Then who loaded them in the car?"

Amelia Ann brushed a hair from her cream suit. "Oh, Rob Donner. He's a senior in high school from next door. Nice boy."

Tory bit her lip. This anthropologist was getting the lay of the land. Men and women had carefully defined roles in this town, it seemed. Well, she could respect traditions—to a point.

"Let's get Rye." Plus, she hated the thought of him standing alone like that, clutching the fence like it was a life preserver.

Amelia Ann stopped Tory with a gentle touch. "Please, not yet. I was hoping we might talk privately for a little while we have the chance."

Just what she wanted to avoid, but she nodded. She followed Amelia Ann into the formal living room and took a seat across from her on the most ornate and uncomfortable sofa she'd ever experienced, cheery in sunny yellow.

"So, what do you think of Rye?" she asked.

"Well, he's nice..." Gosh, her view of him had done a one-eighty, and it would be rude to share her first impression of him as a wild, devil-may-care country singer.

Amelia Ann's lashes fluttered. "When Rye introduced you to me as his cook, I thought he was simply trying to get Mama's blood up by bringing you here. Rubbing her nose in it that you were..."

Beating around the bush was so not her style. "What?"

"Well, it's not like I think that way," Amelia Ann said in a rush. "But Mama has certain ideas about class. I thought you really might be...involved, despite what you said. Especially since he told Mama you were his friend, not his cook."

Tory started laughing and pointed to her chest. "Me and Rye? No, I'm Rye's cook. Do I look like his type? Trust me, the other stuff is all a PR trick."

"But what about the kiss in the papers?" Were the woman's cheeks red?

"Let's leave it at this: your brother brought me here because he likes to eat, and like he said, we're friends...of a sort."

"And you'll be private about all this, I can tell, which is real important to Rye." Amelia Ann tucked a strand of hair behind her ear. "Not that he ever tells the truth about us. He even told a reporter once that he was named after his Mama's favorite drink—rye. Mama's never touched hard liquor. It was quite the scandal before she cleared it up with her friends."

Scandal? That sounded pretty extreme. "He didn't," she said, although she could easily hear him saying that.

Amelia Ann shook her head. "Yes, he did. And you can imagine how well that went over. Rye is an old, honorable name in our family. I understand he only said it because he was hurt."

Yes, there seemed to be to be to be a lot of that going around.

She leaned forward. "Mama was really upset after she talked with Daddy tonight. He told her he's going to one of Rye's concerts when he gets better." She was acting like she was divulging gossip at a church picnic.

"Tell me about Granddaddy Crenshaw." Tory said, both to change the subject and because she was curious.

"Granddaddy's family lost nearly everything in the Depression, but he fought and scraped his way back to the top. He was something of a hell raiser. Divorced the woman his family had wanted him to marry—my Mama's mama—and married a spinster school teacher from across the tracks. They had quite the love affair and were married for decades, but they were too old to have children when they met. Mama was in high school when it happened. I don't think she ever forgave him for the divorce. She blamed him for sullying the Crenshaw name, so she found a sort of...redemption by marrying into the Hollins family."

No wonder Rye respected him and had taken his name. Tory curled her leg under her seat, eager to hear more of the story.

Amelia Ann traced the couch's arm, deep in thought. "But Granddaddy was always around. He had enough money that he could buy his way into just about anything, even if the more traditional families didn't respect him. Daddy always liked him since they shared a passion for golf and the stock market. When Betty, his second wife, died, Daddy insisted he come live here in this guest house. Mama wasn't happy about that."

A new warmth blossomed in her heart when she realized they were staying in his granddaddy's house. That had to mean a lot to Rye.

"He and Rye were close. The man died of a heart attack with a glass of whiskey and a can of chew by the bed, just like he would have wanted to go out. His funeral was the last time Rye was home. Three years ago. Mama had this house redecorated after he passed. Daddy fought her at first, but he gave in.

"Granddaddy would have hated what she's done to his house. So will Rye, but Daddy thought he'd like to stay here anyway. Rye spent a lot of time in this place. It holds good memories."

"Speaking of Rye, how about we go get him? Besides, those groceries shouldn't be in the car in this heat."

It was still over ninety degrees according to her last check on her smart phone. She'd heard about Southern heat, but even so. They both rose and headed for the door.

"I left the car running with the A/C on, so they should be okay."

"Still, we shouldn't leave them out there forever. Besides, I'm hungry." She rubbed her stomach for effect.

Amelia Ann placed a comforting hand on Tory's arm. "Oh, bless your heart. Let's get Rye *this instant*. We don't want you blowing away with the wind."

Blow away with the wind? Who said that? "Why don't you go get him? Be nice to talk to him in private, I'm sure." She could heft the groceries in by herself and start dinner.

"When I went to Ole Miss, I managed to slip away and see him for the first time in a long while. After that, I tried to see him a few times a year. Mama didn't find out until recently. That's when Rye shoved that rude man at the charity event. Mama had called him that day, forbidding him to come to my graduation or contact me anymore. It was all my fault he got in trouble." Her eyes were glistening with tears.

Goodness. So that's what had set him off. "That's not true," Tory said, placing a hand on her arm. "We all make our own decisions."

Amelia Ann's hand patted Tory's before falling away. "I pray Daddy's desire for peace will allow Rye to come back to me. I miss him so much."

Her love for her brother was as warm as the night they'd just walked into. "I imagine that means a lot to him."

Amelia Ann looked off at Rye, who was still standing at the fence, looking like he hadn't moved an inch. "I think so, but he rarely talks about his feelings."

"Go get him then."

Tory watched her walk down the gravel path.

It was at times like this that she wished she had a brother or sister.

***

The groceries Amelia Ann had brought made for a grade-A dinner. She pan-fried steaks and zucchini and whipped up some mashed potatoes, one of Rye's favorites.

The siblings' murmured words drifted in from the living room. Her stomach was growling, so she decided to start without him, not wanting to interrupt their talk. She had finished half her plate when Rye strolled into the kitchen.

"Why didn't you say dinner was ready?" he asked.

"I didn't want to interrupt your talk with your sister. Besides, you said you weren't hungry."

"She just took off. Said to say bye." He pulled out a chair at the kitchen table and sank wearily into it. "And technically I'm not hungry, but it's like having a hard-on in the morning. Even if you're not really interested, the hunger is still there. I find it hard to pass up your food. It's always on the edge of my mind."

She arched an eyebrow at his rude metaphor, but rose to reheat his dinner. When she placed the plate in front of him, she picked up her own plate.

"Where are you going?" he asked.

"I was going to let you eat alone."

"Sit down and eat with me. You're probably starving."

Sitting back down, she speared another piece of her steak and dabbed it in the blue cheese cream sauce she'd thrown together. "Yes."

Rye pushed his zucchini around with his fork. "Well, I'm glad this little drama hasn't ruined *your* appetite. Amelia Ann told me about your little chat."

Tory finished chewing. He was in a mood, there was no doubt. "So was she right? Did you bring me here to piss your mama off?"

"No, I damn well did not." He leaped up and started rifling through the cabinets.

"What are you looking for?"

"Some booze. My mama probably threw it out like everything else when she redecorated Granddaddy's place." China rattled at his force. "He'd tan her hide if he could see what she's done."

She hesitated a moment before sighing. "There's some Jack Daniels in the cabinet over the refrigerator. Amelia Ann brought you some from the house."

"Well, bless her heart. I hope she brought a case." Rye took a healthy swig from the bottle.

Tory winced. Watching someone drink from a bottle made her stomach queasy. She didn't know what to do for him, so she stood with her plate. "I'm going to finish this in my room. You should eat your dinner. It always makes you feel better." She prayed it would work tonight.

"No need to run from me, honey. I won't hurt you."

That infernal *honey* again. "No, but you're hurting yourself, drinking like that, and I'm not sure I want to be around to watch."

Rye smirked and leaned back against the refrigerator. "Careful, darlin', you almost sound like you care."

Her heart rapped against her ribs. Now that he said it, she realized she did. Alarm bells clanged in her head. The last thing she needed in her life was to care for this man. "There's no need to get mean. You're hurting, and I understand that. Best to leave you alone."

She'd made it halfway across the kitchen before Rye grabbed her. Her skin tingled where his big hands held her arms. "Honey, I *am* a mean man. Best know what you're dealing with."

"No, you're not. I can't imagine reconciling where you came from with where you are now."

His eyes narrowed. "Stop trying to understand. There's nothing to reconcile. I know who I am. I'm Rye Crenshaw, dammit."

He'd taken the name of the granddaddy who'd broken tradition after finding true love. It spoke volumes. Small-town culture being what it was, it must have been a huge scandal back then.

Tory set her plate down on the table. "I know who you are."

"Dammit, you don't." He picked up the bottle of Jack and took another swig.

Her face grew hot. "You're just spoiling for a fight tonight. I'm going to leave now before you do something you'll regret."

The bottle slid a few inches across the counter when he set it down. "Honey, Rye Crenshaw never has regrets. And he doesn't run from anything."

When he reached for her, she swatted his hands away. "Stop calling me honey. You're acting like a child. And everyone has regrets, so don't give me that bullshit. Enough of this playacting. Have the decency to be honest with me. After all, we're friends, aren't we?"

A chuckle escaped, soft and harsh. "Yes. Yes, we are."

She softened, touched his arm. "Rye, I don't know what good I can do for you here."

He stared at the floor for a long moment before looking up and meeting her eyes. "Just do what you do best. Cook. And, ah...listen to me."

Redness streaked up his neck, showing his embarrassment, and this evidence of his vulnerability squeezed her throat. "So I'm like your cooking confessor," she joked to ease the tension between them.

"I like you, Tory," he said. His Adam's apple moved. "Maybe I...have a thing for you."

She stilled. Oh no. While the attraction between them was unspoken and deep, she hadn't imagined he would call it out like this. He shifted on his feet, his face the color of a ripening tomato.

"Don't say things you don't mean," she murmured, a tingle of fear and excitement shooting down her spine.

He took his hat off. His thick hair was matted on the top, the ash-brown curls sticking to the back of his head. She wanted to twine her fingers through them like knitting needles.

"I don't say things I don't mean. You...darn well know that."

Her eyes widened. The fact that he stopped himself from swearing—for her—had her heart rapping a spastic rhythm against her ribs.

"We've become...close, haven't we? And I think you're ...about as lovely as sunlight kissing the leaves of a birch tree in autumn."

She didn't think his face could turn any redder, but it did. Somehow it did. Poetry? From him? It was the last thing she'd expected.

He exhaled in a whoosh. "I need you here, or I don't know if I can get through this. It's...hard. That's why I asked you to make the trip with me."

"Rye—"

"You don't have to do anything for me, Tory, except be here."

"Okay," she whispered, overwhelmed by his words.

His hands suddenly framed her face. "I don't know what it is about you."

Ditto. He wasn't the type of man she'd imagined herself with...but now he was the only one who entered into her thoughts. Her breath stopped. She tried to pull back to maintain the last vestiges of professionalism between them, even though she felt herself blossoming under his sweet hazel eyes. "Rye, this isn't- "

"Shh, don't talk." He leaned in and kissed her, a gentle pass across the lips.

It might have been friendly, but the heat between them was undeniable. Tory pulled back to meet his burning gaze and couldn't look away. Then he brushed his lips over her mouth again, nipping at her bottom lip this time.

It wasn't enough. Tory opened her mouth, wanting more of him. Rye tangled his tongue with hers and took the kiss deeper. He groaned, the sound reverberating across her skin, leaving a trail of goose bumps. She fisted her hands in his hair, seeking his mouth like cool water until she couldn't breathe. Moaning, she let her head fall back for a moment, drinking in air with shallow breaths. Rye kissed the column of her neck before pulling her mouth back to his. The wet, deep kiss had her knees shaking. She sagged against him, tasting the spiciness of the whiskey he'd drunk. When he pulled her against him, she could feel his arousal.

Tory moaned again and clutched his shoulders. Rye picked her up bodily, and her legs wrapped around his waist to hold on.

Part of her knew they were out of control, but she just couldn't seem to stop.

He pressed her against the kitchen wall, his hand tugging at her shirt and slipping inside her bra to cup her breast. She gripped his neck when his fingers tugged on her nipple, her head arching back to hit the wall. When he replaced his fingers with his mouth, laving and then sucking, her hands dug into his biceps. Had anything ever felt this good?

"Oh, God," she cried, her breath choppy.

"You really are a little thing."

Was he talking about her breasts? Suddenly embarrassment dug in, and she wanted to cover herself. "That's not very nice of you to say."

He gave her a gentle kiss on the lips. "You misunderstand, darlin'. I've always heard people say good things come in little packages." His fingers caressed her breast. "Seems they're right."

Tory rolled her eyes. "Must be a news bulletin to you."

He pressed his forehead against hers suddenly, an endearing caress. "There she is. I was wondering where that sassy girl had gone."

Could he be any sexier? "I'm at a loss here," she heard herself saying. "I don't know what to think."

He kissed her softly on the nose. Moved on to her eyelids. "Neither do I. Can't we take a time-out from being Rye the singer and Tory the cook while we're here in Meade and just be together?"

She let her legs loosen from around his waist and stood shakily in front of him. "I'm not too good at that."

Falling into bed with a man was rare for her, and it wasn't something she took lightly.

He pushed a curl behind her ear. "You're one of those commitment types."

"Yes. What's wrong with that?"

"Nothing. I just don't have anything to offer a woman in the long-term."

She lowered her gaze to his throat. "I'm sorry that's what you believe."

"Are we at odds, then?" he murmured.

God, she hoped not. She didn't want to be deprived of his touch. "No," she said, "but we should probably stop. I work for you, and you said—"

"I know what I said." His hands took a leisurely stroll down her arms, making her shiver. "I don't usually have regrets, but I'll regret it if I don't make love to you."

So would she. "We can't always have what we want."

He finally stepped back and picked up his hat. "You usually can in my world. I don't feel much like eating, after all. Good night, Tory."

"Good night, Rye."

He put a finger to the brim in a salute. As he left, she sought comfort in cleaning up the kitchen, but tonight it didn't bring her peace.

When my parents died, I was only twelve, and my grandma must have wondered what to do with me. When I came to live with them, they hadn't had children in the house for decades, but I never felt like I didn't belong. Grandma brought me into her magical world of cooking, which helped heal my grief. One of the first recipes she introduced me to was sugar cookies. Now most people make these at Christmas, but Grandma, well, she believed you could make them any time of year. So, we'd make the dough, and then pick from the cookie cutters she'd been collecting for years. If we didn't have the shape we wanted, we'd improvise and make our own, using frosting to decorate instead of colored sugar. For me, it was better than cutting out paper dolls on a rainy day.

Sugar Cookies

1 cup butter
1 cup sugar
3 eggs
3½ cups flour
1 tsp. soda
2 tsp. cream of tartar
1 tsp. vanilla

Cream the butter and sugar. Add the eggs. When the mixture is fluffy, add the remaining ingredients. Blend well. Refrigerate until the mixture is cold and hard. Roll out into the desired thickness. Cut into shapes. Bake 375 degrees for 10-12 minutes. Decorate.

Tory Simmons' Simmering Family Cookbook

CHAPTER 10

T ory was stirring scrambled eggs with a red spatula when Rye strolled into the kitchen. He'd gone for a run. His T-shirt was covered in sweat spots and his hair looked like he'd taken a shower. And he looked freaking sexy.

"Christ, it's muggy out. Going to be bitchin' hot today." He pulled a bottle of water from the refrigerator and swigged the entire contents.

Tory turned back to the eggs, not wanting the zip of attraction that shot through her. She'd tossed and turned all night, her body still warm and flushed after their rendezvous in the kitchen. Today she was plain grumpy.

A black-and-white dog padded into the kitchen and headed straight for Rye. Her spatula clattered onto the counter, and she pressed herself against the cabinet, her heart rate spiking. The dog barked at her, revealing sharp teeth when it opened its mouth.

"Where'd that dog come from?" she rasped.

"It's my Daddy's hunting dog, Buster," he said, petting the animal. "Our property manager, Mr. Pullins, takes care of him and the horses. Buster here kept me company on my run. Makes me miss my own dogs, but I know my pal J.P. is taking great care of them like he always does when I'm on tour."

"Rye, could you please take the dog outside?" she whispered, her old fears making her hands sweat.

He wiped his mouth with the back of his hand. "What's the matter?"

"I'm afraid of dogs." She pressed her hand to her chest when it became hard to breathe.

Rye studied her for a moment. "Something happened, didn't it?"

Her lips trembled as the memories rode in like an unwelcome guest. "My parents swerved to avoid hitting a German shepherd once." She could still feel the cold glass of the window as she crashed into it. Hear her mother cry out in alarm.

Rye grabbed the dog by the collar when it tried to approach her. "What else?"

She gulped in air. "A tire blew. My dad lost control of the car. We hit a tree."

"That must have been scary," he said. "Keep going."

She couldn't take her gaze off the dog. Her ears were ringing, and sweat broke out on her temples. "My parents died on impact. The car didn't have airbags."

"Oh God, Tory. I'm so sorry."

Her arms wrapped around her middle. For some reason, hearing him say the words meant more because it wasn't perfunctory. "The dog didn't go away. He came up to the car and started barking. Wouldn't stop. I thought he was trying to hurt me. The police officer who found us later told me he was trying to help. They're smart, he said, and the dog knew people were injured inside the car. Still, I couldn't get out of my seatbelt for almost thirty minutes, I was later told, and the whole while I just heard him barking."

Her hands had clawed at the belt until they were bleeding, and she'd screamed until she was hoarse. That was when she'd started crying, having realized her mom and dad couldn't help her, would never be able to help her again. "Finally a car stopped, and an older man helped me out and then called the police. But even then the dog wouldn't stop barking, and the man had to set me down and chase him off."

Rye's hand tightened around the dog's collar. "I can't tell you how sorry I am. Let me take him out, and I'll be right back."

She jumped when the dog let loose another bark. "It was a long time ago." And she'd tried to work on her fear of dogs with one of the school's counselors, but it hadn't abated. While she knew it wasn't rational, it didn't matter. The old fear was always there, simmering beneath the surface.

He gave her one last look before turning to leave, and the look in his eyes made her feel like crying. She took slow, deep breaths and turned to stir the eggs.

His tennis shoes squeaked on the floor a few minutes later, and then his hands settled gently on her shoulders. He turned her around and brought her to his chest. Giving in, she nuzzled her face against his sweaty T-shirt. When he kissed her temple, she wanted nothing more than to curl into him and let him help her forget.

"My poor Tory," he murmured.

The dam of her tears threatened to break, so she pulled back.

"You'd best hit the shower. Breakfast will be ready in a few."

Fortunately, he gave her space, only stopping to trace her cheek with one fingertip before leaving the room. She moved to the stove and turned the now overcooked eggs. When she dumped them on a plate, she leaned against the counter and watched the steam rise. Reining in her emotions was like pulling in a canoe during a storm, but after a few minutes, she managed to shove them into the box where she always stored them.

Tory made Rye a plate and decided to take a walk before he came out, wanting some air. When she opened the door, she scanned the yard for Buster. No sign of him. She tiptoed outside, only resuming her normal pace after she made her way past Rye's truck.

The humidity and heat were suffocating. Sweat broke out on her upper lip and between her breasts. Swatting away mosquitoes the size of small birds, she walked to the gravel road that led from the house. Unlike Kansas, the shade from the trees didn't make the heat any more palatable. Firming her shoulders, Tory scanned her surroundings, grateful for the distraction. The land was beautiful and lush, and there were about a thousand different shades of green. Ferns thrived in the natural hothouse, and moss grew around the bases of the trees and dripped from their bark. Branches towered over her, thick with leaves, blocking out the sun.

She hadn't gone halfway down the road before realizing she'd need to shower when she returned. How did people function in this heat? Or before air conditioning? She remembered how Southern women constantly fainted in old movies, falling over in their hoop skirts and lace. As she trudged through the suffocating veil of moist air, she formed a new understanding of that phenomenon. Wearing a corset out in this heat could be an Olympic sport. Tory could barely breathe, and she wasn't even cinched up.

She turned onto the main road. A shiny white BMW SUV slowed as it approached. Tory stepped to the side, eyeing it with caution. When she recognized Tammy through the windshield, she prayed she would pass and leave her in peace.

As the car came to a halt, Tory realized her luck hadn't been so great lately.

***

Tammy forced her mouth to relax when she saw Tory power walking on Kraven Hill Road. What in the world! She hit the button to roll her window down. "Tory, what are you doing on the road? Someone could have hit you."

The woman visibly shuddered before striding forward. "I was taking a walk."

A walk? The woman seemed nice, but despite being educated, she didn't have a lick of sense. It was sweltering out, and even if it hadn't been, no one *walked* on the road. It just wasn't done. Perhaps she hadn't realized, since she was as out of place in Meade as a Kansas blizzard.

"Well, you shouldn't be out here. People don't walk on the road around here." Except vagrants, but she didn't add that.

Tory lifted her hand above her eyes as the sun emerged from behind a cloud. From the rear view mirror, Tammy saw Annabelle wave from the backseat. Rory simply stared.

"Rye went running this morning. Where did he go?" she asked.

Tammy tapped her fingers on the steering wheel. "Knowing Rye, he probably ran on the road, but he's always done what you shouldn't do. You'd do better not to take after him."

Her words weren't very nice, but she couldn't help it. Having him back here was downright discomfiting, and Mama had been in a mood all morning because of it.

Tory reached down and re-tied one of her shoes. "Would you be able to give me a ride back to the guest house? It's a lot hotter out here than I expected." She fanned herself.

"I'll have to drop you off after I leave the kids at the big house."

"That's fine." Tory came around to the passenger side.

"Hi guys. What are you up to today?" Tory asked the kids after putting on her seatbelt.

Guys? That's right. People in the Midwest used that term for everyone. Tammy tried not to frown. Eyes flicking to the rear view mirror, she saw Annabelle lean across Rory to better see Tory, but he gave her a gentle push back into her seat. He wasn't fond of anyone getting too close. It worried her. Did all boys push people away or just hers?

Annabelle bounced up and down. "Mama has a meeting, so we're going to stay at Grandmama's house today."

"That sounds nice," Tory replied.

Even Tammy could hear the insincerity. No doubt Rye had filled this woman's mind with all sorts of bad stories about Mama. Tammy knew she was difficult, but she was still her mama. That meant something.

When they arrived at the house, Annabelle grabbed Tory's hand, ever the open-hearted child.

"Mama, can Miss Tory stay for a while and play with me?"

Tammy picked up her Coach purse and shut the door. "No,

Annabelle. I'm sure Ms. Simmons has things she needs to do for your Uncle Rye." Hopefully Annabelle would understand Miss Tory was too informal, but she was still learning manners.

Tory swung Annabelle's hand in hers, making an arc. "Actually, I don't have a thing to do. I'd love to stay and play. I bet you have some pretty dolls."

Her daughter grinned. "Yes, I do. We can have a tea party. My dolls love them."

"Well, we'll have to fix something nice for them."

She wasn't sure why, but Tammy pulled on Annabelle's other hand. "Honey, you shouldn't bother Ms. Simmons."

"It's no bother, really, and please call me Tory. Let's go inside, Annabelle. You can show me your dolls."

So Tory was ignoring her request? "My children are expected to use their manners when addressing adults."

The pause was slight, but telling. "Of course. How about Miss Tory? I feel ancient when I'm called Miss Simmons."

Tammy still thought it was too informal, but she nodded.

"Why don't you come along with us, Rory?" Tory asked.

He shook his head. "Boys don't have tea parties."

Tammy reached out a hand out to caress his cheek, but he darted away, his eyes wide and watchful.

God, his fear of being touched kept her up at night. Had Sterling done something to him when she wasn't around? Acid poured into her stomach.

"Well, come and find us if you change your mind, Rory," Tory said.

The revving engine of a fast approaching car sounded behind them, and they all turned to look as Rye's truck sped toward the house. He slammed the door when he got out, making her jump in her heels. Did he have to be so forceful?

He strode over to Tory. "Where were you? I couldn't find you when I came for breakfast. You were pretty upset before."

Now, wasn't this interesting? Tammy cocked her ear to hear the answer.

"I went for a walk."

He put his hands on his hips. "In this heat?"

Well, he clearly hadn't lost all sense. "And on the main road."

"You were walking on the main road?" he asked her.

"Why is that such a problem?" the woman asked, her voice exasperated.

"Honey, we don't walk on the main road here. You could get hit."

"Isn't that where you went running this morning?"

Rye tapped his boot in place. "Hell, no. Sorry, Tammy. Kids."

Tammy shot him a look and then caught Tory's smirk. So, she'd been caught in an exaggeration about Rye. She waited to see if the woman would say anything.

"Well, I like to walk, so if there's somewhere better..."

Tammy let out a breath in relief. The last thing she felt like doing was hashing things out with her brother.

"There's a path in the woods. I'll show you later, but tell me when you're leaving next time. I was...worried."

"I'm sorry. It won't happen again." Her face softened as she said it. Curiouser and curiouser.

Rye hooked his thumbs in his belt. "Did you walk all the way here?"

"No, Tammy was kind enough to give me a ride, and Annabelle and I are going to have a tea party now."

Tammy glanced at her watch. "I'm going to be late. You two be good for Grandmama. Annabelle, don't be a bother to Miss Simmons."

Annabelle sashayed, swirling her yellow dress. "I won't, Mama."

"Then come and give me some sugar." She leaned over so her daughter could kiss her cheek. "Go inside now. I'll be back after lunch." Taking Tory's hand in her own, her girl scampered off toward the house.

Rye put his hands on his hips. "Nice to see ya, sis."

She made her mouth move, but it probably didn't look much like a smile. His infernal words didn't deserve one.

"I'll see you later, Rory. You be a good boy."

He didn't turn toward her, but Rye did and met her eyes. Was that sadness in his face? He glanced away before she could tell. Once inside the car, Tammy checked her lipstick in the mirror. Her reflection looked a little sad too, so she reapplied some blush. She drove off with a tight throat.

Rory hadn't moved.

Neither had Rye.

***

Rye looked up at the sky and sighed. Tammy wasn't his mama, but she sure reminded him of her, just like she always had. Daddy wasn't the only one he had to make peace with, and the way they grated on each other, he wondered if peace was even possible with Mini-Mama.

Rory was still standing there, too, and while his nephew was cute, he had no idea how to interact with the boy.

"What are you waiting for, son?"

The boy's face scrunched up. "You weren't nice to my mama."

Rye chuckled at his honesty. "No, son, but she wasn't particularly nice to me either. We've been fighting like cats since we were your age. You best treat Annabelle better. It's no fun growing up that way."

Without another word, Rory turned and walked to the house. After retrieving his hat, Rye followed. He slapped the Stetson against his thigh. The desire to flee was strong. He wanted nothing more than to get into the truck and haul ass, but he wanted to see his daddy. He froze when he stepped inside.

"Mama."

Her face was as hard as the diamond studs in her ears. "You can put that hat on the hat rack, Rye. Your daddy knows you're here, and he's asked to see you." She lowered her head, looking down her nose at him.

There it was. That famous expression.

"Rye, I don't want that woman playing with Annabelle. I will tolerate her as a guest, but that's the extent of it. I expect you to make that plain to her since Tammy failed to do so."

Rye bit his cheek to keep himself from raising his voice. "Mama, Tory is not some cheap woman you can order around. Like I told you, she's a doctoral student and a friend. She's a good woman, and Annabelle clearly senses that. Let it go."

"She's your cook, and God knows what else." Margaret's spine straightened. "Am I supposed to believe that you didn't bring her here just to needle me?"

"She's my friend, first and foremost." Rye curled his lip. "Mama, any woman other than a carbon copy like Emeline would needle you."

"Emeline was the best choice for you, and you threw her away," she said harshly.

"No, Mama. She was *your* choice for me."

"So I'm supposed to believe this Tory is the best choice now?"

"As I said, she's my friend." His mind momentarily flashed to that moment in the kitchen last night. She was more than that, but he wanted to protect her. "As for why I brought her here, the whole world doesn't revolve around you. Don't give yourself airs."

Margaret sucked in a breath. "You are as rude and common as ever."

He bowed. "Thank you, Mama. That's what every son wants to hear from the woman who gave birth to him. I'm here for Daddy.

Understand that."

Margaret fingered the gold necklace around her neck. "I am against this reconciliation. And whatever you say, I don't want that woman you brought making attachments with my grandchildren or *anyone* in this family."

Rye chuckled bitterly. "No surprise there. I don't know where this will lead, but Daddy's making an effort. The least I can do is to make one too."

"It doesn't change anything between you and me."

"Fine, but understand this. If Daddy and Amelia Ann want to see me, you will not stand in the way. I won't have you setting Daddy's health back because of your hatred for me."

Her mouth pressed together in a hard line. "How could you think I would hurt him? He's my husband."

The old wound up and bled on him again. "Well, I'm your son, and you've done plenty of damage to me."

He strode to the stairs, taking them two at a time. Chatty voices and giggling spilled out of Tammy's old room when he reached the second floor. He peered inside. Tory and Annabelle were sitting together on the antique brass bed in the middle of a mass of dolls, talking in animated voices. It was good to see her happy after her horrible confession this morning. Hearing how her parents had died had near broken his heart, even more so because of the brave way she'd held back her tears.

Just then Tory ran a hand down Annabelle's blond hair, and Rye froze. Emotions he couldn't identify clamored through him, sending off alarms in his brain. But he couldn't look away. The peaceful, happy looks on their faces made his heart clutch.

She was good with kids. Why was he surprised? Worse, why did it affect him so?

He jumped when he saw Rory standing in the next doorway—his old bedroom—looking like he was doing the same thing Rye was, watching them. How many times had he stood alone in that doorway dressed like a perfect boy instead of getting dirty playing outside with the other kids? Rory stared at him and then turned away, his shoulders slumping.

Rubbing his chest hard, as if to stop the emotions roiling through him, he realized he was going to have to toughen up if he wanted to survive this visit. Then he realized he was being too hard on himself. He'd known all along that coming here would be hell. There was no reason to get confused by the unexpected way watching Tory with Annabelle had affected him. Or how seeing his sister's lost little boy had reminded him of himself. He straightened,

134

preparing for his sit down with Daddy, and ran a hand through his hair before opening the door.

Hampton smiled when he saw him, and Rye let loose a breath of relief. His daddy looked less pale today. "Good to see you, son."

Hearing the endearment today was less jarring than yesterday, and he took it as a measure of progress. "You bored yet?" Rye asked. "How about we pass the time by playing some poker?" He pulled the cards he'd brought from the back pocket of his jeans.

When his Daddy nodded with a grin, Rye drew a chair next to the bed. "I hate to warn you, sir, but I play a ton of poker on the road. And one of my best friends is Rhett Butler Blaylock, who's won—"

"The World Series of Poker," Daddy finished. "I told you I've kept up with you. But to give you fair warning in return, where do you think I go on Wednesday nights?"

The cards felt good in his hands as he shuffled them. "I thought you always worked late on Wednesdays."

Hampton grabbed the cards from him, shuffling the deck like a professional in a Vegas casino. Well, well.

"I have a standing poker game. Seems we have something in common."

Rye gave his first easy smile of the morning. "Seems so. Why don't you deal the cards? Just don't cheat. I can't abide cheaters."

Hampton chuckled. "Neither can I, son."

As his father shuffled the cards, Rye caught sight of Mama peeking through the crack in the door. He turned away, giving his Daddy his full attention.

"I'm glad you're home, Rye."

Rye picked up his cards. "Me, too."

And in that moment, he meant it.

***

After making sure his Daddy was settled for a nap, Rye headed downstairs and followed voices into the kitchen. Amelia Ann was standing next to Tory, and Annabelle was perched on the kitchen island, her feet swinging. They all had spoons in their mouths and were making humming noises.

"Oh, my gosh. This has got to be the best cookie dough I've ever tasted," Amelia Ann cried.

Annabelle waved her spoon like it was a magic wand. "Let's not make cookies. We can eat it all like this."

Tory caught sight of Rye. "Want a taste?"

His eyes immediately went to her mouth, which was slightly

135

wet from licking dough. Yeah, he was going to have to talk her into kissing him again—and more. "Can't think of anything I'd rather taste."

Her whole body seemed to ripple. Good, he was getting to her.

Amelia Ann crossed the room to kiss him on the cheek. "Hi sugar. How's Daddy?"

"Great. He's taking a nap now." It seemed like a good idea not to mention that Daddy had won two hundred dollars off him in poker. The man had to have been counting cards.

Tory offered him a spoon, and he ran a hand down her arm before taking it. "Thanks."

"What have you two been doing up there?" his sister asked. "Mama looked pretty upset when I returned from town. She promptly announced that she had some errands to run, and she never runs errands on Wednesday."

Rye winked at Annabelle, who was gazing up at him with big eyes, her spoon back in her mouth.

"Daddy and I were...conversing." It wasn't exactly a lie. Then he took a bite of the dough. "Sugar cookies," he purred.

Sheer bliss couldn't describe it.

"Miss Tory thought we could make them into shapes and decorate them while Mama's out," Annabelle told him.

"That sounds like a great idea!" He spooned some more batter for Annabelle and handed it to her.

After taking it, she scooted across the counter and hugged him. "Will you help us, Uncle Rye?" He froze when the little arms reached around him, breathing in the smell of children's shampoo and baby powder.

"I know where Grandmama keeps the cookie cutters," his niece announced with a smile. "Help me down, Uncle Rye."

He caught her as she pushed off the counter. "Where's your brother?"

Her shrug made him want to tweak her nose, it was so cute. "He doesn't like cooking or tea parties."

"I'll bet he likes to eat though, right?"

She nodded her head, her thin, silky blond hair swinging around her heart-shaped face.

After opening a few drawers, Rye found a spoon and swiped some more batter. "I'll go find him." He hadn't been able to shake the image of that solitary boy while playing poker.

He strode past Amelia Ann, whose eyebrows rose in surprise. When he found Rory sitting at a small white desk, quietly reading a book, Rye's insides gripped like wrung-out sheets. His Mama had updated his room, but the perfect order and sterility were the same as they'd ever been. Messiness had *never* been tolerated, and to this day, he couldn't stand places that were this...orderly.

The boy stood up, his posture as stiff as the toy soldiers displayed on the shelf. "Sir?"

Rye waved the spoon. "Your sister said you like cookies. I thought you might like some batter."

"Food's not allowed upstairs, sir."

"We had that rule when I lived here," Rye said as he dropped to one knee in front of his nephew, "but sometimes it's okay to break it. Don't worry. It'll be our secret."

Rory narrowed his eyes, looking suspicious.

"Well, if you don't believe me, you can always come down to the kitchen and eat it there."

Silence descended, and the boy looked at the spoon he held. Finally he nodded after a long pause.

"Let's go then."

Laughter spilled from the kitchen as they entered the room. When Annabelle saw Rory, she raced forward.

"Rory, we're making sugar cookies. Did Uncle Rye give you some batter?"

"Annabelle, you know that we aren't allowed to eat food outside the kitchen."

She frowned. "I forgot."

Rye shoved the spoon at Rory. "Well, you're in the kitchen now."

After he took the spoon, the boy turned away like he was hiding a bad secret.

The dough was being rolled onto the kitchen counter by Tory, who kept sprinkling flour on it between passes. "Rory, Annabelle already picked out her cookie cutter. Do you want to pick one out too?"

"Boys don't cook."

Amelia Ann put her hands on his shoulders, but he jerked away. She bit her lip as she met Rye's eyes.

He had needed to unlearn a whole heap of bullshit like that when he left this place behind. Maybe he could help the kid.

"Well, that's mostly untrue. Haven't you ever heard of chefs, son? Granted, Tory here is a lady chef, but there are plenty of men who cook."

The boy's spoon was perfectly clean when he set it down. "My daddy and granddaddy don't cook."

"No, they don't, but I'm going to help Tory make cookies with your sister and Amelia Ann. And we could use your help."

He was grateful the boy hadn't asked him about his culinary skills. Part of him couldn't believe he was offering.

Annabelle grabbed Rory's hand. "Come on. You can sit with me. Uncle Rye, can you help me up again?"

"Sure, darlin'." He hefted her onto the counter and then reached for his nephew.

"I can do it myself."

There was anger in his tone, so Rye didn't offer again.

For the next two hours, laughter was the main sound in the kitchen. Tory orchestrated the entire production, helping them roll dough, cut cookies, and then peel them off the flour-dusted counter and onto a cookie sheet. Coloring the frosting added another piece of fun with Annabelle trying to achieve the perfect shade of pink.

Rory finally relaxed and was swept away. He didn't get the giggles like Annabelle, who was clearly on a sugar high, but he smiled more and acted less guarded. Rye couldn't hold back a grin as the boy settled closer to him, announcing that the two of them were making *manly* cookies with *manly* icing.

When Tammy and Mama walked into the kitchen, cookies covered every surface. Rye was helping Rory finish decorating his soldier while Amelia Ann and Tory were adding the last silver ball to one of Annabelle's princess cookies. Rye braced himself for a return of the tension.

"What is going on?" Tammy asked, a frown on her mouth.

Annabelle held up her princess, smearing the pink frosting with her fingers. "We made cookies, Mama."

Rye watched as Rory walked over to Tammy, his posture as stiff as it had been in the room upstairs.

"Daddy needed to rest, so we brought the kids down here to make sugar cookies," Rye said. "Tory has a family recipe. I'll be sure to get it from her, Mama."

Rather than replying, Mama smoothed a crease in her pale yellow suit. "Your daddy was no doubt exhausted from playing poker with you."

Silence descended, and Amelia Ann and Tammy stared at him open mouthed. So he'd broken another of Mama's rules: no gambling in the house. He had to grip the counter to hold back a nasty reply.

Annabelle's eyes teared up, the tension clearly upsetting her. "Mama, would you like to have one of my princess cookies?" She carried it over to Tammy, the princess bobbing in her shaking hand. "Grandmama, do you want one too?"

"Annabelle, you and Rory have spoiled your supper," Mama said, her voice cool, reminding him of what it had been like to be disciplined as a child.

The ice in her voice could be as cold and punishing as hail when she had a mind. Like she did now.

"No, we didn't, Grandmama," she said, her voice trembling. "We only decorated them."

That was it! Rye stepped forward, but Tory grabbed his hand, clenching it tightly. He didn't heed the squeeze. "Amelia Ann, why don't you take the children upstairs for a little while? Tory and I will clean up. We'll see you kids later."

Annabelle and Rory looked over their shoulders as his sister led them out, her mouth grim. The remaining adults stood silent until the sounds of them going upstairs faded.

"Look," Rye said, waving his hand across the room. "I don't care what you do or say to me, but don't bring the kids into it. This is no big deal. They were only making cookies."

"Rye, I think we should excuse Miss Simmons," Mama said, calmly crossing her hands across her chest.

Tory started to leave, but Rye stilled her with a hand. "Right, we don't discuss family matters in front of guests." Even to his ears, his laugh was cruel. "Who gives a damn? She saw what happened."

Mama's mouth thinned. "Well, we can only hope she is discreet. It would be bad for your *career* if she were to talk about her visit here, right? Or would it help? Making cookies with children after you made those disadvantaged little ones cry? Your fans haven't been too happy with you. At least Miss Simmons appears to be helping your image."

Damn, his Mama always knew when to raise a sore point. Rye squeezed Tory's hand. "The main reason I brought Tory here is that she's a friend, as I've told you. But not to worry, I know she won't say anything about our family drama."

"I think that's just about enough," Mama replied. "Tammy, you should take the children home."

"No, I want to finish this. Tammy, don't you see? They're only kids. And they're suffocating, just like we did. Don't make the same mistakes with them. Don't make them feel bad for enjoying something so simple and harmless."

Even though he knew he was out of line, he couldn't stop himself from speaking the words.

Tammy's hand moved over her string of pearls at her throat. "Rye, you have no right to speak to me this way. How dare you judge me? Not all of us feel suffocated here. My children are happy."

He dropped Tory's hand. "Happy? Have you looked at them? Their clothes are perfect. Their manners are excellent. Annabelle's still pretty resilient, being so little, but not Rory. He doesn't play easily, and he's afraid to run around or make a mess. Trust me, Rory is not happy, and when the life is snuffed out of Annabelle, she won't be either."

Wasn't that exactly what he'd discovered after breaking free? That twenty-five years of being miserable had been way too long.

"It's not true," Tammy whispered, biting her lip.

"Let her alone, Rye," Mama said. "You're the one who brought the kids into this by allowing Tory to be here and cook in *my* kitchen. You simply couldn't be content having your Daddy and Amelia Ann on your side. See yourself out."

Wrapping her arm around Tammy, she led his sister from the room. Their heels clicked away in the silence.

He bent his head, rubbing the back of his neck. "Christ."

Tory laid a hand on his arm, and he pulled her against him. "I need to get out of here," he whispered in her ear. The smell of cookies was now as assaulting as Clorox.

"Go," Tory whispered, stepping back. "I'll clean up."

He ran a finger across her cheek. "I'm sorry."

What must she think of him now?

***

Tory heard Rye slam the front door as she hurried to find containers for the cookies. Her stomach was a ball of knots, and all she wanted to do was make a speedy exit, too. Then there was the patter of footsteps beyond the kitchen, and she heard the door close again, more quietly this time. Probably Tammy and the kids. Tory was closing the last Tupperware container when Amelia Ann entered the room.

"It must have been ugly down here. Tammy looked like a corpse when she came upstairs to get the kids, and Mama has the door to her sitting room closed. I thought you might want a ride back. It's muggy out. Rye seems...to have left without you."

"Yes." She understood why he'd needed to escape, but the haze from the humidity was visible through the window, and the last thing she wanted to do was walk back to the guest house. "I'd appreciate it."

Amelia Ann pointed to the containers. "Do you want to take some for you and Rye?"

"No, thanks." All the joy they'd brought had evaporated.

"Tammy didn't even take any home. I'll drop some off later tonight. The kids should have their cookies." She suddenly pressed a hand to her stomach. "Oh God, why does it always have to be so hard?"

Tory had no answers, so she gave none. All she did was put her arm around Amelia Ann. They walked out of the kitchen as a unit, moving slowly and quietly across the hall.

Amelia Ann drove them without haste in her sporty BMW convertible, the top closed, of course. Tory suspected she didn't want to go back to the main house alone. When they came to a stop in the driveway, Tory asked, "Do you want to come in?"

"No, I'd better not. Mama will only be harder on me if I'm gone too long. She already thinks I'm on Rye's side and not hers." Her hands clenched the steering wheel.

The dynamics in their family were completely foreign to Tory.

"Where's your family?" Amelia Ann asked, turning in her seat to look at her.

The question made the ever-present hole in her heart grow a little wider, especially after reliving the memories this morning. "Ah, I don't have any. They're all dead."

Her face fell, and she placed a hand over Tory's. "Oh, I'm sorry. Were you close?"

"Yes." The word almost felt too simple, too small.

"We're not, as you can see. I prayed Daddy's heart attack might change that, but it's only making things worse. I'm glad Daddy and Rye have reconciled, but Mama won't stand for it for long."

Amelia Ann slumped back in the seat. It was the first time Tory hadn't seen her with perfect posture.

"I'm not perfect enough for Mama, either, not like Tammy is. I try, but I just can't do it." She wiped some dust off the dash. "And I don't want to anymore. I have some thinking to do."

There was something mysterious about that last comment, but all Tory could think to do was nod, sitting silently as the A/C blasted her chilled skin.

"I should get back. Thank you for what you did today. For all of us. You shouldn't let what Mama and Tammy said bother you. It's a blessing to have you here." She sniffed. "Now, you'd best leave me alone. I'm about to have a good cry."

She gripped the door handle, the opposing desires to comfort and escape doing battle within her. Escape won out. "Bye."

"Take care of my brother, Tory."

The request made her want to head away from the guest house, not toward it. Take care of him? The problem was, the desire to do so was only getting stronger as she saw how deep his wounds went. She shut the door gently behind her and stood there long after the car's tail lights had disappeared. Shivering despite the heat, she rubbed her arms and went inside to find Rye.

"Rye?" she called, searching the rooms when he didn't respond.

He'd left the guest house, she realized, which explained why she hadn't seen his truck, and worry spread through her. His recklessness scared her, especially when he was hurting this much. She tried his cell, but it went straight to voicemail. Sinking onto the couch, she clutched her knees to her chest.

When her grandpa had died, she'd thought there was no one else to worry about but herself.

Clearly she'd been wrong.

I don't want no responsibility.
I just wanna be free.

Roll your window down.
Crank the music up loud.
Let the breeze rush over your face.
Let it set you free.

I don't want no responsibility,
Taking control of me.
Don't wanna live my life that way.

'Cause life's too short.
And I'm too free.
No responsibility is taking control of me.

Rye Crenshaw's Top Ten Hit, "No Responsibility"

CHAPTER 11

When Rye walked into the house shortly after ten o'clock that night, Tory was reading on the couch. Sitting there in the muted lamplight, she looked heart-stoppingly beautiful. Somewhere along the way, her small and slender figure had transformed into a tight and sleek little package that he was just waiting to unwrap.

"I hope you didn't make supper," Rye said shifting on his feet when she didn't glance over. "I couldn't have eaten anything."

She placed one of her Africa books on the coffee table and removed her glasses. "I didn't think so. I wasn't hungry either."

Yeah, he'd wondered how she was feeling, but he'd been too raw to call her. He sank wearily onto the couch next to her. "I'm sorry. The only appetite my family should affect is mine."

It seemed natural when she rested her head on his shoulder.

"I couldn't help but be affected. Where were you? I was worried."

Her presence soothed the angry, reckless energy that had been running through his body all afternoon. Rye wrapped his arm around her and tucked her close. He wouldn't analyze why she felt so good against him. "I went out driving. Then I stopped at an old haunt and did some shooting. It doesn't always make me feel better, but it helps."

"You carry a gun in your truck? And just what in the hell were you shooting? It's dark out."

"No, I rented one, and the range has lights," he said, chuckling at the incredulity in her voice. "They were just beer bottles. Nothing big."

She fiddled with a crease in his shirt. "I'm glad. For a minute I thought you were one of those crazy hunters who has night vision goggles."

He ran his hands through her silky hair. "No, I leave the owls alone. They're mostly endangered and don't taste good anyway." He smiled for the first time in hours.

"So, we had a pretty bad day. I know you didn't want company, but I might have liked to shoot some bottles tonight. I didn't like being alone here, worrying about you."

Surprise rippled through him over a layer of something darker. He hated to think he'd hurt her by being gone. "Do you know how?"

"No," she said, "but you could have taught me. I'm a quick study."

Visions of her bracing her petite body for impact ran through his mind. "Well, there's a news flash. I mean you've been in school for something like a hundred years. Makes a man wonder at your acuity." He grunted when she playfully elbowed him in the ribs.

"I needed the stress relief. Being here and seeing my daddy does something to me. He wants..." He sighed. The longer he was here, the more stirred up he felt. Was reconciliation with at least part of the family even the best thing for him?

She didn't ask him to explain himself, which made it easier to continue.

"I don't know if I can give him what he wants. Let's change the subject, okay? I should take you to Jack's Shack. It has the best Southern food around. I think you'll like it. It's not Diner Heaven, but it's never failed this ol' boy."

Food never failed to be a refuge for him, which he knew she understood.

"Sounds good."

He tipped his head down. Her green eyes looked sleepy, and his gaze immediately dropped to her mouth. He didn't think twice before pressing his lips to hers in a gentle kiss, and instead of pulling away, she gently caressed the side of his face. When Rye raised his head, Tory stared at him. He stared back. Neither of them spoke. And before he knew it, he'd cuddled her closer. He refused to think about the fact that he never cuddled with women.

How long they stayed that way, he didn't know. Her breathing slowed, and she fully relaxed in his arms. When he realized she was asleep, a warm glow spread inside his chest that he didn't recognize. Rye made no move to disturb her. Just continued stroking her hair, listening to the evening sounds that were barely audible through the window. He fell asleep, her gentle breathing music to his ears.

He awoke the next morning to a splash of sunlight peeking through the open curtains. He shielded his eyes, forgetting where he was for a moment, like he often did when he was on tour. Tory jerked awake when he moved.

"What?" she cried.

Her hair was all mussed, and she looked downright cute.

"Mornin'."

She slowly lowered her forehead to his chest. "Oh, it's you." And there was significance in the comment, like she wasn't used to waking up with a man, something he'd already guessed.

"We might need to work on your enthusiasm."

"Hah," she said, and then pushed herself up.

Rye tugged her back down gently. "Take a minute. We're both tired, and you're still all warm and soft."

"I should get up," she said. But she lowered her cheek to his chest.

He stroked her hair, pressing his thumb into her nape in a gentle massage. "After yesterday, we deserve a quiet morning."

The undemanding ease of the moment started to evaporate as Rye became conscious of her body, the slim, delicate lines. Awareness and need rose up inside him. Still, he made a show of being gentlemanly because she deserved it.

She gave a small stretch and rubbed her back, probably as stiff as he was from sleeping on the couch. Rye's eyes took in the slight undulation. Where the hell did being gentlemanly get any man? He turned them onto their sides, trapping her against the upholstery. His finger caressed her cheek and played in her short black hair.

"You have a spattering of angel kisses on your nose," he said.

"What?"

"Freckles."

"Oh. Angel kisses, huh? I've never heard that one."

"That's what they call them around these parts, although most women don't like them. And you do come from Diner Heaven, so you should know all about angel kisses."

Her mouth tipped up. "The only kisses I got at the diner were from grease splatters or aggressive customers."

He didn't like to think about customers ...or any man, touching her. "I'll beat them up for you."

"Nah. That pretty face of yours might be ruined if they got a punch in."

He hugged her. "Good, you're getting your mouth back. It stops working when you're upset."

"Some things aren't worth making smart comments about. They only make it worse."

Memories of yesterday's scene in the kitchen played in his mind. "Okay, enough of that. Let's try to enjoy ourselves for a little bit before we have to go back to hell."

Tory caressed his chest. "Why don't you let me make you a good breakfast? How do blueberry pancakes and maple bacon sound? As

I recall, you asked for them once. You always feel better after you eat."

She was right about that. Neither of them had eaten the night before, and her food did something to him. He knew he should let her go, but he pulled her down for a quick kiss. "Kissing you ranks up there with your lemon meringue pie. Good texture and complexity with just enough bite."

Tory laughed as she pushed away. "That sounds hokey enough for one of your songs." She walked toward the kitchen, unaware of him watching her backside. "Lemon meringue, indeed."

Rye crossed his arms behind his head. All that smallness and sass had drawn him in, and he wanted her more than he'd care to admit. He couldn't believe it, but she'd actually managed to make him feel happy here in odd moments. When the wings of panic fluttered in his gut, he willed them away.

When he crept into the kitchen she was humming Beethoven. The cadence was crystal clear, and it made him wonder what her singing voice sounded like. She had her back to him, washing a dirty pot at the sink, and he snuck his arms around her waist. She screamed and jumped in his arms.

"Never let anyone tell you that your volume matches your body. You've got some serious pipes there."

Tory unclenched her hands from the pot as the water continued to run. "You scared me. Don't you know better than to sneak up on a person? You're lucky I didn't whack you with this pot." She waved it in the morning sunshine streaming through the window above the sink. "It's not funny, Rye."

He grunted. "That's what you think. That was priceless. Seriously though, your humming has a nice musical quality to it. Why don't you sing something for me? I suspect that you might have a decent voice."

Her hands continued scrubbing the pot. "If there's one thing I never plan to do for you, Rye Crenshaw, it's *sing*. How stupid would that be? I mean, you're a professional."

"Oh, come on. Sing me something."

"No. Now, why don't you hit the shower? You smell like someone who got a little reckless and shot up some beer bottles last night."

Her eyes sparkled like the water in his favorite fishing spot upriver. They both knew he didn't reek of old beer.

"That's the scent of a man you're detecting, darlin'."

Her laughter followed him out of the room.

***

Tory was flipping bacon when she heard a car pull up outside. She frowned when she looked through the kitchen window. Amelia Ann was heading toward the house, carrying a container of cookies from yesterday. She had on a pink linen dress belted with a white sash. When Tory opened the door, she noted the delicate pearls at the woman's neck.

Amelia Ann forced a smile. "Good mornin'. I hope it's not too early for me to drop by."

Returning the smile, Tory put one bare foot over the other to cover up her lack of shoes and smoothed her hair behind her ears, praying she didn't have bed head. She felt practically undressed next to the other woman.

"No, of course not. I'm making breakfast. Rye's in the shower, but he should come out soon. I left bacon on the stove. Come on in."

Still clutching the container to her chest like it was stolen treasure, Amelia Ann nodded and followed her inside, waiting as she put the bacon on a paper towel.

"I managed to save some cookies," she explained when Tory was done. "Mama dumped the majority in the garbage, but the phone rang, and I managed to save what was left while she was talking with Kim Jenkins. I thought we could keep them here until we could take them to the kids. Mama and I are going to a ladies' luncheon, or I'd hide them in the car. But it's going to be a hot one today. The frosting would melt."

"Don't worry. We can keep them here."

"I talked to the kids last night. Annabelle cried on the phone. She wanted her princess cookies. Rory didn't say anything, but he never does."

Her heart broke, hearing that. The poor kids.

"You must think we're monsters." She twisted her pearls. "To treat children like that."

Tory, who'd been checking the blueberries for stems, looked up at her with a soft smile. "Amelia Ann, you were in the kitchen making cookies with the rest of us. And now you've gone to all this trouble to make sure the kids get what they made. You're a good aunt."

Amelia Ann sniffed, reached into her small white purse, and pulled out an embroidered handkerchief.

The woman had an embroidered handkerchief? Tory hadn't seen one of those since her grandma died.

"I'm really not. If I was a good aunt, I'd stand up for the kids like Rye did."

She delicately blew her nose, managing not to make a sound.

Tory was impressed—she always sounded like a goose.

"That's why I came this morning. I did some serious thinking last night, and...I want to talk to Rye." Her usual grace was gone as she stutter-stepped forward. "I want to make a break from family tradition like he did."

What could that mean? "Amelia Ann, I don't usually give advice, but you need to find out what's best for you. It may not be the same as what's best for your brother."

"I know that, but..."

Rye walked into the kitchen wearing only a pair of worn jeans. Beads of water still clung to his chest. Did the man have something against drying off and wearing a shirt or was he purposely teasing her?

"I'm hungry. Breakfast about ready?"

Right. Breakfast. Her mind had gone blank, erased by that mouth-drying, awe-inspiring chest. "Yes, I was waiting to put the pancakes on until you came out."

He turned to his sister. "Mornin', Amelia Ann. Ah...I didn't have anything to eat last night, so I ran out of the shower before dressing properly."

Even Tory thought it was a lame explanation.

"Be right back," he said and turned and left.

Embarrassment crept across her cheeks.

"*My, my*, are you sure there's nothing between my brother and you?" his sister asked with a sly smile. "I know what you said, but... He was raised to never walk around shirtless unless we were at the lake."

Tory had to bite her cheek to keep from laughing. "Have you seen his promotional materials? His chest and butt are prominently featured, guaranteed to inspire salacious fantasies in even the most repressed schoolmarms."

Amelia Ann smoothed an invisible wrinkle in her dress. "Yes, but that's business. And that's not here. I figured he'd revert back to some of his old habits."

Tory did laugh this time. "I'm sorry, but are we talking about Rye Crenshaw?"

"You can laugh, but people who were raised in a rigid and structured environment tend to do two things. They keep following the straight line like Tammy. Or they swing too far the other way— like Rye. I'm hoping to end up somewhere in the middle. But I need help. That's why I'm here."

Tory studied the young woman closer. She might look like a frothy confection from an elite bakery, but there was more substance to her than Tory had originally expected. "You're absolutely right, Amelia Ann."

She smiled, and this time there was a barbed edged to it. "Being a cultural anthropologist, I thought you would have understood something about my brother. Rye Crenshaw is as big a fake as Rye Hollins was. He still hasn't figured out who he is."

Tory felt her chest tighten. Yes, she had begun to suspect that very thing. The man she had slept with on the couch last night was so much more complicated than she'd originally thought. And more endearing. There was trouble there—and heartache.

She didn't want to think about why she wasn't running away from it.

***

Rye strode into the kitchen wearing a white T-shirt. He'd noticed Amelia Ann's surprise when he emerged bare chested. It irritated him to think about how he'd turned tail and run from the kitchen because his sister had caught him trying to make a move. Where was his mojo? Hell, he was used to fifty people milling about and taking pictures of him in revealing clothing.

Tory was flipping pancakes on a smoking griddle when Rye walked up and kissed Amelia Ann on the cheek. He froze when her arms clamped around him. This was not her usual embrace. *Uh-oh.*

"What's the matter? It's not Daddy, is it?"

"No. I'm just so glad you're here, Rye."

He smoothed a hand over her blond hair and closed his eyes. "I've missed you, too."

She took a deep breath and stepped back, and he braced himself for what she was going to say next.

"Rye, I... Ah, I need your help. I got into Vanderbilt law school, and I want to go." The words rushed out faster than the usual cadence of her speech.

If his mama had streaked at a church picnic, he wouldn't have been more shocked. "You what?"

Her brow furrowed, and her lip trembled for a moment. "I said that I got into Vandy law school."

"I know, but..." Was he sputtering?

"I took the LSATs and scored a 180."

"A 180!" Holy shit. He'd only scored 172, and that had been considered superlative. "But I don't understand. You've never mentioned wanting to do this before. I'm plumb flabbergasted, Amelia Ann."

Her voice fell to a whisper as she confessed her darkest secret. "I joined the debate team at Old Miss, Rye, and I loved it. From then on, it's been my dream to become a lawyer."

Debate? His sister? She never stood up for herself at home.

"And I'm good at it, too. When I make an argument and win? Well, it's probably the best I've ever felt in my whole life." Her eyes twinkled at that.

"This is a huge decision, honey," he said. Mama would raise holy hell, and he wasn't sure what it would be like to have his sister live so close to him. His lifestyle wasn't exactly...upstanding. "Are you sure—"

"I don't want to end up like Tammy or Mama," she whispered, her eyes suddenly wet with tears.

His mouth opened, but nothing came out. Oh, shit. What could he say to that? "I know you don't...and you won't. You're nothing like them." But a lawyer? His baby sister?

Her face practically glowed in response. He craned his head to look at Tory, hoping to change the subject. "Breakfast ready yet?"

She nodded and set a platter of steaming pancakes on the kitchen table. "Why don't you both sit down, have some breakfast, and talk?" She poured them coffee, her face carefully blank. "I'm going to take a walk in the woods."

Don't go, he nearly called as she walked away. He loved his sister, but he didn't have a clue what to say to her.

Amelia Ann smiled as brightly as a used car salesman as she sat down. "Well, isn't this just the best looking breakfast? That Tory sure can cook. You're lucky to have found her. Too bad there's really nothing more than friendship between you. She seems lovely, Rye. Just lovely."

Her well-trained artifice was worse than toothpicks under his fingernails. When she reached for the platter with trembling hands, Rye sat down, grabbed them, and squeezed gently. "Stop. You're killing me here."

She looked down at her lap.

"All right, you've clearly thought this out. Tell me more."

The women in Mama's family graduated from Ole Miss before marrying, and the Hollins men went to Vandy for law school and married after that. This would be a big break with tradition, and she knew it. No female in their family had ever done anything like it.

Amelia Ann finally met his eyes, and in them he saw a fierceness he'd never seen before. "I want to go to Vandy like all the Hollins men, Rye. Mama will have me married next spring if I don't leave here. She already has Barton Pembroke picked out. We've had three dinners with his family since I've been home this summer, and Mama keeps mentioning him. It's been near impossible to stay away from his pawing hands when no one is around."

Oh, Christ, this was just getting worse. He'd always hated Barton Pembroke, a mama's boy with a predilection for seersucker and pinching girls at church picnics when the adults weren't looking. And his sister was right. His mama would do everything in her power to force her to marry into that venerable family if she'd set her mind to it. Hadn't she done the same with Tammy?

"I don't want to be like Tammy, Rye," she whispered. "Sterling's not a good husband. He's never home and doesn't spend time with the kids. There's talk that he runs around on her."

A frown spread across his face. Part of him wasn't surprised, but even though he and Tammy didn't get along, he didn't want her to suffer.

"Tammy hasn't mentioned it," Amelia Ann continued, "but I know she's not happy. And now it's spilling onto Rory and Annabelle."

His mind was spinning around like the cotton candy machine at the state fair. "Let's back up here. Going to law school to escape marriage is downright extreme, darlin'."

"I'm not doing it because of that. I've never wanted anything like I want this," she said. "Will you help me talk to Daddy?"

He took a gulp of his coffee and singed his lips. He stopped the swear word from leaking out. "Why haven't you mentioned this before?"

"I was afraid," she whispered, lowering her head. "I know you don't think I'm very smart, and I wasn't sure I was brave enough...to bear the consequences. After what they did to you...well, I was afraid to lose my family."

Who wouldn't be?

"Mama always says intelligent women aren't attractive and men don't like them, so I've always pretended not to care about my studies. Well, I'm tired of pretending."

Yeah, he knew all about pretending.

Growing up, she'd never shown an interest in school other than as a place to hang out with her friends and socialize, just like Mama had expected. While she'd done her homework, she'd been a solid B student, not too smart and not too dumb—just like every other girl Rye had grown up with in Meade.

"I was going to tell you at graduation, because I wanted to ask for your help in person, but then everything went sideways and... I was made for the law, Rye, I just know it. I can remember just about anything I hear or read."

He was excited for her, but he knew her decision would lead to a whole heap of trouble. "Well, you are a Hollins. We're all pretty smart." Even if it wasn't part of his public image.

She beamed. "Exactly. Who cares that only the Hollins men have been the lawyers in the past? It's the twenty-first century. Can I help it if I have the lawyer gene?"

"It makes me happy to see you this happy, Amelia Ann. It really does."

But it also terrified him. Mama was going to pitch a fit, and God only knew what Tammy and Daddy would say. "But you know that it's not that simple, right?"

She bit her lip and stuck out her chin, embodying both fear and courage. "I know. That's why I've kept quiet. I sat on my acceptance letter for as long as I could, but I finally had to tell Vandy my decision..." She gulped. "I told them yes, praying you'd help me. Then this happened."

He wasn't following her. "What happened?"

"Daddy's heart attack and his desire to reconcile with you. I was rather hoping that since Daddy seems to have taken a different view of *you* now, he might be willing to form one of me too. And I wouldn't have to lose everybody."

Oh Christ.

"Will you talk to him for me?" she asked again. "I know it will be a shock, and I thought perhaps he'd take more kindly to it if he knew you'd look after me while I'm at Vanderbilt. But I'm not sure I want to work at his law firm. You know how they view women lawyers around here. There isn't a single one. I'd have to practice in a bigger city to...fit in. Like Nashville. Plus it would mean I'd be close to you."

Responsibility twined around his feet like a creeping vine, tying him down. This was getting complicated, but how could he refuse to help her? This was her dream. "I'll do what I can."

She came around the table and squeezed him tight.

"Today?" she pressed.

He took a deep breath, inhaling her signature magnolia perfume. She might be a bright and showy bloom like her favorite plant, but she'd have to have its leather-hard leaves to withstand the Hollins' wrath.

"Yes, I'll talk to him." He kissed her hair. "But I strongly suggest you prepare your argument in advance and compose it as persuasively as you can."

Her arms tightened around him again. "I've been doing that for at least six months, Rye."

She pulled back and looked at him. "I love you, Rye," she whispered.

"I love you too, Amelia Ann," he murmured back, the words rusty on his tongue.

But he felt their power as a new-found warmth swept into the cold, isolated place he'd inhabited since he'd broken with his family to follow his own dream.

When it comes to comfort food on the sweet side, there's nothing better than combining a chocolate chip cookie flavor in a flaky pie crust. I like to add a little cocoa for extra bite. This sucker is pure decadence and perfect for Sunday dessert with fresh whipped cream or heated to warm on a school night. You can barely keep your eyes open after the first bite, least of all form a complete sentence. It makes even the most sensible senseless. My friend served it when her difficult mother-in-law came for a weekend visit. She gave her guest a piece every day she was there and said it was the only time the woman didn't find something to complain about. So, if you're in need of comfort food, chocolate with your pie, or you want to shut someone up—this pie is for you.

Tory's Chocolate Chip Pie

¾ cup butter
½ cup sugar
½ cup brown sugar
3 eggs
½ cup flour
2 tbsp. cocoa
1 cup chocolate chips
1 cup pecans

Cream the butter and sugar. Add the eggs. Mix. Add the flour and cocoa. Stir until combined. Add the chocolate chips. Pour into an already baked pie crust. Cook at 325 degrees for 50 minutes.

Tory Simmons' Simmering Family Cookbook

CHAPTER 12

The house was struggling to keep itself cool, the air conditioner kicking on as regularly as the quarter chimes of the antique Seth Thomas clock above the gray stone fireplace. Tory was reading an article on her laptop about the hunting traditions of the Maasai and the impact of safari groups.

She didn't know where Rye and Amelia Ann had disappeared to after finishing breakfast, but she appreciated that they'd cleaned their dishes. And she couldn't wait to hear more about their conversation. Amelia Ann was going to law school? Rye's head had to be spinning. The revelation had been a surprise to her too, and she barely knew the woman.

Pushing back a lock of hair that was still damp from her shower, she tried to concentrate on an anthropologist's description of the importance of hunting lions to the Maasai tribe in Kenya. How the men were judged by their prowess in tracking and killing the ferocious beasts. She sighed. She couldn't help but think how much she'd prefer to look at food websites. Now, *that* was fun.

She was plodding through her third article when she heard a car drive up. She walked to a window to see who it was, and heaved another sigh. Tammy was climbing out of her sparkling white BMW SUV all perfect and pressed in a matching powder-blue linen suit. She could have doubled for Grace Kelly in that movie with Jimmy Stewart where they watched people from their apartment. Was it *Rear Window?* Oh, who cared?

Was she ready for another visit from Rye's family? No way. Then, she remembered the cookies and ran to get them. Hopefully Tammy would leave after she dropped them into her arms.

It wasn't like she had to invite her in for tea.

***

Tammy smoothed the fronds of a fern hanging on the porch. Her feet had turned leaden and shaky. Rye's visit was raising so many questions inside her about her life, her family. Was he right? Were her children really unhappy, especially Rory? She knew she had to find out, and Tory was enough of an outsider that she might just be honest about it.

"Hello, Tory," she said when the woman opened the door, the name sounding odd on her tongue. "I was hoping I might catch you."

Surprise raced across Tory's face. Tammy tried to smile, though it felt more like a grimace. "Rye's still at the house with Daddy. Mama and I just got back from a luncheon. The kids are with the babysitter, so I thought I'd stop on my way home."

Tory crossed her arms "Did you come for the cookies?"

She gripped her white clutch purse against her stomach. "Yes. Amelia Ann mentioned she'd brought them here." When had the tension in their family become so intense that they were forced to hide cookies from Mama like they were drugs?

"I thought so," she said, reaching behind her to pick up the lone container on the bureau in the entryway.

When she thrust them out, Tammy almost frowned. Didn't this woman know that visitors, even uninvited ones, should always be welcomed inside? "I was hoping we might chat."

The woman didn't blink for a moment. "Come in then."

Tammy followed her into the kitchen. Were those tabloid journalists right? Was Rye really involved with this woman? Amelia Ann didn't seem to believe Tory's denials, and Tammy had to agree with her. What else would have compelled their brother to make sugar cookies?

"The kids were terribly upset when we left without the cookies," she said. That was an understatement. She opened the box and drew out a baby-pink iced princess cookie, so pretty and delicate. "Amelia Ann said she couldn't save Rory's soldier cookies, but she mentioned that Rye had done a good job helping him."

"Yes, he did." The woman crossed her arms over her chest.

"Can I ask you a question?"

Tory nodded reluctantly.

The muscles in her face trembled, but she had to know. "Do you think my children are unhappy? Rory especially? Like Rye said."

Without answering, Tory stood and reached for Tammy's arm, leading her to the kitchen table. "Why don't we sit and have a cup of coffee?"

Coffee? She couldn't squeeze it past her tight throat. "No, it's okay. You don't have to coddle me. Amelia Ann likes you. She says you speak plainly. I figured you might tell me what you see as an outsider."

"I don't want to get into your business."

She almost laughed. The woman was knee deep in it, like it or not. "Rye involved you when he brought you here, so, please, I would appreciate you answering my question."

Was she ready to hear the truth? Tammy still wasn't sure. But she hadn't been able to banish the memory of Annabelle's tears all morning.

Tory took a breath like someone who was preparing to dive off a cliff. "I'm not exactly an expert. Annabelle seems to laugh some."

Tammy didn't miss the fact that she hadn't mentioned Rory. "I watched them last night, and when I took them to play group this morning. They're cautious and polite. Annabelle is less so, but I can still tell it's happening... She's slowly sliding into what's expected of her. They're remarkably *clean* for their age, don't you think? Mama always says you can tell a lot about children by how clean they are." And how quiet. Hysterical laughter bubbled up suddenly, and her head buzzed with it. "I need...I think I'll take a walk."

Dear God, Rye was right, Tammy thought. They were becoming as unhappy as she was.

"Can I leave the cookies near the door? That way I can just reach in and grab them without bothering you." She didn't want to see Tory again when she was like this.

"Of course."

Tammy's legs trembled when she stood. "You'll have to give me your recipe...so I can make Rory his soldier cookies." She couldn't stop babbling. Her cotillion teacher would have taken her to task. "He would never complain, you see, but I don't want Annabelle to be the only one with cookies."

No, he never complained, but he so rarely smiled either. And he didn't like to be touched. Oh God.

Fortunately, Tory stayed silent and let her leave in peace.

When the humidity enveloped her outside, she wanted to run, but her training was too deeply ingrained.

Besides, where could she run to? There was nowhere.

*****

Tory watched Tammy stumble down the hall, her perfect posture no more than a memory. She gazed at the cookies and pressed her fingers to her temple. She'd never witnessed so much bottled up emotion in one person. It was like shaking a champagne bottle without opening it. The poor woman was suffering as much as her children. Should she mention their conversation to Rye? Yeah, that was a good plan. He was struggling as much as everyone else around here. His family was like the walking wounded.

She needed to quiet her mind. There was no way she could focus on her research now. She'd do what she always did when she felt so mixed up... She'd make a pie. Maybe her famous Chocolate Chip Pie would help Rye's mood. Hell, how about hers? She could use a little comfort food. And she'd put a roast in the oven too. Peel some potatoes to boil and mash later.

She was pulling the pie out of the oven when she heard the front door slam against the wall, propelled by a gust of wind. When she went to inspect the sound, she found Rye in the hallway.

"Is Tammy here?" he whispered.

"No, she's out...walking." It had been over ninety minutes since she'd left, which worried Tory.

Rye pressed the bridge of his nose, heading into the kitchen. "Walking? My sister? In this heat and wind? There's a storm brewing. Why did she come here, anyway?"

Tory leaned against the doorway. "She came to pick up the princess cookies that Amelia Ann brought over." Part of her was brimming with curiosity about what had transpired with his youngest sister and his father, but she'd let him tell her in his own time.

Rye grabbed a glass, filled it with ice and water, and chugged it. Refilled. Then he sniffed. "God, why does it always smell so good when you're around?" His eyes tracked to the pie. "What kind did you make?"

"Chocolate chip. One of my comfort foods."

"My God, woman. You nearly bring me to my knees with your cooking. My stomach was queasy before, but it's already feeling better just from the smell. Sorry, your pie got me off track. Why did Amelia Ann bring the cookies here?"

"Your mother was throwing them away. Amelia Ann managed to save the princess ones."

Rye slumped against the counter. "Christ, she threw away the cookies?" he asked, his jaw ticking.

Her nod was perfunctory.

"That storm is moving in fast," he said, turning and staring through the kitchen window. "Wind's kicking up something fierce."

There was no music in his voice, only the flatness of despair. "Don't talk about the weather with me, Rye Crenshaw. I'm not some Southern belle."

His back muscles bunched visibly under his shirt. He slowly

turned, eyes glaring like an angry wolf's. "No, you're not, but you know what? Talking about the superficial is a hell of a lot easier than talking turkey, let me tell you."

Didn't she know it? She crossed her arms.

His angry strides brought him across the kitchen until they were nose to nose. "What? Do you want to hear about how I just told Daddy that Amelia Ann actually wants to be a lawyer? Like all the Hollins men have been for four generations until me. That she's decided to go to Vandy rather than marry the starched shirt Mama picked out for her."

Amelia Ann's mother had picked out a husband for her? Part of her was shocked, but having seen Mama Terminator in action... Tory's compassion knew no bounds for Rye's sisters. "What did he say?"

He chuckled—a mean and ugly sound. "After I realized he wasn't going to have another heart attack? Well, I won't go into all the details, but he said he would support her. He doesn't want to make the same mistake with another of his children." He slammed his hand against the wall. "Not like the one he made with me. Goddammit! Doesn't he know what that kind of talk does to me?"

Unhinges him, she thought, and dredges up all the pain he'd turned into anger years ago. Tory's eyes burned at the anguish on his face, and she suppressed the urge to comfort, fearing he would only slap it away. "I'm glad for her."

His chest was rising and falling in quick, raspy breaths. "I need some air."

When he walked away, Tory followed. She closed the door he'd left open and walked right off the porch. The first big drops of rain hit her. The sky was dark and packed with gray thunderclouds, just like he'd warned her. She had almost reached Rye when she saw Tammy running toward the house.

"It's going to rain," she called.

Her suit was slick with sweat, her white sandals coated in mud. Her pantyhose had a run in one leg, and her hair had escaped her coif, clinging in tendrils to her neck and face. Mascara ran down her cheeks.

Rye darted toward her. "Tammy?"

She jerked to a halt, her ankle turning in the gravel.

The rain started to pelt the earth as he took her shoulders. "Honey, you look a fright! What's the matter with you?"

The laugh that burst from her was high-pitched and slightly crazed. "Do you think you're the only one around here who can get dirty?" Three more barks of laughter escaped before she pressed a shaking hand to her mouth. "I need to get the cookies. I need to go home." Then she looked down at herself. "Oh God, I'll scare the children looking like this. I've *never* looked like this."

Tory believed that, all right. She pushed Rye aside and grabbed Tammy's arm, leading her into the house. "You can take a shower and wear some of my clothes."

The rain was pounding down now, the sound deafening. Once Tammy was safely inside, Tory turned to wait for Rye, but he still stood there in the driveway, soaked to the bone.

"Rye, come inside!" she shouted.

He shook his head before taking off in the opposite direction.

That infernal man. The last thing she needed was for him to get struck by lightning. Pulling the door shut, she ran into the storm and jumped when lightning flashed close by. When she caught up to him, she grabbed his arm. "Rye. Come inside. Please."

"I can't," he shouted. "It's tearing me apart, being back here."

When he started to move away from her again, she planted herself in front of him. "I know you're hurting, but there's no going back now. Your family needs you."

"Leave it alone, Tory."

When he started forward, she blocked him again.

"*Leave me alone.*"

"No!"

Through the veil of rain, his eyes shot fire at her. "This is none of your business."

She ignored his menacing tone and stepped closer. "You're wrong. You made it my business when you brought me here."

He put his hands on his hips as thunder cracked and rolled. "What the hell do you care? If you had any sense, you'd be the one taking off."

She pushed dripping hair out of her eyes. "I thought about it, but I'm staying to help you see this through."

"Why, dammit?"

"Because I care about you, you idiot! And you're lucky you still have a family."

His arms caught her against him. "I told you. I don't have anything to give you."

"You're wrong," she said, twining her arms around him.

His hazel eyes burned a hole inside her belly. "I'm not wrong, and God help you."

His mouth swooped down. The kiss was charged, as if it were feeding off the storm roiling around them. Tory clutched his back and opened her mouth. She wanted more. She wanted him. Teeth scraped. Hands fisted. He picked her up, and she wrapped her legs around his waist and held on with all her might, rain running in rivulets down their skin. Warmth from his body seeped through her soaked clothes. Rye changed the angle of their kiss and took it deeper.

Desire rumbled through her body like thunder, shaking her slender frame. She groaned. He growled. The feasting continued. When lightning flashed close to them, Rye broke the kiss and pressed his forehead hard to hers.

"God, I want you so much. *Right now*."

Her belly tightened. There was no going back. Steam rose from his wet hair.

"I want you too, but it'll have to wait." She slid down his body. "Come inside with me."

Her dripping hand extended toward his. He studied it as lightning flashed in his eyes.

"Tammy needs you right now." She smiled with effort. "I can have you later."

His Adam's apple bobbed up and down as he swallowed, and then he took her hand. They trudged back into the house, shoes squishing water, as the storm thundered behind them like the angels battling Lucifer.

Tory heard the shower running in the bathroom when she headed into her bedroom to change. She found some clothes for Tammy and waited in her room, sitting on the edge of the bed, towel-drying her hair.

Rye ducked his head inside. He'd changed, too, and had run a brush through his wet hair. He tucked his thumbs into his belt loops and rocked back on his heels.

"I found some clothes for her," she said when he glanced toward the bathroom door.

"Good. Well...I'll go make coffee."

"Good idea. I'm sure we could all use some."

He nodded and disappeared.

When the shower finally shut off, she knocked on the door. "Tammy? I have some clothes for you."

The door cracked open, steam escaping. When Tammy stuck her hand out, Tory pushed the clothes at her.

"They're not your usual, but they're clean and dry."

"I'm sure they'll be fine. Thank you."

The door shut with a sharp snap, and Tory headed straight for the kitchen. Rye was hunkered down, staring at the coffee maker like it was advanced molecular science.

"Couldn't figure it out, huh?"

"Mama clearly bought this," he muttered.

"Perhaps it's child proof," she said to add some levity.

He snorted. "What? They're trying to prevent some kid from making coffee and stunting his growth? What's this world coming to?"

"Perdition, I'm sure." And she'd landed smack dab in the middle of it. She got the coffee started and then stepped back, rubbing her cold hands together.

Rye leaned against the counter. "You were joking about the child proof part, weren't you?"

"Yep."

His gaze lowered to her mouth. "I'll make you pay for that later."

Oh, please, her body said, but her mind had started working overtime too. "Rye..."

"Uh-oh. When you say my name like that, it tells me you've been thinking." He sauntered forward. "Don't."

If only. "Look, when we first met at the diner, you said I could keep my job so long as I didn't sleep with anyone in your band like your last cook. Now..." She dropped her gaze. "We're heading that way."

His sigh competed with the sound of the percolating coffee. "So, you're wondering if I'll fire you the next morning?" He settled his hands on her shoulders and squeezed. "No."

"Then..."

"Tory, you have my word. You have your job independent of what happens with us. We both know this is probably temporary anyway. You have to do your research and finish your dissertation. And I'm heading back to Nashville to start my new album."

It hurt, his acknowledgment that their time together would come to an end. When had he become so important to her?

He tucked a damp lock behind her ear and tilted her face up. "Tory, if you don't think you can handle that..."

She didn't, but she also knew she'd regret it her whole life if she didn't make love with him. "No, it's fine. It's good to be clear, that's all." It seemed wise to step away to give herself some space from those warm kneading hands on her shoulders.

"Tory, look at me," he said. "You need to know that I don't want to hurt you."

Like he could control that. "Let's get some coffee and wait for your sister. She should be out soon."

As for her, she'd just have to learn to enjoy the moment. You'd think by now she would have figured out that nothing was permanent.

***

Tammy felt bad listening to Rye and Tory, but she hadn't wanted to interrupt them. So there *was* something between them. She found herself hoping it would work out.

If there were any chance she could have left the house without them knowing, she would have tried. She'd made enough of a fool of herself. Best get herself home, but it was getting harder to feel safe there. She tried to be the perfect wife and mother, but Sterling's anger seemed to be getting worse, regardless of what she did or didn't do. And here she was in a strange woman's store-bought clothes, a complete wardrobe disaster for Sterling's "perfect" wife.

Summoning all her breeding, she walked into the kitchen and made a beeline for the cookies. Her wet hair trailed down her shoulders, the heavy feel of it making her want to wince. She never wore her hair down. "I'll just get out of your way."

"Stay for some coffee," Tory said. "Be good to settle your nerves before you head home."

There was that word again. Home. She clutched the container as if it were a life preserver.

"Besides, it will give your hair some time to dry."

Yeah, she hadn't found a hair dryer. Granddaddy Crenshaw had been bald, so it wasn't like he needed one, and Mama hadn't seen fit to furnish the bathroom with one.

Rye pulled three mugs out of the cupboard, saying nothing, and started pouring. She'd never seen him do a domestic thing in his life, so she sank into the chair. Rye nudged Tory toward the table, almost as if he didn't want to be alone with Tammy, and who could blame him.

The silence was unnerving as he set the mugs down.

"I'm glad the clothes fit," Tory said. "You look good in jeans, Tammy."

She rubbed the rough material with her thumb. "I don't own a pair."

"Well, maybe you should get some."

Silence descended again. They all turned their heads when a loud knock sounded on the door.

"I'll get it." Tory darted out of her seat, and moments later, Amelia Ann walked into the kitchen with her, looking radiant.

"Good heavens, Tammy, what happened to you?"

"We're having some coffee," Tory interrupted, for which

164

Tammy was glad. "Do you want some?"

Rather than replying, Amelia Ann continued to study them. Everyone had wet hair, and Tammy could all but feel her sister's speculation. "I got caught in the rain," she explained.

Amelia Ann made a clucking sound. "Don't you keep an umbrella in the car?"

"I...must have taken it inside and forgotten to put it back."

Amelia Ann didn't ask about her clothes, thank goodness—she just grabbed Rye's hand. "Rye, I just finished talking to Daddy." A grin spread across her face.

Tammy hadn't seen her look this happy in ages.

"He's agreed to pay my tuition for Vandy. I'm just over the moon with joy. Oh thank you, Rye. Thank you!" she cried, bending over to hug him.

Vandy? What *was* she talking about?

"Wait a minute," Tammy said, her stomach knotting up. "What's this all about, Amelia Ann?"

As her sister filled her in, Tammy sank against the back of the chair. Law school? Like the rest of the Hollins men? My heavens. Mama wouldn't recover. Hadn't she already picked out Barton Pembroke for Amelia Ann? She looked from her sister to Rye, and back again.

"Isn't that great, Tammy?" Amelia Ann asked, but even she seemed to hear the tremor in Tammy's voice.

She fell back on manners. "Yes, that's *lovely*, darlin'. I'm so happy for you." But she wasn't. She hated her Daddy for giving Amelia Ann what she wanted when he'd never done anything for her, never given *her* another choice.

"Oh, Rye," Amelia Ann nearly sang. "We're going to have so much fun, living so close. And I won't have to marry Barton or anyone else Mama tries to force on me, making me miserable all the days of my life."

The gasp came from Tammy's mouth before she realized it.

"Oh, Tammy, I'm so sorry!" her sister said.

Her heart felt like a frozen glacier in her chest. "It's all right. I know you didn't mean anything." Rising, she shuffled to the doorway. "I'm happy for you, darlin'. Really, I am."

Tory rose and headed her way.

"I'll have these clothes back to you tomorrow, Tory. Thank you for letting me borrow them. I'm sorry I was such a bother."

"You weren't a bother. Why don't you stay and finish your coffee? We can...talk some more."

About what? There was nothing more to say. Everybody's life

was changing but hers.

"Thank you, but I need to get back."

When Tory handed her the cookies, Tammy took them in a daze. "Oh, how silly of me. Here I cause all this trouble and forget the reason I came in the first place."

Rye's long strides ate up the ground until he towered over her. "Tammy, stop it. You don't have to act this way."

She saw Amelia Ann press a hand to her heart, her face pale.

A laugh bubbled up her throat. "Act? That's a good one. That's the only way some of us get through the day."

"It doesn't have to be this way," her brother said.

"Yes, it does. I'm married with two children. I have to make the best out of what I have." Isn't that all she did? There was nothing more. Nothing else. "You and Amelia Ann can live the lives you want, Rye." When his warm hand settled on her shoulder tentatively, she jerked away. "I'm too far down the road."

She walked stiffly out of the kitchen, leaving behind silence. It was a sound she well knew. It was the main sound in her own home.

Only she wasn't sure she could take it anymore.

When I was little, I watched Gone with the Wind *with my grandma. The movie captured my imagination. The women seemed so elegant in their hoop skirts, dancing the Virginia Reel with men sporting wickedly handsome slim mustaches. Houses like Twelve Oaks with their curved staircases seemed a dream. Being an only child, I frequently imagined friends like Scarlett or Melanie for my tea parties. Using my grandma's lace-edged napkins, I'd serve what we termed French éclairs. They were actually cream puffs, but again, we used our imagination. Scarlett wouldn't eat cream puffs. Depending on how much time my grandma had, sometimes we'd serve the éclairs with vanilla pudding, which we called French custard. Other times, I simply settled for French Chantilly cream. Back then, I used Cool Whip with a dash of ginger. Now, I can make all these things from scratch. But as a child, those cream puffs were magical. And my imaginary friends in their fine gowns were always pleased.*

Cream Puffs (or French éclairs a la Tory)

1 cup water
1 stick of butter
1 cup flour
4 eggs

Boil the water and butter until the latter melts. Add the flour and mix, forming a yellow paste. With a wooden spoon, add 4 eggs, one at a time, and beat well. Drop with a tablespoon onto a greased cookie sheet. Bake at 400 degrees for 30 minutes. Slit the cream puffs and fill with custard or cream, depending on your preference. Or fill with something else that sounds good to you. These airy, golden brown pastries work well with many fillings.

Tory Simmons' Simmering Family Cookbook

CHAPTER 13

The sunlight shone in bright patches across the yard the next day. Birds chirped. Squirrels chased each other, bending thin tree branches before leaping into the air. It was almost as if nature had forgotten the torrential rain of the previous day. Tory watched it all from the window with a jumping stomach.

She and Rye were going on a date. He'd actually *asked* her last night. Said he wanted to romance her a little.

They both knew they were going to make love, so she appreciated his gesture. It confirmed she was making the right choice with him.

When she heard Rye call her name from outside, she smoothed her hands down her sage cotton blouse and checked her white linen A-line skirt for stains. Today, she was wearing Amelia Ann's clothes and her gold sandals. When Tory had asked to borrow an outfit, Amelia Ann hadn't reminded her of what she'd said a couple of days ago—that there was nothing between her and Rye—she'd just smiled and volunteered to do Tory's hair and make-up, too. It felt strange, being so dressed up. She hadn't gotten this fancy since her grandfather's funeral.

Tory took a last look in the mirror and headed out to meet Rye. She blinked when she saw him. Gone were the cowboy hat, jeans, and T-shirt. He was wearing khaki pants and a blue button down dress shirt still showing the fold creases, and she had a moment to wonder if he'd bought the outfit on his errand in town.

When he stared at her without saying anything, nerves started a complicated tango in her belly again. She raised her chin and walked carefully down the stairs, unaccustomed to the three-inch sling-back sandals.

"Hi. Nice car." She eyed Amelia Ann's sleek blue BMW convertible.

Suddenly, under the shadow of the big plantation house up on the hill, there was romance in the air.

***

Rye stood there stupidly. Surely, the heat was making him light-headed. She looked like Tory, but the packaging had altered dramatically. He couldn't decide where to fix his eyes—at her sexy legs or the delicate crease of cleavage winking out from her green blouse. The pearls at her neck and ears made him tug at his collar, which suddenly felt three sizes too small. Amelia Ann had given her Grandmama Crenshaw's jewelry to wear. Did his sister have any idea what it did to his blood pressure to see Grandmama's pearls on Tory? Yeah, he'd bet she did. He could still see Grandmama stroking them as she sat next to Granddaddy Crenshaw, laughing as he opened his birthday presents. They'd been the picture of happiness, a rare sight for him growing up.

He tripped as he walked to the passenger side of the car and fumbled with the handle before opening it. "I thought it would be nicer than the truck."

Her brow rose, but she ducked inside and let him close the door after she settled into the tan leather bucket seat.

He shook himself as he hunched his frame to fold himself into the driver's side. The car was no bigger than a tin can, and there didn't seem to be anywhere for his legs to go. He saw Tory bite her cheek to stop from laughing and almost swore.

"So where are we going?" she asked.

"It's a surprise." He had filed away her comment about how much she loved that infernal movie, *Gone with the Wind*—no disrespect to his friend, Rhett Butler Blaylock, intended—and now he was taking her to a place he knew she'd enjoy.

"Okay. Can we put the top down?" she asked, gesturing to the ceiling.

Was she nuts? It was about two-thousand degrees outside with a haze so thick a baby could cut his teeth on it. "You want it down?"

She nodded.

He bared his teeth in a forced smile. "Sure, darlin', whatever you want." If she wanted the top down, he'd do it. Isn't that what courtin' was all about? It had been his idea to go for a real date, after all. She deserved it after everything she'd done for him, and deep down, he wanted to do something special for her.

She burst out laughing suddenly. "Oh, no, what *have* you done with Rye Crenshaw?"

"Huh?"

"Were you really going to put the top down in this heat just because I asked?"

He frowned. She had his number, and it was early yet. "You might be nicer when I'm trying so hard with this courtin' stuff."

"Courtin' stuff?"

Did she have to repeat it? Heat crept up his neck. "Well, I sing about it, so I should be able to do it." Even though he hadn't. Not since Emeline.

"You also sing about checking out a stacked blond hottie as she's draining a long neck."

Great, so she was going to be that way. "Look, I was trying to make this a nice date for you to show you how much I appreciate you being there for me. I didn't want to just take you to Jack's Shack for BBQ."

"Besides, you were hoping to get lucky."

He hadn't thought she was going to call him out on it. "Christ, Tory."

"Oh, that's so sweet. Your ears are getting red," she said, her smirk carrying over into her voice.

He whipped around to face her and pulled her to him, kissing her roughly. Her lips softened. Her mouth opened. She all but melted against him.

"I think I've got you figured out," he murmured, nipping at her mouth once more. "You get even sassier when you're nervous. You only shut up when you're sad. And since you've already shot me up pretty good today, I'll take that to mean that you're more nervous than usual."

She pulled back and secured her seatbelt. "You're right. I am nervous, and I'm sorry I teased you."

He started the car and put it into gear. They hummed down the driveway, the tight engine showcasing its perfect engineering.

Halfway there, Rye took Tory's hand and laid it on his thigh. "You look beautiful, by the way."

She turned away from the lush countryside dotted with farmland.

"You look good too."

He squeezed her hand, and they rode the rest of the way in comfortable silence.

When he turned onto the oak-lined driveway to Bedford Plantation, Tory sat up straighter in her seat. The place hadn't changed a bit. Gardens packed with a whole bunch of pretty flowers covered the front of the property. The rose brick antebellum mansion with white columns and black shutters held all the gravitas of a former age. Gravel crunched under the tires as Rye pulled into the circular driveway.

Rye was halfway around the car when Tory slammed her door shut. "You're supposed to wait for me to do that," he said.

"I am?" She gripped her necklace and gave a soft smile. "I'll do better next time."

To the right of the house, a fountain gurgled near a stone bench that was situated under a white arbor covered in a purple flowered vine. If it hadn't been so hot, he would have led her there and simply held her hand, taking in the eye-catching sight of the gardens.

There was peace here. This place. This woman.

"It's so beautiful," she murmured.

Rye heard the awe and whimsy in her voice. "Yes, I thought you might like it, since you mentioned liking *Gone with the Wind* and all. The family still lives here. It's more out of the way than the cluster of plantations just south of here, so it doesn't receive as many visitors. Makes it more private." The air carried the scent of fresh cut grass and a faint whiff of honeysuckle. He extended his hand. "Shall we?"

She took it, her fingers curling around his. "Yes, let's."

After knocking, an elegant white-haired woman opened the door. "Mr. Crenshaw. Ms. Simmons. I'm Emily Bedford. Welcome to Bedford Plantation."

She led them inside that place of grandeur. After getting them drinks—a mint julep for him and a peach champagne cocktail for Tory, the peaches fresh from their orchard—Emily Bedford gave them a tour of the house, telling stories of her family's rise to wealth decades before the Civil War, or the War of Northern Aggression as they called it around here, and their struggle in the aftermath.

Rye listened with half an ear, unable to take his eyes off Tory. He loved the way she listened intently when Emily answered one of her frequent questions, how her face brightened when she laughed at a funny anecdote.

Nearly an hour later, Emily showed them to a private garden for dinner. She explained how the carefully selected plants glowed when the moon's rays kissed them, which was why it was called a Moonlight Garden. The hydrangeas were white and plentiful, intermixed with pale, silver ferns.

Arranged in the middle of the garden, the dinner table was set with the Bedford family china of roses and heather, the silver gleaming on the white tablecloth. After Rye and Tory sank into the cream-colored cushioned chairs at the table, Emily introduced them to their waiter and excused herself.

Rye glanced at the French doors across from him. He'd reserved the garden suite in case Tory wanted to stay over. God, he hoped she would. He shifted in his seat and dropped his napkin in his lap, letting his eyes rest on her.

Bedford had never held any allure for him the many times he'd been forced to come in his youth. It symbolized a history and tradition he rebelled against. But he'd wanted to do something just for her, and coming here seemed a small sacrifice after everything she'd done for him, become to him. Yet, tonight, seeing it through Tory's eyes, it was charming and inviting, and his old opinions faded away. He reached for his pewter cup, twirling the mint sprig.

Tory was fascinated by the marble carriers that ran water around the garden's perimeter, serving as an old-fashioned air conditioner, which allowed them to eat outside in the heat. She told him about the gardens of Alhambra in Grenada, Spain, where the same device was used, something she'd learned in one of her history classes, her undergraduate minor.

He realized there was so much he didn't know about this woman. And so much he wanted to know.

The first course of sun-kissed artichokes against a bed of greens arrived as the shadows lengthened, and the sun began to dip in the sky. Crickets and cicadas sang over the clink of silver against china as they sampled a chilled apple soup dotted with smoked bacon. He and Tory didn't talk about serious matters—there was no mention of his family or hers or the tour. Her love of cooking was something she happily shared when their entrée of pecan-crusted trout arrived, and he listened without interrupting, watching her eyes glow like emeralds, especially when she made him laugh by concentrating on a single bite of the trout and telling him what spices the chef had used.

As the moon rose, the garden came to life with glowing white light. Their waiter served them peach pie with custard ice cream. Tory swore it was the flakiest crust she'd ever tasted, and suddenly Rye could wait no longer to touch her. He rose and walked to her side of the table, pulling her from her chair. She tasted of peaches and cream when he kissed her, and in that moment, he never wanted to let her go.

Tory slid her hands into his hair as he tugged on her bottom lip and slid his tongue inside to rub lazily against hers. Fitting her against his hardening body, he circled his hips. Her head dropped back, and he kissed a trail down her neck and filled his hands with her breasts, brushing her tightened nipples through her blouse.

"Rye." She pressed a hand to his chest. "We need to stop. We're in the middle of dessert."

"Yes, we are," he teased.

Her eyes closed when his mouth nipped at her nape and moved the pearls aside to gently bite where neck and shoulder met. The shiver that coursed through her body made him smile.

"There's a lovely bedroom waiting for us right through those

French doors," he told her. Because he knew he would see the truth in her eyes, he looked straight into them as he spoke. "Is that what you want?"

Her eyes darkened. "Yes, it's what I want."

His fingertips caressed her delicate cheek. "Then let me make love to you."

Even though he'd never referred to the act that way, it seemed appropriate for this moment, this woman. Rye picked her up and carried her across the patio. He didn't question the gallantry. It simply felt right.

The air conditioning was cold on his skin when he entered the suite, pulling the drapes to the French doors closed with one hand. The room was cozy and intimate, and on the small table to the side of the doors was a crystal vase filled with red roses. It was perfect. After all, what woman didn't like roses? The leather-back books artfully scattered across the antique furniture looked nice, but he had to wonder... Did anyone really come here to read?

He smiled when he saw the bed. Now, that's what he was talking about. The dark wood four poster was massive, and his feet wouldn't hang off the end. Someone had already turned back the covers, revealing the inviting pale blue linens. There was another crystal vase brimming with white hydrangeas on the bedside table.

He couldn't have done any better. Somehow, this first time with Tory deserved this elegance, this romance.

And he wasn't going to ask himself why it mattered so much.

***

Tory scanned the room. Her heart was going to burst. She'd never imagined being surrounded by such loveliness—or having a man take such care with her. Who would have imagined Rye Crenshaw could read the cue cards in her mind?

His breath tickled as he kissed her neck. Oh yes, that spot.

"I want you," he whispered in her ear.

Heart racing, she turned in his arms. She knew she was smiling like a fool, but she couldn't help it. Didn't want to. She linked her hands around his neck.

"That's convenient. I was thinking the same thing."

His mouth tipped up. "Can't you be serious for once?"

But if she was, it would only scare him—and her, for that matter. They both knew this was temporary, and she had to keep reminding herself of that. "About this? No way."

He caressed her hips with his thumbs. She saw his dark eyelashes flicker down. Heat pooled in her belly. This man knew how to look at a woman.

"You're not planning to use that smart mouth to poke holes in my technique, are you?"

Even if she had enough experience to do that, she would never have been that cruel. She trailed her hands up his chest, wanting to feel his hardness, his strength. "I'm sure your technique is just fine. I was planning on using my smart mouth on other things tonight." To demonstrate, she opened a button on his shirt and pressed her lips to his warm skin.

The rush of her skirt's zipper sliding down sounded in the quiet room. "Works just fine for me."

When Rye slipped his hands inside her skirt and grabbed her butt, Tory jerked against him.

"Like that, do you?"

About as much as licking a spatula coated in warm chocolate ganache. She continued to undo the line of buttons, frowning when she reached his belt. "You want to take this off or shall I?"

"Ladies' pleasure," he murmured, reaching for the buttons on her blouse next.

His voice was making her crazy. "Oh, I do like that phrase. You Southerners have such a way with words." She shivered as he caressed the creamy skin above her bra. "Put your hands on me, Rye."

"Happy to oblige, ma'am."

Her head fell back as he undid the front clasp of her bra. "Oh, that feels good, but Rye? Don't call me ma'am." She tugged his shirt up and ran her hands up his naked back.

"Then what do you want me to call you?"

"Just Tory."

When he lowered his mouth to her breast, she moaned.

"Tory," he murmured, the name like music on his lips. "Tory."

When he kissed her nipple and took it into his mouth, he made her forget her name. And everything except having him inside her.

He pushed her skirt to the floor, and she reached down to slip out of her sandals and then ran her hands up his legs until she reached his belt and unclasped the buckle. When she tugged his shirt off, a sigh escaped her at the sight of his bare chest. Her fingers slid across his defined pectorals and the waterfall of abdominal muscles.

How had she gotten so lucky? "God, you have the most incredible body." She pressed kisses against his heated skin.

He slid her underwear to the floor and stepped back, gazing at her, the longing in his face as obvious as his arousal. "You're beautiful."

Her smile was soft despite her heart thundering in her ears. "Glad you approve."

He framed her face in his hands. "I'm going to take my time lovin' you tonight."

"Then you'd better take these off." And, full of bravado, she tugged on his pants.

He slid his hand into the pocket and threw a couple of condoms on the bed before stepping out of his underwear and pants. Her gaze slid down his chest, stopping when it reached his arousal. She knew her eyes widened, but she couldn't help it. He was large, and he wanted her badly.

"Come here."

She shivered at his voice. It had gone shades lower and each syllable was drawn out. When their skin met, fire seemed to ignite between their bodies. He ran his hands down her back and settled them on her waist. Rocking against his hardness, she angled her head for a kiss, which he provided with slow, lazy passion.

He circled them until they stood at the edge of the four-poster bed. Then he leaned her against the post and proceeded to kiss his way down the front of her body. When he finished, he turned her around and started down her back. How had she never realized her back was one long erogenous zone? Tory gripped the post and pressed back against his mouth and hands. Her hands slipped as sweat broke out across her body, caused by a flash of heat so hot it could have melted steel.

"Rye," she cried. Did he know what he was doing to her?

He scooped her onto the bed and covered her body with his. That was more like it. She delighted in his weight, and when he leaned over her and took her mouth in a drugging kiss, she ran her hands along his back, scraping her fingernails across the skin. He groaned into her mouth and slipped his hands between her thighs. She stilled as the fire spiked inside her and then let out a quiet, agonized moan when he pressed his palm down.

"Sweeter than honey," he whispered and plied her with his fingers until her legs opened wider and her hips jerked against his hand.

"Rye," she called. "Now."

He kissed her stomach while continuing to caress her. "Not yet. I want you out of your mind with pleasure first."

When his mouth lowered, he had his wish. She quaked and trembled with a violence that caused her muscles to knot and then shake.

Her hand fell across her eyes as he slid her legs open wider and settled between them. Panting, she lowered her arm and forced her eyes open, watching as he sheathed himself with a condom. Then he leaned over her on his elbows and, reaching a hand between their bodies to guide himself, pressed inside her. Taking her hands in his, he raised them above her head to the headboard.

His smile was wicked and desperate. "Better hang on."

His first thrust made her moan long and loud. For a while, he kept the rhythm slow and easy, clenching his teeth. When he lowered his head to her breasts and took one in his mouth, Tory arched her back, moving her body in time with his, and released the headboard so she could grip his hair in a vice. His lips moved to her neck, and she grabbed his head and pulled his mouth to hers. God, she wanted that mouth. Their tongues pressed and dueled as he kept up a steady rhythm between them.

She moaned when Rye increased the pace. To brace herself, she gripped the thickly carved wood behind her again, the texture only making her hands tingle more. Rye came to his knees and laid his hands over hers, making the strokes harder and deeper. Their eyes locked, and she felt stripped all the way to her soul. Then he went deeper still, and she saw stars.

Her moans were like a chorus now as their flesh slid together. The rush started at her toes and slammed across her body. She arched and bucked against him, and when he pressed his mouth to her neck, it only enhanced her pleasure. Then he took her hips in his hands and lifted her for three deep, long strokes and followed her over the edge, calling out her name.

***

When the buzzing in his head stopped, Rye became aware of Tory stroking his back in lazy circles. He forced himself onto his elbows with shaking arms and looked down.

Her smile was lush and forbidden, like the Garden of Eden. His heart pounded hard against his ribs, and his mouth broke into an answering smile.

"Thought you were asleep."

"Dead is more like it."

She chuckled softly. "Well, hello again, Lazarus."

He dispensed with the condom and rolled them onto their sides, tucking a strand of damp hair behind her ear. The earring winked at him, giving him a funny flutter. "You look good in pearls."

Tory reached to take them off. "I should have been more careful with them."

He brought her hand to his mouth for a kiss. "No, leave them. They look about as luminous as you do right now."

Cuddling against him, she said, "You're so good with words, Rye."

Not in this situation. Usually he didn't say much after sex and the thought had him clearing his throat. "It's my job."

She rose on an elbow. "No, Rye. You have a gift."

She would use that word. There was a beauty in the way she saw people for who they were, how she helped them. His finger traced her collarbone and the depression in the middle.

"I'm going to want you again tonight." He couldn't imagine tiring of their bodies coming together. All that heat, friction, with the underlying glimmer of deeper emotion, like the flickering of sunlight through a thicket of trees.

Settling back against him, she made a humming noise in her throat. "I'm glad we're of the same mind. Do you happen to know if this room comes with one of those old, enormous claw-footed tubs?"

"I think it's a good bet."

Pressing a kiss to his mouth, she slid away. "Let's go see."

Venus in all her glory padded naked across the room and slipped through the bathroom door. When had he ever thought petite wasn't perfect?

She peeked her head out, eyes twinkling. "Guess what?"

"Found a claw?"

Her hand made the shape. "Yep. Come on, cowboy. You got anything against a bubble bath?"

He'd never taken one, but tonight seemed to hold a lot of firsts. "Not if it comes with you inside it."

When her finger made a crooking motion, he almost hauled her back to bed. "Funny," she said, "that's what I was going to say to you."

He playfully stalked her into the bathroom, and she retreated inside, giggling, the sound music to his heart. When he caged her against the counter in front of the mirror, he realized he looked sated—and happy—something he hadn't been in a long time.

He turned away from his reflection and set his hands over her white skin all over again.

Being from the Midwest, my family cooked a lot of roasts for dinner. Obviously, the same old, same old, gets old. So, we'd make a Chinese pot roast every now and again. I'm not sure what made it Chinese. Perhaps the ginger and soy sauce. Heaven knows, we added potatoes to the mix, not rice. But it was always a winner. The meat's flavor simply explodes in your mouth, and the broth makes the best juice for the potatoes. It's a simple dish to make with some lead-time—one of those all-in meals that's perfect for families or days when you're on the run. My grandma was fond of fixing this before we'd go to church. We'd return to a splendid smelling house, set the table, and feast.

Chinese Pot Roast

1 chuck roast, about 4 lb.
2 garlic cloves, minced
A dash of nutmeg and cinnamon
2 tbsp. brown sugar
1 tbsp. sherry or red wine
¼ cup soy sauce
1¼ cup water
3 peeled and sliced carrots
3 potatoes, peeled and cubed
1 celery stalk, sliced
2 tbsp. cornstarch

Marinate the meat in the next six ingredients for at least 3 hours. Place the meat in a roasting pan at 325 degrees for 2 hours. Add the vegetables 45 minutes before cooking time ends. Voila!

Tory Simmons' Simmering Family Cookbook

CHAPTER 14

ory was putting a Chinese pot roast in the oven when she heard a car pull into the drive. She smiled, hoping it was Rye. She missed him. They'd awoken that morning in tangled sheets, feasted on each other again, and then had breakfast in their private garden before returning to Hollinswood. Since it was their last full day in Meade, he'd promptly gone to see his father.

They would be leaving the next morning.

She'd been daydreaming all day, and while she knew she was in trouble, she cut herself some slack. Who wouldn't be whimsical after such a romantic, steamy night?

When a knock sounded on the door, she headed to the front of the house to answer it. So, not Rye then... He wouldn't have knocked.

"Yes?" she asked the older man on the doorstep. Dressed in a navy button-down shirt with tan slacks, he had thick white hair, bright blue eyes, and an aquiline nose. There was something immediately familiar about him, but she couldn't put her finger on it.

"Miss Simmons, I'm Hampton Hollins."

Confusion reigned. "Mr. Hollins! I thought Rye was with you. Is everything all right?"

"We're both fine. He's running an errand that we both agreed was long overdue, so I decided to come down here and meet you."

Well, this was a surprise. "Oh. Please come in."

"Smells good in here. Rye tells me you're an incredible cook. Let's go into the kitchen, so you can watch what you're cooking while we sit a spell."

Good. She was always more comfortable in the kitchen. "Can I get you some coffee?" she asked. "We have decaf. I know you can't have the real stuff with your heart."

When they reached the kitchen, he settled back into one of the chairs around the table. "Now, how would you know that?"

The memories were still fresh enough to squeeze her chest. "I took care of my grandfather until he passed away a few months ago."

"I'm sorry for your loss."

"It's okay," she said like she always did. "I know he's in a better place." At least, she prayed he was.

"So, I understand from Rye and Amelia Ann that you're pursuing your doctorate."

"Yes, at the University of Kansas in cultural anthropology," she replied, getting the coffee set up.

"Amelia Ann tells me you've been a great help to everyone during your time with us."

"I haven't done much," she immediately said, wondering what else his daughter had told him.

"I expect you're modest to a fault. Amelia Ann told Rye part of the reason she finally found the courage to talk to Rye about law school was how proud he was of your studies."

The mugs she'd taken down hung limply in her hands. "I had no idea."

"Well, I expect you understand the importance of social and cultural cues from your studies. You know, I couldn't be happier that she's planning to go to law school at Vanderbilt. One of my children will be following in my footsteps, and although they won't be close to home, it will comfort me to know they're together." The look he sent her was pure mischief. "And it will keep my son involved in this family. We need him more than he knows."

It was exactly what she'd hoped for him, but there were still a lot of issues to work through, particularly with Rye's mother.

"I thought that the Vanderbilt tradition was dead when Rye dropped out," he continued, "but it seems I will get my wish after all. The first female lawyer in the family. Pop Crenshaw would have been delighted."

Setting the mugs down seemed like a good idea, since she was about to drop them. "Excuse me, sir, but did you say Rye dropped out of law school?"

"So, he hasn't told you yet. Well, he doesn't like to talk about it. He and his record label buried it as best as they could." He stroked his chin. "It doesn't exactly fit with his anti-establishment persona."

Oh, that big faker—giving her a hard time about too much education. Tory poured the coffee with shaking hands and brought the mugs over. "May I offer you something else?"

"No, I'm fine. I'm on a restricted diet now. The coffee is perfect. So, tell me how you met Rye."

Hampton knew how to get people to talk. He had her at ease in ten minutes, her fingers loosening their death grip on the cup. Tory found herself confiding in him, and he had her laughing at an old story about Rye when the man himself stalked into the kitchen.

"Daddy? What are you doing here? Are you okay?" He strode forward and put a hand on Hampton's shoulder.

"I'm fine. I decided to come down and meet the lovely Miss Simmons, whom I've been hearing so much about." He gave her a wink. "And all the good things I've heard about her are true."

Rye only grunted.

"Please call me Tory, Mr. Hollins. There's decaf coffee," she said to Rye. "Do you want some?"

He pressed her back into her chair, his hands gentle. "I'll get it. So, what have you two been talking about?"

"About you going to Vanderbilt law school."

Rye's jaw clenched as he poured himself coffee. "That's old news."

Not to her. Of course, she'd guessed long ago that he was smarter than he liked to admit, but still, it wasn't easy to be admitted into Vanderbilt. "To some, I guess."

Hampton picked up his coffee. "How did the errand go, Rye?"

Rye's face darkened as he sat down and raised his own mug to his lips. "Fine."

Her eyes zeroed in on his scraped knuckles. "What happened to your hands?" When she made a move for them, he pulled back.

"It's nothing."

Nothing? "Have you been fighting?"

Rye cleared his throat and looked away from her. "Well, it wasn't much of a fight. He crumpled into a ball after taking one punch."

Wonderful. And just when she'd thought he'd put *The Incident* behind him.

"I'm not surprised. Good job, son." Hampton toasted Rye with his mug before taking another sip.

So his genteel father had been in on this? "Who did you hit?"

His sigh was deep and long-suffering. "Sterling Morrison."

Oh no. This was not good. If the media got hold of this... "Tammy's husband?"

"You haven't met Sterling yet, or you wouldn't be surprised."

Hampton patted her arm. "I take full responsibility. I should have had a conversation with Sterling some time ago. Unfortunately, I was plagued with a certain problem before my heart attack."

"Oh, I'm sorry. What was it?" she asked.

He started laughing and looked at Rye. "I was a horse's ass. Wasn't I, son?"

Rye grinned. "I guess we both were, sir."

The men were still chuckling when someone gave a hard rap to the door. Tory was out of the chair before the men could move. Another visitor. *Great.*

Maybe Mama Terminator had come to pay a call.

***

Tammy straightened her shoulders, pain radiating through her muscles with every movement. She could handle this. Didn't they understand? She couldn't take any more interference.

They wanted to help, but they were only making things worse. Sterling's angry words over the phone still echoed in her mind. Annabelle and Rory stood beside her, clearly sensing something was wrong. She straightened her daughter's collar, reminding herself what was important here. Her children. She had to accept her life for them. Make them a stable home. How dare Rye interfere with that?

When Tory opened the door, Tammy nodded at her and then bent down to address her kids. "You go play in the backyard, but keep clear of the horses, do you hear? I have to talk to your Uncle Rye. Is he here?" she asked, turning toward Tory.

Tory nodded. "Hi guys," she said as the kids gave her a muted greeting and reluctantly shuffled off.

Tammy followed the voices to the kitchen. The cozy scene between father and son had her clenching her hands into fists at her sides.

"Daddy? I thought that was your car. What *are* you doing here? Mama will throw a fit when she discovers you've left the house."

Hampton ran a finger around the rim of his mug. "Don't be dramatic, Tammy. You make it sound like I orchestrated a jail break. Besides, your mama's still at the beauty parlor."

Rye just looked at her, saying nothing.

Well, with Daddy here, at least she'd have an ally against Rye. He would never approve of what his son had done, even with this reconciliation in the air. "Daddy, you won't believe what Rye's done."

"Coffee, Tammy?" Tory asked.

"No, thank you. Daddy, Rye assaulted Sterling at his office," she said.

Rye snorted. "All I did was punch him."

He was going to be glib? She marched him down. "How *dare* you assault my husband! I know you're a bully and a...bad-ass, but you have no reason to go after my family."

Daddy put a gentle hand on her arm. "Yes, he does, Tammy. Rye and I agreed this morning that a talk with Sterling was long overdue. Your husband needed to hear from one of the Hollins men about how he's treating you. If I hadn't been such a captive to convention, I would have done it years ago."

Her heart stopped in her chest. No, he didn't know. He couldn't. A fresh bruise on her shoulder throbbed in time with his words "What are you talking about, Daddy?" she asked, terror spilling over her like cold rain.

"Tammy, you don't have to pretend anymore," Daddy said. "We know all about the affairs."

A buzzing sounded in her ears.

"Everyone does, honey."

A pained gasp escaped her mouth before she pressed her hand to it. Hard. No, this could not be borne.

The grooves in Daddy's face deepened, and he suddenly looked as tired as he had in the hospital when she'd first visited him. "I'm sorry you've had to shoulder this alone for so long, but we're here for you now."

No, this couldn't be. She could tolerate the affairs if no one knew. Say nothing when Sterling came home smelling of another woman's perfume. Even remove the lipstick stains from his collar before sending his shirts off to the dry cleaner.

But not if people were talking about her. *Pitying* her. Oh the shame...

Suddenly it was too much. "This is all your fault," she said, pointing at Rye. "You've done this. Where do you get off acting like the prodigal son after throwing everything we value in our faces?"

Tory just looked down into her coffee mug, silent. That this strange woman should witness Tammy's personal business...

"And how dare you interfere in *my* marriage," she raged, "and tell me my kids aren't happy." The truth that they weren't didn't matter in that instant. Rye had ripped all her illusions from her, and they were the only things she had to hold onto.

"Who do you think you are?" she whispered.

"Tammy, you're wrong," Daddy said.

"No, I'm not."

Rye stood slowly. Why did it look like his eyes were full of pain? *He'd* done this to *her*. "I didn't know how it would be when I came back here, but I came. It was damned near the hardest thing I've ever done. I'm not some prodigal son, but I'm here. I haven't been home long, and even I can see that you're not happy."

Why was everyone using that word all of the sudden?

"You said you made a choice," he continued, "and that it's too late."

He stepped closer, towering over her. She wanted to back down. She hated when Sterling did the same thing to her.

"Well, you're wrong, and I'll be damned if I'm going to sit by without helping."

"You think beating my husband up is *helping*? Maybe in your hick country world, but not here. Do you have any idea what people will say when they find out you hit my husband?"

"But they're *already* talking, aren't they, honey?" Daddy said. "And at least Sterling's got the message, and the town knows your family won't tolerate him runnin' around on you."

Her chest grew tight as she imagined the whispers. Tammy Hollins wasn't woman enough for Sterling Morrison, or he wouldn't fool around. Her eyes started to burn. "All you've done is make it worse." After his angry words, he was sure to hurt her again when he came home tonight. Oh, God.

How could she hold her head up anymore? Now she'd have to hole up at the house, where she never felt safe.

Daddy held out his hands. "I'm sorry you feel that way. And I have to ask, do you love him, Tammy?"

Her mouth opened, but no response came out. Had she ever? If so, she couldn't remember. He'd been Mama's choice, and she'd accepted him willingly enough, as was her duty. "Who cares?" she finally said. "I'm a wife and a mother of two young children. This is my life now."

His sigh was audible. "It doesn't have to be, honey. You're so young, and I don't want you to feel trapped."

Trapped? When had she been anything but? How dare he say this to her now after rearing her on duty? "Do you love Mama, Daddy?"

His face turned white.

Bitter laughter poured out of her mouth, and she wondered absently who this woman was, talking this way. "You should be more careful before you start encouraging people to change the status quo, Daddy. It begs larger questions."

"Tammy," Rye called.

His raised voice had her muscles clenching in fear. For her, anger had come to mean the punishing grip of Sterling's hands on her body. "It's only fair for him to answer the same questions he's asking me."

Daddy's jaw clenched. "We didn't raise you to be cruel."

A tear spilled over before she realized it, and her hand quickly dashed it away. The pain felt like a bomb inside her, ready to explode. "Well, maybe you should have. It would have made life a lot easier."

"It hurts me to hear you talk like this," Daddy rasped.

Did he think it didn't hurt *her*? "Well, then it's a good thing we never really talk."

Daddy rose shakily, leaning heavily on the chair for support. "I don't want it to be that way anymore."

"Well, that's too bad, Daddy, because my life is all set, and it's too painful to talk about."

She briskly left the room, fleeing the people who knew her secrets.

But they didn't know the darkest secret, and wasn't that the worst part?

***

"Oh God, what have I done?" Daddy murmured, and his anguish snapped Rye out of his own emotional funk.

"No, Daddy, you did right. I'll go after her." Seeing Tammy like that had broken his heart clean open. "Tory, stay with him."

Without another word, he sprinted after Tammy. When he thundered onto the front porch, he heard her calling Rory's name frantically. He took in the scene. Annabelle was curled into a fetal position on the chaise lounge in a white dress dotted with sunflowers, sucking her thumb. Her eyes were huge and glistening. When he knelt by her side, she took her thumb out with a popping sound.

"Rory ran away."

Jesus. Had the kids heard them? He hadn't even known they were out here.

Rye picked her up and hugged her tight. "We'll find him, baby. It's gonna be all right." He carried her into the kitchen and handed her to Tory. Their eyes locked as she stroked Annabelle's hair. "Take care of her. I'm going to help Tammy find Rory. He's taken off."

Daddy slowly rose, and Rye could see that his strength had left him.

"Daddy, sit back down," he commanded.

"Don't worry about me. Go."

When Rye left the house, he spied his sister near the edge of the woods. "Tammy!" he called and ran to her. Tears were falling freely from her eyes now. God, this was killing him. He couldn't remember ever having seen her cry.

"It's all my fault," she cried, clutching the lapels of her suit. "He must have heard us. I couldn't leave them at the house alone. I should never have come here."

Rye wrapped his arm around her, their first embrace in God only knew how long. She fought him at first and then slumped against him. His heart pounded in his chest as he scanned the woods. Where had the boy gone?

"I brought Annabelle inside. Go check on her while I start looking." He grabbed her shoulders and stared into her pained eyes. "We'll find him, Tammy. I promise."

As she hurried off, he turned to look at the massive expanse of trees fluttering in the breeze. He'd explored these woods often enough to know how many hiding places there were for a little boy who didn't want to be found. And Rye understood that feeling. Hadn't he escaped here himself when times got too hard?

For the first time in a long time, he sent up a prayer. He hoped God would overlook his faults and grant his request.

Rory hadn't done anything wrong. He was just a scared little boy.

***

Rye was examining the ground when Tory found him. "What are you doing?" she asked, dumbfounded.

"Looking for the boy's footprints. It rained yesterday. I need to get Buster. He'll be able to track him."

His mention of the dog made goose bumps break out across her arms, but she knew he was right. A hunting dog could help.

"I told Tammy to stay with Annabelle, that I'd help you look for him."

"Oh God, Tory, what have I done?" Rye said hoarsely.

Desperation and doubt were rare for him, but now his voice nearly shook with them. "Let's leave that for later. We just need to find him." She looked around, trying to think like a little boy. "I don't think Rory would have headed for the main house—he'd guess that's where we'd look first. You take the woods on this side. I'll take the one that angles around the pasture."

He cupped her face. "What did I ever do to deserve you?" Then he kissed her swiftly and took off.

Tory had played outside frequently as a child, and while the woods could be a magical place, she remembered the fear of being lost in them as the sky darkened. She looked at the sun and heaved a sigh. Fortunately, they had a few hours of daylight left. She couldn't bear the thought of the boy being alone and afraid in the dark. Her pace was brisk, but she paused to listen every few yards.

She was sweaty and bug bitten when she reached a shiny red barn above the pasture. The caretaker wasn't there, and the stables were empty because the horses were still out in the field. Ears straining, she heard a small sound, like something brushing across the floor. It only lasted a second, but she went on instinct.

"It's Tory, sweetheart. I know you're in here." She decided to give him a reason to come out. "Rory, your Granddaddy isn't feeling so well at the moment, so I came to get you and bring you to him." Clasping her hands together, she prayed he would take the bait.

Her teeth bit into her lip when his small body slowly climbed down the ladder from the loft. He looked so small. His eyes were swollen from crying, and streaks of dirt and mud covered his blue-and-white seersucker shorts and white polo. He had a nasty scratch on his cheek, and his eyes were wary.

"Has Granddaddy had another heart attack?" he asked.

She crouched down, meeting his gaze. "No," she immediately assured him, "but he's done a little too much today and needs you to help him back to the main house."

"I'm running away," he told her.

Oh, you poor boy. "Are you now? Where are you going?"

He kicked at some hay. "I thought I might stay here. Mr. Pullins can bring me food. He's real nice, and that way, Annabelle can still come and see me." When he lifted his head, his sad blue eyes cut Tory's heart into ribbons. "She needs me, you know."

Tory blinked back tears. "I'm sure she does. She's lucky to have you for a brother. I always wished I had a brother."

He studied her with a seriousness beyond his age. "Don't you have a family?"

"No, I don't," she said softly. "My grandpa just died. He was the only one left."

"What happened to your mama and daddy?"

"They died in a car accident when I was little."

"Oh." His brows knit together like he was trying to figure out a puzzle. "So, your whole family's in heaven?"

Tory wiped away a tear before it could fall. The little boy's faith seeped into the cracks of her heart, and in that moment, she had a surer answer to that question than she'd been able to muster for some time. "Yes, I hope so."

"That's sad. Do you miss them?" he asked.

"Very much," she responded.

His body edged closer, smelling of boy sweat and forest.

"Do you think my family would miss me if I ran away?"

Oh, baby. She wanted to hug him, but knew it would be the wrong move. "Of course they would. Your mama was crying when I left, and so was Annabelle." She raised a tentative hand and brushed the damp blond hair off his forehead.

"My Daddy wouldn't. He doesn't love us."

In that moment, she was glad Rye had punched Sterling. If he hadn't, she would have. How could he make his own son think such a thing? Tory put an arm around him. "I'll bet he does. You're a sweet boy." She could lie to a little boy about something this important, right?

Rory rubbed his head against her shoulder. "No, he doesn't. I heard Mama fighting with Granddaddy and Uncle Rye. I'm glad Uncle Rye hit Daddy. *I hate him, I hate him, I hate him.*"

Tory hugged the boy tight. His usual reserve snapped, and he clung to her. She smoothed his hair and rubbed his back—anything to give him comfort.

"Rory, even if only *one* person loved you like your mama does, it would be worth going back."

Pushing away, he put a finger to his lips like he was thinking. "You're right. Annabelle and Mama love me. And Granddad and Grandmama and Amelia Ann." He leaned into her again, ducking his head into her shoulder. "I like you too. I'm glad our names sound alike."

Could she choke out an answer through her tight throat? "Me too," she whispered. When she held out her hand, he took it. "How about we see if that three-wheeler over there has a key? That way we can get home faster."

"It does," he told her.

He was right, and as soon as they were both situated in the vehicle, wearing helmets, she turned the key dangling in the ignition. The engine thundered to life.

"You hang on tight now."

His little arms gripped her waist. She hadn't ridden a three-wheeler since high school, but it came back to her with ease, and she headed in Rye's direction. When she spotted him and Buster near an enormous oak tree, she braced herself as the dog came bounding toward them.

"You found him," Rye called. He plucked Rory off the seat and hugged him tight against his chest, and the boy wrapped his little arms around him.

His hazel eyes met hers, shining so bright, and in that moment she knew she loved Rye with all her heart. There was no holding back now.

"Thank God."

When he pressed his face into the boy's hair, she bit her lip as the dog danced around them, wired from the chase.

"You scared us, son."

"I know, sir," he murmured. "My tummy hurts."

"No doubt." Rye eased back. "Let's get one thing straight. I'm your Uncle Rye, not *sir*. I know we don't know each other well yet, but that's about to change."

As he hugged the boy again, Tory stepped off the three-wheeler, keeping a wary eye on Buster.

"Why don't you take him back?" she said. "I'll walk."

"No!" Rory yelled. "We're not leaving her." He shrugged free of Rye's embrace and took Tory's hand.

Now what was that all about?

"All right, son," Rye said. "She goes with us. I didn't want to leave her behind either." He sent Buster home with a firm command. "Do you know he picked up your scent, Rory?"

"He's a good dog, Uncle Rye."

He picked Rory up and placed him in front before settling into the seat. When he turned to look at Tory, he gave her a big smile. "Good thing you're so little. It's going to be a bit tight, but it's not far, and I'll go real slow."

When she climbed on, she pressed her face into his back, struggling with tears. Oh this man. This boy.

They'd barely cleared the woods when Tammy screamed out Rory's name. Rye halted the three-wheeler and killed the engine, then lifted Rory from his seat and unbuckled the boy's helmet.

"Run to your mama, son. It'll make her feel better."

Rory took off, arms pumping. When he reached Tammy, both of them fell to their knees, clutching each other, making room for a crying Annabelle to join them.

"What did you tell him to make him come back?" Rye asked.

Tory took her helmet off and rested her chin on his shoulder. "I told him that so long as there's one person who loves you, it doesn't matter how bad things get. You always have to go back."

Rye turned and caressed her cheek. "You're one hell of a woman."

She slid off the three-wheeler, and it seemed like the most natural thing in the world to go into his arms. His embrace was sweet, his kiss gentle. Then he tucked her under his arm and led her back toward the house.

Hampton raised one hand in greeting, using the other to grip the porch rail. His face was haggard.

You all right, Daddy?" Rye called.

"Aged me twenty years."

"Me, too."

Rory pulled away from Tammy as they approached and crooked a finger at Tory. She went down on one knee in front of him.

He leaned forward and whispered in her ear, "You don't have to be alone anymore. I'll be your family, I promise."

She blinked back tears as she smoothed down his hair and rubbed a spot of dirt from his face. "That's the most precious thing anyone has ever said to me. You go home with your family now, sweetheart. I'll see you tomorrow."

As he ran to take Tammy's hand, Tory took a moment to study Rye's sister. She was disheveled for the second time in their acquaintance, her hair in wild clumps, mascara streaked down her face. She looked vulnerable—and like a stranger to the woman she'd first met, all smooth and polished. Her unpainted mouth trembled.

"Thank you, Tory. And Rye," she added in a whisper, grabbing Annabelle's hand with her free one. "We're staying at Hollinswood tonight."

"Good idea," Rye responded. "I'll take Daddy and follow you. We'll talk to Mama with you."

Rory tugged on Tammy's hand. "I want Tory to come too. She shouldn't be alone."

His sweet words humbled her. "I'll be all right, Rory," she said. "You go with your family."

"No, you're coming with us." He walked over and grabbed her hand. "You remember what I said?"

How could she forget? And while she didn't want to go to the manor house, she nodded because Rory wanted it.

"Then that's enough of that," he said in a grown-up voice.

Tammy's eyes widened, and Rye strode forward. "Rory, you sound like your Granddaddy Crenshaw. How about I tell you and Annabelle about him at bedtime tonight? You would have liked him a whole lot."

"I need to turn the stove off," Tory murmured, suddenly remembering the pot roast.

"I just checked on it," Tammy said. "Why don't you bring it up to the house?"

"That's a good idea. I'll go pack it up. Be right back."

Tory arranged the food in a couple of brown grocery bags. When Rye strode in, she nodded her head to the counter. "Could you grab the chocolate chip pie and one of the sacks?"

"What did Rory say to you?" he asked, doing as she'd asked.

"That's between us for now." It held so much meaning for her that she wasn't ready to share it, not even with the man who held her heart.

He stepped in front of her. "Why won't you tell me?"

Her heart pounded faster with his closeness. "Because it meant a lot to that little boy, and I'm not sure he wants anyone else to know." There was truth in that.

"Do you think I would do anything to hurt him?"

"Never. I'm just not ready to tell you."

His jaw clenched, the only sign that he didn't like her response. "We need to go. They're waiting for us."

Rory waved out the SUV window when Tory emerged. She smiled at him, her eyes burning with held back tears again. When had she become so involved with this family—this dysfunctional, hurting family—that she was willing to risk being hurt?

Rye took her bags and started arranging the food in the back of his father's SUV. It felt normal, somehow—like domestic moments like this happened all the time with them. She wedged the pie in the corner so it wouldn't slide and heaved a sigh. Perhaps her food would help the others.

"Buckle up," he muttered, opening the back door for her.

Hampton turned around in his seat as Tory slid in. "Seems like the men in this family really like you, Ms. Simmons. I hope you know how rare that is. We're not easy to get along with."

She didn't believe that anymore.

I don't want silent dinners no more.
Where even the dog don't come 'round anymore.
And all that can be heard is a fly,
Beating against the screened porch.

I want a healthy dose of noise.
My woman watching me with joy.
Smiling her sweet smile.
The one reserved just for me.

I want my kids to chatter about their day.
Giggle over little things and play.
And bow their heads to pray.

Silence with others around is hell.
I don't want to hear that sound again.
I don't want to hear it anymore.

Rye Crenshaw's Number One Hit, "Silent No More"

CHAPTER 15

After just a few moments at the house Rye wanted to duck back out. Mama immediately took Rory to task for being filthy and gave Rye a scorching look that told him as clear as any words that she'd heard all about his skirmish with Sterling. Then she gave Daddy a piece of her mind for disappearing, but he shut her down and announced they were having a family dinner. Unaccustomed to Daddy challenging her authority, everyone waited in silence to see how she'd respond. She finally tapped two perfectly manicured pink fingernails against her emerald necklace and gave a full-watt smile, announcing her intention to make cocktails. Rye wanted a bourbon—straight up.

At the threshold to the parlor, Mama said, "Tammy, dear, why don't you take Rory upstairs and clean him up? He looks like he's been rollin' around in the dirt. And Tory, since my son seems to think so highly of your cooking abilities, I'm sure you can finish everything up in the kitchen."

Rye ground his teeth. "Leave her be, Mama."

Tory just squeezed his hand before heading off with the pot roast.

When they sat down in the dining room, the gold damask tablecloth showcasing the Hollins china—white porcelain with a gold rim—everyone was as silent as a tomb. Mama looked like she'd sucked the lemon in her cosmopolitan, and Amelia Anne's eyes fairly shouted questions about what had happened earlier. Rye noticed Rory grab Tory's hand and wondered again what the boy had said to her.

Fortunately the roast she'd made was large enough to serve their crew, and she'd wisely created a few additional sides of sugar snap peas and green beans to add to the potatoes.

After taking the first bite of Tory's food, the tense atmosphere at the table changed. Rye almost smiled, Daddy's eyelids fluttered, and Annabelle outright giggled. Everyone reached for more—except for Mama. She didn't touch the food, well aware that it was a grave insult to the chef.

"This is so good," Annabelle cried, spooning in another carrot. "What's it called again?"

Tory's mouth lifted. "Chinese Pot Roast."

"Like people in China?" Rory asked. "I thought they ate rice."

Tory gave a nervous laugh. "Well, I don't know why my Grandma called it that, but I'm glad you like it."

Hampton lifted his glass to her. "It's wonderful. Thank you for sharing your talent with us. I can see why Rye thinks so highly of your cooking."

Rye winked at Tory, whose face instantly went red. When the doorbell rang, Mama rose quickly. Since no one solicited at dinnertime in Meade, Rye had a bad feeling. Everyone's eyes followed her.

Rye heard Tammy's sharp intake when the sound of low conversation filtered to the table, and he instantly knew who it was. Mama had invited Sterling. He started to stand, but Daddy put a hand on his arm.

When Sterling came in, his arm linked through Mama's, Rye wished he'd punched him in the face. Still, he'd known that would generate more talk, so he'd gone for the stomach.

Mama smiled, but her face remained frozen, as if she'd received a Botox injection at the beauty shop that afternoon. "I called Sterling to join our family dinner."

Daddy rose to his feet, which was when Rye realized why he'd stopped him. This was *his* house. He was the one who needed to make a stand.

"Until his behavior changes, he is not welcome here," Daddy said.

Mama gasped. "But Hampton—"

"Your help is not needed, Margaret. Rye and I have already spoken to Sterling. Haven't we, son?"

His use of son was intentional. Sterling's face paled.

Rye let his sneer loose. "Yes, sir, we had a right pleasant conversation. Didn't we, Sterling?"

Mama straightened her spine as if she were preparing for battle. "Amelia Ann, please take the children up for their bath. It's been a long day for them. Tory, you can clean up the dishes. And the rest of us can retire to your study, Hampton."

"No, I want Tory to come with me," Rory cried.

She met Rye's eyes as she took the boy's hand. "Okay, I'll come with you guys if your Aunt Amelia doesn't mind."

His sister's nod was little more than a wobble of her head. When they walked out, Rye was comforted by the thought that the little ones would be well cared for. He walked to Tammy's side in a show of support and settled a hand on her shoulder, but he broke the contact when she flinched.

Daddy walked forward. "It pains me to say this, Margaret, but I think it would be better if you went upstairs to get ready for bed, too."

Her hand flew to her throat. "Hampton!"

Go Daddy.

"Sterling, let's go to my study," he said, gesturing to the entryway. "Rye, please bring your sister."

He took Tammy's elbow in his hand, taking care to be gentle so she wouldn't flinch again, not sparing a look at Mama as they walked past her. Rye hadn't been in his Daddy's study since he'd been disowned, and his stomach went from queasy to greasy as the memories came rushing back.

Daddy conducted business from home at times. His office could impress and intimidate, depending on the reason the person found himself or herself sitting across from him at his massive, freshly polished mahogany desk. When Daddy settled back into his high-back leather chair, he reached for his antique letter opener, said to have been used by Stonewall Jackson during the War of Northern Aggression.

There were two chairs in front of the desk, and Rye gently nudged Tammy into one, gesturing for Sterling to take the other. Now that he'd had some time to process the unexpected turn of events, his brother-in-law didn't even look upset.

"Well, it appears we have some things to discuss," Daddy began.

Privilege had run through so many generations of Sterling's family that he acted like it was part of his DNA. He settled back with his typical arrogance, casually crossing his ankle over his knee like they were going to talk about golf or something. God, he'd always hated this son of a bitch growing up.

"Sir," Sterling began. "I'm not sure what mendacious thoughts Rye has been putting in your head, but none of them are true. He's had a dislike of me since childhood. While he abandoned his family, I've been here, taking care of mine."

Rye's gut burned. It would have been a good tactic if he and Daddy hadn't reconciled. Clearly, Sterling hadn't believed it possible.

"Sterling, I'm sure it will surprise you to learn this, but I've heard stories about you running around on my daughter for years—since your first year of marriage, in fact."

Tammy gave a small yelp, like a dog being stepped on.

"Women hear their gossip at the beauty shop. Men hear it on the golf course." He made direct eye contact with Sterling like he was a hostile witness in court. "I chose to let it be your business. That was my mistake. I've made lots of them. But recent events have made me realize that it's not too late to make amends—or change the status quo. Margaret and I raised our children to respect marriage, but unfortunately, we also instilled a horror of divorce. I don't want Tammy to feel she needs to put up with an untenable situation, whatever the reason. And repeated and flagrant adultery falls into that category."

Sterling clenched a fist in Rye's direction. "You son of a bitch. This is your fault."

Daddy tapped the letter opener on his desk like a judge's gavel. "Enough, Sterling. Rye may have been the one to pay you a visit, but I can assure you he and I are of one mind. We do not want Tammy to feel alone any longer."

"By assaulting her husband over something little like this?" he said, running a hand through his blond hair. "She doesn't care. Look at her. She's not saying anything. She never does. The only thing at issue here is appearances and her pride."

Daddy put the letter opener down. "You're mistaken." He finally looked at Tammy. "It's not a little matter, is it?"

***

Oh heavens, why did Daddy have to ask her that? This was their show, wasn't it?

Then she saw Sterling's smirk, the way his mouth tipped up to the side. It always did that when he expected her to cave and do nothing. She tugged on her skirt and noticed a spot of dirt she'd missed earlier. The dirt made her remember Rory—why he'd run away. She fingered her sleeve, remembering the bruise on her shoulder. Would he ever hit the kids? Had he when she wasn't looking?

It was time to take a stand for Rory and Annabelle. And for herself, she realized.

When Rye placed a hand on her shoulder again, she didn't flinch. His touch wasn't intended to harm her, and it made her feel less alone. Sterling couldn't hurt her here.

"No, it's not a little thing." The muscles in her face trembled. "The children deserve better. I'm tired of seeing Rory and

Annabelle's disappointed faces when they go to bed before you get home because you're out with some woman. And I deserve a better husband." There, she'd said it, even though her throat had squeezed to the size of a thimble.

"You deserve better?" Sterling drawled, uncharacteristically tugging at his tie. "I give you and the kids everything. Don't you have the best house, car, and clothes? Do you think it's easy to come home to a frigid bitch every night?"

How could he say that out loud? Shame shot through her, heating her face.

"Shut up!" Rye shouted. "You don't talk to her that way."

When her eyes met her Daddy's, she only saw compassion there, and it gave her the courage to say the things she'd locked inside her heart long ago. "Why do you think I act that way? I know where you've been. It doesn't inspire *wifely* affection, Sterling. But the children shouldn't suffer for it."

His shrug enraged her. "I don't do anything to the kids."

"That's the problem. You don't love them, Sterling." Her voice shook as she finally admitted her worst fear. "You don't even like them. Rory's old enough to realize it, and Annabelle will soon too." She twisted her wedding ring, hating the weight, the symbol. "I won't tolerate it anymore, Sterling."

Sterling's mouth twisted as he shoved out of the chair. "You won't *tolerate* it? Don't talk to me like that, Tammy."

His anger scared her, but Rye and Daddy were here. "I mean it, Sterling."

"And what exactly are you going to do about it?" he asked, flexing his hand.

Her mind flashed back to other times. His hands—always his hands—on her arms, her wrists, her waist, digging into her flesh hard enough to bruise.

"We can do this easy or we can do this hard, Sterling," Rye finally said. "You've had a taste of easy. I'll be more than happy to show you hard."

"You're going to pay for what you did to me, Rye. Do you think beating me up is going to make me love my wife? You must have turned as stupid as the hick you pretend to be." He pointed at him, sneering. "You think you're some hot-shot, but I'll make you pay. I'll charge you with assault. I have witnesses."

Witnesses? Who? And what would they say about her?

Rye only laughed. "If you'd like to admit that you're a big enough pussy to have crumpled after one punch, that's your business. Press charges. See if I care."

No, they couldn't bring the law into this, and the media would get a hold of this, which he didn't need right now. Rye had been only trying to protect her.

She rose swiftly and grabbed his arm. "Rye, I don't want you to get into trouble."

His gaze softened, and he rested his hand over hers. "It's okay, Tammy."

Sterling clucked his tongue and stood up. "Well, isn't that precious? Who knew country-club Tammy still cared for the black sheep in the family?" He lifted a hand and stroked a lock of her blond hair before she could knock his hand away. "Seems there's an easier way of handling this all 'round."

Daddy raised a brow. "And that would be?"

Sterling rocked back on his heels. "Well, since you've taken a dislike to me runnin' around on your daughter, Hampton, and I don't want to change my ways, I'm thinkin' you should pay me to divorce her."

Tammy inhaled like she'd taken a punch to the stomach. A divorce? She looked at him to see if he were serious. He'd always said he'd never let her go.

Sterling flicked a piece of lint off his suit. "After all, you've just said I'm not much of a husband and father. So why should we stay married? I can find a replacement soon enough. You're a good mama, Tammy, but you're not much of a wife."

"I'm going to beat you into a bloody pulp if you say anything about her again," Rye hissed.

Oh the shame. It made her want to disappear from view.

Daddy slammed his hand on the table. "That's enough maligning. State your terms, Sterling."

He tilted his head to the side. "A million dollars, or I'll make things worse for everyone."

He wasn't serious, she realized. When Sterling didn't want to do something, he made the terms so high that they couldn't be met. His lawyer training.

"Done," Rye responded, shocking her.

She slid into the chair when her legs wouldn't support her.

"You'll get half the money now and the other half when the divorce papers are signed. And you'll sign over full custody," Rye added.

She watched for Sterling's reaction. His eyes widened, and then he blinked. So she was right—he hadn't expected anyone to agree to his terms. Then his mouth quirked up at the corner, and she knew it wouldn't be enough. That she and the kids would never be free—

exactly like he'd always threatened.

"I want another million for giving up custody," he said.

Tammy lowered her head, already thinking of his retribution.

"Don't push your luck," Rye said, acid in his voice. "I'm already being generous." His fist slapped his other palm. "Best not to provoke me right now. As you've heard, I can't always control myself."

When she looked over, Sterling was swallowing like he'd choked on a June bug at a picnic. "Fine. So long as we're done."

Daddy pulled open his desk drawer and drew out legal stationery, like it was the most natural thing in the world for them to sit down together and outline the terms of her divorce. He picked up his personalized fountain pen and started to write in the special ink Tammy had found him in Charleston.

"Since we have an agreement," he said, "I'm going to draw this up right now. That way there will be no need for us to meet again. I will file formally for Tammy tomorrow. Since we're so generous, we'll state 'irreconcilable differences' and not adultery. We'll deal with the other details in the coming weeks, but I warn you not to fight me on this, son. I'd like nothing better than to destroy you."

Tammy watched his bold handwriting cover the paper. People would know the reason anyway. Meade was a small town. She was surprised by how little she cared.

When Daddy turned the papers toward Sterling, he approached the desk. "I'll sign this, but I want half the money now."

Rye pulled out his cell phone. "You know your bank account number?"

Sterling nodded.

Rye talked to Georgia, whom she'd met briefly when she'd flown to his concert stop. After a brief chat, he repeated the bank account number Sterling clicked off. It was one she didn't know about, which made her wonder what other secrets he'd kept from her.

She pressed her fingers to her throbbing temples. It was hard to take everything in. "How could you do this?" she asked Sterling.

"Let's not lie to each other," he said. "I never loved you, and you never loved me. This was an arrangement between your mama and mine, wanting the Hollins and Morrisons to come together. Now that any advantages I received from being in this family are gone, I'm going to cut my losses."

"And the children?" she whispered.

"You're right. They're nice enough, but I've never liked kids. Only had them because it was expected."

Since she had no rebuttal, she said nothing in response.

Sterling drew out his phone, ostensibly checking his bank account. "Okay, I have an email saying the money's in the process of being transferred into my account. I'll just see myself out."

Rye stepped forward, touching his boot tips to Sterling's loafers. God, she'd always hated those shoes.

"You're a fucking prick," Rye growled.

"And you're a bastard. Nice doing business with you." Sterling sauntered out of the room after tapping his finger to his temple in a mocking wave.

In the silence, the cold hard reality crested over her. "What have we done?" she cried. How could her reality have altered so significantly so fast?

Rye knelt by her chair. "We just got rid of a no-account asshole who treated you like trash and didn't even ask to say goodbye to his kids."

He was right. "Oh God." She leaned forward, wrapping her arms around her queasy stomach. "What am I going to do? What am I going to tell everyone? I won't be able to keep my head up in this town."

Rye awkwardly patted her back as Daddy circled his desk to face her.

"Then you need to leave this town," Rye said.

Leave? It was the only place she knew. "But I don't have anywhere else to go."

Rye took a deep breath, like he was preparing to dive underwater. "Yes, you do. You can come to Nashville with Amelia Ann. You and the kids can live with me."

With him?

Daddy's mouth gaped open for a moment, and it was clear he was as shocked as she was. Then he smiled. "That's an excellent idea, Rye."

Her hands clenched. "Are you serious?"

His eyes had a glassy look, but he said, "Sure. I have lots of room."

Suddenly the future seemed too opaque, with her present so new and raw. Pain spread across her body, making her feel like Sterling had bruised her all over. Tammy bent forward, rocking herself. "I tried so hard to be a good wife. Oh, God."

Rye pulled her from the chair and pressed her head into his shoulder. "I know you did."

His words and his touch brought tears to her eyes. She wasn't used to being comforted by men. Actually by anyone. "The kids.

What am I going to tell them?"

"We'll tell them as much of the truth as appropriate," Daddy said, running a hand down her hair like she was a child. "And then we'll tell them they're going to live with their Uncle Rye."

Rye's face looked pale when she pressed back to look at him, and it wasn't hard to imagine this was as shocking to him as it was to her. He'd gone from being the black sheep of the family to being their champion in a matter of days.

Still, he said, "It'll be all right, you'll see."

She couldn't imagine this ever being all right. The whole world she knew was gone. Forever. "But the money...Rye, I can never pay you back."

"Stop. It's just money. Hell, I have more than I can ever use. Don't think about it."

Not think about it? How could she not? "What will I tell Mama?"

"You leave that to me," Daddy said, his voice stern. "She should not have called Sterling tonight." When his eyes locked with Rye's, he smiled. "But I guess it all worked out. We showed him that we take care of our own."

When Daddy extended his hand, Rye took it.

She watched them shake with a sense of disbelief. It seemed they'd also carved out their own deal. Her two protectors, united in helping her.

But where did that leave her now?

***

After untangling herself from a sleeping Rory, Tory went in search of Rye, rubbing the crick in her neck. Rory had stared at the wall silently, holding her hand, as she read him *The Stinky Cheese Man*.

Amelia Ann caught her at the top of the stairs and filled her in on what had happened downstairs. From start to finish, it was a shock. She'd be hard pressed to say who was more surprised by Rye's suggestion that Tammy and the kids move in with him—her or Amelia Ann. Tory wondered how Tammy was feeling. Tonight had changed the course of her life and the lives of those sweet precious children.

When she asked where everyone was, Amelia Ann told her Rye was in the gazebo, and Tammy and Daddy had retired, the latter joining Mrs. Hollins, who had not emerged from her room. Amelia Ann declared that she was going to head to bed as well, but she gave Tory a spontaneous hug before she left.

The house was silent as Tory let herself out and walked across the back lawn, past the point where the glow of the porch lights stopped. The white gazebo was luminous in the distance, reminding her of the Moonlight Garden. She could make out the shape of a man holding something with a red tip.

When she reached the structure, she leaned against the doorway.

"I didn't know you smoked," she said, wrinkling her nose at the cigar.

Rye took another drag and blew out a slow stream of blue smoke. "I started when I quit law school and launched my career. Gave it up pretty quick. Bad for my voice."

And his voice seemed none too steady tonight.

"This just seemed like a good time to revisit the habit," he said, tapping it on the railing, scattering ashes. "Daddy keeps some nice cigars around."

"You want to talk about it?" she said.

"Who told you?"

"Amelia Ann. She was waiting for me when I came out of Rory's room."

A lone bat streaked across the sky, flying recklessly and madly, and the crickets sang in time with the cicadas.

"The boy's taken a right shine to you," Rye drawled, turning his back to her. "I guess that's a good thing. Little tyke will need lots of support now."

Something about his tone—the vulnerability, the need—made her wrap her arms around his middle and pull him close. She rubbed her face into his back. The cigar fell, and he stomped the glowing embers before grabbing her hands.

"I didn't expect any of this when I came here," he whispered.

Of course, he hadn't. The man from the hot tub would never have come if he'd known the responsibility for his broken family would fall on his shoulders. As she caressed his forearms, the repeated shrill of a nearby frog could be heard.

"Life's funny that way."

He sighed. "Yeah, she's a prize bitch."

"It's not all bad though, is it Rye?" she asked, needing to know how he felt about her. Sinking into quicksand alone was too scary.

He turned slowly. The moonlight was stark on his hard jaw, dark eyes, and strong chin.

"No, it's not all bad. One of the best parts is standing in front of me."

The quicksand feeling went away.

When he lowered his mouth to hers, she tasted the spiciness of nicotine and unfulfilled need. Rising to her tiptoes, she wrapped her arms around his neck.

"I need you." He pressed his face to her neck, and his raw emotion called to her. "Right now."

She framed his face in her hands and met his eyes. "I'm here."

He pressed his mouth to hers again, and demand and desire dueled as they took the kiss deeper. Rye pulled Tory across the railing to press her against one of the posts of the gazebo. His fingers shook as they jerked up her T-shirt. She wrapped her legs around him to keep from falling and lifted her arms. Then he pulled the shirt off and threw it behind him, his fingers tugging her bra off an instant later until her breasts filled his hands.

Between the humidity and the heat spiking through her body, beads of moisture formed on Tory's skin. She moaned as Rye lowered his mouth to her breast, sucking deeply, making guttural sounds in the back of his throat. She pulled at his shirt, and he drew it above his head and pressed his bare chest against hers, their moist skin rubbing and sliding, their breathing ragged. Tory reached out a hand and rubbed his defined pectoral muscles. He swallowed thickly as her hand trailed to his belt buckle, and he helped her unhook it and then open his jeans. When she slid her hand into his briefs and caressed him, he leaned into her and reached for the post, groaning in time with the evening sounds around them.

He took her mouth again and pulled her off the railing, holding her against him while he unfastened her pants and tossed them aside, quickly rolling on a condom. Steadying her against the post again, he fitted her legs around his body. Her muscles tensed as she waited for him to enter her. She'd never wanted anything more.

"I won't let you fall," he whispered. "Trust me."

She grabbed his shoulders and pressed her head back against the wood as his fingers trailed between her legs. When he touched her, sweat beaded and fell between her breasts, and she opened her legs wider.

"Rye, please."

Her ears were ringing when he slid inside, pressing deep. Tory felt the imprint of the beam against her back and strained against his thrusting body. She tilted her body to take more of him, and he reached a hand down to rub where they were joined together. Her body revved and then exploded, quaking over and over again.

He pulled her legs more tightly around him. "More, dammit. I need *more*."

She took the pounding. Tried to find an anchor, her hands sliding off his sweaty shoulders. She grabbed his butt, her hands tingling against the rough material of his jeans. He pulled her off the post and worked her over him. She bit his shoulder, feeling her body tighten again. The next climax hit her hard and had her gripping him with clenched thighs.

He pushed her against the post again and thrust deep one more time, finding his own release. When he disposed of the condom, he pulled her against him again. Tory took deep breaths, her body pulsing, and she leaned her head away from his sweaty chest to draw in fresh air. The humidity made it almost hard to breathe, so thick and suffocating. She closed her eyes, awash in sensation. When sweat trickled down her neck, she reached up to brush it away. Her fingers encountered something large and hairy instead. She screamed, her hand slapping madly.

Rye stumbled, holding onto her. "What?"

She wiggled in his arms, continuing to slap the hairy insect creeping across her shoulder. "There's a spider on me," she shrieked.

He knocked something black and menacing to the floor. It raced across the moonlit steps.

"*Kill it, kill it,*" Tory cried.

Rye stomped his boot on the spot. The spider jumped.

Her squeal was deafening, even to her, and her heart rapped hard against her ribs. "Oh, God. It jumped. What is *that*?"

Rye followed it, stomping hard like a flamenco dancer. "A camel cricket."

His boot came down like a sledgehammer, and Tory heard the creepy crawly squish underneath it.

"God, I *hate* those things," he said with a shudder.

Tory leaned weakly against the railing. If her pulse were any indication, she'd need CPR soon. Her heart was going to explode.

"*That* was a cricket?"

"Yeah. It looks like a spider, jumps like a cricket."

Tory gave another wiggle, unable to escape the feeling that there was still something crawling on her. "What the *hell* kind of bugs do you have down here?"

"You should see your face." Rye barked out a laugh. "Mutant bugs are a hallmark down here. You look good, dancing around buck naked."

She slapped a hand to his chest when he grabbed her again. "We're done here, buster. I am *never* having sex with you outside again." Gathering up her clothes, she yanked them on while he made himself presentable as well.

Rye chuckled. "Well, it was damn fine up until then, but I can understand your position."

"Yeah, it was great, but it's hell on afterglow."

Rye crossed over to her and raised her hands to his lips. She jerked, as surprised by the romantic gesture as she was by his sudden touch.

"You still jumpy?"

She only nodded, and even in the moonlight, there was something in his eyes. Something she'd never seen before.

He tugged on her fingers, breaking the spell. "Well, let's get back to the house and take a shower. Then, I'll see to your afterglow. I like holding you after we make love." Then he ducked his head. "Course I like the other stuff more," he added, almost like he was saving face.

And the way he said *make love* made all the love she felt for him rise up inside her. She rubbed her throat to squeak through a response. "Of course. You're a guy."

Before she could think better of it—after all, they were leaving tomorrow, and hadn't they said that would be it?—she linked her arms around his neck. "I'd feel a lot better if you check the bed for bugs." Her tone was playful, even if her embrace wasn't. "Seeing how you're about as scared of them as I am."

His mouth twitched. "Honey, you think what you like, but fear of camel crickets is akin to fearing werewolves. Some things just aren't natural. Besides, you remember who killed it." He planted a quick kiss on her mouth. Snaked a finger down her neck.

She swatted it away. His shoulders were shaking with laughter now, so she punched him in the arm.

"Very funny. You'll pay for that."

As he turned away, she leaped onto his back. He laughed and then darted out of the gazebo, making erratic circles, forcing her to hang onto him. They were laughing like loons by the time he stopped, weaving in place. He tumbled to the ground, taking her with him. Tory sat on his chest. She was so not lying on the ground. The last thing she wanted was another up close and personal encounter with a camel cricket.

Their laughter echoed in the dark, and then she heard a mechanical whine. When the black sprinklers rose from the ground, she tried to push away, but Rye held her fast, his laughter demented now. Jets of water slapped across her body, and the mass of sprinklers pumped water like crystal arcs across the yard.

"See, someone got punished," Rye drawled.

She attacked him. They rolled in the grass like excited children, forgetting for the briefest of moments the suffering that lay in the shadowed house behind them.

I don't know what it is about breakfast, but starting off the day right with a good one gives me a better attitude. Granted, my grandma raised me to never leave the house without breakfast. Eggs, pancakes, and waffles were routinely on the table when I came downstairs before leaving for school. I once commented that I wished we could have gingerbread more often one Christmas since I loved my grandma's Gingerbread men, so she found this recipe. These waffles always make me happy. They're a special treat—like unwrapping presents on Christmas morning.

Gingerbread Waffles

½ cup molasses
6 tbsp. oil
1 cup milk
2 beaten eggs

Mix together and add the following dry ingredients together in a separate bowl and then add to the liquid ingredients:

2 tsp. baking powder
½ tsp. baking soda
1 tsp. ginger (fresh is best)
½ tsp. cinnamon
4 tbsp. sugar
2 cups flour

Cook in a waffle iron for 4-6 minutes until golden brown. Serve with a lemon sauce or maple syrup.

Tory Simmons' Simmering Family Cookbook

CHAPTER 16

orning came way too early for Tory after a night of passion and playfulness that lasted until nearly dawn. Rye had certainly seen to her afterglow. If he'd been able to see her heart, it would have glowed like a well-tended camp fire. He'd fallen asleep with his body tangled around hers.

Rye was still fast asleep, and she didn't want to wake him up yet since they hadn't slept much. The drive to Oklahoma City was only eight hours away after all. She'd promised to play with Rory before they left, so she made breakfast and stored bacon and her favorite Gingerbread waffles in the warm oven with a note on the table for Rye. He deserved something extra special after the way he'd made her feel last night.

She decided to walk to the main house, and a smile spread across her face as she did, particularly when she remembered the sprinklers. Rory was largely quiet, but they read books together and played checkers. An hour later, she heard a guitar and Rye's husky singing voice, so she pushed herself off the floor and moved toward the sound, Rory following. Amelia Ann and Annabelle met them in the hallway, and they all headed toward Hampton's room. When they cracked the door open, Rye was sitting on the edge of the bed, his back to them. While Annabelle jumped up beside him, Amelia Ann and Rory walked ahead and leaned against the bed, snuggling up close to Hampton.

Rye's voice was so deep and filled with emotion that it raised the hairs on the back of her neck. He hadn't sung like this at the aborted concert she'd attended. No, not like this at all.

She decided to stay just outside the room, not wanting to intrude on this family moment. Likely their first in a long while. Her eyes were burning when she felt a presence behind her.

"I'd like to speak with you, Miss Simmons."

Even whispering, Mama Terminator inspired fear. Tory took a breath and turned around. "Yes, Mrs. Hollins?"

"Shall we go downstairs?" Her suit was periwinkle blue. Her lipstick a pale plum. She looked as immaculate as ever.

"I promised Rory I'd stay close." It wasn't quite the truth, but she had no desire to go downstairs with this woman.

Margaret's mouth thinned, and she quietly closed the bedroom door. "Fine, I'll say what I want to here. At first, I blamed Rye for all the changes going on around here, but I've revised my opinion. I think you're the one at fault."

"Me?"

"Yes, Rye has thought of no one but himself since he left this family. Hampton might have decided to make amends, but Rye wouldn't have been open to the overture without some encouragement. And his offer to help Amelia Ann and to have Tammy and the children live with him just isn't like him." Her hazel eyes narrowed, making her look mean and hard. "And if you have anything to do with his sudden generosity, I can promise you this. He won't be taking my daughters away from me."

She heard applause break out in the bedroom, followed by Rye's warm chuckle, and she wanted nothing more than to leave his mother in the dust. "Rye's not taking your daughters away from you, Mrs. Hollins. He's helping them."

"My daughters don't need help. They're fine the way they are."

Could the woman not see the truth before her eyes? "They don't seem to think so," she said softly.

"Don't judge me." Her hand gripped her pearls as if she were seeking comfort from the family heirloom. "Don't you *dare* judge me."

Her vehemence made Tory's stomach quiver.

She planted her hands on her trim waist and looked Tory up and down. "You aren't even a lady. Trailing around after my son as his *cook*. I saw you last night. You rolled around with him in my back yard." Her voice rose. "Blood *always* tells."

"Mama, please," Tammy said, appearing by their side, looking pale and exhausted. "That's enough. There's no call to talk to Tory like that."

Mrs. Hollins' huffing sound was close to a growl. "How dare you. I raised you better than to talk to your mama that way."

Tammy flinched. "Mama, you also raised me better than to insult a guest. Tory has shown herself to be a good friend of this family, regardless of what you think. She found my son yesterday and talked him into coming home, for which she has my eternal gratitude. As for Rye, well...he's done right by me. More than I have by him, which I hope to change now."

When her voice started to shake, Tory reached for her hand and squeezed it tight.

Margaret's lips quivered before she turned on her lady-like heels and walked downstairs.

"I'm sorry if she hurt your feelings," Tammy said.

She wasn't sure when, if ever, she'd overcome the embarrassment of knowing Margaret had seen her and Rye in the backyard, but there was nothing she could do about it. "It's okay. She's pretty unhappy too, don't you think?" It was the nicest thing she could think to say, and it had the advantage of being true.

"Yes, she is," Tammy said, "and I'm finally starting to realize it. Let's go inside and listen to Rye. I've...never heard him sing in person."

A warmth spread through Tory's heart. The transformative power that forgiveness and reconciliation were having on this family awed her.

When she and Tammy entered the room, everyone looked over. Rye continued singing, and Tammy pressed a hand to her chest as her gaze locked on her brother. It was as if she were seeing him for the first time.

After a few more songs, Rye set aside his guitar and grabbed Annabelle, pulling her onto his lap. "We'll have to have another concert soon, and we'll be talking about getting you all settled in Nashville, but unfortunately, Tory and I need to go. We've got a long drive ahead of us."

She hated to leave, too, but they were going to get in pretty late.

Hampton rose and held out his hands to Tory, which she took in her own. "I hope we see each other again. You've been nothing but wonderful. Thank you, my dear."

Her eyes burned as she wondered if she would ever see them again. In a few days, she'd come to care about this family, flaws and all. "You take care of yourself, Mr. Hollins."

"Hampton, my dear," he corrected, and he squeezed her hands as he said it.

Then he placed his hand on Rye's shoulder. "Amelia Ann and I were talking this morning, and we were wondering if it would be all right if we came to see your last concert in Memphis. And we could celebrate your birthday together. It's been a while since we...have." He had to clear his throat.

It took a moment for Rye to say anything, though his Adam's apple moved. "Of course, Daddy. It would be great to have y'all there," he said in a hushed voice.

Hampton tugged Rye in for a hug. Tory felt tears gather in her eyes, and she noticed Amelia Ann dash away a tear.

"Thank you for coming," the older man said hoarsely. "Thank you for everything."

Rye nodded jerkily and turned away, only to be gathered into a fierce hug by Amelia Ann.

"I'll see you soon. I just can't believe I'm going to be living in the same town as you and can see you any time I want." She wiped away more tears when he eased back.

"Me either," he said, kissing her cheek.

Annabelle gave Rye an easy hug and laughed when he tugged on her braids. His nephew, as always, was more serious. Without moving from his place by the bed, he said, "You take care of Tory for me, Uncle Rye."

Suddenly Tory was the one dashing away a tear.

"Let's shake on it, son," Rye said without trying to add any levity to the situation.

They did, and then Rye turned to Tammy. Their embrace was brief, but both smiled shyly when they gazed at each other.

"I'll have someone contact you about packing up the house," Rye said, stepping back. "You tell them what you need."

"Great," Tammy replied softly. "I think we'll come to your concert, too."

His eyes fairly gleamed at that. "I'd like that."

Suddenly there was a gentle tug on Tory's shirt. When she knelt down, Rory was in front of her, and he engulfed her in a hug. Since he wasn't prone to shows of affection, it meant that much more.

"I'll miss you," she whispered, kissing his hair. In that moment, she prayed she'd be lucky enough to have a little boy like him some day.

When she rose, Tammy surprised her by giving her a brief hug, too. "I hope we'll see you in Memphis later this summer."

Tory swallowed thickly, and in that moment, she knew this family was going to work things out. When Rye held out his hand to her, she grasped it, and they walked downstairs together, followed by the others. When they passed the parlor, they saw Mrs. Hollins standing there at the window.

Rye paused. "Good bye, Mama."

She didn't acknowledge him, which filled Tory with sadness, but this time that sadness was for the frigid woman pushing her family away, not for Rye.

As they drove off, the family waving to him, she turned to him. "It won't take me long to pack up."

"No need. I did it for you so we could just take off," he told her.

So, they wouldn't be going back to the quiet little house. In many ways, their time together had been a break from reality. Here in Meade, she hadn't felt like his employee, and he hadn't acted like a bad-boy country singer. What was going to happen now?

"You turn off the stove?" she asked to distract herself.

"Uh...yes. Those were the best waffles I've ever tasted, by the way." His hand squeezed her knee. "But I missed you this morning."

Delight spread through her as she reached inside her bag for a book.

Suddenly she wasn't as afraid of what awaited them when they returned.

Maybe there's something wrong with me,
Even though you bring me to my knees.

I've gotta let you go.
Nothing lasts.
Don't you know?

Regrets aren't for me.
Accept me for who I am.
Or leave me be.

Doesn't mean you're not special to me.
This is what I am.

But I can't help thinking,
On a cold, quiet night.
Maybe something's wrong with me.

Rye Crenshaw's Top Ten Hit, "Something Wrong with Me"

CHAPTER 17

Getting back to the grind always sucked, but add the tabloids back into the mix, and it double sucked. Rye strode into Georgia and Clayton's bus, nodding to crew members as they called out greetings.

Georgia ended her call when she saw him. "Welcome back."

When Clayton appeared, he took a seat next to Georgia. Rye took a deep breath and held up the gossip rag in his hand. "You plant this?" It was impossible to keep the anger from his voice.

Georgia lit a cigarette. "Clay and I were just discussing that this morning, and we were about to call you. We didn't plant it, but the story about you taking Tory home to meet the family after your daddy's illness is good PR. We thought Tory might have shared it." She took a deep inhale and blew the smoke out in three rings.

Rye threw the magazine across the room. "It wasn't her." Not after everything they'd shared.

"Then who?" Clayton said.

"I don't know, but you'd better find out. Check the bus for listening devices. Hell, some reporter got access to private information about my trip, and I want to know how."

"Rye," Georgia said, rising, "you're not seeing straight. Who else could it be?"

"It's not her, I'm telling you." He wasn't going to mention everything he and Tory had gone through together in Meade, what she'd done for his family. "It might be my brother-in-law, Sterling Morrison. There's some bad blood between us, even though the reason for it would be more embarrassing for him than for me. Hire an investigator. Find out. Whoever it is, I want them punished."

Georgia rose and rested her hand on her hip. "Already done. I've been doing this type of work since before you were born. But let me make a suggestion. You need to stop sharing anything with Tory until we know for sure. Might even be good to move her off your bus."

"No." He shook his head. "I'll say it again. It's not her."

"Okay, Rye," Clayton murmured, ever the peacemaker.

"If we're clear, I need some help with another matter."

Georgia flicked ash into her butterfly ashtray. "Whatever you need, honey."

The words wouldn't come out at first. "I need you to secure off-campus housing for my sister, Amelia Ann, around Vanderbilt. She's going to law school in the fall."

Clayton's mouth dropped plumb open.

Rye's lungs burned, and suddenly the enormity of what he'd agreed to washed over him. "Then I need you to hire a designer to go to my house and...decorate a few rooms. One for a fancy Southern lady, one for a four-year-old girl, and the other for a six-year-old boy. And a play room. My sister and niece and nephew are coming to live with me."

Georgia dropped her cigarette and made a dash to pick it up before it burned the rug.

"Tammy and her kids are coming to *live* with you and Amelia Ann is going to Vandy law school?" Clayton shook his head. "I must not be hearing right."

"No, you are. I need everything in place shortly after the tour ends. And obviously, I need to have your ideas on how we're going to present it to the press. My family is going to be back in my life."

"Must have been some reconciliation," Georgia drawled, and even her stellar poker face was blown to smithereens by this news.

"It was," he only replied. "Now fill me in on what I've missed."

When he was done, he went to find Tory. She must have seen the tabloids, too.

They hadn't really talked since getting back last night. After a late rehearsal with the band, he'd returned to the bus with the hope of hashing some things out, but she was fast asleep. Since they hadn't talked about continuing their relationship when they returned from Meade, he didn't crawl into bed with her, although it had been tempting. They were back to business, but he was terrified of losing their connection.

When he stepped off the bus, he caught sight of her red shirt first. What the hell was she doing, striding across the parking lot? Panic erupted. Yeah she knew about the story if the hard clips of her steps were any indication. God, was she leaving? A cluster of fans started screaming his name from behind the barrier. He started jogging, not wanting to call out her name in case the press were around, so they could talk privately.

"Where are you going?" he asked when he caught up to her.

Her face was covered by a pair of oversized sunglasses, which she pushed up higher on her nose. He wanted to yank them off so he could see her eyes.

"I'm going to a coffee shop to work." She gestured to her laptop case. "You should go sign some autographs."

He took her arm and didn't let go. "I know you saw the tabloids, and I'm as upset as you are, but I can promise you that it didn't come from any of us."

"Would you let go of my arm?" When he did, she tugged her bag up higher on her shoulder. "Who else could it be? How am I supposed to believe that after the way you've used me for press before? It's not fair to me. And it's certainly not fair to your family. Regardless of how much trouble your image is in."

"I told you I never wanted anyone to know about the trip, so why would I do that?"

"Clayton and Georgia might have felt differently."

Clearly she had thought this out.

"No, they wouldn't go that far. Look, we have a leak, and we're going to find it, I promise."

"Who else knew besides you, me, your family, Clayton, and Georgia?" Then her mouth dropped open. "Oh, God, you thought it was me again."

She marched off.

"No, I didn't for a moment. I told Clayton and Georgia it wasn't you," he said and tugged on her arm so she stopped her forward march. "Will you come back to the bus so we can talk about this? We have an audience here." His fans had their cell phones out and were snapping pictures of him.

She shook her head. "No, not right now. I need some time to think."

He edged closer, casting a shadow over her. "Please, Tory. I don't want you to be upset."

"Too bad. I need a break. Back off right now."

For once, it didn't bother him that people were witnessing a private moment in his life. He cupped her face in his hands. She trembled, making his heart pound even faster. Didn't she see? He hadn't cared about someone this much in so long that he didn't know what to do, how to act, what to say.

"Tell me how to make this right."

She removed his hand from her face. "I don't know. Everything's been so... I just need some time."

His heart hurt, and he realized she'd become a vital part of his life. And being back with the tour hadn't changed his desire to be close to her. "I don't want it to be like this."

"Neither do I. I saw a side of you in Meade that made me hope there was more to you and hope for us. Then I saw the comments online about the story. People are finally taking your side. Georgia and Clayton have wanted this all along, so it's hard not to believe this came from your people. Right now, I'm confused... And I just need you to let me go."

Let her go? He didn't think he could do that. But she took off, his fingers only touching her fast-moving shadow, leaving him alone in the blazing sun.

It seemed trust went two ways, and right now, he was on the losing side.

***

The coffee shop was quiet, the perfect balm for Tory. She was clicking away on her laptop, working on her outline again.

"Hey there," a man said, making her look up. "Luke, remember? Lighting. We met—"

"At the bull riding," she replied, falling into an easy smile as he grinned at her. "Hi. Good to see you again."

"Looks like you're working hard. Researching recipes for Rye?" he asked.

No, and she wasn't planning on making him dinner tonight either. She needed some more time to work through her feelings. She wanted to believe him. His words had pulled at her, drawing her in just like those sincere hazel eyes. And while Georgia and Clayton had pushed boundaries before to get a good story, why would they accuse her if they'd done it themselves? Oh, what a mess! Right now, she had no idea what to believe.

"No," she replied. "I'm working on something else. You in between breaks?"

"Yes," he replied easily, taking a seat at her table. His coffee was steaming, which made her remember hers was probably cold. She'd gotten engrossed in her work, the one thing she could always count on for escape, the one thing she never had to worry about leaving her while the dear people like Rye came and went.

"So you're just back from seeing Rye's family, huh?" he said. "From the papers, it sounds like he's got a lot on his plate. He's lucky you could go with him. The whole crew's been talking about it all day. How are you feeling, hon?"

Maybe it was because he was older, but it didn't feel weird for him to call her that. It seemed like a fatherly thing to say. "I don't want to talk about it. Really." And she wouldn't, even to Myra. After the first tabloid incident, she kept their conversations superficial, not wanting to create any more problems.

Now this.

Luke patted her hand. "You poor dear. I've been around Rye for years, and he's like this incredible tornado. You can't look away from him, but sometimes he's, well...out of control."

Well, if that didn't characterize their time together, she didn't know what did. "Well, I do come from Kansas," she said, "so you'd think I'd be used to tornadoes."

"Tell that to a trailer park," Luke joked. "Listen, I need to get back, but if you want to talk about it, just call me. Let me give you my number. We all need a friend on tour, and honey, I hate to tell you this, but you look like you need one real bad."

Wasn't that ever the truth? "Thanks," she said, storing his number in her phone to be polite. He was a nice man, but she wasn't about to talk to him or anyone else about this situation.

Not after Rye had accused her of selling him out in the beginning.

"All right, Tory, you hang in there." He tipped his John Deere ball cap at her. "I'll see you around."

"Thanks, Luke," she said, and he winked before heading out.

She'd enjoyed talking with him, seeing a friendly face. She didn't know many of the people who worked for Rye, and only a few by name. Most didn't approach her, clearly unsure of what to say or how to act. And who could blame them, given how the tabloids had described her association with him?

What in the world was she doing with him?

Sipping her cold coffee, she decided their return to the tour had been a demarcation point. The time in Meade was over, and if she were smart, and she was, it would be better to cease all personal involvement with him.

Her heart broke at the thought, but she firmed her shoulders. It was for the best. Their time together was going to come to an end anyway, so why continue to be intimate with him when she'd have to say goodbye anyway?

Of course, she was already in love with him. She'd fallen for him in Meade. There was no lying to herself about that.

It would be awkward at first, going back to being friends, but it was for the best. Rye probably wouldn't mind too much. He'd been upfront about having nothing to offer her, after all, and he had more practice moving on than she did. Maybe it wouldn't be terrible.

Yeah, right. Except at night when she wanted to lie in his arms. Or at breakfast when she wanted to feel his hands settle around her waist when she was at the stove.

Okay, that so wasn't what she needed to think about right now. She dove back into her work, hoping to find consolation there.

But as usual, there was none to be found.

***

She waited until the concert started before returning to the bus, texting him out of politeness to say she wasn't up for making him supper. Fortunately, instead of pushing her, he'd only replied, *Okay*, making her feel less guilty about shirking her duties.

At bedtime, she plugged headphones into her ears, putting on some soothing Brahms, so she could convince herself she wasn't listening for his footsteps. She jerked out of sleep when she felt something on her neck, and—still unconsciously jittery from the whole mutant spider experience—she swung a hand out to slap it away.

"Whoa! Hey!" Rye called out, sitting on the side of her bed in boxers and a T-shirt, visible from the light streaming through the open door.

Tory pulled the headphones out of her ears and peeked at the clock. It was well after one in the morning. And he wasn't dressed professionally.

"That mad at me, darlin'?"

Tory backed up against the side of the bus and tugged at the covers. When his eyes dipped to her chest, her skin started to tingle. "I've told you I don't want you calling me that."

"Well, then we'll have to find another endearment. 'Tory' doesn't work for me in some situations. Like this one. I understand that you need space, but a day is all I'm okay with."

She arched a brow at that. "So I have a time limit?"

"No," he said urgently. "I just...I was worried about you. Hell, I even missed two cues tonight. I never do that."

They'd known each other long enough for her to know when he was in prime form, and like her, he clearly wasn't. His face was haggard, and the hand he ran through his hair was shaking.

"After Meade... Well, I'm not sure how you could think I'd pull a PR stunt like that, but I don't know how to prove to you I didn't." He gripped her sheet. "I thought about having you talk to Georgia or Clayton, but I know you won't believe them because they work for me."

She swallowed thickly. His beautiful hazel eyes were anxious. He was right—she'd seen a different side of him in Meade, and she *didn't* think he was capable of something like this. When her shock had worn off, she'd remembered how private he was about his family, and logic had won the day.

But it still smarted that Clayton and Georgia suspected her.

"I believe you," she said softly.

His exhale was like a wind gust, and he reached for her hand, running his thumb over her palm. "Thank you."

"But I need to tell you something else," she said and steeled her heart. "I think we should go back to just being friends."

"What?" he asked, his face falling.

"Meade was... Well, we both know there's no future, and I think...it's made things between us more complicated."

His hand left hers, and she bit her lip so it wouldn't tremble. She waited in silence for his response. "I know you're right, but...the thing is ...what happened between us in Meade. Well, I don't want to stop being with you."

"What are you saying?"

"I just..." When he met her gaze again, her heart almost exploded at the intensity she saw there. "I want to be with you—like we were—at least until you go back to school. Will you...be with me?"

She fisted her hands in the sheet. And even after all the promises she'd made herself today, it came down to this: this man, the vulnerable one she'd seen in Meade, was not to be denied. Not when he seemed to be falling for her as hard and as fast as she'd fallen for him. "All right."

"That's it?" he asked, his shock evident.

"Do you want a dissertation?" she responded, releasing her grip on the sheet. "I'm already writing one of those."

"No. I just want to hold you."

When she made room for him, he eased down beside her and caressed her cheek. "I...really care about you, Tory."

Knowing him, the words were tantamount to a declaration.

"I care about you, too," she whispered, unwilling to fully expose herself by revealing the truth—that she loved him.

"Will you come to bed with me?" he asked, ducking his head, and it was almost shocking to see shyness in him.

"Rye, we are in bed."

His mouth tipped up. "True, but my bed is bigger, and that's not what I meant."

"I know," she said, feeling shy now too.

He brought her hand to his lips and kissed it. "I didn't want to assume...or rush you after today. We can just..."

"Cuddle?" she suggested, unable to stop her smile when his ears turned red. Yes, there was no doubt. Meade had changed everything for them.

"If you want," he replied, and her smile grew. The old Rye Crenshaw would never have cuddled.

"Rye?"

"Yes?"

"Kiss me."

And he did.

They didn't make it to his bigger bed.

Oh, Elvis don't you know?
Aren't you alive somewhere in Mexico?

You had it right.
Life's tender.
Full of light.

You sang us songs.
Gave us your all.
We miss you.
Feel so alone.

Memphis still chugs to your mem-or-y.
Your legend still sensory,
Along the mighty Mississippi.

Please come back.
Teach us more.
We're students at your feet.
Eager to learn more.

Rye Crenshaw's Number One Hit, "Elvis, Come Back"

CHAPTER 18

In the following weeks, they found a neutral corner and were happy there. He performed his concerts and handled business. She cooked and worked on her dissertation and cookbook. July rolled into August and, over meals, they talked about his family coming to join him and all the preparation that entailed.

But there were some things Tory never talked about: the new bills Myra kept sending her, the fear that she'd never be able to sell her grandparents' house, and the sinking feeling that she wasn't as passionate about her graduate work as she should be. She set all her worries aside when she was in Rye's arms each night so she could experience the magical time with him, accepting that all the challenges in her life wouldn't go away, that she would just have to face them when the tour ended.

They didn't deviate from their routine, and fortunately, there were no further tabloid incidents to upset their delicate balance, although the source of the leak was still a mystery.

Her dread about the end of the tour grew with each day. They hadn't talked about it at all, except for Rye promising to show her Memphis, the final stop. Her heart felt as warm as an oven as she listened to his stories about how he'd learned to enjoy life in Memphis, which is why he always ended his tour there, celebrating his birthday the next day. Frequent trips during his college and law school days had sealed his special regard for the town. But while Beale Street had given him an appreciation for the blues, his love for Elvis had come from his daddy.

When they arrived in Memphis on a hazy August morning after driving all night from Louisville, she could see why he held it in such high regard. Memphis was a feast for the senses. The heat and humidity were as constant as they were debilitating, and the muddy Mississippi River added to the steam-like shroud that enfolded the downtown area. New buildings shared their blocks with foreclosures; sidewalks sported weed-filled cracks and flowed into fresh pavement. Dereliction was decadence's neighbor. It was a city of contrasts, with both flashy money and abject poverty living side by side.

The final concert would be the following night, and Rye's birthday was the day after, August 31. Tory was scheduled to leave the next day, since Rye would be heading down to Padre Island with some friends, another tradition at the end of his tour. They hadn't spoken about her departure other than when she'd casually mentioned that she had her ticket home. He hadn't responded.

They were staying at The Peabody Hotel, and Rye indulged her by standing by her side as the Peabody's famous ducks marched into and out of the lobby at eleven o'clock in the morning. He even suggested that they catch the show again with Rory and Annabelle when they arrived with the rest of his family, sans Mrs. Hollins, the next day. Rye had to sign a slew of autographs and pose for a dozen pictures when the guests in the lobby went crazy at the sight of him, but he claimed it was worth it to see her enjoyment.

He told her he was taking her on a personal tour of Memphis, but he had a surprise for her first. She just smiled secretly, since she was working on a surprise of her own. Because she wasn't Clayton and Georgia's favorite person, she'd called Luke to ask if there was a kitchen at FedEx Forum where she could make Rye a birthday cake. Luke had been happy to help her and had arranged for her to use it.

She was thinking about making his cake a few hours later as Rye was preparing to finally share his surprise, back from a rehearsal with the band.

"You ready, darlin'?" he asked from the bathroom.

Sitting on the bed, she couldn't contain her grin. What in the world did he have in mind?

"Ready."

When Rye walked into their bedroom, her mouth dropped open.

"What do you think? No one's gonna recognize me as an Elvis impersonator."

He smoothed a hand over a sleek black wig and struck a pose. His body was not the older Elvis. It was the hot, make-chicks-scream body out of *Jail House Rock*. He put a hand to his stomach and did that hip gyration that had made countless women swoon.

"*Oh. My. God.*" Sometimes Rye Crenshaw defied words, and this was one of those times.

"Do you like it?" His voice was sultry and low, mimicking the King.

Tory jumped up and circled him, noting how good his butt

looked in the white jumpsuit with the buckskin fringe. "You shaved your goatee," she accused. It felt odd seeing his face without it, especially with the wig and press-on sideburns.

"Part of the collateral. Elvis only went for sideburns."

His strong chin had a sexy dent, she noticed for the first time. "You are certifiable." And so sweet for doing this, she almost added.

He ran a finger down her nose, making her aware of the numerous rings on his fingers. "It's the perfect disguise. Now I can show you the city without fans stopping me every five feet."

Her throat grew tight. He was doing everything he could to keep things private between them, and it only made her love him more.

"I love it," she said, instead of *I love you.*

He leaned in to kiss her lightly on the lips. It felt weird to kiss him without his goatee, and he clearly felt the difference too, since he pulled back with a grimace.

"You're going to have to do better than that. You're my girl for the evenin'."

She laughed, hoping a little levity would ease the tension in her chest. "Please, Elvis wouldn't be seen with a girl like me. I don't have big enough breasts." Tory let her hands cup them. "Or big enough hair."

His eyes narrowed. "Don't you dare say that! You're about as perfect as they come."

So much for easing the tension in her chest. She could all but feel the clock ticking down the rest of their time together.

God, how was she ever going to leave him?

"I'm gonna show you Memphis," he said, kissing her on the lips. "Feed you BBQ from Rendezvous. Fried chicken at Gus'. Show you Beale Street."

"Sounds like an awful lot of food," she mused, and what a change of pace not to be the one cooking it.

"Honey, one of the reasons you come to Memphis is to eat. Speaking of which, have you ever had fried pickles?"

"No."

"Then you're in for a treat. They're incredible."

She stroked the side of his face. "It sounds wonderful."

Pulling her close, he ran his hand down her hair. "Good. I'll give you anything you want tonight, Tory."

Since their time together in Meade, he'd done nothing but. He bathed her in pleasure, anticipating anything she could ever want. Sat with her while she worked. Played his guitar for her and sang her requests, laughing at some of her taste in music. Soon her life would be empty again, and she couldn't bear to think about it.

"Do you have any ideas about how we're supposed to handle the heat?" she asked in an attempt to distract herself. "It's hot as Hades out there."

He led her to the door. "We'll find you a super-size hurricane. You won't notice the heat after that."

He was right. Her first raspberry-colored Hurricane did the trick. It also began a decadent evening of food crawling. They popped into all his favorite food joints, from Rendezvous to Bigfoot. The BBQ was incredible, falling away from the smoky bone with barely a bite, and the fried pickles were a strange new delight, full of tartness and crunch. By the time he led her down to Beale Street, she was clutching a full stomach. So far no one had identified him, and she'd gotten used to people greeting him as Elvis.

Beale Street was flashy and packed with people. Loud bars played competing and complimentary types of music, from blues to country to Elvis, and Rye hummed along as they went by. Electric signs cut across the hazy night sky. They passed street performers with guitars and drums. One of the men had a set of spoons that he used to create a beat against his knee. And there were men doing back flips and handsprings down the middle of the closed-off street. Police patrolled, looking bored, like there was little they hadn't seen before. Rye pulled her to a take-out window bar to order another Hurricane.

When they reached Club 152, one of his favorite haunts, he led her inside, and they wound their way to the back. Another Elvis impersonator was performing on the well-lit stage, and he gave Rye a collegial nod. She and Rye found a table in the corner, and they both sat down.

Tory took in their surroundings. The club was an open, airy space that featured a combination of brick walls and dark wood paneling. While the stage was small, it only gave more gravitas to the Elvis look-a-like in his black jumpsuit bejeweled with rhinestones. He had fake side burns like Rye's and dark, retro sunglasses. His chest hair protruded from the X stitching on his chest. A white sash was wrapped around his relatively trim waist like a Civil War soldier, and he was wearing French cuffs that trailed to six golden nugget rings on his fingers. The microphone in his hand sparkled as brightly as the disco ball above his head.

The patrons clapped along to a lively rendition of "Viva Las Vegas."

Rye ordered whiskey sours for them. She hated mixing, but tonight was special. His family was arriving in town tomorrow. It was the last time she'd have him to herself.

After another four songs, the crowd had grown quiet, and a few people left.

"Well, folks," said the man on the stage. "It seems I'm not the only Elvis on Beale Street tonight. Perhaps we can get the other guy to show us his stuff." He tipped the microphone in a challenge at Rye. "Then y'all can decide who you like better." He strutted forward, his bell bottoms swinging.

A few of the patrons gathered closer to the stage, intrigued by the prospect of a competition. Tory thought his strategy was ingenious, but she knew something he didn't: he was going to lose tonight.

Rye stood and rubbed her arm. She caught his devilish wink and smiled after him as he walked onto the stage like the star he was. There were perhaps thirty people in the audience. Little did they know that they were getting a free concert from country music mega-star Rye Crenshaw.

Rye gave a nod to the other Elvis. He'd relinquished the stage to his competitor for the moment and was sitting at the bar with a beer. Rye put the microphone to his hip and scanned the crowd— giving each person just enough attention to feel that he was really looking at them.

"Well, it seems we have a lot of good lookin' ladies in the house tonight. It makes me want to sing something special for y'all. Honey, why don't you come on up here with me?"

Since he was pointing at her, she frantically shook her head. *No freaking way.*

"Why don't you folks put your hands together for my girl? She's a bit shy. And it's her first visit to Memphis." He crooked his finger, giving her a challenging look.

That did it. She never backed down from a direct challenge. Taking a fortifying gulp of her drink, she climbed onto the stage.

"Now, that's what I'm talking about." He grabbed a silver bar stool from the back of the stage and gestured to it grandly. Tory sank into it, heat breaking across her body as the lights beat down on her.

Rye rubbed her shoulder. "So, y'all, what song do you want to hear?'

"'Love Me Tender'," a woman called out.

"Ah, one of my favorites. Ladies, I hope you'll find a man who can love you tender—just like Elvis sang it."

His deep voice took on that magical Elvis quality as he began to sing, "*Love me tender, love me sweet...*" He made eye contact with the audience and had them in thrall before turning those deep hazel eyes on her. The words made her heart burst open.

As he continued, singing about how she made him complete and he never wanted to let her go, she blinked back tears. His eyes seemed to glow under the lights, and there wasn't a hint of a smile on his face...

It was too easy to believe he meant every word.

She reminded herself that someone had requested the song, but her heart didn't care about that logic, and her throat grew thick with emotion.

He gave the song his all, managing to watch both the audience and her. A few of the women in the audience sighed, as if they were as transported as she was. Well, why wouldn't they be? He was a beautiful man crooning out a beautiful love song. People edged closer to the stage, spilling over from the bar, as Rye took the song home—and with it her expectant heart.

Applause reverberated in her ears. Rye turned to her and kissed her hand before putting the microphone close to his chiseled lips and giving a perfunctory, "Thankya very much." Bowing, he led Tory down the steps and handed the cordless microphone to the other Elvis, who looked glum, his plan having backfired quite epically.

"Can we go back to the hotel?" she asked as they left the club, the excitement of being on Beale Street gone.

"Sure thing," he replied, taking her hand.

When they arrived back in their room, she turned to him. "Make love to me, Rye."

He tossed the wig aside and tunneled his fingers into her hair. Tory surrendered, desperate for the distraction. Her mind was still playing "Love Me Tender," and her heart was still eager for more.

***

The arms clutching him were unusually desperate, and Rye felt his own rawness answer hers. He thought back to the way she'd looked under the stage's lights while he sang to her. God, she was beautiful, and it was getting harder and harder to accept that he wouldn't get to keep her.

Every moment counted. As he stripped off his clothes and hers, he treated each touch as if it were their last. He wanted their lovemaking to be slow, and he wanted to memorize her face as he made her come again and again.

When his hands covered her breasts, she traced his chest in an answering touch, and they continued to caress each other with their hands and mouths, paving a trail of desire.

He brought her to her first peak, and then licked his way up her body, igniting her all over again. His name was a hoarse cry on her lips, and in that moment, he could no longer hold back. He slipped between her legs after putting on a condom and slid slowly into her until he was fully sheathed, knowing she liked him deep. Her eyelids fluttered, and her body rose to greet him.

"Look at me," he whispered.

Their eyes met, and all his senses were attuned to her—her skin, the way her neck arched when he stroked in deep. Soon they both needed more, and he picked up the pace as they fisted their hands together. When he lowered his mouth to kiss her, she tugged on his bottom lip.

"Come with me," he urged, drawing her knees up higher.

She moaned and moved with him, lost in the sensation of them coming together. When she came, he followed her over the edge.

When he regained his senses, Rye rolled to his side and pulled her against him. "Making love with you is damn near perfect," he whispered in her ear. And it was true. He couldn't imagine wanting anyone else after her. He pushed aside the thought.

Tory pressed her face against his chest. "For me, too."

His emotions, which had been tangled since that moment in Club 152, picked up on her melancholy. "What's the matter?"

She let out a jagged breath. "Nothing."

It was a lie, but he didn't press. He didn't know what to say, so he tilted her face up, stared at her for a long moment, and then kissed her.

The gentleness and quiet passion in that kiss was mixed with something more potent. When she finally pulled away, Tory burrowed her face into his side.

Rye ran his hand up and down her arm. "About tomorrow night. As you know, my family is coming for the concert... I was hoping you might go with them."

The first and last one she'd been to was in Minneapolis.

"I wouldn't miss it," she whispered.

"I've got another surprise for you tomorrow," he rushed on. "But I promise it's not a PR thing. Will you trust me?"

A gentle smile spread across her face. "Yes, I'll trust you."

The simple words had his heart pounding, his ears ringing. "Good," he said, so grateful that they'd learned to trust each other. He knew it didn't come easily for either of them.

When her body relaxed and her breaths lengthened, Rye was still awake. She hadn't talked about how she felt about him or said anything about staying in touch. And while she'd become a vital part of his life, she had her Ph.D. to finish, and he was facing the new challenge of integrating his family into his life. The timing was bad for a long distance relationship.

And beyond that, there was the issue they'd faced since day one: he was a country singer, and she didn't like to be in the public eye. Plus, she was the marrying kind, and while he cared for her deeply, he feared he would eventually resent the idea of being tied down.

But under the lights, singing "Love Me Tender" to her, he'd felt something more powerful than he'd ever experienced before and had almost bumbled a few of the lyrics.

Letting her go would be the hardest thing he'd ever done, but like everything else in his life, he'd just have to suck it up and do it.

I met an angel in a place called Diner Heaven,
Her eyes were a shiny bottle green,
She had a smart mouth,
Perfect for me.

She's a bull-riding fiend,
And oh, what she cooks for me,
Makes me fall to my knees.
Oh baby, baby, please set me free.

She's strong as steel,
And as tough as they come,
Life's been one hard road.

But she don't quit.
Keeps ploughing on.

But I know she has to go,
We're at the end of the road,
'Cause even in the country,
Angels have to go back to the heaven that sent them.

Rye Crenshaw's untitled new song

CHAPTER 19

Seeing his family and Tory close to the stage gave Rye a jolt more powerful and heady than any normal performance adrenaline. It wasn't the wild cheers and screams he craved tonight, but the amazed look on Tory's face when he angled closer and sang directly in front of her. Rory's guarded delight. Annabelle's giggles. The expression of pride mixed with happiness in his daddy's eyes. The sight of his sisters, hand in hand.

After his opening set, he gave his band the signal. The audience quieted with the exception of periodic shouts from adoring women. "We love you, Rye," one screamed at the top of her lungs.

He gave a husky chuckle. "I love you too, darlin'." He took the stool one of his crew members brought him and sat down. "So, it's my last concert on this tour, and I couldn't be in a better city. I love you, Memphis. I really do. That's why I always end my tour here. Can't imagine anyone can top your hospitality."

More cheers and whistles punctuated the Forum. The JumboTron in the middle broadcast his serious face to his fans in the nosebleed seats. Silence descended.

"This concert is special for me. I have some people in the audience who mean a lot to me, and I'm grateful they're here." He cleared his throat, lowered his head, and caressed Old Faithful.

"I got my love for Elvis from my Daddy, so I'd like to sing you his favorite song. Seems fitting tonight. Daddy, this one's for you."

The stage lights dimmed and turned blue. When he launched into "Hound Dog," Rye saw Amelia Ann reach for Daddy's hand as the crowd started clapping and singing along. When he lowered his voice and brought the song home, Daddy nodded to him. Who would have thought it? Hampton Hollins at a country music concert? Rye had to clear his throat before starting the next set.

The concert was as special as the first one he'd ever given. Halfway through the performance, he dedicated a song to his sisters and Rory and Annabelle. While the rest of his family swayed to the music, Tammy's posture was as stiff and correct as always until Amelia Ann bumped her with her hip, causing a reluctant smile to break out across her face.

As he reached the end of his performance, his nerves kicked up again. Funny, he never felt much stage fright. But seeing Tory out there, knowing what he was about to do... Well, he was glad he hadn't eaten. He wiped his face with a towel and sat on the stool again with Old Faithful. The audience grew quiet.

He took a deep breath. "So, I've probably made more dedications in this one concert than all the others, combined, but you'll have to indulge me. I have one more. It's dedicated to a woman who came into my life recently, one of the best people I've had the pleasure of meeting in a long while."

He looked at Tory, but didn't use her name, exactly as he'd done with the rest of his family. This wasn't about PR. It was about honoring the people who were important to him.

"She's helped me figure out a lot lately. Thank you, sweetheart—for everything." He played the first chords, praying he wouldn't fumble. His fingers felt thick and awkward. It was as close to a ballad as he ever got—the lyrics poignant, the music a slow caress.

"This is a new song," he murmured. "I hope y'all like it." He hoped *she* liked it.

He kept his eyes on her while he played the melody. She pressed a hand to her mouth, and he saw Amelia Ann grab Tory's hand.

I met an angel in a place called Diner Heaven,
Her eyes were a shiny bottle green,
She had a smart mouth,
Perfect for me.

She's a bull-riding fiend,
And oh, what she cooks for me,
Makes me fall to my knees.
Oh baby, baby, please set me free.

She's strong as steel,
And as tough as they come,
Life's been one hard road.

But she don't quit.
Keeps ploughing on.

But I know she has to go,
We're at the end of the road,
'Cause even in the country,
Angels have to go back to the heaven that sent them.

When he repeated the last phrase again in a quiet whisper, he saw Tory bite her lip. Did she understand this was the only way he could tell her how he felt? His hands fell from Old Faithful.

No one made a sound in the arena. Then the audience's applause and cheers crashed over him like a final summer storm. Their eyes locked, and he saw Tory wipe away a tear.

He slapped his guitar with one hand to break the moment and signaled his band to start their final set. The crowd's response was deafening when he walked off the stage after the final song, letting the noise build before returning for the encore.

Georgia gave him a wink, and Clayton slapped him on the back when he reached them.

"I didn't think you could top the concert in Dallas in 2009, but you just did," Clayton drawled.

"Clayton's right," Belle said. "It was your best concert ever."

He stood in the wings as the lights dimmed on the stage. He couldn't take his eyes away from his family and Tory.

The curtain parted, and Tucker from the band wheeled out a cake lit with candles. A single spotlight shone down on him, his white cowboy hat as bright as an iceberg beneath it.

"You know, it's nearly midnight," he said, "and seeing as how Rye's just turned thirty, we thought we'd ask you to start the celebration. Y'all up to singing 'Happy Birthday' to him?"

Fans screamed across the stadium.

"Then let's sing it and see if we can get him back out here." His voice started the chorus, but the crowd quickly joined in, and the familiar song grew louder.

Rye walked back onto the stage, bowed when they finished the song, and blew out the candles. "Thanks, y'all. There's so many darn candles I thought we'd set this place on fire. There's nowhere better to celebrate a birthday than Memphis." He pulled on his guitar strap. "Y'all ready for some more music? How about this old favorite?"

A lone violin sounded behind him, and the crowd started clapping in time with the beat.

"It was my first hit single, so it holds a special place in my heart. I've had a few birthdays between then and now, but it's nice to remember where I started."

And hadn't he come a long way? After all this time, he was finally coming to peace with his past.

"Thank you, Memphis!" Then he began to sing.

***

The crowd was still calling for Rye's fourth encore when a crew member came to escort Tory and his family backstage. Rory put his hands over his ears as the din from the crowd continued unabated, and Tory could understand why. Even hers were ringing.

When he finally came backstage, Rye was grinning. He strode toward them, ignoring the bottle of water thrust at him and pressing Old Faithful into the chest of an assistant.

"I'm so glad you came, Daddy," he said, grabbing the man in a hug.

Hampton had looked as proud as a new papa all night and had surprised her by singing along with the crowd. He knew all of Rye's songs word for word.

"I wouldn't have missed it for the world, son," Hampton said, slapping him on the back. "I'm so proud of you."

Rye chuckled as Amelia Ann charged him, shrieking, and Annabelle grabbed a hold of his leg. After greeting them both, he moved on to Tammy, who quietly smiled and rose on tiptoes to kiss his cheek. When he reached Tory, he nodded to Rory, who was still holding her hand.

"Do you mind, son? I have a woman I need to kiss."

Rory frowned, but he let his mother pull him back.

After taking his hat off and perching it on the little boy's head, Rye cupped Tory's face in his hands. He was sweaty, his hair matted to his head. And his clean shaven face was so very dear to her.

"So, what'd you think?" he murmured.

There were too many thoughts racing through her head, especially about his song, for her to vocalize them. His words had moved her, and she knew how hard it must have been for him to write that song. But he had also made it clear that he thought their time together was at an end, and any hidden hope for a future had died.

"It was incredible," she said, making her smile bigger than usual.

He studied her for a moment, as if he knew there was something more behind her words. Then he kissed her firmly on the mouth before she could stop him. Cameras flashed and, feeling like she was on display once again, she pushed away.

Someone called his name, and when he looked behind him, Georgia waved him over. He nodded and turned back with a frown. "I have to go do some interviews. Meet some people. Y'all get some sleep. I'll see you for breakfast."

After saying goodbye to his family, he met Tory's eyes. "I'll see you soon."

Tory watched people swarm around him, sporadic flashes illuminating his face. He laughed as reporters threw questions at him. Women angled closer. One, who was showing off four inches of cleavage in a blue sequined top, wrapped an arm around his waist. Tory tried not to be jealous.

She turned away from the scene. Well, she had certainly seen Rye Crenshaw the performer tonight.

And she was having trouble reconciling him with the man she'd come to know. It had been easy to forget about his fame in the haven of the tour bus. Her heart tore as she realized he was right— they had to let each other go. Their worlds were miles apart, and she just didn't think they could bridge the gap.

Rory yawned, and Annabelle seemed to be fading fast, too, now that the adrenaline of the concert was wearing off.

"Let's go back to the hotel," she told everyone, "and you can tell me how you've been."

Just as she was doing with Rye, Tory planned to savor every minute she had with this family she had come to love.

God, but I love you.
Never imagined wanting this.
Never imagined, wanting you.

But the risk's too great.
It'll make me break.

Don't want to bleed.
Unplant the seeds.

But I won't forget.
Never wish we hadn't met.

I can't help loving you,
But I can't keep holding you.

The hurt's too big.
Don't wanna break.

I just can't break again.
I just can't break.

Rye Crenshaw's Top Ten Hit, "Don't Make Me Break"

CHAPTER 20

Rye rolled over the next morning and reached out a searching hand. When all he felt was the coolness of empty sheets, he cracked an eye open and frowned. Tory must have snuck out to do something. Damn, he'd hoped to wake up with her and have more of that birthday sex they'd had last night. He rubbed his hand over his chest where his heart throbbed. It hadn't been simple birthday sex. It had been filled with desperation and had ended with quiet caresses.

She hadn't brought up the song, and because he was feeling raw, he hadn't either. He'd always let his music speak for him, but for once he was afraid he'd made a mistake.

He levered himself up and glanced at the clock. 8 a.m.? Where would she have gone this early? He stubbed his toe on the way to the shower and swore.

Clayton was waiting for him in the bedroom when he walked out in a towel. Rye's eyebrows rose, and he didn't even bother to ask his friend how he'd gotten a key.

"You here to give me a special birthday present?" he asked.

His mouth was grim, Clayton flipped over a newspaper. "I wish I were."

The tabloid's headline had his knees going weak, a first. "Crenshaw Pays One Million for Sister's Divorce."

Clayton handed him the paper. "It provides details about your silver spoon upbringing, your estrangement from your family, and your recent visit to Meade. Everything."

Oh Jesus, he thought. This was going to kill his family. They were going to bear the brunt of the ridicule, especially Tammy. The betrayal burned like peroxide on a wound.

"Dammit!" He scanned the article. Clayton was right. It was all there. The most intimate details of his past and his visit to Meade.

"It was written by the same reporter who broke the story when we were in Oklahoma City. Georgia and I are meeting with the investigator right after I finish with you to go over the information we have again. But I have to warn you, Rye, there aren't too many people who knew about this besides your family, Mama, me, and Tory, and so far nothing has popped on your former brother-in-law. Besides, these details would be pretty embarrassing to him, don't you think?"

Rye fisted his hands by his side, reeling from the news.

"And of course the bank employees would know, but we doubt the leak came from there," he continued. Then Clayton's phone burst into a rousing rendition of "The Devil Went Down to Georgia."

He held up a hand, and Rye waited, his mind swirling with the news. This couldn't be happening.

When Clayton snapped the phone shut, he took a deep breath before talking. "That was Mama. We had people reexamine the background checks on the crew and get confirmation on anyone who had a break in employment."

"What did they find?"

"One of the lighting techs, a Luke Mardel, was out of work for a while. He's kept his nose clean, but our investigator called in a favor at the IRS and discovered that he worked for a tabloid about ten years ago. We didn't catch it because we don't go far enough back with the tax records. Mama and someone from security just tried to corner him in the breakfast room, but he slipped away when he saw her coming. When they went through his room, they found his phone charging and... Rye, I don't know how to tell you this, but Tory called him yesterday."

The news was worse than a sucker punch. Why would she know a lighting tech? Least of all call one? The hammer came down on his heart and shattered it. "It has to be a mistake."

"Why would she call him, Rye? And right before the tabloid goes to press with this story! What possible explanation could she have?"

"I don't know." He pressed his hand to his pounding forehead.

"Has she mentioned being friends with him?"

"No, dammit, she hasn't!" *And why would she if she's guilty?* a dark whisper asked.

"Rye I know you don't want to believe—"

"Maybe he was using her the same way that reporter manipulated Myra?" Tory cared about him. She adored his family. She wouldn't do this. The evidence didn't matter.

"Maybe." But he could tell Clayton didn't believe it.

Rye turned around and walked to the window, and all he could see was Tory's smile, all he could feel was her comforting touch. "It can't be true," he muttered, staring across the hazy city.

"You're being blind about this, Rye."

"Don't tell me that!" he shouted. Did Clayton not realize that his accusations were tearing him apart? "I didn't want to dredge up the past before, but don't let your own trust issues sour you here. I've forgotten all about that undercover reporter sleeping with you and pumping you for information about me."

Clayton slapped his hat against his knee, his mouth twisting. "Well, at least I found her out before I told her anything."

Amanda Grant had been an ambitious reporter for a gossip rag in Nashville, and she'd set an enticing lure for Clayton with the intention of learning dirty secrets about country singing's newest star. Clayton had fallen for her hard, Rye knew, and had felt betrayed when he'd discovered it was a set up, even if she claimed to have developed feelings for him. Now his friend kept all his relationships simple and short-term. And he didn't date professional women with any ambition.

"It wasn't your fault, Clay," Rye said softly.

"Leave it. Back to the matter at hand. Has Tory's money situation improved?" Clayton asked.

He ran his hands through his hair, the hurt searing through him. Since she never talked about it, he didn't know. "Why wouldn't she have come to me if she needed the money so bad?" he cried. He had plenty.

Clayton slapped his hat against his thigh. "I don't know, but we'll figure it out. We need to find her and question her."

He suddenly had a thought and rushed to their walk-in closet. Her clothes were still hanging next to his, her suitcase open. "She didn't leave." Didn't that mean something?

"She doesn't know we're...looking into her." He was acting like her guilt was certain. "Call her."

He picked up his phone, and when she didn't answer, he wanted to punch a hole in the wall.

Clayton just shook his head. "We have people looking for her."

"Call them off," he said, something new burning in his gut. "She's coming back. I'll handle her myself. And keep looking into other suspects. Sterling, the bank people."

Anybody.

Anybody but Tory.

His friend studied him for a moment. "Okay, Rye. Look, this is a shit storm," Clayton continued. "You need to tell your family, and we'll make arrangements to keep them from the press. I need to get back to Mama so we can figure out a strategy. Do you want to cancel your party tonight?"

He reached out and caressed Tory's red top, which was still lying on the bed. Party? That's right. It was his birthday. What a way to welcome in a new decade. "No, everyone's in town, including Rhett and Abbie. Let's move it to a secret location. Keep it low-key and closed to the press. No pictures."

He heard Clayton's sigh. "I'm sorry, Rye. Happy birthday."

Yeah, happy fucking birthday.

***

When Rye arrived at Tammy's suite, the family's home base since Amelia Ann and Daddy were sharing a connecting suite, they sent the kids into her bedroom to watch a movie. Tammy knew something was wrong immediately. And then he told them about the tabloid story, and she couldn't stop shaking. Daddy assured her it would be all right, even though his pale complexion told another story. Amelia Ann was quietly crying.

"What are we going to do?" Tammy asked, her eyes searching her brother's.

Rye had been pacing, but he rushed over and placed a comforting hand on her shoulder. "My people are working on it. You have to trust them to do their job."

He sounded like he was trying to convince himself.

Tammy bit her lip when it quivered. "Rye, you don't think Mama would do this, do you? She hates me now."

Daddy pulled her into a hug. "No, honey, she would never do something like this. And she doesn't hate you."

"Mama can't abide airing the family's dirty laundry," Rye said.

"And Sterling has way too much pride, so I don't think it could be him," she said. If there were one thing she knew about him, it was how much he valued his image.

"I still asked Clayton to have the investigator look at him, just in case," Rye said, and hearing that, Tammy clenched her hands.

Amelia Ann put an arm around her waist, and the touch was a small comfort in the sea of agony. "Maybe someone in the bank leaked it. It's a pretty juicy story."

Rye only shook his head. "They wouldn't know the rest of it. About the family."

"Someone from Sterling and Tammy's bank might," her sister added. "They could have put two and two together."

"Perhaps," Rye growled.

Tammy studied him. He knew something. She saw despair beneath the anger in his red face—after all the sadness she'd experienced in her own life, she knew how to spot it.

"I guess it's a good thing we're moving to Nashville, right?" she tried to joke.

Rye pulled her into a hug. "That's right. Besides, who wouldn't be impressed by a woman who's worth a million dollars?"

Who knew her brother could paint a silver lining? Her eyes burned. But she wasn't worth it. She'd only been sold.

"It's gonna be all right," Rye said, rocking her back and forth. "You're not alone now."

And despite the huge fear that took her breath away, she realized it was true.

My Grandma made a lot of cakes, but my favorite was her Lady Baltimore—an old school, spongy white cake that you don't see too much anymore. Maybe it was the name, which reminded me I was special, but I always chose it for my birthday. She'd frost it with a mouth-watering buttercream frosting in the colors I liked best, adding cabbage roses in the corners. Other times, I'd select a "shape" cake, like an elephant or a horse, and she'd cut the cake into pieces and reassemble it, transforming a normal cake into a magical creation. By the time the cake was punctured with candles, it was a work of art. And while you were sad to see the magical cake disappear, you never thought twice about eating it. With one bite, it hooked you.

Lady Baltimore Cake

¾ cup butter
2 cups sugar
3 cups sifted cake flour
3 tsp. baking powder
½ tsp. salt
½ cup milk
½ cup water
1 tsp. vanilla
6 egg whites

Sift the cake flour with the salt and baking powder. Cream the butter and sugar. Whip the egg whites to stiff. Combine milk and water with vanilla. Mix half the flour mixture and milk/water mixture into the creamed butter and sugar. Stir. Repeat the process. When blended, gently add the egg whites in batches until thoroughly mixed. Pour into a buttered and floured pan. Bake 25 minutes at 350 degrees.

Tory Simmons' Simmering Family Cookbook

CHAPTER 21

When she didn't find Rye in their plush celebrity suite, Tory knocked on the door of the suite where Tammy and the kids were staying. Her clothes were slightly damp from spending the morning in the stuffy kitchen at The Forum baking Rye's cake, and she checked her arms to make sure there wasn't flour anywhere while she waited.

Rye opened the door, and his face was so tense she instantly asked, "What happened?"

Amelia Ann rushed forward and filled her in on the whole messy situation. Her heart started pounding in her ears.

Oh my God, she thought, watching Rye's face. Gone was the man who'd lingered over her the night before, driving her to passion and then cradling her so tenderly in his arms. His mouth grim, he stared at her with anger and suspicion in his eyes.

He blamed her. *Again*. After all they'd been through. Shock made her shiver, and the pain of his mistrust was like a spear in her gut.

"That's horrible," she whispered back to Amelia Ann, striving for composure. "I'm so sorry."

They walked into the main room of the suite, where Mr. Hollins and Tammy welcomed her with hugs. Out of the corner of her eye, she spotted Rory and Annabelle sitting on the floor in Tammy's bedroom in front of the TV.

"So, where have you been, darlin'?" Rye drawled.

The petty endearment was like a slap. "I was out getting your birthday present."

"*This early*? Where were you really?" he growled, grabbing her arm.

"Rye." She flinched and tried to pull away. His grip wasn't strong, but the intensity of his anger made her shake.

Suddenly Rory heaved himself at Rye and swung a fist at him. "Don't hurt her!" he cried. Tory's throat closed as the little boy started whaling on Rye.

"Rory!" Tammy cried out, lurching forward to stop him.

The boy's eyes were wild. "You leave her alone."

Rye grabbed ahold of Rory's arms. "Son, it's okay," he said, his voice gentle now. "I wasn't going to hurt her."

The boy's labored breathing punctuated the silence. "You grabbed her arm like Daddy does to Mama when he makes her cry!"

Oh no, Tory thought. Not that. But Tammy was shaking so hard her heel was tapping the floor, and her reaction was all the verification that was needed.

Hampton staggered back into a chair, and Amelia Ann's gasp was audible.

Holding his hands up, Rye said, "I wouldn't hurt her like that, Rory. I promise."

Everyone seemed to have frozen in place, so Tory crouched down in front of Rory. "I'm okay. He didn't hurt me." She pulled him to her and held his trembling body in a tight embrace. It wasn't enough. She picked him up even though he was heavy, and he wrapped his arms around her neck. "There now. It's all right."

Rye's jaw ticked as he watched the scene.

Tammy picked up Annabelle, who had followed her brother into the main room. "Excuse us," she muttered, disappearing into her bedroom.

Amelia Ann followed them, brushing away tears.

"Why don't you go on with your mama?" Tory said to Rory. "It'll make her happy."

When he finally nodded, she lowered him to his feet and kissed his cheek. "Thanks for looking out for me, sweetheart. I'll see you later."

He stared at Rye with narrowed eyes before following the others.

Hampton stood and walked over to Rye, gripping his son's shoulder. "It's okay, son," he said, his voice shaking. "We'll make it right somehow."

Rye just shook his head. "My God, Daddy. Thank God we've gotten them away from him."

"Tory, I'm going to excuse myself," Hampton said, looking ten years older.

Her heart was pounding in painful beats and she watched as Rye headed for the door.

"I have to get out of here too," he muttered.

Tory stopped him in the entryway. "So you aren't even going to ask me? It's written all over your face. I was out baking you a birthday cake just now, if you really want to know! It was going to be a surprise. But go ahead... I want you to ask me. I *want* you to say the words to my face."

His face went from white to green, and he leaned a hand on the doorframe. "Did you sell that article to the tabloid?"

"No. I would *never* do that! How could you even think it?" she asked, wrapping her arms around her middle.

"The lighting guy you called yesterday before the story broke?"

Her mouth parted, and dread stole over her. "Luke?"

"*Luke*, how quaint. Well, your friend used to work for a tabloid, and he took off when Georgia tried to talk to him, so given your call—"

"But Luke's one of the nicest—"

"So you didn't know he was a reporter?" he said, his eyes boring into hers.

"No, of course not," she protested.

"Then why did you call him?" he shouted.

"I asked him to help me find a kitchen where I could bake your birthday cake," she answered, breathing shallowly now in the face of his rage.

"Why didn't you just bake it on the bus?"

"I was afraid you might swing by. You do have most of your things on the bus, and I wanted it to be a complete surprise." Her voice trailed off when his expression remained thunderous.

So, he actually believed she'd done it...

"Did you tell him things in confidence because he was...nice or because he paid you?" he scoffed.

So, he'd already pronounced her guilty in his mind, but he was hoping she'd betrayed him unintentionally?

"I told him nothing. I haven't even told Myra anything after the first incident, and do you know how that feels? Being so isolated and alone?"

Lowering his eyes, he said, "Yes, I do."

"Rye—"

"Tory, look at the evidence. The first story hit right when we got back from Meade, and this one contains information only a few people know. Are you sure you're telling me everything? Are you sure you didn't give Luke any details?"

Her lip started to tremble. "How could you believe I would ever hurt you or your family like that?"

"Maybe it was an accident or maybe you need the money," he said flatly. "You haven't said anything about that lately..."

"Because it's my problem!" Taking a deep breath, she looked

him in the eye. "Yes, I need money, but I would *never* earn it that way. Never! You might as well suggest that I'd go out and hook for it."

"Goddammit! Do you think I don't want to believe you? But I can't this time. I just...can't." Something flickered in his eyes before his expression went blank. "Perhaps it's a good thing you're leaving tomorrow. Go ahead and say goodbye to my family because it's the last time you're ever having contact with them. I just can't risk it now. And Clayton will arrange for you to have another room until you leave."

The door clicked as he let himself out. Tory wrapped her arms around herself, wanting to curl into a ball and cry her heart out. For herself, for all of them.

After all of the pain she'd been through, this was one wound she was afraid would never heal.

***

Rye spent the afternoon in Clayton's suite, going over the information that had been gathered by Georgia, Clayton, and the investigator, only pausing once to talk to his daddy about Tammy and the kids. Hampton had actually cried, which had only made Rye feel more helpless. None of them had realized what a monster Sterling was.

When the investigator confirmed that Tory had indeed made him a birthday cake at the Forum, Rye downed two shots of bourbon, hoping it would ease the pain. It didn't prove she hadn't given Luke the information, but at least she'd been telling the truth about something.

No one had found a connection between the lighting tech and the tabloid that had reported the story, and the investigator said it would take time. When he suggested interviewing Tory, Rye roundly refused. She might have been the leak, but he couldn't bear to have her interrogated.

He just wanted her out of his life.

Clayton arranged for Tory to have another room like he'd asked, and when it came time to change before his birthday party, Rye asked Clayton to get his clothes for him. He didn't want to run into Tory if she hadn't finished packing.

He trudged up to his family's suite for dinner before the main event. He didn't want to hurt them by telling them Tory might have been behind the leak, so when they asked about her, he told them she wasn't feeling well. He could tell no one believed him.

Rory glared at him over room service, and everyone's nerves

were strained—even his always sunny niece looked tense. When he rose to leave for a quick meeting about the information leak, no one pressed to attend his party later that night. None of them was in a partying mood.

When he caught sight of himself in the mirror in the hallway beside the suite of his lawyer, long-time friend, and sometimes songwriter, John Parker McGuiness, he sighed. Christ, he looked like ass, like he'd spent the night puking up drink like a college student, and there was a crease in his forehead from too much tension. Good thing he'd been promised there would be no pictures tonight.

He knocked on the door and tapped his fingers on the doorframe as he waited for his friend to answer. As soon as it opened, he swept through it and headed straight for the bar.

"About time you arrived, J.P." he growled as he poured himself another drink, hoping it would numb his pain.

Tory had somehow betrayed him, and he wanted to tear the whole room apart, the whole world.

"It's good to see you too, Rye," J.P. settled himself on the couch and crossed his arms. "I'm sorry for everything that's happened. I know it's hit you and your family hard."

Leave it to J.P. to make a comment like that. He'd always been the softy of their Vandy trio.

"I've been hard at work since Georgia called me this morning," he said. "I thought you'd want to know that I was able to locate the lighting tech."

"How?" he asked.

"I called his daughter and said we wanted to pay him for information."

Rye downed his bourbon, still standing in front of the bar. Yeah, the investigator wouldn't have that kind of power.

"And?" he said.

"He called me back, and after a little game of sticks and carrots, he confessed that though he tried, he never found enough information about you to share with his old employer. Said Tory was tight-lipped and one of the sweetest people he'd ever met."

Rye had to grab hold of the bar. She hadn't done it. The relief was intense. After hours of not being able to take in a full dose of air, he gulped a couple deep breaths. And then a couple more.

"He said he felt bad about it all and wanted me to pass his regrets along to her," J.P. continued. "Seems he'd gotten in deep with some gambling debts and was trying to dig his way out."

Rye sank onto the couch beside him. "Jesus," he said as the

relief spread through him from top to toe, making him light-headed.

"No need to take the Lord's name in vain," J.P. said. "I also looked into the local bankers who helped transfer the money to Sterling's private account. The leak was definitely not from their end. I haven't dealt with your bank yet, but I doubt they're involved."

His body suddenly as heavy as lead, Rye sank back into the cushions. "I can't believe this," he said. "Any of it." And his mind spun back to Tory.

All his years of mistrust, of being made to feel wanting by his mother, of being used by the women in his life had risen up inside him, and he'd eviscerated her.

"I know this has cut you deep, but you need to keep your head here," J.P. said. "We've got a major issue, Rye. But I have to say that I'm glad it's not your cook—for your sake. Clayton told me he's never seen you like this with a woman."

He lowered his head into his hands. "I hurt her, J.P. When I thought she'd done this, I was so angry..."

And a little boy had stepped up to defend her. Jesus, he was ashamed of that.

His friend rested his hand on his shoulder for a moment, as much male bonding as either of them would allow. "That's natural, and you'll just have to make amends. Look, we need to get you to the party now, or Clayton will have my head."

Going to a party was the last thing he wanted to do. He wanted to find Tory, and he dug out his phone and called her. It went straight to voicemail, and he left her a brief message to call him.

"Let's get this over with then and hope to hell Clayton managed to keep the press out."

"You can count on him," J.P. said.

Yeah, he could. They might lock horns every once in a while, but he knew Clayton had his back.

"Rye, I've also looked at your sister's divorce like you asked to make sure your daddy handled everything appropriately. There won't be a problem."

Rye's hands clenched into fists. "Well, there's gonna be. I think he hit her some." He was still enraged about it.

J.P. turned from his easy-going friend to the ruthless lawyer Rye knew him to be in about a second. "No man should hit a woman."

"No," Rye growled. "I want his blood."

"You'll need to talk to your sister and see what she wants to do. Domestic abuse can be hard to prove, and it could get dirty quick.

Rye, you can't let this be about you. It has to be about her and the kids."

The control he'd been trying to keep a leash on all day finally snapped. "Like I don't fucking know that? They're moving in with me, aren't they?"

J.P. cleared his throat. "It's a big step. You do realize you'll have to make some changes to your current lifestyle, right?"

"I do."

As they walked to the elevator, all he could think about was finding Tory and saying he was sorry, but this time, he didn't think she'd listen. He might have lost her good opinion forever.

"Come on, Rye," J.P. said, pulling him along. "Man, don't you ever get tired of wearing tight jeans?"

His friend's playful sneer snapped him out of his misery a moment. "Christ, I'm glad you're here."

J.P. gave his back a good pounding. "Happy Birthday, Rye."

If only.

All you smokin' hot ladies,
Let me tell ya something about myself,
I'm not that kind of guy,
The one to put stars in your eyes.

I'm not into settlin' down,
So please don't give me that frown,
Oh baby, baby, baby.

So kick up your feet,
Have a longneck with me.
Let me give you what you need.

But it's not gonna last.
I'm not that kind of a man.
So don't give me the look.
It's as old as the good ol' book.

For the long haul, I just can't give ya what you need.
So don't expect too much of me.

Rye Crenshaw's Number One Hit, "Man of Low Expectations"

CHAPTER 22

Rye awoke with a punishing hangover. No one had been able to find Tory last night, and he'd given up calling her phone. This morning, Clayton had persuaded the hotel staff to let him accompany them to her room after she didn't answer the door. The bed hadn't been slept in. All her clothes were gone from his suite and the bus, and the fear that she might have left without a word left a bitter taste in his mouth.

The desolation was too much, and it took serious effort to clean up and go to his family's suite to spend time with them since they were leaving today. He ran a hand through his damp hair as he walked down the hallway, and then knocked on the door.

His heart sputtered when Tory opened it. Her green shirt brought out the color in her eyes, but he noticed there were dark circles around them.

"What are you doing here?" he asked in total shock. She hadn't left.

"Hello, Rye," she said calmly. "I wanted to talk to you."

"Good. I wanted to talk to you too."

"Yes, I heard your voicemail, but I figured I'd rather have this conversation in person." And she took a deep breath.

"Where is everyone?" he asked as she stepped back to let him in, wondering why she wasn't taking a swing at him.

"They'll be back in a few hours." She sat down in a chair and reached for a water bottle with a shaking hand.

Rye stayed where he was, fiddling with his belt loop. He braced himself for the ass-kicking he deserved. "I thought you'd left."

She turned the water bottle over in her hands. "The thought did cross my mind."

"Where were you last night?" he asked.

"Amelia Ann let me stay with her. I needed...some time."

Yeah, he'd never thought to check here, not after he'd forbidden her from seeing his family. Jesus, the very thought of his ugly words made him ill. "Tory, I owe you an apology, and there just aren't enough ways to say it. Luke said you didn't do anything and—"

"I'm glad," she exhaled forcibly. "I was afraid...Well, no matter now. I didn't stay behind to talk about that. I stayed to talk about your family. I...decided there was something you need to hear, and that I might be the only person willing to say it."

Dread swept across his belly, and he waited in silence.

"Rye, Tammy, Rory, and Annabelle are moving in with you shortly. Do you *really* know what you're getting yourself into?"

This is what she wanted to talk about? "Look, it'll be fine. What I really want to talk about is us... I need you to understand how sorry I am."

She held her hands out. "Well, I don't. There's nothing left to say. You can't trust me. Ever. And the truth is you warned me about that a long time ago. I'm leaving today, but you have some very fragile people coming into your life, and I'm worried about them. Do you understand that you can't have any more crazy parties at your house? Can't have women running in and out of hot tubs naked? Rye, I suspect Tammy has been physically abused. And her husband certainly verbally abused her."

His eyes shot to hers, and the anger he felt over what had happened to his sister coursed through him again. "I know that, dammit."

She closed her eyes for a moment, as if composing herself. "I don't know about the kids, but you'll have to find out. They're *children*, Rye. And whatever happened, they need a safe, loving family." She wiped away a stray tear. "The man I thought I met in Meade can give them that, but he needs to show up now. If he doesn't, I'm afraid you're all going to get hurt even more."

Like he'd hurt her.

"Rye, your family needs you to be stable, dependable. Right now, you're caught between the man you used to be and the man you started becoming in Meade. The Rye Crenshaw I first met would never have invited his family to live with him."

Rye felt like Memphis' muggy haze had descended upon him. "But he would have accused you of selling him out."

"Yes," she said and walked toward him. "Don't you see? You're somewhere in between Rye Hollins and Rye Crenshaw. And I'm afraid that if you don't admit that, you'll never be happy or able to truly trust and give to the people around you."

Her words were making his heart crack open like an old sidewalk. "How can I make things right between us? Make up for what I've done?"

"You can't. That kind of mistrust isn't something I'm able to forget. Perhaps if it had only happened once, but..." She pressed her lips together.

He hung his head in silence, wishing he could just yank her into his arms and close the gap between them, but he knew that was impossible. "I'm grateful for everything you've done for us, Tory."

"I don't want your gratitude, Rye. I want you to stop selling yourself short. You're more than some bad-boy country singer. The problem is, you're beginning to realize it, but you don't know what to do about it yet."

Her insights were too sharp, and they cut him into ribbons. Didn't he already know he'd failed her? "Please don't say anymore."

"I've said what I had to say, so I'll be going now." She looked at her watch. "My plane leaves soon."

His eyes darted to the clock on the wall. He realized she'd never told him her flight time. God, there was so much she hadn't told him. About how much money she still owed. About what she was planning on doing when she left him. He pressed his hands to his temples. Christ, he didn't need a hangover making him fumble, not at a time like this.

"I wish you and your family well, Rye."

"You're wishing me well?" His heart pounded in time with his head.

"Yes, of course I am. Isn't that what you usually say when things reach their natural end?" She picked up her purse.

Her calm demeanor made him doubt everything they'd shared. Deep down, he had been sure that she loved him—that they maybe loved each other—but the way she was acting...

She picked up her suitcase, and he automatically reached for it, the desire to stop her and help her dueling inside him.

"No, I've got it."

Her brush-off sent him into a panic. "Come to Padre Island with me, Tory. Let me make this up to you. Don't just leave like this. I...care about you."

"I can't. This time you hurt me too much." She ran her eyes over his face as if to memorize what she saw there. "You asked me to sing for you once, and since I didn't get a chance to...*Happy birthday to you*," she sang softly, and wasn't it a bitter pill that her voice was beautiful, just like he'd guessed it would be. Her voice broke when it crested over his name, but she finished the song, her eyes shining with tears.

It had never happened to him before, but he was sure his lip trembled.

"Goodbye, Rye."

When the door closed behind her, he stared at it for a long moment before finally slamming his fist into it.

When he headed back to his suite and entered the sitting room, a birthday cake was waiting for him there. He approached it wearily, the three layers of white frosting giving him pause. Though elegantly decorated, it seemed almost too simple to be from one of the gourmet bakeries in Memphis. And then he spotted the cake's centerpiece—a plastic Elvis figure in a white jump suit.

His breath rushed out, and he knew in that moment it was the cake Tory had baked for him as his surprise.

There was a cake knife and server, and a plate beside it. As he drew closer, he stumbled. It smelled like her, and he knew it would taste like her too.

There was no fighting the temptation of eating the final thing she'd cooked for him. It lured him like a siren. He forked a morsel, not bothering to cut a piece. The frosting hit his mouth first and then the spongy, white cake knocked his taste buds out of the ballpark. He grabbed a napkin and gagged, unable to force it down. It tasted like it was mixed with the hemlock of broken promises and bruised hearts. As Tory's face swam in his mind, he put a hand out and lowered himself slowly into a nearby chair, sick beyond record.

She was truly gone.

Why did he fear he'd never be the same?

***

The plane ride was terrible. All Tory could think about was Rye's betrayal. Well, what had she been expecting? This was real life—and fairy tales didn't happen to girls like her. Beastly country singers didn't suddenly turn into nice guys. Cooks and servant girls didn't become princesses.

Hadn't she been alone for a while now? You'd think she would have learned from it.

Then she thought of Rory, how he'd told her she wasn't alone anymore, that *he* would be her family, and she had to reach for a tissue to dab away her tears.

By the time Tory made it home via the Super Shuttle—she'd told Myra not to pick her up—her travel Kleenex had run out. She hauled her suitcase into the empty house, and wrinkled her nose at the stuffy smell. Sighing, she carted her baggage to her bedroom.

After taking a shower, she poured herself a glass of wine and settled onto the couch. When she heard the knock on the door, she trudged over to answer it on wooden legs. Myra's smile fell when she opened it.

"Oh, honey," she murmured and opened her arms.

Tory pressed her face into the other woman's shoulder and cried. Myra held her tight and led her inside after a few minutes.

"Okay, now, come on and tell me," she said, patting the place on the couch beside her.

Tory told her everything, not caring about confidentiality anymore. Myra's eyes shone bright with tears a couple of times, but she didn't let herself cry. She rubbed her hand up and down Tory's arm as if to warm her.

"So, he's a troubled and confused man, and he hurt you terribly," she murmured.

Tory leaned against her. "Yes, and I knew it—except there was more to him, Myra. So much more. And then he…"

Myra made a tsking noise with her tongue. "We'll have to hope and pray he comes around then—for himself and for his family. And maybe even for you."

"No, not when everything we shared couldn't balance his inability to trust."

Myra grabbed her hand and squeezed. "Tory, something arrived in the mail a few days ago. I decided to wait to tell you because I knew you were coming home soon. Now seems like the perfect time." The thick manila envelope she drew out of her purse made Tory's heart race.

She tore it open and sped through the letter, pulling out her advance check. "Oh, my God! My grant from Fulbright came through. I'm going to Africa," she said.

For four months. The timing couldn't be better, and since all of her expenses would be covered, it would help her financial situation.

"You can rent the house while you're away," Myra said. "Maybe some student hasn't found housing yet or something fell through. I'll keep looking after the bills, but you'll have to leave your checkbook this time. I don't think you'll have a phone where you're going."

No, she'd be living in a tent, without any air conditioner or running water in sight.

"Tory, don't lose faith. I know this thing with Rye has hurt you, but your heart will heal. There's still a man out there for you, I promise." Myra's wink was saucy. "Maybe you'll even find him in Africa like Meryl did in *Out of Africa*."

"Yeah, and she got syphilis and went bankrupt."

"Good point. Let's stick to a better version."

As Myra continued to chatter on cheerily, Tory focused on steering herself away from the past, trying desperately to erase one thought: how was she supposed to give her heart to someone else when it belonged to Rye?

***

A week later, she was packing, trying not to think about Rye and his sisters in the house in Dare River. He'd spun a magical picture of his home, so much so that Tory could practically see the way the sunlight turned the river into diamonds when he took his fishing pole down there to catch trout or catfish.

Keeping her promise to Rory had been hard, but she'd told the little boy she would keep in touch. He'd written down Tammy's phone number for her in a purple magic marker, and a few days ago, she'd dialed it into her phone. After exchanging empty pleasantries with Tammy, Tory had talked to Rory about her trip and all the animals she'd see in Kenya.

She had a good cry after saying goodbye. It seemed to be happening as regularly as clock-work lately. Part of her hoped Rory would forget her. Calling him was too hard because of the continued link to Rye, especially since the little boy would soon be living with him.

There was more packing to do, so she threw another pair of shoes in her suitcase. She was almost done when the phone rang.

"Hello," she answered.

"Tory, it's Connie Perkins. I know you're trying to rent the house, but I think my news will change your mind."

A few students had come to look at the house, but no one had called her back yet. "*Okay.*"

"Oh, Tory, it's simply the most incredible news." Her voice bubbled like candy before it cooled. "I've just received an incredible offer on the house. And you won't believe who it's from. Rye Crenshaw! Those media reports about you two getting cozy must be true after all."

Her hand fumbled the phone. He'd made an offer on her house! *Why*?

"His manager, Georgia Chandler, just sent in their offer today, and it's twenty thousand more than the asking price as a bonus for you. Can you believe it? Plus, he wants to sign it back over to you. You'll be free and clear of the mortgage, but you'll still have a place to live! Oh, Tory it's simply an answer to prayer. I've heard about celebrities doing things like this, but I never thought I'd play a part."

Anger burned through her. What the hell did he think she was?

Some mistress he could pay off? If it was his way of assuaging his guilt, it wasn't enough. Especially when he hadn't even bothered to make the call himself.

"I just need to pop by with the papers. Is today good? I know you're leaving soon."

Even though it would make her life harder, she knew what she had to do. She'd feel guilty taking his money, and it wouldn't change what had happened between them.

"Tell him no," she said flatly.

Connie's chuckling broke off. "What'd you say?"

"I said, I want you to tell him no, Connie."

"But Tory—"

"I'll find someone to rent it for the semester." And she prayed she was right. "You can put it back on the market when I return around Christmas."

There was a quiet pause. "Tory, you don't seem to understand. Once he signs it back to you, it's yours. You can still rent it out like you planned. In fact that's wise. Give you some extra income."

"Connie, please understand." She took a breath, trying to keep the tremor out of her voice. "I'm not selling this house to Rye Crenshaw. Please tell him we've rejected the offer."

"Tory, I don't know what happened between you two, but you're not thinking right," she continued. "This is your best chance. You know how old that house is, what we're up against in this market."

Tory looked at the ceiling, at the small lines in the plaster like old wrinkles. "I know, Connie, but please don't question me on this. Just tell him no."

"All right, dear, if that's what you want."

"I have to go, Connie." She clicked off and rolled into a ball on the bed, tears falling freely now.

Thank God, she was leaving tomorrow.

***

When Georgia called him and told him Tory had refused his offer on the house, Rye reached for the bottle of Johnnie Walker that hadn't been out of reach since he last saw her. The ocean thundered and cracked against the beach in Padre Island, and he just wanted to punch at it with his fists. Why wouldn't she let him do this? Goddammit, he felt guilty about how he'd treated her, and he hadn't been able to stop worrying about her financial situation.

J.P. looked up from his James Patterson novel, and his long-time friend, poker champion Rhett Butler Blaylock, glanced over with a frown.

"What?" Rhett said. "You look like you're about ready to start another bender."

The shot he poured went down easy. "Tory refused my offer."

J.P. grabbed the bottle away from him when he made another move for it.

"All this drinking's dulled your reflexes," Rhett said. He'd started to act like a mother hen since getting hitched to Abbie Maven. Usually they partied wild when they were together, but not anymore.

"Seems to me this girl has character," J.P. said. "Aren't you going to sober up soon? We leave tomorrow, and traveling with a hangover is hell. Not to mention that your family will be arriving in Dare River in a couple days."

"When did you turn into my fucking babysitter?" he snarled. Since losing Tory, he'd been striking out at pretty much anything that moved.

J.P. stretched back. "Since I lost the coin toss with Clayton, and he bowed out this year, leaving you to Rhett and me."

Rhett tipped his hand to the cowboy hat he wore. They all had on swimming trunks and cowboy hats.

"You don't need any more incidents," Rhett said. "Let me see what the chef cooked up today. If we can't stop you from drinking like a fish, at least we can get you to eat."

J.P. had hired a private chef since everyone who knew Rye knew about his love for good food, but he couldn't even stand the smell of food right now. It reminded him of her, and the fact that she'd never cook for him again.

He was pathetic, acting like a girl, but he didn't know what to do about it.

"You should call her, you know," Rhett said. "Explain why you wanted to buy her the house. How is she supposed to know what to think of that?"

When J.P. only nodded in agreement, Rye heaved himself out of the chaise and threw himself into the hammock strung up between two palm trees. It swung madly, and he had to throw his hand to the ground to keep from falling out. What good would talking to her do? She hadn't accepted his apology in person. And it didn't sound like time would heal her wounds.

"I take it from that growl that you won't," J.P. said. "All right. Have it your way, but if you ask me, she's the first woman who's refused to take money from you. That says a lot."

"I agree," Rhett said.

Rye cradled his hands under his head and stared up at the

swaying palm trees. "Shut up." And he almost winced—he knew he shouldn't talk to his friends that way—but dammit, everyone seemed to be telling him how wrong he was lately. And didn't he know it? Didn't he regret every mistake he'd made with Tory?

And Tory's last words to him kept echoing in his mind. What if he couldn't change and be the kind of person his family needed? She was right. He had to step up for them, and he was afraid he couldn't. He swatted away a fly buzzing around his head.

Nausea rolled over him like ocean waves.

Tory was better off without him, but deep down he feared he wasn't better off without her.

The kernel of good,
Is inside every man.
Even a man like me.

I fight it,
But its power has dug deep inside me.

It whispers in the dark,
Even when I'm partying on the beach.

Yes, I am,
A good man.

Don't fight it.
It won't make me weak.

Yes, I can.
Be a good man.

Come on.
Give into the seeds.

Rye Crenshaw's Number One Hit, "Kernel of Good In a Man"

CHAPTER 23

The day before his sisters arrived with the kids, Rye sobered up and shaved the beard he'd grown, leaving his signature goatee. Rhett, J.P., and Clayton had hung out with him the night before, watching him like a hawk and helping him make sure everything was ready for his family. What an odd sensation it was to see the four rooms that had been decorated for his family. It made his ten-bedroom mansion feel strange, like someone else's home. Like a real home. The kids' rooms—bubble gum pink walls for Annabelle and girly dolls on a twin bed decked out in white and black polka dots, and a sailor-blue trundle bed for Rory with fire trucks painted on the front—made his head spin. Tammy's pale blue room boasted a whimsical four-poster with white netting dotted with butterflies draping the posts.

He was going to let them change anything they wanted, but at least the new décor was more welcoming than his masculine taste had been. And he'd give Amelia Ann his credit card so she could outfit her housing exactly as she wanted, since she wanted to live on her own.

Before flying back to Dare Valley, Rhett had told Rye to call when he wanted to talk turkey. Rhett, J.P., and Clayton were interfering sons of bitches sometimes, but he was grateful for their friendship, particularly now that his whole life was up in the air.

When the gate called to announce his sisters' arrival, he stepped out of the house to meet them, his eyes tracking to Dare River. The first time he saw this house with the river cutting across it, he knew he was home. The red brick plantation-style house had eight columns, a sweeping veranda, tall French windows and doors, a mix of balconies, a gabled roof, two fireplaces flanking the sides, and black shutters. The peace he found here, away from the stage lights and the cameras, gave him fuel for his music. In Dare River, there was a special way the wind blew, the trees swayed, and the river sounded. Something about it just helped him hear the music better.

Now it was time to open this home he'd created to his family. And do everything he could not to let them down like he had Tory.

His exhale was deep as his sisters' BMWs pulled to a stop in his circular driveway. Amelia Ann raced out, her face beaming, and pulled him in for a hug.

"We're here, we're here, we're here," she chanted. "I can't believe it."

Neither could he. He watched as a pale Tammy approached with the kids, who were already being greeted by his golden retrievers, Bullet and Banjo.

"Sit," he commanded, and they immediately did.

Annabelle hugged one dog, and then crooked her finger at Rye. He crouched down and she wrapped her little arms around his neck. God, she was so little. Was she really going to be living in his house?

"Hi, Uncle Rye." She patted his face and smiled. "You've got a real big house. That's good 'cause we brought *everything* in our old house now that Mama and Daddy are getting a divorce. It's going to be fun, staying with you. Like a vacation."

So, she didn't understand the permanence of the situation yet. Well, that would come with time.

Rory stalked forward next, his hands in fists at his side. Clearly the boy knew what was going on. He put his hand on the kid's shoulder, since Rory wasn't the hugging type—well, except with Tory and his mother. The thought sent a streak of pain through him. He grew even more alarmed when Rory shrugged free of his hand.

Rising, he approached Tammy and cautiously kissed her cheek.

"Hi, Rye." She wrung her hands, drawing his attention to her empty wedding ring finger.

What the hell was he supposed to say to her? "The drive go well?"

Tammy ran her hands down her front, smoothing away the travel wrinkles. "Yes, it was fine." She let her gaze roam. "I like the house."

Her ghost of a smile made him realize the irony of him choosing something antebellum.

Amelia Ann linked her arm through his. "Oh, I do, too. I've always wondered what it would look like." Right, she hadn't seen it either. It was hard to believe he'd been so distant from his family, and now this...

"And you have my favorite tree," Amelia Ann continued. "Magnolias," she clarified, pointing to the cluster of them to the right of the house. "Oh, I can't believe it. We're here, and I'm going to Vanderbilt."

Since everyone else had shared their thoughts, he turned to Rory. "Well, son, what do you think?"

Rory glared at him and kicked a pebble in the drive. "I'm not talking to you." His tone was angry.

"Son, you've just gotten here, so I can't have made you angry already."

Tammy crouched down in front of the boy. "Rory, we talked about this."

He mulishly shook his head. "Mama, I'm just telling him how it is." And he looked at Rye with a pinched face before racing off to the car. "Come on, Annabelle, let's help unpack."

As his niece ran off to join her brother, Rye nodded toward Rory. "What's that about?"

Tammy averted her gaze. "He's just upset right now. He'll get over it."

"He's going to be living here, Tammy. I can't fix it if I don't know what's broken."

"He's decided he won't talk to you," she said, lowering her voice. "He's a little boy, so it won't last long."

Suddenly it was like all of the air had been sucked out of him, and he knew why. Tory. Still he asked. "Tell me why."

His sisters exchanged a glance, and then they both looked down at their feet. "Well, Tory called this week to talk to him. Rory made her promise to stay in touch, and it meant so much to him that I couldn't tell him no. He's been through so much, and she's the only one he...reaches out to."

His head started buzzing. When Amelia Ann put a hand on his arm, he knew there was more, and he wasn't going to like it. "When Tory told him she was leaving for a while to do some research, he got angry and blamed you."

His heart pumped viciously. "What do you mean, she's leaving?"

"Well, she got some grant she's been waiting for," Tammy said, shifting on her feet. "She's gone to somewhere in Africa for a few months."

Oh Jesus, it hurt to think of her being thousands of miles away from him. It made things seem more final somehow—like their worlds were further apart than ever.

"Why does Rory blame me?" he said.

"He's got this idea that you made her leave," she said softy. "It all makes sense to him after seeing you...angry with her. I couldn't convince him otherwise."

Rye rubbed his goatee, his mind spinning. He had to know more. "Rory," he barked.

Tammy put a hand out. "Rye, please. He's just a little boy."

The plea in her voice made him feel sick. "I would never hurt him."

Rory came forward, his chin stuck out. "I said I wasn't talking to you."

"Fine," Rye said, crouching down beside him. "You can stop talking to me after you answer some questions." He put a hand on his shoulder. "You talked to Tory." He wanted to ask how she was, but he didn't. "Did she tell you why she was leaving?"

Rory kicked at a pebble. "She said she got her money to study things...in Africa. But I know it's your fault."

"What makes you think that, son?"

He pushed at Rye suddenly, making him fall on his backside. "You made her cry. I heard her the night she stayed with us on your birthday."

"Rory, you shouldn't talk to your Uncle Rye that way," Tammy said. Amelia Ann headed off Annabelle as the little girl ran back toward them, the retrievers following her worshipfully.

"It wasn't his fault she left," Tammy continued. "I've told you that. She had to finish her schooling. She has her own life, baby."

His nephew punched his little fists against his sides. "But now I won't be able to talk to her for a long time. She said so. Everybody leaves," the little boy cried. "Nothing's the same anymore."

Rye grabbed Bullet's collar when the dog butted his arm. He stroked his fur as the pain radiated through his body. No, nothing was the same.

Tammy pulled Rory to her. "She's coming back, sweetie. She'll be home around Christmas, remember? She'll talk to you then."

"How do you know? It's just like Daddy. He said he'd call, but I know he didn't mean it. And I don't care. I hate him." He turned to Rye. "And I hate you!"

"Rory—" Tammy whispered, her face stricken.

He ran back to the car and climbed in, slamming the door behind him.

"Jesus, Tammy," Rye said, rubbing his throat. How was he supposed to recover from what had happened with Tory when his nephew was leveling charges like that at him?

"Rye, I'm so sorry."

He pulled her into a hug. "It's all right," he said, trying to convince them both.

What did they say about kids? Out of the mouths of babes?

Well, shit. He'd just been taken to the woodshed by a sprout.

As he looked over Tammy's shoulder, he could practically see his house morphing into a glass house with cracks starting to shiver up the side, like in the art for his latest album. He planted his feet and made a silent vow.

He'd move heaven and earth if he had to, but the glass was not going to crack again.

***

They settled in over the following weeks. Rory and Amelia Ann started school, and his little sister called him every day to tell him how grateful she was for his help in bringing her dreams to life. But Rory and Tammy were less enthusiastic, and Annabelle's infectious laughter was a much-needed bright spot in their somber family dinners. It didn't help that Rye seemed to be allergic to food—his taste buds acted like they'd been seared to nothingness, and even the most succulent dinners made him ill.

But he dreamed about maple cornbread and pancakes dotted with chocolate chips. And the woman who'd bantered with him as she cooked, green eyes sparkling.

Sleeping had never been so difficult for him, and he couldn't believe he'd ever taken it for granted. He'd taken to sitting on the back porch late at night strumming on Old Faithful. The first time Annabelle snuck out of bed and climbed onto his lap, he didn't know what to do. When he tried to take her back to her room, she started crying and locked her arms around his neck. So he stopped fighting her, terrified by her tears, and let her stay with him until she fell asleep. She came the next night, and they repeated the pattern until he finally stopped trying to make her go. Sometimes they listened to evening sounds, and sometimes she asked him to sing to her. When she fell asleep, he tucked her into bed before heading into his own room.

If Tammy knew, she didn't say anything, so he didn't say anything, either. It was like egg shells covered his floor instead of hardwood.

Rory still wasn't talking to him directly. The boy's accusatory eyes became a form of punishment for all Rye's misdeeds, reminding him to be careful with other people's feelings.

Tammy spent time decorating their bedrooms and the playroom, trying to make it into a real home for her and the kids. Still, Rye would sometimes find a random doll or dump truck lying around in other parts of the house. She'd apologize for the mess before making things immaculate again. When he finally told her he didn't mind a little clutter, she looked so fragile—like he'd shaken her brittle world with those few words—that he didn't know what to say.

He went out less. Found the old easy distractions like women and liquor less easy. His friends talked about his mood, and Clayton claimed he was depressed. Depressed? Rye Crenshaw? He was just adjusting to having his family around, that's all.

But deep down, he knew better. He lost weight. His face grew haggard from too little sleep. Amelia Ann even tried cooking for him when she came home for a Sunday dinner, which was a total disaster not to be repeated.

He sought peace in the one thing that had always made him happy, throwing himself into the songs for the new album. But when he tried to write his catchy trademark lyrics, they felt fake—like when a word that's been read too many times doesn't look right on the page anymore. The trash can in his studio looked like a legal notepad had ended it kamikaze style, and broken pencils lay scattered everywhere. Clayton and Georgia suggested hiring a songwriter. He refused. He told them the problem was temporary, but he worried it wasn't.

The mood in the house remained tense, and when he was on an errand to purchase dog food on a cool October day, he decided to change that. The kids loved his dogs, but Bullet and Banjo were pretty big for them. Standing in the pet aisle, he picked two animals that seemed the perfect size for the kids. He'd always wanted a dog of his own growing up, but Mama had put the kibosh on that idea.

When he returned to the house, his spirits were better for the first time in months. He bundled his purchases under his arms and walked to the front. Bullet and Banjo raced off when he pointed to the back of the house.

When he opened the door, he was smiling. "Annabelle. Rory. Come out here."

He couldn't wait to see their faces. Maybe he'd found a way to help the little ones adjust to their new lives, perhaps even enjoy them.

***

Tammy heard his shout and set aside the magazine she'd been thumbing through for an hour. Why did Saturdays seem to drag on? The kids were reading quietly too, but they scampered off when Rye called for them. Tammy trailed behind, the only thing she knew how to do right now. In this new world, she didn't know who she was other than a mama, and wasn't sure when she'd venture out of this nest to try and find out. She couldn't stay dependent on Rye forever.

Rye stood in the entryway with his fingers tucked in his belt loops, shifting on his feet. "I have something for you kids." He eased open the front door. "Follow me."

Annabelle ran forward in delight, squealing. "Oh my, it's a puppy. Look, Mama, it's a puppy!"

Rye gave Annabelle's head an absentminded caress and leaned down to nudge the miniature Shih Tzu forward. Annabelle picked up the pink leash and pulled the puppy into her arms, giggling when it licked her.

"I thought it might be nice for each of you to have a new friend here in Nashville," Rye said.

He'd bought them puppies? Her eyes burned. Did he have any idea how precious this was? Sterling hated animals and thought they were filthy creatures, so she'd never been able to grant the kids' wish for a pet.

"I'll show the kids how to take care of them, Tammy. You won't have to do a thing, I promise."

She only nodded. Her voice had dried up like an old well.

Annabelle launched herself at Rye. "Oh, Uncle Rye, this is the bestest present ever. Right, Mama? I can't wait to show Aunt Amelia. I'm going to name my dog Barbie."

Rye winced and scratched his chin. "Ah, don't you think you might want to choose something else?" he asked, glancing sideways at Rory, who stood by the front door, his little brow furrowed.

"No, it's a Barbie dog, so its name is Barbie. What do you think, Mama? Isn't she pretty?"

Tammy cleared her throat. "She sure is, precious," she said, leaning down and giving the puppy a hesitant rub. He—she?—curled into her hand.

"Please tell me it's a girl dog," she whispered to Rye.

"Nope," he said with the sputter of a laugh. "Poor Barbie is a boy. Leave it be. She's happy."

Rory still hadn't moved away from the front door.

"Rory, come on over here," Rye called.

Her son took his time, making her nervous. Surely, he wouldn't refuse this gift. He and Rye were still at odds over Tory, but perhaps this could be the first step toward making it right.

"I thought you might like a labradoodle," Rye said, handing him the other puppy's leash. "They're fun and friendly and good companions for boys your age. He's your dog, son. You can name him and everything."

Please take it, Rory, she prayed. *Don't hurt Rye or yourself anymore than you already have.*

"Rory, have you got any names for your dog?" she asked, hoping to soothe the tension between them.

Her boy lifted his chin. "It doesn't change what you did."

"No, it doesn't, son." Rye heaved a sigh. "I didn't buy him thinking it would. I bought him because I thought he'd be a good friend to you." And with that he handed Rory the leash and headed inside.

"I know you're hurting," she said, looking down at her son, who now had a hesitant smile on his face and was patting the dog, "but so is your Uncle Rye."

And this time, after what he'd done for the kids, she couldn't leave him alone with his sorrow. When she reached the staircase, he was already taking the stairs two at a time. She called his name, and he stopped halfway up, one hand on the polished wood railing.

"I can't thank you enough," she said. "For thinking of the children."

"I saw a kitten and thought about buying it for you," he said, avoiding her gaze. "I remember you asking Mama for one when we were growing up, but I didn't know if you'd still want one."

She reached for the pearls at her neck and wrapped her fingers around them. He'd thought of her? He'd remembered? The sweetness of it almost stopped her breath. Where had her black sheep brother gone? Annabelle's favorite nursery rhyme ran through her head: *Baa, baa, black sheep, have you any wool? Yes, sir, yes, sir, three bags full.*

Yes, his hands were full. And he was opening them up to her and the kids. And wasting away before her eyes... After just getting him back, she couldn't stand to lose him again. She was grieving the mistakes she'd made, and she could see him doing the same.

"I'm too old for a kitten, but getting dogs for the kids was so sweet of you, Rye," she said, her voice breaking. "You've been...wonderful."

"They're only puppies, Tammy. If you need me, I'll be in the studio." He tromped up the stairs.

She didn't remind him he was going the wrong way. His studio was on the lower level.

"Mama, there's a man out here," Annabelle cried from behind her.

Tammy darted to the front door, worried to hear that someone had gotten through the gate without her knowing. A man dressed in khaki shorts and a gray T-shirt was crouched down comfortably on the porch, petting Annabelle's dog. He had thick brown hair, and when he looked up, she felt her breath stop at the sight of his dimpled smile and arctic blue eyes.

"Hi there, you must be Tammy." He stood and held out a hand. "I'm John Parker McGuiness, an old friend of Rye's. I decided to finally come over to meet y'all. He's told me a lot about you and the kids. Welcome to Dare River."

Tammy smoothed her hands down her raspberry linen top, grateful that she'd bothered to dress nicely like she always used to...even though she never went anywhere other than to the market and Rory's school. Somehow, seeing that put-together woman in the mirror each morning was a small comfort.

"I'm Tammy." Rye hadn't told her to expect company. The man's handshake was warm and firm.

His mouth curved. "I know that."

Heavens, she was getting flustered. "Of course. And these are my children Annabelle and Rory. And these are the new puppies Rye has bought them."

He tugged on Annabelle's hair, making her giggle. "We've met, doggies and all. Your uncle is really glad to have y'all here."

Rory just eyed him with suspicion and walked to Tammy's side with his leashed puppy, like they were her little guardians. Tammy didn't know what to do with her hands, so she crossed them over her body. "Ah, how do you know Rye?"

J.P. winked at Rory, who stood still while the puppy jumped excitedly around him.

"We went to school together and have been friends ever since."

A Vandy alum? Who knew Rye had college friends? Even though they'd been living together for over a month now, they hadn't discussed such things, wrapped up in their own worlds of grief. Tammy pointed to the mountain bike propped against the side of the house. "You live close by?"

He scratched Rory's puppy, getting him to roll onto his back. "Yep. Up river. About ten miles. It's a good ride."

Ten miles? His tan forearms gleamed with a sheen of sweat, and while she'd never liked seeing men heated from the outdoors, she couldn't seem to look away.

"Rye inside?" he drawled.

"Yes," she murmured. "He's probably in his studio. I'll show you."

His dimple winked again as he stood, all tall and lean, towering over her. "I know my way. It's nice out just now. You should stay out here with the kids and get to know the puppies better. Perhaps Rye and I can put up a tree swing for the kids sometime soon." His eyes tracked across the lawn. "There are some nice trees for it."

Annabelle clapped her hands. "Yes, yes," she cried.

"That would be lovely." Hadn't she promised herself she'd get the kids to play outside more? Get dirty like other kids? She'd become a neat-freak mommy, and it was time for that to stop.

"I'll see y'all later then. It was good to meet you, Tammy."

He strolled through the door. When he faded from view, she fanned herself, feeling warm. Must be the heat. What was wrong with her? Well, she hadn't seen a lot of men for some time. Hadn't Sterling been jealous, angry when they'd come home from a dance at the country club? She'd stopped talking to men, and it was jarring to return to it, especially with one who was so handsome.

Annabelle grabbed her hand, holding the pink leash, the dog on the end chirping out a bark. "Come on, Mama. Let's take Barbie for a walk."

She shook off the memories and extended her hand to Rory. "Come with us."

There was a smile on his face when she took his hand, and hope sparked inside her. She prayed the puppy would help him heal. She couldn't remember him truly being a little boy. And she was deeply afraid it was her fault.

Every night she prayed it wasn't too late.

***

Rye was staring down at his legal pad when J.P. entered the room. He had been so flustered earlier that he'd actually gone the wrong way to get to his studio—imagine that, getting lost in his own house—and he still felt out of sorts..

"Well, lookee here," Rye said when J.P. walked in. "You're not wearing one of your fancy suits for once."

J.P. plopped down on his massive leather couch. "I biked over. It's a nice day. Lyrics coming along any better?"

Rye scowled. "No, dammit."

"Hmm. Well, I met your family. Your niece is as sweet as they come, but the boy's guarded. Your sister is, too, but she's lovely. I can't say I see any family resemblance."

"Ha ha. You just came over to spy since I told all of y'all to stay clear of the house for a while."

He shrugged. "We understand that you want them to have some space after everything they've been through, but as the nicest guy in our set, I was given the honor of coming over to check on you. How are things going in Familyville?"

Rye reached into his mini-fridge and pulled out a couple of

271

beers, handing one to his friend after he popped them open. He took a long draw from the bottle to wet his dry throat. Christ, he felt raw after giving the kids the puppies. And scribbling down gibberish for lyrics wasn't helping his mood.

"I don't know what to do with Tammy. She and I were never close growing up. Amelia Ann's going to be fine. She's got fire. She's been running around Nashville like a newly liberated woman."

"She's been given her freedom," J.P. commented. "Heady stuff."

Yeah, and his freedom seemed to have vanished at the same time. Funny how he wasn't missing it. "Tammy's different. She's controlled and unsure. Doesn't seem to know what to do with herself now that she doesn't have her own house to take care of and appearances to keep up."

J.P. rested his beer against his chest as he leaned back on the sofa. "She's a different woman with different experiences. Can't imagine what it must have been like to be married to that piece of work."

Even now, the memory of what Sterling had done burned Rye's ass. When he'd asked her—in a pretty awkward fashion—if she wanted him to do anything about Sterling hurting her, she'd only responded with a stiff shake of her head. They'd never spoken of it again, and he still had bad dreams about what might have happened between them.

"Her life was blown apart," J.P. said. "Now, she's divorced and a single mama, living in a new city with a brother she doesn't know well, of whom she's never completely approved. Must be hard for her to reconcile thinking of you as a sinner when you've showed recent signs of being a saint."

Rye growled. "I ain't no saint." Hadn't his missteps with Tory proven that?

J.P.'s dimple winked when his mouth tipped up. "Sinners don't buy puppies for children." He chuckled. "Hey, that's a pretty good song lyric. Maybe you can use that."

"Shut up, J.P."

"Your sister needs to discover who she is now and what she wants to become. Right now, all she knows is that she's a mama. Beyond that, I'd say the rest is about as fuzzy as a pussy willow. My mama felt the same after Daddy took off until she became a preacher. Then she was right as rain."

Rye glared at him. He'd swear J.P. must have picked up this annoying therapy talk from his mama by osmosis. "Well, your sisters turned out all right. Not so sure about you."

J.P.'s shoulders shook with laughter. "You really are out of sorts. So, tell me. What does Tammy like?"

He threw aside the legal pad. "Shit, how do I know? Didn't you just tell me that we're basically strangers?"

J.P. raised a brow. "Work with me here, Crenshaw. I'm trying to think of something she could do, on the professional side, to become more independent. Does she like to host parties? God knows you do. Although with the kids around, your future events may need to be more upscale. No more slutty bunny costumes...unless it's Easter."

"Funny." He'd had those parties in the past, ones where women threw themselves at him left and right. Now the thought had no appeal for him. Tory had erased his passion for the two things he'd once loved most: food and women. And he wondered if he'd ever get it back.

"I aim to entertain."

Rye tipped his head back and studied the beams running across the studio ceiling, thinking. "You're right about one thing, Tammy's a Hollins. She was raised to host parties."

"You were raised to be a lawyer. How'd that work out for you?"

"I don't know why I ever let you come over. You're always such a dick."

J.P.'s chuckles filled the room. "Well, you're an asshole and that beats being a dick any day. Nice lyric, but a little too racy for your fans. So, have you finally decided to crawl on all fours to get Tory back?"

Rye jerked at the sound of her name, spilling his beer. "Shit."

"Come on, you're a miserable son of a bitch because you *miss* her. Admit it. You were a wreck in Padre Island. Rhett and I have never seen you drink like that. Even Clayton was impressed when I told him. We're all worried about you, Rye."

Rye grunted. "So, I miss her. What the hell does that change? I screwed up and accused her of selling me and my family out to the tabloids. I hurt her beyond repair. She wouldn't accept my apology. Heck, she's hurting for money, but she wouldn't even let me buy her house."

"You never even told her why you wanted to do it," J.P. said.

"I don't have anything to offer her, J.P, and I can't make things right."

J.P. leaned forward. "You have plenty to offer her, but that, my friend, is your choice." He threw his bottle in the trash can, on top of all the balled up yellow paper. "You're not acting like the wild Rye Crenshaw everyone knew around town, are you? You've poured all your energy into taking care of your family. That kind of thing means something to a woman."

He clutched his beer as he thought back to Tory's parting words. Wasn't he trying to do his best, not just for his family, but to prove to her that he could be the stable anchor they needed? "I'm doing...what needs doing right now."

"Fine. You keep telling yourself that. I've said my piece, and now I'm going to run on home and change. I'm meeting Clayton tonight. You're welcome to join us, but only if you put that junkyard dog persona away. If you're not careful, you're going to scare those new puppies so much they'll take to peeing on your carpet."

Rye took a long pull from the bottle, but he couldn't even taste the beer. "Before you go, please tell me you've found something new on the leak to the tabloid. This is taking too goddamn long and the trail is almost arctic by now."

"There's nothing new, I'm afraid, and I'm just as frustrated as you are." J.P. had a hand on the door when he turned. "Let's review what we know. Whoever did it was careful. The person who did this wasn't after any money. That's why there's no trail."

"My family has sworn to me that Sterling would be too concerned with his reputation to do such a thing, but you should have seen his face when he told me he'd make me pay. My gut tells me it's him."

"We're still looking at him, Rye, but we need to be careful. He's a well respected lawyer, and we have similar associates. So does your daddy."

Rye's hands clenched around the bottle. "I want to cut his balls off for hurting Tammy and the kids."

"Don't worry. We're going to fry whoever did this. After meeting your sister and seeing the kids, I have even more motivation. She's a real Southern lady, and this has cut her deep."

Rye rubbed his neck. J.P. had always been able to read people well. "Yes, it has. I'll think about what you said. About finding something for her to do."

"I know you will. And you're a heck of a lot nicer than you let on. Why do you think we've stayed friends so long?"

Snorting was his best response, since he wasn't ready to have a Hallmark moment with his friend.

"And I have a suggestion for how you can fix your writer's block."

Since J.P. was a master with lyrics, Rye grabbed his legal pad to jot down his advice. "What?"

"Close your eyes."

Rye glared at him before slamming his eyes shut.

"I want you to tell me the first thing that comes to your mind. Finish the sentence. And don't think. Having your heart broken is like …"

Rye's heart sputtered at the words, but his mind popped out a response without effort. "It's like someone's put holes in it with a fucking twelve-gauge shotgun." His eyes opened when a few musical notes popped into his head.

J.P.'s infernal dimple winked. "Write what you know, Crenshaw. But I'd leave 'fucking' out. Oh, and I told your sister we should put a tree swing up. I can come by tomorrow and help if you'd like."

Yeah, J.P. had three sisters, and he knew how to deal with family. Perhaps staying away from his friends had been a mistake. "I'll call you."

"Catch you later, my friend."

Rye heaved himself off the couch and walked to the window. The kids were in the backyard, both of them laughing as the puppies chased them in circles. Tammy was standing near one of the beds he'd hired some hot-shot landscape architect to design, touching a white hydrangea. Then she knelt and plucked out a weed tunneling through the mulch. When she continued to thread her way across his flower beds, he frowned. She didn't need to act like some gardener. He could hire people for that. But when she reached the roses, which were blooming in a profusion of apricot, and broke off a few spent flower buds, he suddenly remembered something. Her childhood science projects had typically involved growing plants from seeds or cuttings. Inspiration dawned.

Letting himself out the French doors, he started across the backyard. Annabelle made a beeline for him. She was sweaty and slightly rumpled, her yellow hair ribbon hanging askew, but her face was filled with a contagious kind of joy. He swung her around, and she burst into giggles. When he stopped, she shouted, "Again, Uncle Rye. Again."

Playing with her gladdened his heart, but he didn't miss the fact that Rory was doing his best to ignore him as usual. God, he hoped his nephew would stop making him feel like an asshole. Tammy had said it would wear off, but it hadn't, and Rye was beginning to think the kid had picked up the Hollins ability to hold a grudge. Wasn't Rye a champ grudge holder himself?

Heart racing from nerves, he finally put Annabelle down—she immediately scampered back toward Barbie—and made his way across the yard. Made himself frown as he neared Tammy. Let the silence lengthen until he flicked a rosebud with a finger.

"You know, ever since I moved into this house, I meant to do something with the yard. I mean, we planted some things," he said, gesturing to the roses. "Yet, something seems to be missing." He waited, watching her from the corner of his eye. "What do you think?"

She turned her head so quickly, her dangling pearl earrings slapped against her cheek. "What?"

He dug the tip of his boot into the grass. "What do *you* think's missing?"

She took her time, and he wondered if he'd misjudged the situation.

"Well," she started, "what you currently have is lovely. It's simple and uncluttered. It allows the grass and trees to define the space with a few flower beds as focal points, leaving the river as the main point of reference."

Define space? Focal points? Well, someone seemed to know landscaping jargon. "But it could look better, right? I mean, it's awfully boring other than this stuff." It nearly stuck in his throat, but he forced it out. "What's this again?"

She followed the finger he was pointing. "An oak-leaf hydrangea."

He shook his head. "Right. Well, you seem to know an awful lot about landscaping. I'm going to be real busy with this new album over the next few months. Do you think you might have the time to do something about this? I mean, I entertain here a lot, so you could spend whatever you like. Do whatever you want." And darn it, if he wasn't acting like an idiot, trying to suggest a new purpose for her.

The way her mouth parted made him want to buy J.P. a whole case of his favorite bourbon. "Really?"

"Heck, if I had time, I might just use some old tires I have in the barn and plant some of those flowers with the faces on them." He bit his cheek to keep from smiling at her horrified reaction. "What are those anyway?"

"Pansies," she said weakly. "Did you say tires?"

When he nodded, she looked ill. He almost laughed. J.P. had done it again.

"I'd be happy to do something," Tammy said in a rush.

"Wonderful," he replied, and when she smiled without reserve, he knew he had her. She looked about as happy as Annabelle did, racing around with her puppy.

"Just don't cut my shrubs into any weird shapes. I hate that."

"Oh, no, I wouldn't."

As he strolled away, he started whistling, and when he passed a white hydrangea, he thought of Bedford Plantation and the night he and Tory had spent there.

There was pain in the memory, but maybe J.P. was right. He needed to write about what he knew. Words about a moonlight garden started to form. Music—guitar, violin, piano—started to play in his head. Feeling his creativity burst forth, he began jogging.

It was early yet, but somehow he knew his writing block was over.

Everyone has something they crave when they're sad or away from home. Being halfway around the world in rural Africa, I realize mine is French toast. Its power to lighten your spirit, soothe your worries, and make you feel closer to home is magical. My Grandma started the tradition by bringing day-old French bread home from the diner where she worked. We were always looking for ways to use it. This recipe worked like a charm—and we never tired of it. Dress it up with a good cup of coffee or mimosa and enjoy its scrumptiousness.

Fan-tabulous French Toast

1 loaf of French bread
¼ cup butter
2 eggs
1 2/3 cups milk
Pinch of salt
3 tbsp. sugar
1 tsp. nutmeg

Slice the loaf into pieces and butter both sides. Line a buttered pan with the bread slices. Beat the eggs. Add the milk and pinch of salt. Stir. Pour over bread and sprinkle with nutmeg. Chill for at least 1 hour (overnight is best). Bake at 425 degrees for 20-25 minutes until golden brown. Serve with warm maple syrup and a side of fruit. Strawberries are especially lovely.

Tory Simmons' Simmering Family Cookbook

CHAPTER 24

Kenya, Africa

Night sounds screamed around Tory. Crocodiles thrashed in the water, fighting hippos. Birds squawked. When she heard steps outside her tent, she grabbed the stick on the floor. Was it another baboon? The mutant monkeys with their red butts were completely unafraid of humans and showed up all the time—day and night. They freaked her out.

"Tory?" Kevin Andrews called. "Can I come in?"

"Sure." She was glad for the company, given that the generator was set to go off in about thirty minutes, plunging them into darkness.

Kevin, a Ph.D. student from New York University and another Fulbright fellow, was the only other student with her in their small camp. They were both studying the impact of tourism on the Maasai people and how it affected life in their family compounds, called bomas. She was more interested in how it affected women and girls, particularly their traditional gender roles as wives and mothers, while Kevin was focusing on the impact on their pastoral way of life, especially the herding of animals. Kevin spoke Maasai and Swahili, which had been a God-send, even though there were an increasing number of Maasai who spoke English because of their interactions with the tourism sector. He darted through the tent flap quickly, swatting to keep the giant bugs outside. His earnest round face was covered in a whole truckload of freckles, and his red hair was fuzzy from the humidity, which never seemed to go away.

"You're working on your cookbook again," Kevin commented, sitting in her other rickety chair.

"Yes, it's my fun time." Her salvation in this strange world, which was a heck of a lot more challenging and alien than she'd ever imagined. The contrasts made her head spin—in Kenya there were thriving, modern cities like Nairobi and Mombasa, and small villages in the savanna, where local people lived in mud huts and still hunted their own food in a largely untouched landscape of golden grass and endless blue sky dotted with elephants, lions, and giraffes. Of course, there was also the spattering of Range Rovers trolling along that same land, tourists on photo safaris leaning out of the cabs to snap pictures of wildlife.

Kevin was holding two beers, and he held one out to her. The local brand, Tusker, wasn't bad, but it was always lukewarm. The condensation on the bottle coated her hand.

"I hope you don't mind me saying so, but you did a great job cooking with the Maasai women today." He ducked his head and glanced away.

She wanted to sigh. The poor guy had a crush on her, and she couldn't be less interested. Why couldn't she find a funny, nice guy attractive? Oh yeah, because Rye had cut her heart out with a melon baller, making a summer salad of her most vital organ.

"Thanks, it was interesting to learn what they do to the meat after the men hunt. How they pack it in salt." Everything else had been...well, not her cup of tea. She knew these people ate every part of the animal, but seeing it had given her a queasy stomach. Calling them sweetbreads in her head hadn't helped.

Kevin fingered her binder. "You ever think of making cooking your fulltime passion?"

Of course. She'd had twin withdrawals on this trip. One for Rye. And the other for cooking. She missed planning what she would cook each day, and that moment when someone's eyes fluttered at the first bite of one of her dishes. Especially wickedly-lashed hazel eyes.

"I love cooking, but my Grandma really wanted me to have an education, and my parents were both educators. I liked anthropology in college, so I kept pursuing it."

The electricity flickered in the tent. Tory's eyes darted to her watch. She and Kevin always shut the main generator off at nine o'clock to conserve fuel while the small one kept their food cold in the mini-fridge. Then, it was pitch black. And the night sounds seemed to crank up in volume like the boom box of her youth.

"Well, don't chefs have educations? I mean they go to school, too." He lifted his shoulder. "It's just that I like you, and you don't seem happy. You've told me about Rye Crenshaw, but I don't think that's the only reason... I've been on a lot of research trips, and...well...are you sure this is what you want to do for the rest of your life?"

Hadn't she been asking herself that question every day since she'd arrived? She'd always expected her true passion for this subject to spring to life when she was in the field, experiencing other cultures live and in the flesh rather than trudging through dry textbooks. Right now, she didn't know what her purpose was, but she hadn't found it here. Scary.

"You know, my grandpa always said you couldn't escape your problems by running away," he continued. "They always caught up to you."

Yeah, Kenya certainly hadn't been the escape she'd hoped it would be, even though the beauty of the land stole her breath away. Giraffes running across the savanna, elephants bathing, and lone lions or cheetahs boldly sunning themselves, ignoring her presence as she drove by.

Kevin swatted at one of the ever-present flies. There were swarms of them, especially when she and Kevin were eating or right before a storm. It was yet another foreign thing.

"Look, I know it might not be my business, but I don't like seeing you so miserable. When I saw you cooking around the fire with the women today, your face...well, it beamed. It's the first time I've ever seen you *really* smile since you got here. I think that means something. Don't you?"

She looked away. The tent's sides rippled from the wind. He was right, of course. Hadn't she felt that elusive sensation—happiness—for a short while today? And what a relief it had been... She'd been worried some switch in her had been permanently shut off in Memphis, condemning her to a life of tears and misery.

"It helps having someone else see it," she said. There was the urge to take his hand, but she didn't want to give him false hope. "I'm glad you said something."

"Good." His round face transformed with his smile. He reached his beer bottle out, and she clinked hers against it. The lights flickered again, and his face fell.

"Well, I guess that's my cue to shut the generator off. Might be running out of fuel."

Kevin had never made a move on her—he'd only given her a friendship she needed so desperately. And that was something else she liked about him.

As he ducked out of the tent, he said, "For whatever it's worth, Rye Crenshaw was a fool to let you slip away."

God, could he be any nicer? And he was right. Rye was a fool. She'd been so good for him. And he'd been good for her until his mistrust had driven an irreparable wedge between them. Somehow, some way, being with him had made her feel like she was part of something bigger than herself, part of a family again.

Every night, even though her prayers for herself had dried up, she whispered prayers for each of them in the darkness of her tent. Hoped they were doing all right.

She caressed her cookbook. Kevin was right. She didn't belong here, observing and analyzing tribal culture. She wanted to spend her days in that special place where life blossomed—in the kitchen, cooking for people. When she finished her dissertation, hopefully in the spring, her promise to her grandma would be fulfilled.

Then she could go back to what she loved.

Cooking.

Maybe not at Diner Heaven, but somewhere else. She hoped her grandma could understand.

The lights went out. Instead of the fear that always shot through her at this time of night, a new peace filled her to the brim like a glass of cold water on a warm day. She fell back on the cot. Even though she couldn't see the stars, she could imagine them.

And she started to whisper to the creator of the skies above.

God bless Rory. And Tammy, and Annabelle, too. God bless Hampton and Amelia Ann.

She rubbed her heart when it fluttered, but didn't fight the words forming in her mind.

And God bless Rye, she whispered. *Help him be the good man I know is inside him.*

A tear slipped out of the corner of her eye and fell into her hair.

***

In the ensuing weeks, Rye was knee-deep in his writing mojo. J.P.'s advice seemed to unlock the words that had been frozen in his head. He found purpose again—in his music and his family. He burned both ends of the candle until he had his songs where he wanted them, and when he shared them with J.P., his friend told him they were the best he'd ever written. Heartbreak and his newfound love for his family looked good on him.

And then J.P. had promptly made a few suggestions. Lawyer boy could make a person weep with his stories, either in court or on the radio, and with a stable full of country singers as clients, he shared his gift for words in both spheres.

Clayton and Georgia loved the new material too, and were delighted by the new image he was creating for himself. This was the new Rye, the one forged in fire in Meade, changed by his time with Tory and his new life with his family. This is what they'd been striving for all along with their various PR strategies.

It was hard not to think back to what Tory had said to him that last day in Memphis, urging him to integrate the different sides of his personality. He'd finally done it through music, as he'd always done, and it pained him that he couldn't tell her about it.

Then he called his band into the studio, and Clayton and Georgia managed the process of creating his new album. It was a crazy, chaotic time.

But through it all, there was the underlying sense that something vital was missing.

His family could sense his lingering sensitivity because they still walked on eggshells around him, but either they'd gotten used to it or there were fewer shells. When Tammy casually showed him her ideas for the property over breakfast one day, her garden design blew his mind with its raised beds and koi pond and other water features. When he praised her, she thanked him and promptly fled the kitchen.

Amelia Ann simply crowed like a rooster about Vandy and started bringing new friends by to meet the family, which was awkward, since most of her friends swooned over him. But he was glad to see her happy, so he had put up with the eyelash flutters and nervous giggles.

Late October was a bit late to plant, but they'd had a warm fall, so Rye told Tammy to go for it when she asked him. Crews dug up parts of his lawn to lay stone paths and fill in the new koi pond by the oak tree. When he asked if he could go fishing in it, it made her laugh—a beautiful sound.

Annabelle started going to a nearby pre-school a few days a week, making new friends as easily as Amelia Ann, but Rory said little about school or anything else, and he still refused to talk to Rye. Fortunately, he seemed glued to his growing puppy, whom he'd finally named Bandit. The kid didn't even laugh when he joked about all their dogs' names starting with B: Bullet, Banjo, Bandit, and Barbie.

But Annabelle did, bless her heart.

He walked along Dare River before dinner each night, taking a few moments for himself, and that was when he let himself brood about Tory. His regrets would rise up, fresh and raw, threatening to consume him.

He started babysitting, a word he hated since it didn't involve much more than keeping an eye on the kids. Annabelle always challenged him, constantly telling him she was bored, and he was pretty proud of the games he'd invented to keep her occupied. With Tammy out at a Junior League meeting, a recent foray back into being social, today's game was paying the kids a dollar for each bright red leaf they found scattered across the property. After he announced the challenge, Annabelle claimed she was going to make a million dollars. Rory just rolled his eyes and threw a stick to Bandit.

When Tammy came home and let herself onto the back porch, he was thrumming the strings of Old Faithful. She sat in the chair across from him, running a hand over the new outdoor furniture she'd picked out.

"How was your meeting?" he asked.

"Good. I recognized more faces today. There are some nice women there. I have two lunches scheduled next week."

"That's great," he replied, wondering if any of the women had given her trouble over the article in the paper.

Her figure had finally stopped its slow decline to gaunt. In the first weeks after moving to Dare River, she'd barely eaten a thing. For that matter, neither had he. Desperate not to think about the reason for his lack of appetite, he turned to watch Annabelle stack her leaves neatly in a pile under the tree. She gave chase when a gust upended her neat arrangement.

"Hi, Mama. Uncle Rye, the wind's ruining my pile," she called across the lawn, clutching leaves to her rumpled green dress.

"Come and bring them to me, Annabelle. We'll count them together." Rye set his guitar aside.

"Do you have my kids picking up leaves, Rye?" Tammy asked with a small smile.

He puffed out his chest, delighted to have thought of it. Too bad no one had him playing that game when he was a kid. He would have done well for himself.

"Yeah, they get a dollar for every one they catch. Of course, Annabelle is cheating, but I'll overlook that since she's little. But we may need to work on it. If she's cheatin' at this age, she'll be running us ragged by the time she graduates high school."

When his sister's face crumpled, he grew alarmed. Was she upset about this innocent game? "What's the matter?"

"You said 'us.'"

He realized he had, and that realization sent a powerful river flowing through his heart. "Of course I did, darlin'. I'll...go help Annabelle."

He darted away as she wiped a tear from her cheek.

"I'll go make us some dinner," Tammy called after him in a hoarse voice.

He didn't want to eat, but he knew he had to. They ate as a family now. Tammy was trying even harder than he was to give

Annabelle and Rory some semblance of a normal life.

He doled out ten dollars to Annabelle and fought a frown when Rory didn't present him with any leaves. Well, he'd already guessed he wouldn't be able to pay his way out of this situation.

Hadn't Tory taught him you could never purchase someone's affection?

***

Later that evening, he was nursing a glass of Jack Daniels on the porch when he heard Annabelle's footsteps. The moon was a silver fingernail, so he couldn't see anything but a small body. He smiled, waiting for what had become his favorite moment of the day—when she cuddled in his lap, and he sang her his new songs.

He was setting his glass aside when Rory came into focus a few yards away. Shifting uncomfortably in his chair, he acknowledged the boy, knowing he wouldn't get any greeting in return. "Rory."

"I know Annabelle comes out here with you most nights," the boy said quietly, and the shock of hearing his nephew finally speak to him caused his heart rate to speed up. "I told her you were in your studio tonight, so she fell asleep."

Was this some new game? Perhaps Rory thought ignoring him wasn't enough punishment, so he'd decided to deny him time with his favorite girl. Still, he asked, "Why tell her that?"

"I wanted to talk to you."

"Okay," he mused, still not sure what to make of the situation. "It's a nice night out. Sit a spell."

"I want to stand."

"Fine," he said, and almost sighed. The kid was as stubborn as ever, and didn't it drive him nuts to remember how similar he'd been at that age. "What do you want to talk about?"

Rory looked down, the moonlight making his hair a ghostly blond. "I overheard Mama talking on the phone with Amelia Ann tonight. She said you're in love with Tory, and that's why you don't look so good most days."

His chest grew tight, and while it didn't surprise him to learn his sisters saw through him, he hoped they wouldn't confront him. So far they hadn't.

"So," his nephew pressed, "is it true? Do you love her?"

Oh, Christ. Was he really supposed to share his secret with her little champion? Well, if it would make peace with Rory, maybe it was worth it. "Yes, I do."

Rory took a step closer after studying Rye's face for a spell. "I love her, too."

The familiar pain started to well up again. "I know, son. She's a mighty lucky woman to have you feel that way."

"If you love her, why aren't you trying to get her back?"

How could he explain how much he'd hurt her to a six-year-old? How any love she might have had for him had been erased by his betrayal.

"It's...complicated," he said.

"If you say you're really sorry and tell her you love her, she'll forgive you. Like granddaddy said, she has a big heart."

Daddy had said that? Well, after all Tory had done for them in Meade, he wasn't surprised.

"I'm not sure that will be enough," Rye said. He knew in his heart it was too late. "You should go back to bed." Talking about this was only making his wounds bleed.

"Then you need to prove it to her," Rory continued, his little fist clenching at his side.

Even Rye could feel Rory's anger brewing, and his hope that this moment would lead to a reconciliation was fading fast.

"I made her a promise," the little boy said, "and when you made her mad, and she went away, I couldn't keep it. She told me it was okay, but a promise is a promise."

His mind returned to the day when Rory had run away. He remembered how Tory had refused to share what his nephew had told her. "What did you promise her?"

"She told me everyone in her family was in heaven. That made me sad, so I told her she wasn't alone anymore. That she had me." He pointed to his blue pajama top. "That I'd be her family."

He rubbed a hand over his throat. The kid was destroying him, reminding him of how Tory had convinced him to go to Meade after Tammy's visit. It all but killed him to think about her being all alone, shouldering a growing mountain of debt. Isn't that part of the reason he'd tried to buy the house for her?

"That's a mighty big promise," he said. "You should head off to bed now."

Rory glared at him. "Mama says you're nice now, and that I should be nice to you, but nice people say they're sorry when they're wrong."

God, he was failing miserably—again—and Rory's anger was bubbling up with each passing second. "I tried, son, but it wasn't enough for her."

"I don't believe you."

"Now, Rory—"

"No! I hate you. I'm never going to be nice to you or talk to you again." He stormed off, leaving Rye alone in the darkness once more.

When he placed his head in his hands, all he could think about was what Rory had said. Could the kid be right?

But how was he supposed to prove his love to Tory? To show her that he'd changed?

Then a new thought emerged. Wasn't that exactly what his new album was about? Suddenly, he sat up. The new album. Everyone in his inner circle had been awed by the change in his music, and how it reflected the change in him. Would she believe him if she heard it?

His friend, Rhett Butler Blaylock, had convinced the woman he loved to marry him by serenading her. But then again, Rhett hadn't done anything wrong.

Well, he'd never know if he didn't try, and he couldn't bear to leave so much unsaid between them. He'd never even told her that he loved her, that he'd cherished their time together, that he never wanted anyone but her to sleep beside him.

His evening ritual blown, he headed inside, a new hope burning in his chest.

But he knew he wouldn't sleep tonight.

***

Dusk was falling in a beautiful layering of crisp blues, warm apricots, and hot pinks when Rye sought Tammy out. He figured she might have a more informed opinion than Amelia Ann about what he was thinking, having been married, but he still intended to ask his other sister's opinion when she got home. He knew the importance of keeping the peace between the two of them.

He brought Tammy a margarita on the rocks as she stood on the back lawn, surveying the newly-dug pond. The kids were busy playing with the dogs. Rory stopped to glare at him before running off to the tree swing, and it only cemented Rye's determination.

"Bringing me a drink?" she said. "How lovely."

"It looks good," he commented because it was expected, pointing to the huge hole in the ground. In reality, it looked like a mass grave.

"You need to look past the dirt and sod to see its potential as a shining pond with exotic water lilies rising from the surface." A blush warmed her cheeks, and she gave a reserved smile. "It's going to be beautiful."

The feeling in his stomach less resembled butterflies than gravel being kicked up on the highway by a semi. He tucked his thumbs in his belt loops.

"I need your advice. As a woman."

She turned, her expression surprised. "Okay."

"Rory talked to me last night," he began, and filled her in on their conversation. By the time he was finished, she was wringing her hands. "I...ah." Christ this was hard. He felt like a total girl, talking about his feelings this way. "I got to wondering what it would take for you to reconsider a man who'd screwed up so royally."

Silence lengthened. In the distance, Rye heard Annabelle giggle and Barbie bark in return.

"Besides an apology? Action."

"Great!" As a confirmation, it was music to his ears. "So, I'm thinking about flying to Africa to share my new songs with her and tell her...that I love her."

Just thinking about getting on a plane made him sick, but his fear of flying wasn't going to stop him—Tory was too important. And as for finding out where exactly she was, well, he had people to do that for him, right? Surely, it wouldn't be too hard. Or so he kept telling himself.

"But you're petrified of flying," she mused.

"I know."

Then his sister smiled. "I'm glad you've decided to do something. Tory...is a special woman. I'm sorry I didn't treat her better. I hope I'll have the chance to apologize for that."

It was nice to hear her say that. He wanted them to get along. If Tory actually... The thought of actually talking to her, seeing her, made him nervous all over again.

"Do you think she'll believe me?" he said, ducking his head down, his embarrassment acute. "She's so tough. And after all I've put her through, I'm not sure what I have to offer will be enough."

"She's not that tough."

"What?" he asked. "Of course she is. She's in freakin' Africa."

"That's different. I've seen her with Rory," she explained. "You don't inspire love like that in a six-year-old without softness. And I noticed the way she looked at you."

Oh, boy. "How'd she look?" he had to ask.

"Like you. In love and scared," she whispered.

He rubbed the back of his neck and decided to ask her opinion on another worry that had been keeping him up at night. "The song I sang to her in Memphis. It was like a breakup, right?" He'd wanted to tell her how special their time together had been, but the gesture seemed more hurtful than romantic now.

"I can't say what went through her mind, but...I can see how a woman might think that. Still, it was a lovely song, Rye."

Those words were her way of softening the blow. Well, Tammy was a softy too, he'd discovered, something he'd been blind to growing up.

"Thanks, Tammy."

"After everything you've done for me and the kids, I'm glad I can finally give something back, even if it's only advice." When she leaned on her tiptoes and kissed his cheek, it was suddenly hard to swallow. "Thank *you*, Rye."

They held each other's gaze, and because he'd experienced it with Tory, Rye recognized the beginnings of a true friendship with his sister. Before this summer, he never would have believed it possible.

"Well, I'm going to get dinner started," she said.

"I think I'll head to my studio for a while."

He had hunkered down in his studio and was stupidly staring at his legal pad, trying to think of some new lyrics for the Memphis song, when Tammy called him and the kids for dinner. She never let him help in the kitchen, and because it reminded him of Tory, he hadn't forced the issue.

After pushing his food around, he returned to his studio, where he kept scribbling and ripping up paper. The new lyrics for the song just weren't coming to him.

When he went to sit outside to wait for Annabelle, he was surprised to see Rory approaching him again. Dread rose.

"Mama told me you're going to Africa to get Tory back."

Over the sounds of crickets and the rustling of trees, he heard something near the door and turned his head. Even in the dim light, he could make out Tammy's shoes, illuminated in the moonlight. The rest of her was bathed in shadow.

"Yes," he said, his chest filling with emotion at his sister's peacekeeping efforts. "You were right. If I love her, I need to tell her I'm really sorry and try to prove it to her."

"Mama says I can't go to Africa because of school, but can I make her a card?"

He'd wanted to come too? Tory's little champion knew no bounds. "You make her as many cards as you want, and I'll bring them."

Rory hiked up one shoulder. "I'm sorry I said I hate you."

It didn't seem possible that anything could relieve the pressure in his chest, but the boy's apology finally did. "That's okay."

"I'll start talking to you again if you promise me not to be mean to Tory or make her go away again."

He chose his words carefully. "If she forgives me and comes back, I promise I won't make her go away again." No, he'd love her all his days, and didn't it figure that music accompanied those words in his head.

"I miss her," Rory said, and Rye's eyes burned with a matching emotion. "I miss her too, son."

When the boy looked down again, Rye gave in to the need to make peace and pulled Rory onto his lap. Fortunately, the boy didn't balk.

"We'll both be her family now, son."

"She'll like that, Uncle Rye," the boy whispered, leaning his head against his chest, and as a surrender, it was sweet.

He ran a hand over Rory's hair. It was thick and curly at the ends just like his had been. His serious little knight—just six years old and already looking out for damsels in distress.

Rory fiddled with his pajama top. "Will you sing to me, Uncle Rye? Like you do with Annabelle?"

It took Rye a moment to clear his throat. "Sure, son. Do you have anything in mind?"

Rory cuddled closer, his warm body soft. "Would you sing that Elvis song, 'Love Me Tender'? Tory told Granddaddy it was her favorite."

Rye felt his breath leave his chest, remembering that long ago night in Memphis. Christ, what a fool he'd been.

"Sure, son. I think that's my favorite song, now, too."

"You'll have to tell her that, Uncle Rye. It'll make her happy."

I hope so, he thought as he started to sing, his deep voice caressing the words. His voice broke suddenly at the memory of Tory in Club 152, and Rory patted his chest with a small hand.

Rye had found his voice again.

But I missed her so,
Couldn't let her go.
So, I got on my knees,
Started a prayer with please,
And asked God to send back my angel to me.

Told Him I'd make her a home,
And love her all my days,
Down here,
In country heaven.

Rye Crenshaw's new verses for the song now titled,
"Country Heaven"

CHAPTER 25

Finding the exact location of Tory's camp in Kenya was taking longer than Rye liked. Myra hadn't felt comfortable telling him where Tory was in light of Tory's refusal to accept his offer on the house. The setback had been disappointing, of course, but he had used the time to record the new version of "Country Heaven" and put a rush on the cover art and new songs. The end product couldn't be more symbolic of the new man he was, and he hoped Tory would understand that.

The art featured him sitting near a glorious autumn tree, his signature black cowboy hat resting off to the side, the blurred forms of his niece and nephew running around in the background by the tree swing. Tammy had been kind enough to agree to the concept, understanding how important the kids had become to him. Rory had asked him to let Tory know it was him running around since his face wasn't visible. The kid was chomping at the bit to find her as much as he was.

His private investigator had discovered that Fulbright had given her the grant, so J.P. had flown up to Washington, D.C., to personally deliver a sizeable donation to one of the board members and work his magic. When his friend called with the information, Rye heaved a sigh of relief and shouted for Rory to tell him the good news.

"We found her, son."

And the little boy jumped into his arms and said, "It's about time, Uncle Rye," which made him laugh.

It was early November, and even though Tory was supposed to be coming back around Christmastime, he wasn't about to wait. And, as J.P. had pointed out, the fact that Rye would be stepping onto a plane for the first time in his life might be an even bigger gesture than the album.

A few days later, he was boarding the private jet he'd commissioned for the trip. J.P., Clayton, and Rhett had insisted on making the trip with him. Part of him wondered if they were coming because they were worried how he'd take it if Tory rejected him. Whatever their reasons, he was grateful for their support.

"Are you sure you want to do this?" J.P. said from beside him. "You look about as sick as a bloated possum after days of being dead by the side of the road."

Not wanting to be groggy, he'd decided against drugging himself for the plane ride. He planned on gritting his teeth the whole way. Except he'd already been doing that for a day and his jaw hurt, and he hadn't even gotten on the plane yet. "I'll be fine."

"Can't tell you how proud I am of you, Rye," Rhett said, slapping him on the back with enough force to send a smaller man flying. "Seems fitting for me to help you claim your woman, since you helped me serenade mine."

Yeah, what a time that had been, playing the piano in the freezing cold as his friend crooned the song he'd written for Abbie. At the time, Rye hadn't believed he'd ever do something so crazy over a woman, and yet here he was, gripping the handrail as he ascended the plane's stairs, about ready to puke.

"I still say you should have videoed that performance, Rye," Clayton drawled. "We all know Rhett can't sing worth spit."

His friends continued to banter as they found their seats and belted themselves in. Rye just concentrated on taking deep breaths during takeoff, and when they reached cruising altitude, he somehow managed to peel himself out of his seat and join the others in the sitting area.

Clayton looked up and grinned, clearly enjoying his discomfort. "I just can't feel bad for you, Rye. Here you are, on a private jet in pure luxury. Terrified. You don't know how scary commercial airlines are. They don't even give you a can of soda anymore."

A snort was all Rye could manage.

"Oh stop riling him," Rhett said, plopping a deck of cards on the table between the men. "Let's play some poker."

Rye lost every hand, which he hoped wasn't a bad omen.

When they stopped to refuel, he stayed on the plane, not wanting to step on land until he was in Kenya, worried he might not be able to make himself get back on. He'd hoped that the longer they flew, the easier it would become.

It didn't.

When they arrived in Nairobi late that night and found their hotel, he took a cold shower and tried to calm his system down. Tomorrow, the guide they'd hired would take him on another godforsaken plane ride to the Maasai Mara, and then they'd drive the hour plus to the site of Tory's camp. He'd been warned the plane was the size of a crop duster, and his stomach roiled at the thought.

Sleep was impossible. But he was closer to Tory than he'd been in months, and even though everything around him was foreign, he took some comfort in that.

He finally fell asleep after reading the card Rory had made for Tory yet again.

Even if she could resist him, how could she possibly resist his nephew pleading his case?

***

The camp was totally empty when they arrived. It was nothing like Rye had imagined, and it made him wonder how she'd lived like this for the past months. There were three tents pitched close together, two private quarters, and one that was stacked with camping gear and cooking equipment. The shower and bathroom setup made him frown. It was outside with barely a cloth to conceal the person using it, and a huge rusted tank overhead with holes punched into it. The fire pit in the middle of the camp drew his gaze, and he wondered how she cooked out here and what she ate. Dear God!

"Makes my summer camp growing up look like a five-star hotel," Clayton muttered.

There was a small river below a steep cliff about a hundred yards off, the waters muddy and filled with shifting shapes. Hippos. Crocodiles.

"Jesus," Rhett breathed out. "It's like *Wild Kingdom*. Why isn't she living with the tribe she's studying?"

"The more traditional Maasai don't like to have people that close to them," J.P. said. He was the expert on the trip, since he'd done a fair share of reading and talked to the Fulbright people. "There are some land and cultural issues, but you don't care about that."

"Where in the hell is she?" Rye asked, kicking at the ground.

"Probably out on a field trip at one of the surrounding villages," J.P. said. "We'll have to wait for her here."

Rye looked around. He'd been hoping for some privacy for their conversation, but he wasn't sure he was going to get it. The sun was hot and the flies were as attracted to him as his craziest female fans.

Yet the beauty of the place was undeniable. The vast savanna was flat and sparse with only one or two knobby trees dotting the landscape. They had seen some giraffes and a ton of zebras and water buffaloes on the way to Tory's camp, and Rhett was right. It was like watching *Wild Kingdom.*

A green Range Rover appeared in the distance, and Rye's breath caught. It was her. Finally.

The vehicle was still miles away, and it took a while for it to come close enough for him to see that it was a young man, not Tory. This had to be the other student. A sudden worry hit him in the solar plexus: could she have fallen for this guy?

When the redhead climbed out of the cab, J.P. crossed over to him, his mega-watt smile radiating charm. "You must be Kevin Andrews," he said. "The people at Fulbright couldn't say enough good things about your grant application. I'm John Parker McGuiness." Then he introduced the rest of them.

When J.P. reached Rye, the young man frowned, and it was obvious he knew something about Rye's connection to Tory.

"I was hoping to speak with Tory," Rye said. "I'm not sure if you know this, but she worked for me this past summer as my cook, and we have some unfinished business."

"Long way to come for business," the guy said, raising his eyebrows. "She's still out in the field."

Well, he hadn't been expecting that. "Can you let us know how to find her? I'd like to see her today."

"Directions out here aren't particularly easy to explain to outsiders," he said.

"We have a driver who knows the area," J.P. said, "and we'd appreciate your help in finding Tory."

The guy gave each of them a lingering look, and Rye could tell he wasn't going to share diddly. "Would it be all right if we waited for her, then?" He wasn't about to leave without seeing her.

"You can wait in the mess tent, I guess. But it's going to be a while. Where are you staying? I can tell her you were here when she returns."

Like Rye would leave something this important to a stranger.

"That's mighty neighborly of you," Rhett said. "We're staying at The Queen's Lodge. But we don't mind waiting. Tory's an old friend."

"I'll bet," Kevin said. "Fine. I have some things to do, so if you'd like to make yourself at home..."

Yeah, the guy had a chip on his shoulder all right.

They ducked inside the mess tent, and Rye took in the sight of an old mini-fridge, a hot plate, and a couple of chipped plates and bowls. This had to be the camp kitchen. Christ, how could she stand to cook under these conditions when she loved cooking so much?

"More poker anyone?" Rhett said as they settled in at the small table, J.P. pulling over two crates to serve as makeshift chairs since there were only two in the tent.

"Might as well," Rye said, looking at his watch. The waiting was getting to him, but he had to stay focused. He was here. She was coming. It would all work out.

For the second time, he lost every hand at poker.

***

When Tory returned at sunset, she noticed the additional Rover and guide waiting near the camp. While she wondered who their visitors could be, she had to go to the bathroom so bad, she didn't stop to find out. The village she'd been working in today was thirty minutes from their camp, and while she could go outside in nature any time she wanted, there were no trees for cover save a lone acacia. The animals in the Mara were incredibly socialized to people, which is why you could pull your Rover over next to a cheetah or lion sunning itself without fear of being mauled, but they were still wild animals.

And she might not have a nice bathroom anymore, but at least it had four sides.

While she was sprinting to it, Kevin emerged from his tent. "Tory, we have some visitors."

"Yes, I saw. Be back in a jiff." She waved and hurried off to handle her business.

When she emerged, Kevin was gone, so she headed to her tent to freshen up and use a wet wipe to clear off the dust and grime of the day. They didn't have visitors often, but at least she could be less sweaty and dirty while they chatted.

Unzipping her tent netting designed to keep air circulating but the bugs out, she stepped inside and immediately turned around to zip it back up.

"Hello, Tory," a familiar voice said from behind her.

She looked over her shoulder and stumbled back against the tent when she saw Rye standing there.

He was hatless and dressed in tan slacks and a white long-sleeve T-shirt and looked much leaner. His hair still curled at the ends, a mix of blond and ash that she'd remembered each and every time she looked out at the savanna. He still had his goatee, and his hazel eyes seemed to drill all the way into her soul.

Her heart pounded in her chest, and a part of her thought for a moment that she had to be crazy, thinking she was seeing him here. With her. After all this time.

Yet he approached her as she stood there, her quickened

breaths audible in the quiet of the tent. Speechless, she watched him reach out and touch the hair sticking out of her hat. "It's longer," he said in a hoarse voice. "I like it."

When his fingers brushed her hair, it snapped her to attention. "What are you doing here? How...did you even find me?"

"We contacted Fulbright." His hands fell to his sides. "I've come a long way to talk to you."

Suddenly it was too much. "Why in the world would you come here? It's been months, Rye." Then a thought hit her. "There's nothing wrong with your family, is there?"

His gaze roamed over her face. "No, everybody's fine. They send their best. Including Rory."

She picked at her white cotton skirt. Oh, that sweet little boy. "Then I don't understand why you're here. There's nothing more for us to say to each other. I've moved on with my life, and I thought you would have, too."

"There are things I need to say to you. Things I want to explain. I should have called you about buying the house—"

"Stop right there," she interrupted, and suddenly the old anger—that he had gone too far, interfered too much—had her seeing red. " Like some personal Dear John letter? Oh dammit, why couldn't you just leave me alone?" She'd been so happy, stepping more into the sun each day, and now she was being plunged back into the darkness.

"No, God, I...I needed to see you. To tell you how things have been. How everything has changed. Tory, I've missed you like you're my last breath."

It felt as though her heart had crashed down against the rocks, miles from shore. "Stop saying things like that. It's too late. Don't you understand? I came all this way to get you out of my head, and now you're here."

She edged away, but he reached for her shoulder, and that old ping of attraction between them blew through her defenses. This time it was unwelcome, a devastating reminder of everything they'd lost.

"Tory," he whispered hoarsely. "I love you. Please just calm down and let me talk. I have something I want to show you."

At one time hearing those words from him would have given her hope, but all they did now was engulf her in familiar pain. "Stop this! You don't love me. If you did, you never would have believed I'd betray you."

He hung his head and ran his fingers through his hair. "I'm sorry. I'm ashamed of that. I've never asked anyone this directly before, but I'm asking you... Tory, will you forgive me?"

So, this was about his guilt, after all. Studying him, she realized her first impression of how lean he'd become was spot on. He was haggard, and he didn't radiate star quality quite like he had when she'd worked for him.

Her lip started to quiver. "It's not so easy as that, Rye. You hurt me. Not once, but twice."

"I know that, and I'm sorrier than you could ever know. Please forgive me, Tory. So we can begin again. I'm a changed man, and I brought something to show that to you."

He wanted her back? Her hand flew to her throat, and she pressed her lips together to keep from crying out. Would it even be possible after all the betrayal and hurt he'd put her through?

"Tory, are you all right?" Kevin called, and the sound of her tent unzipping made her look away from Rye.

"If you'd just give us some privacy," Rye barked.

"I heard raised voices," Kevin said and walked over to her. "Is everything all right? Do you want him to leave?"

Rye stepped forward in a move designed to intimidate, but Kevin didn't back down.

"Oh stop it. Both of you," she said. "I need to think. Rye, I...where are you staying?"

If she had time to think, then she'd be better prepared for the next time they spoke.

"Tory, please don't send me away," he said, and cast a cutting glance at Kevin. "Please let me stay and tell you about my family and how things have been with them."

It was a low blow, and he knew it, using her love for his family to sway her. But she felt like she was emotionally freefalling, and she desperately needed to regain control. Otherwise she was afraid she'd start yelling at him or crying over spilt milk, and she had too much pride for that.

"No, you sprang this on me. Coming here out of nowhere. I need some time to process all this."

His sigh was long suffering, and he put his hands on his hips, looking defeated. "All right. I'll give you your time. I'm staying at The Queen's Lodge. Do you know it?"

Of course. It was the most luxurious safari park around, frequented by celebrities. "Yes, I do. I'll...find you. When I'm ready to talk."

Rye inclined his head to Kevin. "Can you give me a moment here?"

Her friend looked over at her for guidance. "It's okay, Kevin."

When he left the tent, Rye took a deep breath and gazed at her with such intensity, she could feel all the tears she'd suppressed rising up in her chest.

"I do love you, and I've changed. Like I said, I brought proof...or at least as close to proof as I can get." He crossed the space and picked up a manila envelope from her small sitting table. "This is for you. I hope it will help you see..."

She took it when he pressed it into her hands, and then he covered her hands with his. "I do love you, and I'm willing to do anything you want to show you just how much."

A huge pocket of emotion flew out of her as she exhaled sharply.

He crossed to the tent flap. "Will you promise me you'll come talk to me when you've done your thinking?"

Since she couldn't squeeze a word out, she nodded sharply.

His mouth tipped up to the side. "Okay, then I'll see you soon."

When he left, she succumbed to the storm inside her. The pain was fierce, the tears hot. Her head and nose grew stuffy, and she had trouble catching her breath when she curled onto her cot.

Did he really love her? Why would he wait to tell her until now? It was insane. And then another thought surfaced, something she hadn't remembered until now. He was terrified of flying, and yet he'd faced that fear for her.

She reached for the package, and the first thing she pulled out was a CD. On the cover, Rye sat hatless under a tree with two kids playing in the background near a tree swing. Her heart stopped, and she knew the kids were Rory and Annabelle, dressed in matching outfits of crisp white and powder blue. Above his name was the album's title, *Country Heaven*. Since Myra had been a long time fan of Rye's, Tory had seen plenty of his other album covers. They all showcased his spectacular body in motion, solidifying his reputation as a bad-boy country singer.

But not this time...

Then she pulled a blue card with a garden scene on the front with the words, *Thinking of You*. It looked like something Tammy might have bought. Inside were two pieces of construction paper with a child's big, awkward red letters.

Dear Tory,
I miss you. I hope you're having fun. Listen to Uncle Rye and his songs. He loves you like me. I didn't talk to him until he said it. Come home soon and see my puppy, Bandit. He bought him for me.
Love, Rory

So her little champion thought Rye loved her? He was no pushover. Tears leaked out of her swollen eyes, and she knuckled them away.

Her gaze fell to the CD again. *This* was the man she'd met in Meade.

She tore off the cellophane and popped the disc into the mini-player that was in the bottom of the envelope. Her heart pumping in vicious beats, she hit play.

The first track shared the name of the album, and when she heard the opening chords of a guitar and his quiet voice, she shivered, realizing it was the song he'd sung for her in Memphis. Bracing herself to hear the words that had broken her heart, she was shocked when the lyrics were different.

But I missed her so,
Couldn't let her go.
So, I got on my knees,
Started a prayer with please,
And asked God to send my angel back to me.

Told Him I'd make her a home,
And love her all my days,
Down here,
In country heaven.

She pressed a hand over her mouth as she started to cry again. "Oh God, oh God, oh God," she chanted, rocking herself. So it was true. He loved her. He really did.

Pulling the lyrics sheet from the cover, she scanned the Acknowledgements, where he thanked his Daddy, Amelia Ann, Tammy, Rory, and Annabelle for coming back into his life. And the last line on the page was To T.S., with love. Always.

For a moment, it felt like lightning had struck her heart.

She read the lyrics for the rest of the songs as if her life depended on it. They were all about his broken heart, sitting a spell with his favorite little girl in the evening, and the power of forgiveness. Her finger caressed the album cover as she listened. She noticed his cowboy hat resting to the side in the picture. Rye Crenshaw without his hat? Surely it meant something. He was telling her—telling the world—that he was setting aside his old image, wasn't he?

And she'd sent him away.

What in the heck did she need to think about? Everything was exactly as she'd always hoped it would be.

Panicked, she picked up her keys and ran to her Rover. Kevin emerged when she started the engine.

"He loves me!" she shouted. "I'm going after him."

"Good luck," he said with a smile, but his shoulders fell as she drove away.

She had only been to The Queen's Lodge once, for a special lunch, and while it was grandiose, she barely paid it any mind as she crossed the lobby to the main desk.

"Can you tell me what room Rye Crenshaw is staying in?" she asked the receptionist.

"I'm sorry, miss, but we're not able to divulge the name of our guests," he replied.

"Then can you call him, please, and tell him that..." She broke off when she saw Clayton and another man walking out of a nearby room. She cried out his name, rushing toward them.

His mouth curled at the corner, while his friend regarded her warily.

"I'm here to see Rye," she said in a rush. "Can you take me to him?"

"Are you planning on breaking his heart anymore than you've already done?" Clayton asked.

"No," she said quietly. She'd broken his heart?

"Well, good," he replied.

"I'm John Parker McGuiness, by the way, another friend of Rye's," said the man next to him. "It's good to finally meet you, Tory. Why don't you come with us? We'll take you to Rye."

"Thank you," she said. Suddenly she was nervous.

"I'm really glad to see you here," John Parker said. "Rye's terrible at waiting."

The first makings of a smile formed on her face, and it felt good. "I know."

"Seems I owe you an apology," Clayton said. "Georgia raised me to speak plainly, and it sometimes comes off too gruff. I'm sorry I doubted you."

Her mouth parted slightly in shock. "Thank you," she simply responded.

They followed the path to the pool and then curled around it, heading to the largest bungalow on the property. When they reached the door, J.P. squeezed her arm. "Just wait here for a moment."

The wait was interminable, and she tapped her foot, all the

things she wanted to say to Rye spinning through her mind in an endless loop.

When the door opened again, J.P. and Clayton emerged with another very tall man, who looked her up and down and whistled. "Lady, for being so little, you sure know how to cause a whole heap of trouble," the stranger said. "But I'm glad you're in love with my friend because I'm a hopeless romantic now that I've gotten hitched myself. But go easy with him. He wasn't sure he'd convinced you about his feelings, so he went a little crazy."

"It'll be fine," J.P. said. "Just tell Rye how you feel."

And with that, they left her alone at the mahogany door. She only needed to open it.

Every good cook has a signature dish. Even though I'm not of Italian heritage, one of my signature dishes is lasagna. The wonderful thing about cooking is that you can go anywhere in the world simply by cooking in your own kitchen. Since we didn't have any money to travel to mysterious places when I was a kid, I started cooking recipes from countries I wanted to visit. When I was first introduced to Italian cuisine, I felt that I'd found my second home. Their approach to food—simple, family style with fresh local ingredients—seemed to blend with my own vision of what makes a good meal. Serve it to your family with a good red wine. Light some candles. And celebrate togetherness.

Tory's Mouthwatering Lasagna

2 packages sausage
1 lb. hamburger
6 cloves garlic
2 tbsp. Italian seasoning
1 can tomato paste
1 small can crushed tomatoes
1 carton of cottage cheese or ricotta
2 beaten eggs
1 tbsp. Parsley
¾ cup Parmesan cheese
Mozzarella cheese

Fry the meat and when cooked, add the garlic and Italian seasoning. Then add the tomato paste and crushed tomatoes. In another bowl, mix the eggs, ricotta, parsley, and Parmesan cheese. Boil the lasagna noodles in salt water until *al dente*. In an oil-coated pan, layer in two stages: noodles, meat mixture, creamy mixture, and then top with mozzarella. Bake at 375 degrees for 50 minutes until golden brown.

Tory Simmons' Simmering Family Cookbook

CHAPTER 26

She was reaching for the door when it was wrenched open. Rye stood there on the threshold, breathing hard. His face seemed to tighten as he looked at her.

"Do you believe me?" he whispered.

She had to fight a fresh onslaught of tears. "Yes," she whispered.

"Thank God," he cried. "Come inside. We can talk..." Then he shook his head. "Screw this."

He pulled her to him, his mouth swooping down and finding hers. The kiss was rough and untamed, but she didn't care. Under the force of his embrace, there was an agony she understood.

She rubbed her fingers over his face, tracing the angles, as the kiss went deep and wild. He pressed his body into hers, cupped her bottom, and pulled her inside, slamming the door. Her hands ran over his shoulders and then reached under his shirt to caress the strong lines of his back, desperate to feel his naked skin.

He pulled back and shook his head as if to clear it. "We have some talking to do."

Her heart was pounding in her chest, and it was almost impossible to hear past the buzzing in her ears. Her head bobbed a *yes*, and she let him take her hand and lead her into the main sitting area. Decorated in earth tones, it boasted an incredible view of the savannah.

When they stopped in the center of the family room, he raised her hand to his lips. The sweetness of the gesture made her eyes burn.

"I missed you, sweetheart. God, how I missed you. You finally listened to *Country Heaven*?"

"Yes," she whispered. "Rye, it's the most beautiful thing I've ever heard."

His eyes gleamed. "I meant it. Every word. You are an angel, *my* angel, and I came halfway around the world to tell you that I can't live without you anymore."

This, this was everything she'd hoped for, but never thought possible.

"I need to hear you say it," she said, and he gave her that special smile reserved just for her.

***

How long had he waited to tell her? He framed her delicate face in his big hands. "I love you, Tory Simmons. God, how I love you."

She bit her lip as tears filled her beautiful green eyes. "I love you too, Rye Crenshaw."

"I'm sorry. I'm so sorry for everything I did to you." He pulled her close and rocked her, tunneling his hands into her hair.

"I'm sorry I hurt you, too. I didn't know I broke your heart," she said, her tears wetting his face.

"I broke it by acting like a prize ass. Don't cry, love. You're cutting me to pieces." He kissed her eyelids. "I'm the one who should be saying I'm sorry for the rest of my life after everything I've done. I wasn't ready for you, for what was between us. Will you forgive me?"

"Yes," she said, putting her hand over his heart. "And you're not scared anymore?"

"No, I was just afraid I'd come all this way and fail. And I wasn't sure how I'd tell Rory..." His voice broke.

A tear slipped down her cheek. "I'm here," she whispered. "I'm here."

His whole body seemed to unwind with relief. "Thank God. Hang on a sec. I have something for you." It was so hard to step away from her, but he left the room and headed into his bedroom.

When he came back, he stopped in the doorway and watched her for a moment. She wrapped her arms around her body like Annabelle did. She was a study of contrasts—black hair, green eyes, porcelain skin. He wanted to remember this moment forever.

"Have I ever told you how beautiful you are?" he said in a hoarse voice.

A blush spread across her cheeks. "Maybe."

He sauntered forward. "Well, it bears repeating. You take my breath away and then you give it back." He lowered to one knee.

When her face froze, he felt some of the pressure return to his chest. "Will you marry me, Tory?"

She blinked rapidly, like she had something in her eye. "You're *serious*?"

"Do you think I would have traveled all this way when I'm

deathly afraid of flying if I didn't have marriage in mind?"

"No." Her hand clutched her throat. "Was it bad?"

"Not as bad as fearing I'd lost you," he said, flicking open the black box he'd concealed in his hand. The square-cut emerald shone like her eyes, and the small diamonds clustered around it were radiant against the white gold setting. "My sisters helped me pick it out. I hope you like it."

She sank to both knees and stared at the ring. "Oh, Rye."

"I love you. I want to marry you, and for us to be a family." And for some reason, Rory's promise popped into his head. "I don't want you to be alone any more. And *I* don't want to be alone any more, either."

A tear stole down her ashen face.

"Are you going to answer? My knees are starting to hurt here." They weren't, but he was dying for her to say the words.

"Yes, Rye, I'll marry you."

He reached for her hand and slid the ring on her finger. Damn, if Tammy hadn't been spot on about the size. "That's better. Tammy thought you might like something less traditional, something with color. But if you don't like it—"

"She's right. I love it." She ran delicate fingers over the setting.

"I love you," he said, pulling her close. "No, there's more to say. We have some things to talk about."

"Like what?"

"Well, for one thing, you're currently living in a tent in Africa."

Her brow wrinkled. "But I'm coming back next month. I won't be gone much longer."

But any time apart seemed like too much after everything they'd been through, though he didn't see any way around it, since he couldn't stay in Kenya for that long. She had her work, and he had his, not to mention his family.

"Okay, what about when we're married?" Rye asked.

In response to her blank stare, he pointed. "Aha! Well, I have two options for you to consider. We can live in your house in Lawrence until you graduate, or you can come live at my house in Dare River, and we'll travel to Kansas when you need to go up for school. You're mostly finishing up your dissertation, right? I'll keep my performances and events to a minimum until you're done. Of course, Rory and Annabelle are hoping you'll choose option number two. They miss you. We all do."

"You'd move to Lawrence to be with me?" And even he could hear the surprise in her voice.

"Of course! I want to be with you. I *need* to be with you."

She threw her arms around him and tackled him to the floor. "You really *do* love me."

"Of course I do. Haven't we established that?"

"Yeah, but I didn't really get it until just now. I'm a slow learner."

"Hell, you're about as slow as a rocket. Sweetheart, you're going to be the more educated one in this marriage. Aren't you lucky that I'm not the type of man who cares?"

"That's because under that 'good olc boy, aw shucks' routine, you're actually pretty damn smart."

"Picked you, didn't I?"

She punched him in the ribs. "Took you long enough. You were beastly."

"Yes, I was, and I'm sorrier than you can imagine." And still was, thinking of how much he'd hurt her and all the time they'd lost.

"Stop," she whispered. "You're forgiven."

And he wrapped his arms around her and held on tight.

"I figured out some things here about my career," she said, "and you were right."

"Music to my ears," he tried to joke, easing up on his grip. "About what?"

"That I don't like anthropology as much as I do cooking. That I was only doing it for Grandma. I miss cooking for people, Rye, especially you. Perhaps I can be your ongoing tour cook, and do some catering in the downtime, I'm open to all sorts of possibilities, so long as I can create incredible meals for people to appreciate." She leaned back and touched his face. "I still want to finish my degree, though. I want to feel like I honored my promise to her."

His hands stroked her face. "I'm glad for you sweetheart." She'd changed, too, in their time apart, and finally seemed ready to leave the past behind.

"Oh Rye, I wish you could have met my family. They would have really liked you."

He thought of his own family. Not too long ago, he'd been like her—alone—but by choice. He hated that she didn't have a choice. But at least he could give her a family, exactly as Rory had promised.

He put his arms around her again. "I know, sweetheart, but I feel like I know your Grandma every time you cook for me. She lives on through her recipes, Tory. And through your cooking."

"I want to publish the cookbook, Rye," she confessed.

"I think that's a great idea," he said. "I couldn't eat anything after you left, you know. It was like my taste buds had broken. Just like my heart."

She made a moue with her lips. "No wonder you look like you lost weight."

"Christ, you make me sound like a girl." He framed her waist with his hands. "Seems like you did, too."

"Haven't cared too much for food lately either. But I promise to cook for you when I come back to the States. You haven't had my famous lasagna. It's the perfect meal to kick off our first family dinner."

"Everybody will love that," he said, and he could already see her cooking in his kitchen, letting Annabelle and Rory help. It would be a dream come true.

"Tell me everything that's happened with your family."

And while the night broadcast its savannah melody, he held her in his arms and filled her in on the past few months.

"I'm so glad everything's worked out for them, Rye," she whispered when he finally finished. "I'm so proud of you."

Her praise meant the world to him, so he kissed her hair.

"Rye, I hesitate to bring this up, but did you ever find out who fed the tabloids the information about Tammy's divorce?" she asked quietly, her eyes darkening.

How had he ever thought she could hurt his family? God, he'd been such a fool. "No, we're still looking into it, but we'll find out. That I promise." He still had his brother-in-law pegged, but there was no evidence. Rye was a patient man, though, and someway they'd pay back Sterling for what he'd done to Tammy.

"You seem to be making a lot of promises lately," she mused.

"I'm a new man."

Her mouth tipped up. "That you are."

He ran a hand over her curves. "I'm also a man who's missed you terribly. Tory, I need to tell you…there…haven't been any women since you."

"Oh, Rye," she whispered, tears filling her eyes again.

"I didn't want anyone else."

"Me, neither."

When she slid a hand tentatively across his chest, he covered it with his. "I want to make love to you," he whispered, and the desire he felt for her was as great as his love.

"I want that, too," she said quietly. "It's been so long."

Didn't he know it? "Great minds think alike," he said and swung her up like she was a princess, which she was to him.

"And where might you be taking me?" she asked, her eyes locking with his.

"Didn't I promise to take you to country heaven?"

Her hands caressed his cheek. "Indeed you did, love. Indeed you did."

And as the African night reigned, they found their country heaven in each other's arms.

Home.
There's no other place I want to be.
Home.
Never imagined it was for me.

I have it again.
I am reborn.

Home.
There's no other place I want to be.

Tory Simmons' suggested lyrics to her fiancé,
Rye Crenshaw, for his new song, "Home"

EPILOGUE

Tory's first sight of Rye's house in Dare River made her heart burst in her chest. As they passed through the wrought iron gates and drove down the road lined with towering trees, she squeezed his hand. It was her first visit to his home, just in time to spend Christmas with him and his family. Her engagement ring winked on her finger, and everything felt right in the world.

The red brick house with the black plantation shutters and massive white columns reminded her of the houses she'd seen in Meade, and she wondered if Rye knew he'd chosen a place that looked like home. The Christmas decorations, carefully chosen by Tammy, no doubt, made it even more inviting, from the gigantic toy soldiers flanking the door to Santa's sleigh, eight reindeer and all, angled across the black-shingled roof. White lights blinked in the bushes, and a gigantic inflatable snowman swayed in the front yard.

But what enchanted her most was Dare River, sparkling across acres of manicured lawn dotted with garden beds. She couldn't wait to walk along the bank of the river later, hand in hand with Rye.

"Welcome home, Tory," Rye said, pulling the car to a stop, and leaning over to kiss her.

Home. This was going to be her home? She could scarcely believe it.

The massive double doors opened then and out streaked Rory and Annabelle, running straight to the SUV, followed by Tammy and Amelia Ann. Tory opened her door, and Annabelle plowed into her immediately, talking a mile a minute as she threw her arms around her.

Rory waited for his turn, and when his sister stepped aside, he smiled up at her. "Uncle Rye promised me he'd bring you home to us."

When his little arms tunneled around her, she crouched down and hugged him with all her might. "Oh, I missed you," she said. "Thank you, Rory. Thank you for keeping your promise to me."

"You're family now," he announced, pulling back. "Isn't she, Uncle Rye?"

Rye swung the boy up into his arms, making him laugh. "She sure is, son."

Next, she hugged Amelia Ann, who commented on how long her hair had gotten and how happy they were to have her here. Then Tammy came forward and wrapped her into a warm embrace, and the change in her was remarkable.

"Now you have to meet the dogs," Annabelle said. "There's Bullet and Banjo, Uncle Rye's dogs, and Barbie, my dog, and Bandit, Rory's. Uncle Rye said you're afraid of dogs. But you don't need to be afraid of ours. They already love you because I've been telling them all about you forever."

"That she has," Rye announced, taking her hand. "We have them penned up, so you don't need to worry about that quite yet."

She'd told him she was ready to face her fear and put that part of the past away forever. "Okay."

Annabelle continued to chatter, and Rory skipped alongside her and Rye as they walked up the steps to the veranda. Gone were the quiet, watchful children she'd met in Meade, and she couldn't be happier to see the change.

A wreath decorated with gold bells and red flowers graced the door, and she gasped when he swung it open. Garland wrapped around the curving staircase, and a fourteen-foot tall Christmas tree decorated in white ribbons and gold tinsel stood sentry in the entryway. Everything was elegant, yet inviting.

"Tammy's redecorated since she's a sight better at it than the woman I hired when I moved in," Rye said.

"Oh, it's nothing," his sister said with a shy smile, but Tory saw new pride in her eyes.

"Tammy, it's incredible," she said.

As they walked into the main room, she looked all around her, taking in the way the modern colors and gleaming antiques living in harmony with children's clutter—toy trucks, a small red shoe, and a ballerina doll. Her heart softened. A family lived here, and now she was part of it.

Rye kept squeezing her hand as if to reassure himself she was there, and she squeezed right back. Their long-distance relationship had been hard on them both, but now she was home. And after Christmas, they were heading back to Lawrence to pack up her things and move her here for good.

When they stopped in the center of the family room, he raised her hand to his lips.

"So this is country heaven?" she asked, her eyes burning.

He only smiled.

As he leaned in to kiss her softly on the lips, Annabelle said, "But Mama, I thought heaven was in the *sky*."

Rye's gaze didn't leave hers when he said, "That heaven is, Annabelle, but this one with Tory and y'all, well it's right here in the country."

And as he pulled Tory close and danced the two-step with her, the kids laughing and elbowing their way in, she knew he couldn't be more right.

Dear Reader,

COUNTRY HEAVEN might be the first novel in the Dare River series, but I'd fallen in love with Rye long before I wrote this story. He captured my heart as Rhett's best friend in *THE GRAND OPENING* and *THE HOLIDAY SERENADE*. This book stretched me with the writing of thirteen country music songs. Wow! As you know, since I'm a former chef, all of Tory's cookbook entries and recipes are a total delight for me. And if you're wondering who the tabloid leak was, stay tuned. That will be solved in *THE CHOCOLATE GARDEN*, Tammy Morrison and John Parker McGuiness' story.

I also released two specially priced companions to COUNTRY HEAVEN since readers loved the songs and the recipes. Check out the COUNTRY HEAVEN SONG BOOK and the COUNTRY HEAVEN COOKBOOK. The cookbook has extra recipes and reflections from my own family in addition to Tory's. If you love The Pioneer Woman, you're going to love this cookbook.

If you enjoyed this book, I would really appreciate it if you would help others enjoy it too. I would love for you to let me know what you think by posting a review. If you do post a review, kindly email me at ava@avamiles.com and let me know so I can personally thank you. Please also consider recommending it to your book clubs and discussions boards.

Next up is the newest book in The Dare Valley series, *THE PARK OF SUNSET DREAMS*. Rhett's former poker babe in *THE GRAND OPENING* and *THE HOLIDAY SERENADE* and now dog walker, Jane Wilcox, falls for Grandpa Hale's great-great nephew, lawyer Matthew Hale.

In case you missed my other books, keep reading. I included brief snippets of them all. Also please consider signing up for my newsletter at www.avamiles.com and liking my Facebook page at www.facebook.com/authoravamiles to keep up with all of my exciting news and enter my fun giveaways. Happy Reading!

Lots of light and blessings,

Ava

OTHER BOOKS BY AVA

All books can be enjoyed as a stand-alone if this is your first time reading. Enjoy!

The Dare Valley Series
NORA ROBERTS LAND: Book 1
Meredith and Tanner's story

A journalist returns to her hometown to debunk the Nora Roberts' romance novels her ex-husband blamed for their divorce only to discover happy endings exist when she falls for a hero straight out of a bona fide romance novel.

FRENCH ROAST: Book 2
Jill and Brian's story

A small-town girl mixes business and pleasure with her childhood BFF until his own Mrs. Robinson returns, making her question their friendship and their newfound love.

THE GRAND OPENING: Book 3
Peggy and Mac's story

A cynical single-mom cop discovers she can't bluff her way out of love when a mysterious poker-playing hotel magnate shows her it's worth the gamble.

THE HOLIDAY SERENADE: Book 4
Abbie and Rhett's story

A professional gambler prepares a holiday serenade to convince a single mom and Martha Stewart wannabe to give their love a second chance.

THE TOWN SQUARE: Book 5
Harriet and Arthur's story
An ambitious journalist returns to Dare Valley to start a newspaper empire, but is soon caught up with his mysterious secretary, not realizing she's come to his small town for revenge.

THE PARK OF SUNSET DREAMS: Book 6
Jane Wilcox and Matthew Hale's story
During sunset walks at the dog park, a woman with a mysterious past and a new candidate for mayor move from friends to lovers until her secret threatens to unravel his campaign and their love.

About the Author

USA Today Bestselling Author Ava Miles burst onto the contemporary romance scene after receiving Nora Roberts' blessing for her use of Ms. Roberts' name in her debut novel, *NORA ROBERTS LAND*, which kicked off The Dare Valley Series and brought praise from reviewers and readers alike. Much to Ava's delight, *USA Today* Contributor Becky Lower selected it as one of the Best Books of the Year.  Ava based her original series on a family newspaper, modeled after her own. Her great-great grandfather won it in a poker game in 1892, so Ava is no stranger to adventurous men and models her heroes after men like that—or like Tim McGraw, her favorite country music singer. Now Ava shares the Dare River series, set in the deep South, telling the story of a country singer and a beautiful cook. A former chef herself, Ava used her culinary background to infuse the story with family and personal recipes, but she also used her love for music to write country music songs to set the stage in the novel, creating a unique book experience. Ava—a writer since childhood—now lives in her own porch-swinging-friendly community with an old-fashioned Main Street lined with small businesses.

If you'd like more information about Ava Miles and her upcoming books, visit www.avamiles.com and connect to Ava on Facebook, Twitter, and Pinterest.

Made in the USA
Lexington, KY
04 October 2014